To my family

THE GUARDIAN

DAVID HOSP

PAN BOOKS

First published 2012 by Macmillan

This edition published 2013 by Pan Books
an imprint of Pan Macmillan, a division of Macmillan Publishers Limited
Pan Macmillan, 20 New Wharf Road, London N1 9RR
Basingstoke and Oxford
Associated companies throughout the world
www.panmacmillan.com

ISBN 978-1-4472-0624-8

1 3 5 7 9 8 6 4 2

A CIP catalogue record for this book is available from
the British Library.

Typeset by Ellipsis Digital Limited, Glasgow
Printed and bound by CPI Group (UK) Ltd, Croydon, CR0 4YY

Visit **www.panmacmillan.com** to read more about all our books
and to buy them. You will also find features, author interviews and
news of any author events, and you can sign up for e-newsletters
so that you're always first to hear about our new releases.

HISTORICAL NOTE

One of the most sacred relics in all of Islam is kept in Kandahar, Afghanistan. Carried into battle by the Prophet Mohammed, it is believed by many Muslims to give great power to whoever possesses it. Ahmad Shah Durrani, the founder of the last great Afghan dynasty, captured it in the eighteenth century, around the time of the unification of what would become modern Afghanistan.

It has been exhibited in public only three times in modern history. The last time was in 1996, following the withdrawal of the Soviet Union and during a time of civil war, when Mullah Omar, the leader of the Taliban, held it aloft before a group of *ulema* – religious scholars – and thousands of his supporters. Many believed that display conferred legitimacy, and shortly thereafter he defeated his primary rival and established the rule of the Taliban. That rule lasted for five years, until the invasion by the United States.

To this day, many believe that only the power of the relic can unite a nation that is still torn apart.

PROLOGUE

2002

Akhtar Hazara crept along the hallways of the mosque at the center of the ancient city of Kandahar. He was thirteen years old, and the weight of the Soviet-era assault rifle slung across his back cut into the muscles of his narrow shoulders. It was late in the evening and the day's last prayers had been said. The world was quiet for the moment.

The mosque was modest by the standards of the great halls of Islam in Riyadh and Istanbul and even Kabul. It was a smallish cubed structure, its exterior covered in filthy blue-and-gilt mosaics. In a city as poor as Kandahar, though, it was considered an oasis of luxury and safety. In the court-yard the goat that kept the grass cropped could be heard braying softly. Outside the walls, traffic had ebbed along Khuni Serok – the 'Bloody Road' – the main thoroughfare that carved through the area.

Akhtar slipped along the passageway until he came to the door. He put his ear to it and listened for a moment, confirming that the room was empty. Once he was certain, he took the key from his pocket and unlocked the door, pushing it open.

The anteroom was unfurnished. There was no rug to cover the cold tile floor. The paint on the walls was in need of a fresh coat.

He stepped in and closed the door. There were no windows, and the room went instantly pitch. He inched forward, his hands raised above his head, waving back and forth until one of his fingertips brushed against the naked bulb that hung from the ceiling. Raising himself up on his toes, he switched the light on. The bulb was weak, and it cast a wan yellow light, but it was enough for him to find the door at the far end of the room. He moved silently to it and took hold of the knob.

He hesitated. Breathless. Shaking.

He turned the knob and pushed the door.

There was barely enough light from the bulb in the anteroom to see within the small inner chamber. The paint was peeling here as well, but at least there was a threadbare rug covering the floor.

The chest was against the far wall. It was wooden, with ornate carvings and gold inlay, and it rested like a miniature coffin upon a brass base. It seemed to be glowing, though Akhtar attributed that to the irregular shadows cast by the deficient bulb behind him. The mere sight of the chest took his breath away. He moved slowly toward it, terrified and desperate.

He bent down and examined it closely. There was a latch and a set of hinges on the side. With trembling hands he unhooked the latch and reached to pry it open.

'What are you doing!'

The irate shout came from behind him. Akhtar spun and

faced a heavyset man in his late-thirties with a long beard and a thick turban. His face was contorted in rage.

'I . . . I . . . I . . .' Akhtar stammered.

'You are forbidden to be here!' the man yelled.

'I only wanted to see it,' Akhtar protested.

The man's frown remained, but his tone softened somewhat. 'That is not permitted, Akhtar!' he said. 'Not for anyone!'

'I know, Uncle. I just thought . . .'

The man walked over and put a hand on the boy's shoulder. 'I know what you thought,' he said, relenting. 'Your time will come, Akhtar. Our family has protected Mohammed's treasure for more than two centuries. It is a greater responsibility than you can yet imagine. You must learn to take that seriously. It is one of the most sacred objects in all of Islam. It is the beating heart of our nation.'

Akhtar stared at the chest for a moment. 'Are you afraid of it?'

His uncle shook his head. 'I am afraid for *it.'*

'Why?'

'Because it has great power. And power can be used for both good and evil.' He took his hand from Akhtar's shoulder and looked down upon him.

'Is that why my father was shot?'

'It is. Men will kill for it. Nations will go to war over it. It is said that he who controls it controls Afghanistan. That is why we must protect it.'

'How do we protect it? We are so few.'

His uncle smiled at Akhtar. 'With Allah's assistance,' he said. He reached out and tugged at the rifle. 'And old Russian guns.' The two of them gazed at the chest for another moment.

Akhtar's uncle said, 'Come. It is time to check on the rest of the mosque and make sure it is secure for the evening.'

They left, closing the doors and turning out the lights behind them. Inside the inner chamber, a glow remained. Outside, on the Bloody Road that bordered the mosque and beyond, the war for control of Afghanistan raged on.

CHAPTER ONE

2012

Hassan Mustafa's heart raced as he walked out into the cool autumn air of the Virginia evening. It was after eight o'clock, and darkness had enveloped the neighborhood where the largest mosque in America looked out over houses and schools and lives. The façade was smooth, polished limestone, unbroken by windows or architectural flourish. The sides of the building receded into an unadorned dome that rolled to an apex seven stories above the street. The building squatted in the middle of the traditional mid-sized American town like a giant riddle.

Mustafa checked over his shoulder as he hurried along Sycamore Street, where upper-middle class condominiums were marshaled in stentorian defense of the American dream. Warm light fell on the sidewalk from inside the apartments, broken only by the occasional harsh flicker from a television set – the great American opiate.

He crossed the street, looking back behind him again. A light rain had been falling on DC's greater metropolitan area throughout the day, but it had let up for the moment. The uneven bricks that lined the sidewalk were slick and puddled. His feet slipped several times, slowing

5

his pace, and he cursed quietly under his breath. He was tempted to break into a run, but it would only draw attention, and he knew that would be unwise. Besides, the coffee shop was only another block and a half away. Once he walked through the door he would be safe. He was so close he could almost breathe normally again. He put his head down and pressed on.

It was hard for him to believe that he felt this frightened again. Growing up in Afghanistan, he couldn't remember a time when the world around him was not on fire and collapsing. His nation had been at war for his entire life, and his childhood had been filled with dangers more profound than most people could comprehend. He'd thought he was immune to fear. He'd been wrong.

The coffee shop was in sight. Through the window he could see the man waiting for him. He had jet-black hair and an angular face. He was less than twenty yards away. It was almost over.

The figure emerged from the alley in front of him before Mustafa knew what was happening. He was a huge man, broad-shouldered and dressed in a loose waterproof garment with the hood pulled over his head. He moved onto the sidewalk so abruptly that Mustafa almost collided with him. He stopped and looked the man in the face. Mustafa recognized him instantly from the sharp features beneath his shaved head, and a new wave of terror washed over him.

'Sirus,' Mustafa croaked. 'What are you doing here?'

'I thought you were going home.' The man tilted his head slightly, the way a predator might just before eviscerating its prey.

'I am,' Mustafa said.

'Your apartment is in the other direction.'

'I am stopping off to get a cup of coffee,' Mustafa said. He nodded toward the coffee shop. The man inside was looking directly at them.

'It must be very good coffee,' the man in the raincoat said, 'for you to come this far out of your way.'

Mustafa gave a weak smile and a shrug, but said nothing. There was nothing to say.

The man moved so quickly, Mustafa never saw the gun. It came up from his side, his arm swinging with the speed and precision of a cobra strike, the muzzle pressing into Mustafa's chest between the third and fourth rib and sinking deep. The man pulled the trigger, letting Mustafa's body deaden the sound, and Mustafa gasped as he sank to his knees.

'You see, Mustafa?' the man said. 'The same fate comes to all those who betray us.' The man was gone as quickly as he had appeared.

The world tilted as Mustafa fell to his side. He could see the man from the coffee shop rushing toward him. He was shouting into a small cell phone, calling for help.

The man with the dark hair reached him and rolled Mustafa over onto his back. 'You're going to be okay,' he said, as he ripped open Mustafa's shirt to examine the wound. Mustafa could hear the doubt in his reassurances. 'It'll be okay,' he repeated. 'Can you talk?'

Mustafa tried to get some words out, but found it difficult. His lips moved, but he had breath only for a whisper.

'Who did this?'

'They will have it,' Mustafa lipped. 'They will have it soon.'

'What?' the man asked. 'What do they want?'

Mustafa's strength was almost gone. His vision was narrowing, the streetlights going dark around him. *Oh God*, he thought, realizing that it was over. *I'm sorry.* He could feel the tears running down his face. *I'm so sorry.*

'What are they after?' The man's voice was desperate. He grabbed Mustafa by the shirt collar and for just a moment Mustafa's focus returned. He could see the man's face, and could sense his urgency. 'What happened, Hassan?'

Mustafa struggled to make his lips form words. 'They . . . must . . . be . . . stopped.'

'Who? Who must be stopped?'

He could hear sirens in the background, growing in volume. Mustafa reached and took the man's hand, gripped it for a moment as he fought against the pain – fought to get the words out.

And then the fight was over.

CHAPTER TWO

Jack Saunders sat quietly at the table in the coffee shop, his head down, his jet-black hair damp. He was in his late-thirties, thin and wiry. So wiry that some mistook him for slight, weak even. It was a mistake no one made twice.

Outside, the lights from the ambulance still flickered, flashing red off the wet pavement and the drops of rain that still clung to the window. The lights were just for show now. Hassan Mustafa was dead before any of them arrived. His body still lay out there, underneath a sheet.

Saunders picked up the Styrofoam cup and took a sip of the coffee that was now stale and cold. He didn't notice. His mind was racing, going over every moment from that evening, measuring out his reactions in seconds and fractions-of-seconds, trying to gauge whether there was anything else he could have done.

He put the cup down, and a stain on the outer edge caught his eye – a dark red smudge near the rim. He wondered for a moment whether a woman had used the cup before and left a lipstick smear. Then he realized it was blood. Looking down at his hand, he saw the dark wet patch near his wrist.

The door to the coffee shop banged open and Lawrence

Ainsworth walked in with one of the local cops. Ainsworth was three decades older than Saunders. He was tall – over six feet – and he carried with him the visible fatigue of a man who has seen too much in his lifetime. He paused by the cash register, whispering to the cop as the two of them looked over toward Saunders. Then Ainsworth gave the cop a kindly pat on the shoulder and walked over toward the table.

He slid into a seat across from Saunders. 'He's the police chief out here,' Ainsworth said, nodding to the man with whom he'd just been talking. 'Name's Quentin. Former fed. They'll do what they can.'

'They won't find anything,' Saunders said. He took another sip of his coffee, avoiding the bloodstain.

'No, probably not,' Ainsworth agreed. He sighed. 'Still, it's good to know we're not dealing with Barney Fife.' He sat there in silence for a moment. 'Did Mustafa tell you anything?'

'Not much,' Saunders said. 'I talked to him on the phone last night. He said the message came in yesterday. Something important. He said he needed to talk in person.'

'Why did you wait to bring him in?' Ainsworth asked. His tone was sharp.

Saunders sat back in his chair and looked directly at Ainsworth. 'I told you last night, this was how Hassan wanted it. He couldn't get away until tonight, and he wanted me to put a protection plan together for him. He wanted to see that the Agency would stand by him. That's why I brought you in on logistics.'

'Well, at least he died knowing how committed we were.' Sarcasm dripped from Ainsworth's words.

'You think I should have handled it differently?'

'Maybe.'

'Then maybe you should have trained me differently. Maybe I should have been some pencil-pushing, ass-covering bureaucrat. The Agency can never get enough of those, can it?'

Ainsworth smiled in spite of himself. 'Yeah, I know it,' he agreed. He took a deep breath, motioned to the waitress, pantomiming the pouring of coffee. She went behind the counter to get a cup and a pot. 'Look, Jack, no one questions your contributions to the Agency – least of all me. I found you, for Christ sake, locked away at Harvard speaking dead languages to the four or five other people in the world who shared your interests. Hell, I've got more time in on you than anyone else I've ever worked with.'

'That's why you need to trust me,' Saunders said.

Ainsworth shook his head. 'It's not about trust, Jack. It's about results. That's why I had to pull you back from the field, and you know it.'

'You didn't approve of the results I got in the mountains?'

'It doesn't matter whether I approve or not.'

'I did that for Sam, for Christ sake. You of all people . . .'

'You disobeyed a direct order. What you did had political ramifications that—' Saunders started to object, but Ainsworth held up a hand to keep him from talking. 'You and I may not like it, but it is how the world works. Now we have to deal with this issue tonight, or people are really going to start questioning your judgment. So let's go back over this. When, exactly, did Mustafa first contact you?'

Saunders shook his head in annoyance. 'Two days ago. Nine a.m.'

'Why you?'

'I knew his brother when I was in Kabul. His brother trusted me, so Mustafa was willing to trust me.'

'Did he give you any idea what this was about?'

Saunders frowned. 'Not much. Not enough to be helpful.'

'Anything?'

Saunders replayed his conversations with Mustafa over in his head as he spoke slowly. 'He said he had information about an operation one of the Taliban splinter groups was running. He said a message was being delivered that would give the details, but that the key was here in the States.'

'The key to what?'

'I don't know. He didn't get the chance to tell me.'

'Did he say anything else?'

Saunders shook his head.

'Did he have any idea where this key was?'

'Boston,' Saunders said. 'The message was going to tell them more.'

'Boston,' Ainsworth said, blowing his breath out in frustration. 'Well, at least that narrows it to a city of five million people.' They lapsed back into silence.

'I know a way we can get more information,' Saunders said quietly after a moment.

'Do you?' Ainsworth sounded skeptical.

Saunders nodded. 'You'll have to trust me, though.'

Ainsworth thought about it for a moment. 'You realize

you're already just barely hanging on here, right? One more fuck-up and even I won't be able to protect you.'

'I know that,' Saunders said. 'Just give me the men I need for two hours, and I'll get some answers.'

Ainsworth sipped his coffee, staring out the window as the ambulance pulled away. 'I guess I don't have any choice, do I?'

CHAPTER THREE

Cianna Phelan sat in the passenger's seat of a rusted Nissan Sentra on Reverend Burke Street in South Boston, staring out the window at Building 29 of the Old Colony Housing Projects. A thick, late-September mist had rolled in off the harbor and hung in the air like an omen. In the driver's seat next to her, Milo Pratt gripped the steering wheel nervously. His normally weak chin had receded to the point where it looked like little more than a bump between his lower lip and his Adam's apple, and she wondered for the thousandth time how he'd ever come to this line of work.

'It's okay,' she said to him. 'It'll be fine. Are you sure she's in there?'

He nodded. 'I followed her earlier.'

'Okay, then,' she said. 'Let's do this.'

She got out of the car and walked across the street. Milo followed. She had to give him credit, he didn't back down, no matter how ugly things turned or how scared he got. She liked that about him.

The three-story building was one of hundreds in the Colony, perfectly rectangular and devoid of architectural charm or individuality, lined up like some oversized trailer park cast in brick permanence. The green door at the center of the building lolled halfway open, daring them. They paused on the sidewalk, regarding the gap in the entrance warily.

'You ready?' she asked.

'I guess.'

'Remember, show no fear.'

'It's all I've got,' he said. She chuckled, and he gave her a weak smile.

The door creaked as Cianna pushed it all the way open, and she could hear Milo suck in a lungful of stale air. There was no one in the hallway that ran through the center of the building. Half of the lights were out, adding to the gloom. Trash gathered in the corners. She stood there for a moment, and pushed away the blanket of child-hood memories that tried to smother her.

'Which apartment?' she asked.

'Last one on the left,' Milo said.

She walked down the hallway, head high, shoulders back, wishing she had a gun. There was nothing she could do about it, but she wished it anyway.

She heard the music long before she came to the door. It was the bass-heavy, expletive-laden, misogynistic fare that seemed to echo through the hallways of too many places she'd been in her life. The door was the same dark green as all the others, with several deep dents in the metal and chips in the paint where it had been struck throughout the years by angry boyfriends or girlfriends or parents or children or enemies or strangers. In truth, anger didn't need a reason in a place like this. Anger grew from the bricks.

She squared her shoulders once more and put on her

game face. Reaching out, she slammed her fist against the center of the door.

The voices that could be heard over the music ceased for a moment before the stereo was turned down. A voice called out 'Fuck is that?' in a thick Boston accent.

'Open up!' she shouted back.

'Who the fuck is it?'

'Now!' Never answer a question. It lets them think they're in charge, and she aimed to make clear that *they* were not.

A moment later, the door cracked open, and a rat-faced kid of around twenty peered out at her. He was skinny and pale, with zits on his face and up the arms that dangled from his enormous sleeveless Celtics jersey. He looked at her, and a wide smile broke over his face as he opened the door even wider. His teeth were brown and dying. *Four out of five dentists surveyed recommend sugarless crack for their patients who smoke crack*, she thought humorously.

'Shit, boys,' the kid said over his shoulder to the others in the room. 'Check out the fox!' He stepped back and swung his arm inward, inviting her to enter. She had on jeans, a dark T-shirt, and her black leather jacket, but from the way the kid was leering at her you'd have thought she was wearing a G-string and was leaning on a pole. It was a compliment of sorts, she supposed, but one she would have preferred to forego at the moment. 'Just what this fuckin' sausage-fest needs.' He licked his lips, and Cianna choked back a gag. 'I don't know what the fuck you're doin' here, but can I get you a fuckin' beer, honey?' All three 'R's in the sentence got caught in the kid's gingivitis. They came out as *yaw*, *heeya*, and *beeya*.

There were five young men in the apartment. Standing behind the toothless scarecrow in the kitchenette was a three-hundred-pound adolescent with a wisp of a beard and bulging eyes. He was turning from the open refrigerator to look at her. That his attention could be diverted from any appliance dispensing food she took as another stunning, if unwelcome, compliment. Two identical twins with crew cuts and piercings covering the outer rims of their ears sat at a battered card table in the living room, glaring at her with a disturbing mixture of lust and anger. On the card table sat a glass pipe, a butane lighter, and several clear plastic bags of substances ranging in consistency from hard-white to powder-brown. The alpha male was in the corner, sitting with his leg draped over the arm of a torn, half-reclined La-Z-Boy. He had long greasy dark hair and the sharp face of a hustler. She had little doubt that a decade earlier he would have been exactly the type of guy she would have gone for. Thank God those days were behind her.

Cianna stepped into the room, looking around to see whether there was anyone else. No one. The place smelled of beer and chemicals, sweat and piss. The skinny crack addict started to close the door and it banged off of Milo, who was moving in behind Cianna. The kid looked at Milo as though seeing him for the first time. 'Fuck are you?' he demanded.

Milo took a deep breath and said in a loud, clear voice, 'We're here for Jenny. Where is she?' Cianna was proud of him. Not a single quaver. She'd taught him the breathing trick a week ago, after his inability to control his voice had nearly gotten them shot.

The other four looked nervously at the young man spread across the over-sized chair. 'Jenny?' he said. 'I don't know any Jennys.' He gave her a sickening smile, and the others in the room laughed as though reassured.

She fixed him with a hard stare. 'Does it look like I'm kidding?' she asked. 'Where is she?'

Just then a girl's voice came from the back of the apartment. 'Jesus Christ, Vin! There's no fuckin' toilet paper in here!'

Cianna raised an eyebrow at the young man on the chair. His nonchalance seemed shaken, but only for a moment. 'Use the paper towels on the sink!' he shouted back, turning his head slightly, but never letting his eyes leave Cianna's. It took a moment, but he forced the smile back onto his face.

No one moved or said anything else until a young woman walked out of one of the bedrooms. Her head was down, and as she pulled her eyes up and saw Cianna, she stopped in the doorway, completing the frozen menagerie. She was wearing pink mesh leggings, a short skirt, and a tight long-sleeved white shirt. Her hair was pulled back and pushed up in a thick wave. Her cheeks were sallow and sunken, and her eyes were red. She had the look of someone about to drive off a cliff. *Make the most of the good years, kid,* Cianna thought, *'cause it only gets harder from here.*

'Jenny, I presume?' Cianna said to her.

Vin, on the chair, spoke before the girl had the time to react. 'Naw, that's not Jenny, her name is Flower, right babe?' The girl looked back and forth between Cianna and the guy, the expression of confusion slowly morphing to jealousy and anger.

'Who the fuck is she?' she asked. She was talking to Vin, but staring at Cianna like she gave off a stench that was more than she could bear.

'Don't worry about it, Flower. Why don't you just come over here, where you're comfortable.' He patted his crotch.

The girl took another look down her nose at Cianna and walked over and wriggled her leather skirt into his lap. 'My name is Flower,' she said defiantly. Vin draped his arms over her shoulders, and they both sat there staring at Cianna. Her eyes were filled with hatred; his less so.

Cianna looked behind her at Milo, and he moved what was left of his chin up and down in an affirming nod. She turned back to Jenny. 'You're coming with us, Jenny,' she said.

'No, she's not,' Vin answered for her. His face grew hard.

Cianna ignored him and spoke to Jenny. 'Let me explain this to you once, Jenny. Me and Milo, here, are your only chance. You're on parole, right?'

For the first time, doubt crept into Jenny's eyes.

'Right,' Cianna answered her own question. 'That's why we're here. You blew off your meeting with your PO today. That's violation number one.' She looked around the room. 'I see at least another eight violations here, any one of which would get you sent back inside. You come with us now, and you get a pass. Just this once. That's the way this works, you understand?'

The doubt on Jenny's face had spread like a rash. 'You're with the Parole Office?' she asked nervously.

Cianna shook her head. 'Not officially, but we work with them. We can get you one pass if you come now.'

Jenny hesitated. 'Where's your daughter Maggie?' Cianna asked. It was her trump card, she hoped. Jenny's eyes went to the floor. 'That's what I thought. Play-time's over; you need to come with us.'

Vin spoke before Jenny could move, and all trace of flirtation was gone from his voice. 'I said she's staying put.' He removed one of his arms from Jenny's shoulder and dug around in the chair's cushions. A second later the hand reappeared, now holding a semi-automatic pistol.

. . . And that's why it'd be nice to have a gun on this job.

He brought the gun up and traced it along Jenny's arm, caressing her with it, running it up along her neck and under her chin. Her eyes were wide with fear as he used the barrel to twist her head back around toward him until he could kiss her aggressively, forcing his tongue into her mouth, his eyes closed in a pantomime of ecstasy. Her eyes remained open, and tears began forming in the corners.

When he was done, he released her and let the gun drop so that it was resting under her left breast. 'See?' he said to Cianna. 'She wants to stay here with me.'

Cianna hadn't looked at or spoken to him since Jenny had entered the room. Now she realized that she was going to have to engage him. She frowned as she looked him in the eyes. 'It's Vin, right?' she said. She didn't wait for an answer. 'Vin, you have to understand something: Jenny is going to come with us. I don't give a shit how you spend the rest of your life, but you're not going to fuck up hers. At least not tonight. Do you understand? Or should I speak a little slower?'

The two twins at the table pushed their chairs back, leaving them with a clear run at her. From all appearances, it was on. 'Do you understand, Vin?' she repeated.

He looked at her, and the sick smile returned. 'What I understand is that we're guys.' He gestured to his underlings. 'And guys need to get laid.' He shrugged. 'That's just the way things are; we need to clean the pipes every once in a while, or we go all fucked up in the head.' He twirled the barrel of the gun around his ear as if to illustrate. 'Now, that's not a problem for me, as you can probably guess. I can get pussy any time I want. But these guys . . .' He pointed his gun at each of the other four. 'These guys ain't all that great with the ladies. That's why I told them that we could have a little party tonight, and once we're all good and fucked up and Jenny and I have had some fun, they can all have a turn with her.'

The blood drained from Jenny's face and her tears gathered speed. He looked at the side of her face. 'It's only fair, Jen. I mean they do good work for me, and besides, by then you'll be so fucked up that you won't give a shit.' He looked back at Cianna. 'Hell, she probably won't even know it's happening.' His eyes were so dark now, they seemed dead.

He pushed Jenny off his lap and stood up. It took two slow steps for him to be in front of Cianna. 'I am a businessman, though,' he said, gesturing over toward the drugs on the card table. He took the gun and ran the barrel lightly between Cianna's breasts, then up her neck and across her cheek. 'So if you have a counter-offer, I'm more than happy to reach an agreement.' He put his face close to hers. 'I'm Irish; I've always loved redheads.'

'I was hoping you'd go in that direction,' Cianna said. She breathed deeply, almost in a pant, as slowly she ran her fingers up his arm, over his shoulder, and around to the back of his neck. She was close enough to feel him harden against her stomach as he pressed against her.

'I had a feeling you were,' he said.

'Oh, yeah,' she breathed to him. He began to move his hips against her and she matched his rhythm as her other hand slid lightly up the forearm that held the gun against her cheek. He was groaning, and his eyes were half-closed. 'You see, now that she's seen who you really are, it will be that much easier for Jenny to walk away.'

He was so engrossed that he wasn't listening. Even if he had been, she acted too quickly for him to defend himself. She twisted the hand that held the gun hard, out away from his body, and heard the clean snap of his wrist. He screamed out in pain, and released the gun. His knees buckled as he used his other hand to grab his wrist. She grabbed hold of the hair on the back of his head and pulled down with all her weight. His head snapped back, and his spine bent to try to keep the hair from being pulled out of the scalp. His mouth was open, and he was screaming louder now, and she raised up his gun and drove the butt into his nose, drawing a fountain of blood.

Vin collapsed on the floor at her feet. It had happened so quickly that no one else in the room reacted. She turned and looked at the other four. The twins and the crack addict and the fat kid by the refrigerator all just stared at her, mouths dangling. She pointed the gun at them. 'You tell him when he wakes up that if I find out anyone has gone near Jenny or any of her friends or family, I'm coming back, and I'm going to shoot all of your balls off, understand?'

The four stood there, paralyzed.

'You understand?' She asked it louder this time, raising the gun at their heads for punctuation.

'Yeah,' they muttered.

Cianna looked at Jenny, who was standing next to the chair, where Vin had moved her. 'Are you coming?'

Outside, Cianna climbed back into the passenger seat of the rusted Sentra. Jenny got into the back seat and Milo got behind the wheel. They all sat there for a moment in the silence, staring straight ahead. She reached over and put the gun into Milo's lap. 'You need to take this,' she said.

He looked down at the gun. 'Are you afraid you might go back and finish the job?'

She shook her head. 'I can't have a gun.' He gave her a quizzical look and she scowled at him. 'I'm on parole, too, remember?'

Milo dropped Cianna off at her place on Mercer Street in South Boston, less than a half a mile from the Old Colony Projects. He would take Jenny home; dealing with emotional and psychological wrecks was his special talent. Handling the physical challenges of their job was hers. It was what she had been trained for, after all.

Her apartment was in a big, square, three-story clapboard house with two residences on each floor. Hers was on the south side of the third floor: 600 square feet of scarred wood floor with a bathroom that had a freestanding tub from the 1940s. The furniture was old and stained: a queen-sized bed, a pea-green couch with a crate in front of it for a coffee table, a dining-room table with one chair, and a makeshift desk. Still, it was home, and it was the one place where no one could tell her what to do.

She climbed the staircase wearily, and made her way down the landing to her apartment. The last of the adrenaline from the evening's encounter had almost fled her system, leaving her with the crack-jittery, strung-out feeling of a crashing addict. She noticed that the light on her landing had burned out and would need to be replaced. It made it a little more difficult to find the right key in the dark, and the keys jangled as she located the right one. She'd just unlocked the door when she felt the hand on her shoulder.

For a moment she was frozen. Her job was dangerous. It was one of the reasons she'd taken it – that, and the fact that Milo was one of the few employers who would hire an ex-con. Milo believed in redemption. Cianna wasn't as convinced, but she was grateful to be given the benefit of the doubt, and was willing to help people if there was a paycheck in it. It was a small neighborhood, though, and you couldn't ruffle greasy feathers without expecting some attempts at retribution. The hand on her shoulder let her know that one such attempt had arrived.

Without thinking, her hand came up and took hold of the attacker's wrist just below where the hand rested on her shoulder, pulling and twisting at the same time. The assailant gave a pained scream as he toppled forward, off balance, and she used his momentum to her advantage, driving his head into the wall just to the side of the door. He screamed again, but now it came out as a confused yelp. 'Wait!' he cried.

She barely heard him. She kicked the man in the side as he tumbled to the floor.

'Get off of me!' he screamed.

She was getting ready to fully incapacitate him before calling the cops, but as she raised her fist his last plea for mercy penetrated her consciousness. There was something about it that was eerily familiar. Like a scent that touches deep within the memory, the rhythm of his wail brought her back to another time, another place. Suddenly, she was back in the Projects, fourteen years old, kneeling on the arms of a skinny kid two years younger than she. She saw herself torturing him by letting a long thin line of spit dangle from her lips, dropping slowly until it almost touched his face as he squirmed away, before she sucked it back into her mouth, laughing. He wriggled and squirmed to try to get away, but she had always been stronger. And every time he tried to get away, he would cry out pitifully, '*Get off of me!*'

Cianna leaned forward, trying to see the man's face through his upraised arms. 'Charlie?' she said tentatively.

'Christ, Cianna,' the man said, lowering his arms just enough to look back at her, though still keeping them high enough to provide some protection. 'What kind of a welcome is that for your little brother?'

CHAPTER FOUR

Jack Saunders was sitting at the head of a large semicircular table on the sixth floor of CIA headquarters in Langley, Virginia. An array of television screens paneled the wall in front of him. The room was dimly lit and hushed except for the periodic rasping of closed-circuit radio communications in the background.

Four others sat at the table with him. Lawrence Ainsworth, the Assistant Director of the CIA in charge of operations – Saunders's friend and boss – sat directly to Saunders's right. Colonel Bill Toney, the Director of the NSA, sat next to Ainsworth, his expression telegraphing his disgust. Saunders thought Toney was a first-class asshole, and figured Ainsworth had strategically separated Toney and him to prevent trouble. To Saunders's left was Gerald Hoag, the Assistant Director for counterterrorism at the CIA, and Sonny Kopecki, a close advisor to the newly elected President. Hoag was ineffectual but harmless – a master paper-shuffler who'd advanced by keeping a low profile on the bureaucratic escalator. Saunders didn't know anything about Kopecki other than what he'd read in the papers. The reports didn't bode well.

Saunders could feel the stares from the other men around the table. He'd never been a clean fit with the management crowd in the intelligence community; they were all spawn of old-line families with powerful connections and political ambitions. Saunders was a mutt. If it hadn't been for Ainsworth's support, he would have been banished from the Agency years ago. And now his ass was really on the line.

It didn't bother him. He figured that's what asses were for. He'd made his reputation across enemy lines, running more successful missions than anyone could remember. At thirty-nine, he had more practical experience than all of the others around the table put together. That was the only reason the rest of them allowed him to be there, choking down stale, re-circulated air. Because, whether they liked it or not, Saunders knew what he was doing, and people who could claim that truthfully were in short supply.

'My men are in place,' Toney said. *His* men. *What a prick*, Saunders thought. The men were actually with the FBI – the CIA had no technical jurisdiction to operate within the boundaries of the United States – and were on loan to a joint operation over which Toney had little operational oversight. Legalities, titles and official chain of command aside, it was an Agency op through and through.

Ainsworth took a deep breath. 'Okay, Jack,' he said. 'You're calling the shots.'

Saunders picked up the headset sitting on the table in front of him, looked at the twelve monitors on the wall. Each showed a slightly different view of a small house in Alexandria, Virginia. Ten of them were beamed from the helmet-cams worn by the operatives in the field. One was an overhead satellite shot. One was from a stationary camera that had been mounted on a nearby telephone pole. 'Team Leader, this is Base,' he said. 'Status?'

One of the radio reports crackled loudly. 'Base, Team Leader. No movement. We have five inside. Two male. Two female. One child.'

'Weapons?' Saunders asked.

'Unknown.'

The man on the other end of the line was Nick Johnson. Good man. Twenty-nine years old. Former marine, now with the feds. Well-trained and battle-hardened. Married, two daughters, the oldest in third grade. Saunders knew the names of all ten of the people on the ground. He was pretty sure Toney couldn't say that about any of '*his*' men.

Saunders took a beat before giving the order. 'Team Leader, proceed.'

'Roger that,' Johnson said. 'Team One, Team Two, move in.'

Ten of the images on the monitors shifted, jostling loosely, scanning as the house grew larger on the screens. The overhead satellite image focused in more closely. The image from the static camera on the telephone pole a hundred yards from the front door remained unchanged. Saunders's attention was on the images on the wall, following each of them, searching for the danger. It was out there, he knew.

The house was the residence of Tariq Kaleada, a doctor prominent in the Muslim community. According to Saunders's intelligence, he was the primary communications conduit delivering messages for the radical Islamists in the area, including two fledgling Al Qaeda cells and some of their allies. It was likely that any messages delivered to those on whom Mustafa was spying came through Dr Kaleada, and he might still have the evidence. *Might* meant there was around a 25 per cent chance. Twenty-five per cent in Saunders's profession was considered a slam dunk. Any way you looked at it, it was the best chance they had to find out why Mustafa had been killed.

'You gonna announce, Saunders?' Hoag asked. He was making irrelevant notes on a pad bearing the Agency's logo.

Saunders shook his head. 'Team Leader, you've got the ram,' he said into the radio. 'Five up front, five in the rear. Take it quick.'

'Roger that.'

Bill Toney rocked back and forth in his seat. 'Jesus fucking Christ,' he muttered. 'What if your intel is wrong, Saunders? What if your informant had shit?'

'If he had shit, why was he killed?'

'Who knows?' Toney said, his voice getting louder. 'Maybe he was just an asshole. Look who he hung out with, after all.' Saunders shot Toney a vicious look. 'Do you know what the Arab Anti-Defamation League is gonna do with this if you're wrong?' Toney continued. 'I'm not even sure this is legal.'

Saunders clicked off the microphone on his headset. 'Go to law school,' he said. 'Let us know if it's legal when you graduate. Until then, shut the fuck up.'

'I went to law school, asshole,' Toney shot back. 'I went to Harvard! Where did you go to school?'

'Mogadishu, prick,' Saunders muttered.

'Please, gentlemen,' Ainsworth soothed. 'You two can compare genitalia when this is over.'

The images on the screens showed that Team One had reached the front door, and Team Two was rounding the corner in sight of the back door. Saunders clicked his mike back on.

'Both teams in place,' Saunders said. 'Team Leader, you have a go. Break it down.'

The radio crackled. 'Team One, Team Two, this is Team Leader. We have a go. On my mark: three, two, one . . .'

Members of both teams swung heavy metal battering rams into the doors, just below the door handles. Front and back doors exploded simultaneously, the wood from the frames splintering inward. For a moment the noise was disorienting, as ten agents, heavily armed and clad in dark riot gear, moved into the house, yelling, 'Federal Agents! Nobody move! Hands where we can see them!'

The television screens on the wall took on the quality of a kaleidoscopic lens as each member of the team broke off into narrow halls. Two Middle Eastern-looking men were sitting at a table in the kitchen, frozen, their hands half-raised, their eyes wide. They were in their late-thirties or early-forties, and they had long beards. 'What is the meaning of this?' one of them demanded. 'We are American citizens! You have no right!'

'Don't move!' was the response from one of the agents. 'Heads down on the table!'

'This is not right!' one of the men yelled back. His hand slipped below the table, and the agent moved without hesitation, swinging the butt of his assault rifle into the man's forehead. The man was knocked from his chair, and slid across the linoleum floor. A phone skittered to a corner, dropped from the man's hand as he grasped his forehead, which was already bleeding profusely. 'No!' he cried. 'I was calling my lawyer!'

Just then, two young women were ushered downstairs. One of them was carrying a baby wrapped in a blanket. She screamed when she saw the man bleeding on the floor. 'What have you done to my husband?' She handed the baby to the other woman and ran to the man. She reached up to the sink and grabbed a dishtowel to wrap around his head. 'What have you done?'

'Ma'am, keep away, please!' the agent yelled at her. He put a foot in between husband and wife and physically separated them.

'Why, why, why?' the woman was screaming through sobs, reaching out to her husband.

'Please, ma'am,' the agent repeated. 'No contact.'

'This is illegal!' shouted the man remaining at the table. He stood. 'By what right do you do this?'

One of the other team members pushed the barrel of his assault weapon into the man's chest. 'Please, sir!' he barked. 'Sit back down!'

Saunders watched Johnson's camera angle as he stepped forward. 'Sir, please remain still. We are executing a lawful search.' His voice was calm but firm, almost robotic. He knew that the entire operation was being recorded. Saunders silently thanked God that none of the ops he'd run when he was younger had ever been recorded. Saunders was nowhere near as diplomatic.

'Where is your warrant?'

'It will be provided to you in due course,' Johnson said.

'That is illegal!'

'No, it's not. Once the search has been completed, you

can contact a lawyer to confirm that. Until we are done, you need to stay here. If you don't, I will place you under arrest. Is that understood?' He looked down at the bloodied man on the floor, turned to one of the other agents. 'Agent Salvino, provide that man with first aid.'

Salvino put his assault rifle down and knelt by the injured man.

'Get away!' the man's wife screamed. 'Get away, I tell you!'

Salvino looked up at Johnson, and the team leader just shrugged.

The search took forty-five minutes. Two team members remained with the residents the entire time, watching over them. The others went through the house with microscopic precision. Through drawers, through cabinets, under beds and in mattresses. They even pried up floor boards where a seam looked askew. The search turned up nothing.

Back at Langley, the four other men around the table stared at Saunders. 'Goddammit,' Toney muttered. 'I told you. I fuckin' told you, but you wouldn't listen, would you?'

Saunders said nothing in response. There was no point. He had no cover, and everyone knew it.

'You can't treat this Agency as your own personal commando unit, you asshole!'

'That's enough, Bill!' Ainsworth shouted.

Johnson's radio microphone crackled. 'Base, this is Team Leader. We've got nothing here.' There was frustration in his voice. He looked around, and on the television screen hooked to his camera Saunders surveyed the mess in the house.

'Search them,' he said.

'Roger.' Johnson turned to the two men. 'Sirs, please stand against the wall, feet shoulder-width apart.'

'I will not,' one of the men responded.

'Yes, sir, you will,' Johnson responded. He nodded to Salvino, who reached down and lifted the man off his chair. Two of the other team members conducted the search, probing far more aggressively than the frisk most people are used to at the airport.

The women were next. Johnson summoned Beverley Samuels, one of the team members, to conduct that search, and ordered his men to turn their heads during the process. 'Nothing,' Johnson said into his microphone when it was over. 'We've got nothing.'

'Congratulations, Saunders,' Toney said. 'You've got yourself an official shitshow. The suspension that's been coming your way for years looks like it has finally arrived, asshole.'

Saunders just sat there, his mind working furiously.

Toney continued, 'Don't think I'm gonna take one inch of this fall for you. Don't you have anything to say for yourself?'

Saunders clicked back on the microphone on his headset. 'Search the baby,' he said.

'Say again, Base?' Johnson's voice was unsure.

'Search the baby,' Saunders repeated.

'Mother-fucking-Christ-on-a-popsicle stick!' Toney shouted. He turned to Ainsworth. 'Lawrence, you need to take control and shut this cocksucker down. Do it now! Otherwise, I'll file a report that will shake the whole Agency to the core. I swear to God, I will. You and I have been friends for a long time, but I don't care.'

33

Ainsworth looked at him. 'We've never been friends, Bill.' He looked at Saunders and shrugged. 'Your operation, your call.'

'Team Leader, do you copy?' Saunders said into his microphone.

'Roger that.' Johnson walked over to the woman holding the infant wrapped in a blue blanket.

'No!' she screamed. 'You leave my baby! Animals! Leave him!'

'Ma'am, hand me the baby,' Johnson said.

'No!' she screamed again.

Johnson motioned to one of the other agents, who stepped forward and held the woman by the arm. She continued to scream. Johnson pulled the child away from his mother and the baby began to cry in long, loud shrieks of fear. Back at the bunker, Saunders could hear several different people yelling, but the baby's wails cut straight through to his eardrum.

Johnson laid the baby down on the kitchen table and unwrapped the blanket. On the screen, Saunders watched as the baby, no longer safe in his warm cocoon, shivered and sputtered. Johnson ran a gloved hand down around the baby's back. Nothing. He reached in and flipped his hand through the folds of the blanket. After a moment, his hand stopped. The screen was still. Slowly, his hand pulled back from the blanket, and grasped in his fingers was a 12-megabyte memory stick. He held it up to his face, giving those back at the bunker a clear look.

'Bingo,' he said quietly.

'Bingo,' Saunders repeated.

Suddenly there was a shriek followed by several rounds

of gunfire. In the confined space of the kitchen it sounded like the world was exploding. Everyone was shouting, and the cameras jostled, spinning around in a panic, seeking out the source of the gunshots. Johnson's camera spun from the baby and the lens came to rest on one of the two men who had been sitting at the kitchen table. He was standing now, and he had a black Glock in his hand, pointing it just below the camera. On the screen, they could see two bright flashes from the muzzle, then the camera spun and flipped, and came to rest staring at the ceiling. More shouting followed, and then several bursts of automatic rifle fire. After a moment, all that was left was the sobbing coming from one of the women.

'What the fuck happened?' Saunders shouted into the microphone.

A voice came back. 'He got Sal's gun! Special Agent Johnson's been hit!'

Saunders surveyed the television screens, trying to piece the scene together. One showed one of the women, bent over the body of her husband, blood pooling under his body. She was rocking back and forth, wailing. Another showed Nick Johnson's face. He was lying on the ground, ashen, gasping for breath. 'I'm okay,' he said over and over. 'I'm okay, I can hack it.'

'We got you, boss,' the man kneeling over him said. Then he turned and looked back toward the hallway. 'Get a goddamned ambulance here!' he screamed. 'Somebody get a fuckin' medic!'

He turned back to the wounded man, and the screen showed Nick Johnson's face again. It had grown paler. A thin river of blood leaked from the corner of his mouth.

'We got it,' he choked out, raising a clenched fist. The man leaning over him held out his hand, and the memory stick slipped out of Johnson's hand. 'We got it,' he said again. His eyes rolled up into his head.

One by one, the other men in the sixth-floor bunker walked out, none of them saying a word. Saunders stayed there, though. He sat alone for several hours, watching as the ambulance arrived, and Nick Johnson's body was loaded into the same vehicle as that of the man who had killed him. He watched as the other members of the operational team passed each other, the faces on the screens tight with pain and anger. He sat until the last of the cameras had been shut down, and the screens went blank, and he was sitting in complete darkness in the command center, wondering whether any of it had been worth it. Wondering whether Nick Johnson's third-grade daughter would care, even if it was.

CHAPTER FIVE

Cianna held a towel to her brother's forehead as he sat on the sofa. Her assault on him had opened a cut just above his right eyebrow. The bleeding had stopped, and the cut was small, but she still felt guilty. 'I think maybe you need stitches,' she said.

'You kidding?' Charlie said with a wry smile. 'I get worse cuts shaving.'

'You're shaving now?' He laughed at that, but she could hear the pain it masked. He'd always been short and slight and acutely sensitive to intimations about his masculinity. 'When did you get out?' she asked, changing the subject.

'Two weeks ago,' he said. 'My discharge came through last month.'

'Why didn't you let me know? I would've put on the dog. How often does my baby brother come home from war?'

'I was a supply sergeant,' he said with a touch of embarrassment.

'In Afghanistan,' she pointed out. 'I don't give a crap what anyone does; if you're doing it in a combat theater, you're a combat soldier, as far as I'm concerned.'

'Not in the same way you were,' he said quietly.

She took the towel away from his head and stood up,

not knowing what to say. 'Yeah, well,' she stammered. 'I'm guessing most people would choose your military record over mine.'

He looked down, avoiding her eyes. 'Sorry. I didn't mean to bring it up.'

'No problem,' she said emotionlessly. 'I haven't had a chance to talk to you since it all happened.'

'You want to talk about it now?' he asked.

She thought about it for a moment. 'You know what? Not tonight. I had a long day at work.'

'Where are you working?'

'I've got a job with a non-profit group here in town.' She tried to make it seem worthwhile, even glamorous. She could tell by the expression on her brother's face that she had failed.

'A *non-profit*? What the fuck is that?' he asked. 'A company that tries to lose money?'

'It's like a charity,' she said. 'It's a good thing to do.'

'What's it called?'

She hesitated. 'Guardians for Youth.' She knew what was coming.

'You're shittin' me?' Her brother let out a loud sarcastic laugh. 'You're workin' for a charity called *Guardians for Youth*? That's rich.'

She threw the towel with his blood on it at him. 'Shut the fuck up,' she said with a smile. 'It's a decent place. We work with the parole board to try to keep young kids just out of juvie or prison out of trouble. We're like the first line of defense. People start to slide, we step in and try to get them back in line before they get to the point where they're gonna get sent back in. It's rewarding.'

'Rewarding, huh?' Charlie said. 'Does that mean it pays well?'

Cianna waved her arm at the apartment. 'Oh, sure, can't you tell? I'm makin' a mint.'

Charlie looked around. 'It's not big, but at least it's a shithole.'

Cianna shrugged. 'You know what they say: location, location, location,' she said sarcastically.

'Right. Three more strikes. I thought you wanted to be a cop?'

Her expression went flat. 'That dream died the minute I put on my prison fatigues.' She took a deep breath and struggled to pull herself out of a brief slide into self-pity. She didn't want her brother to see her that way. 'It's okay, though. I really like what I'm doing, even if it is a kinda shitty job. Milo, the guy who started the place, is an okay guy. You'd like him.'

'Would I?'

'Well, maybe not right off. I get the feeling that he grew up rich and he's a little weird, but he's trying to do the right thing, and he's got his good points.'

'Can't wait to meet him.'

'What are you going to do now that you're back?' she asked, changing the subject. 'Not a great time to be out of work.'

'I've got something lined up,' he said. 'It should set me up for a while.' He looked serious for a moment. 'Maybe longer than a while.'

She tried to smile and failed. 'You were always the dreamer, Charlie.'

'It's not a dream this time,' he said.

She just nodded. 'I'm tired, Charlie,' she said without turning around. 'I'm gonna go get ready to sleep. You can take the bed, I'll pull a blanket on the couch.'

'No,' Charlie protested, but she would have none of it.

'It's the least I can do after beating you up.' She walked over to the tiny bathroom and closed the door.

She was lying on the couch twenty minutes later when Charlie stuck his head out of the bedroom door. He had on a T-shirt and pajama bottoms, and silhouetted against the streetlight through the window he looked so much the way she remembered him as a child. She'd spent a lifetime trying to protect him from the world. She'd been okay at it, too, when they were younger and things were simpler. No more. She was no longer sure she had the wherewithal to be of any use to him, and it frightened her.

'Are you sure about this?' he asked. 'I feel really bad about putting you out of your own bed.'

'I'm sure, Charlie. Go to sleep.'

He hesitated for a second. 'If you ever want to talk about it, you know I'm here, right?'

'I know,' she said. 'I'm fine.'

'Okay,' he said. 'Sleep well.' He went back into the cubby of a bedroom, closed the door.

But Cianna knew she would not sleep well. She hadn't slept well in two years. Dreams of the past haunted her. As she rolled on her side and closed her eyes, she hoped that when the dreams came for her that night they would be of the good, not the bad.

*

It was still dark when Cianna Phelan opened her eyes. The electric fan strapped into the window whirred pitifully, pushing the warm early morning air into her corrugated living quarters. By noon it would be over one hundred and ten degrees. Kandahar in July made Washington DC in August seem temperate.

At least it's a dry heat.

That was the running joke. It was so dry it felt like God had shoved the whole barren wasteland into an oven. As she took a breath she could feel the dust collect in her nostrils. It was better here at the airbase, though, than on the humps the combat units took through the arid mountains, where the dehydration became bad enough that hallucinations set in and muscles cramped so tight men sometimes preferred open combat to walking.

She felt Haley Jones stir next to her in the cot as she looked up at the window. The sun would be up within the hour. She was crazy to have him here with her.

'You need to leave,' she whispered.

He grunted softly, like a bear in hibernation.

She rolled over and looked at him. How old was he? Maybe twenty. Maybe not yet. At least five years younger than she.

She was definitely crazy.

Looking at him she was drawn again to his youth. A fragment of a poem she'd read back in high school flashed through her mind; something about the beauty of an athlete dying young. It had seemed so absurd back then, so divorced from any reality she could imagine at the time. Now, though, the notion resonated. She resolved to find the poem and give it another chance.

Jones still wasn't moving.

She sat up on the cot, straddled him. She was wearing only an OD green T-shirt. 'Private!' Her voice was quiet, but her tone was Army.

His eyes shot open, and she recognized the fear in them. The disorientation of being startled awake heightened the terror that lived in every soldier. It was not a fear of death, but of being surprised – of being unprepared. It took a moment for him to gain his bearings, and then the fear dissipated. He looked up at her and smirked. 'Sarge,' he said.

'You need to get back to your barracks.'

He turned his head and looked out the window. 'It's still dark.'

'Not for long. B Company is doing a clear and hold today. You need to be sharp.'

'I'm always sharp,' he said, stretching. 'You running support?'

She nodded. 'We'll mop up whatever you pry loose.'

'Fuckin' Kandahar,' he said.

'Fuckin' Kandahar,' she repeated.

'Could be a shitshow.'

She agreed. 'Could be.'

'That's why they're sending in the big dogs,' he said with a 20-year-old's bravado. He flexed his biceps like a body-builder and winked.

'Don't get cocky,' she said.

'Me?' he asked. 'How about you?'

'I don't get cocky,' she said.

He reached over to the table by the side of the bed, and grabbed the small leather case sitting on top.

'Give me that!' she said, lunging for it.

He held it away from her, though, as he flipped it open and read the citation. 'For gallantry in action against an enemy of the United States.' *She watched him admire the contents. 'Silver Star,' he marveled. He looked back at her. 'And you say you don't get cocky?'*

'It doesn't mean anything,' she said.

'It means everything,' he replied. 'What do I have to do to get one?'

She sighed. 'Something stupid enough to get yourself killed, probably. Trust me, it's not worth it.'

'You going soft, Sarge?' He laughed at the notion.

'No, Jonesie,' she said. 'But the Army's invested more than 50,000 in your training. Be a shame to leave that kind of investment bleeding out on the street in a shithole like this.'

'Aw, that's sweet.' He laughed again.

'Get back to your barracks,' she ordered.

'Okay.' He nodded, but his hand slid up the inside of her leg.

'Jones!' She tried to put a warning in her voice, but her chest was tight, and it came out flat and breathless. His fingers moved back and forth lightly between her legs. She looked down at his face, wondering why she'd given in to him; wondering what she felt for him. It wasn't love, she knew. She would feel love more deeply if it ever came. But it wasn't mere lust, either. There was something about him — something about his eyes, about his close-cropped dark hair, and his lithe muscular build — that made him beautiful. In many ways, they were physical counterparts, tight, fit, and strong. Army Strong. *For a moment, looking at him, she could see all of the men with whom she had served, all those who had been lost. The men and boys she had fought with.*

She thought back to the times growing up in the grit of South Boston on the edge of the genteel New England city.

It seemed as though she'd been fighting for her entire life. She was attractive, and that made her a target on the street, so she'd learned to defend herself early. She'd been taught to be dangerous, and she'd been in and out of trouble through high school. One of her court-appointed counselors suggested the Army out of desperation, and it had been a perfect fit. She'd trained hard and honed her skills and her instincts. Here she could fight for something other than herself without worrying about watching her back. Her men trusted her, and she trusted them. And every once in a while, as long as she was discreet, she could teach one of them some of the other things she'd learned on the street.

She closed her eyes as he continued touching her. 'I told you to leave.'

'You want me to stop?' he asked. The pace of his fingers quickened.

'If you get caught in here, it's my career,' she said. She'd already surrendered, though, and they both knew it. Her hips moved involuntarily, and she could feel her nipples harden as they brushed the inside of her shirt. 'If anyone finds out – if you tell anyone . . .!'

'Who am I gonna tell, the Lieutenant?' Her face darkened at the notion, and he retreated quickly. 'Don't worry, Sergeant Phelan,' he said with a tilted smile, 'I take orders better than anyone.'

'Yeah, right,' she said.

'Come on,' he said. 'Does anyone outside your squad come to attention as reliably as me?'

She slid her hand between his legs. He wasn't lying. 'When we're done, you leave immediately, you understand?' she said.

'Hooah.' He was breathing almost as hard as she was now,

and his free hand snaked under her shirt, over her breasts and around her back, pulling her down on him.

'I mean it,' she said. 'That's an order.' She guided him to her with her hand as she lowered herself onto him, taking control even as her body began to shiver.

CHAPTER SIX

Lawrence Ainsworth's office was on the fourth floor at Langley. It was necessarily opulent, fit to receive powerful politicians and heads of government departments and convey a sense of omnipotence and control. The anteroom where his secretary sat had thick deep-blue carpeting and textured cream wallpaper. Several polished wooden chairs lined one wall, where those anticipating an audience with the Assistant Director could wait in stiff comfort.

Ainsworth's secretary, Agnes Shoals, had been with the Agency for longer than anyone could remember, and she had an aristocratic air to her. She sat behind a Queen Anne desk wearing a high-necked white blouse under a cashmere sweater, and her hair was perfectly styled. She was probably in her sixties, but could pass for decades younger in a pinch. There was a rumor that she kept a loaded pistol strapped to the underside of the desk in case of an emergency.

Saunders walked through her door and nodded to her. 'Agnes,' he said. 'He's in, I take it?'

She smiled at him as though he were a favorite, wayward nephew. 'Jack, you can't go in,' she said.

He was still moving toward the door to Ainsworth's inner office. 'I can't?' he said. 'That can't be right.' He

46

reached the door and grasped the handle. 'Let me try.'

'Jack!' Her voice was sharp, and her smile had disappeared. 'I will not allow it! He gave explicit directions that he didn't want to see you.'

'You must have misunderstood,' Saunders said, turning the handle.

'Jack, don't!' she barked. Her hand disappeared under the desk.

He smiled at her. 'I've always wanted to know,' he said. 'Is it standard issue, or something more personal? I envision a silver-plated revolver. Something understated that would go nicely with the pearls.'

Her face softened. 'I should shoot you.'

He nodded. 'You should, but you won't. That's why we've always gotten along so well.' He pushed the door open and walked into Ainsworth's office.

Ainsworth looked up from his desk with the pained expression of exhausted patience. 'So much for Agnes's resolve,' he said.

'She threatened to shoot me, if that makes you feel better.'

'I specifically authorized deadly force, so it doesn't.' He sighed. 'She was a fine field agent when she was younger. She's lost her nerve.'

Saunders walked over and sat down in one of the chairs across from Ainsworth's desk.

'Please, have a seat,' Ainsworth said.

'What's going on, Lawrence?' Saunders said. 'It doesn't take a full day to analyze a 12-megabyte memory stick. Why haven't I heard anything?'

'Because it doesn't concern you.'

'You want to tell me what the hell that means?'

'It's not your case, Jack.'

'Why not?' Saunders demanded.

'Because you're about to be officially on suspension.'

Saunders had no idea what to say. It was like he'd been hit with a baseball bat. 'What the fuck are you talking about, Lawrence?' he demanded.

'I'm talking about a dead FBI agent, and a raid that went wrong with everyone watching, that's what I'm talking about.' He shook his head. 'You just don't get it, do you? I wasn't given a choice in this. Toney wanted you executed.'

'Toney's an asshole,' Saunders said.

'Toney's the Director of the NSA. That puts him above me on the governmental org chart. He was also the head of Military Intelligence in Afghanistan for three years, so he does add value on this front. And you're the asshole, my boy. This was just the excuse they were looking for. You've been on the chopping block since you were called back from Afghanistan.'

'You've got to be kidding me. I did what needed to be done over there, and you know it.'

'You were under express orders to leave it alone. But you couldn't, could you? You had to take matters into your own hands.'

'They killed our people, Lawrence. Murphy and Desouza and Keller and Schmidt . . .'

'I know.'

'. . . and Jeffs and Klein . . .'

'I know, goddammit!' Ainsworth shouted. The outburst took Saunders by surprise. His boss was famous for his equanimity. Saunders couldn't remember ever seeing him shout before. His son's death had shortened his temper. 'You don't have to tell me their names; I recruited every goddamned one of them! You think I didn't feel it when they died?'

'And Sam?' Saunders said quietly. 'What about him? Didn't he deserve justice?'

Ainsworth struggled to keep his composure. His face went red, and his breathing was heavy as he stared at Saunders. After a moment he was able to speak. 'My son chose his profession,' he said.

'Your son chose to follow you. Just like I did.'

'He knew the risks. So did you.'

Saunders nodded. 'He did. That's what made him a hero. He did what he did knowing the risk. He, like you, loved this country enough to put his life on the line. To me, that deserves our respect. To me, that deserves justice.'

'I don't disagree,' Ainsworth conceded.

'And yet you pulled me back off the field. You're not allowing me to do my job. Why? Because I did what you would have done? Because I did what others wouldn't do?' Saunders shook his head. 'Do these fucking bureaucrats really expect us to fight a war when we're not allowed to kill the people who are killing us? It's absurd.'

'It's about winning their hearts and minds, Jack,' Ainsworth said.

'That's bullshit, and you know it,' Saunders retorted. 'We're winning just enough hearts and minds to prevent us from using effective tactics. We might be better off pissing people off more and letting everyone know that, in the end, we're willing to do whatever it takes to come out on top.'

'We don't have that kind of mandate. This isn't Pearl Harbor, Jack. Hell, it's not even Iraq. Most Americans think the Afghans are our allies, and they view the number of soldiers we lose every month as little more than an annoyance. Until that changes, an all-out war just isn't feasible. The American people won't stand for a greater commitment.'

'So you've kept me here, out of the game.'

'I kept you here because no one else would work with you. I kept you here because there's an *Assistant* in front of my title, and I don't make the final decisions, you got me? I was trying to protect you, don't you understand that? All you had to do was lay low for a little while, but you couldn't do that, could you? Well, this is where it's gotten you. It's not what I wanted, but there it is. I'm sorry, you know that, don't you?'

Saunders sat forward on his chair. 'Yeah, Lawrence, I know.'

'Good.'

Saunders sat back in his chair. 'But the data's been analyzed, right?'

Ainsworth rolled his eyes. 'You really are unbelievable. It's like talking to a brick wall.'

'What did we find?' Saunders pushed.

Ainsworth shook his head, opened up a file on his desk, looked it over for a few seconds. 'There wasn't much, really. Most of it's coded, and a lot of it's nothing but chatter. Lots of references to Allah's omnipotence, and platitudes about the evils of the West. Lots of propaganda to be spread.'

'But there was something about Boston.'

'There was.'

Saunders sat there for a moment, waiting for his boss, the man who had long ago recruited him for a life of deception and danger, to say more. 'Well?' he finally demanded.

Ainsworth slumped heavily in the chair across from Saunders. 'It's incomplete. There are references, but none of them make any sense.'

'What do they say?'

The old man brought his hands together at the fingertips in a contemplative gesture. 'They say that the Heart of Afghanistan is in Boston.'

'*The Heart of Afghanistan is in Boston*,' Saunders repeated slowly. 'What the hell does that mean?'

Ainsworth shrugged. 'We don't know. The message is garbled. It says to locate Charles Phelan. It says that he has it.'

'Really,' Saunders said. 'Do we know who Charles Phelan is?'

'Maybe,' Ainsworth said. 'There's a Charles Phelan from South Boston who was just discharged two weeks ago. His last billet was in Afghanistan with the 154th Quartermaster Corps. We're assuming it's referring to him at the moment, but we have no way to know for sure.'

'Do we have an address in Boston for him?'

The Assistant Director of the Central Intelligence Agency shook his head. 'His father skipped out on the family before Charles was born, and his mother split a long time ago. He has no permanent residence, as near as we can tell. He was discharged from Fort Devens near the Cape, so it's a safe bet that he's somewhere in the area. He has a sister – Cianna Phelan – former Army, too. For the past three months she's been renting a place in South Boston. They were both stationed at Kandahar Airbase until two years ago.'

'After that?'

There was a noticeable pause before Ainsworth answered. 'She left. He stayed. Finished out his tour, came home.'

Something about the manner in which Ainsworth phrased his answer struck Saunders, and he looked at the old man for a moment before he spoke again. Ainsworth met his stare and didn't blink. 'You said *she left*,' Saunders said finally. 'You didn't say she finished out her tour.'

'That's true.' Ainsworth crossed his legs, looked at his shoe.

'Is this twenty questions?'

'She got herself into some trouble. She had to leave, come back to the States.'

'Where in the States?' Saunders asked slowly.

'Leavenworth.'

Saunders raised his eyebrows. Leavenworth was the largest military prison in the United States. 'What for?'

'Manslaughter,' Ainsworth said.

'Really?'

'The original charge was murder. The panel of officers found there was enough justification to convict her only on the lesser charge. She was decorated, so the Army kept it out of the press, and her sentence was reduced to two years. It's just as well; any publicity about her conviction would have gone down badly for the Army.'

'Why?'

Ainsworth took a deep breath. 'She wasn't an ordinary soldier. She was part of an experimental Delta Force unit and she'd been given special training. The kind of training most women are not permitted to have.'

'What do you mean?'

'Under Army regulations, women can't serve in combat roles. They can be in support units – the Military Police, the Medical Corps, even 'non-combat' pilot positions – but not in direct-combat units. It often ends up being a distinction without a difference, particularly with the MPs, where she served, who are regularly placed in full-combat positions. But the Army still tries to recognize the division. As a result, certain types of combat training are not given to women. But over in Afghanistan, the Army was getting creative. They had certain needs, and she filled one of those needs. Some believe the training she got led directly to the killing. No one wanted to go there with an investigation, so a deal was cut.'

'Who'd she kill?'

'That's classified.'

'I've got clearance,' Saunders laughed.

'No you don't,' Ainsworth shot back. 'Your clearance was revoked when you were put on suspension.'

'You need me out there,' Saunders said. 'You don't have any field agents in the country who understand Afghanistan the way I do. Who are they going to send to Boston to check this out?'

Ainsworth shrugged. 'I've submitted the analysis to the

Director and the NSA, and it's all being looked at. If they find it worth pursuing in his office, they'll assign someone.'

'*If they find it worth pursuing?* Mustafa bled out on the street in front of our eyes! How can this not be worth pursuing?' Ainsworth held his hands out, palms up, in a gesture of helplessness. 'Jesus, it's gonna be days before they even make up their minds. By then, whatever this is will be over. You think Toney has the balls to do anything? We'll be reading about shit blowing up in the *New York Times* before he or the Director puts anyone on a plane!'

'What do you want me to tell you, Jack?' Ainsworth demanded. 'I just work here. I do what I'm told.'

'That's bullshit, and we both know it. You've never been a guy who *just does what he's told.* Neither one of us has ever been that.'

'Maybe I've changed, then, because I'm sending out an official suspension notice today. It will arrive at your house within two days and is effective as of then. After that, I do not want to see your face in this building. If I find your car parked in the lot, I'll have it blown up. Do you understand me? It's a paid suspension. There will be a formal hearing in three weeks. After that . . . we'll see.'

'What the hell am I supposed to do for the three weeks while I'm on suspension?'

Ainsworth was looking at the file on the table in front of him again. 'Get out of town,' he said. 'Go somewhere.'

'Where am I supposed to go?'

It took a moment for Ainsworth to answer. He raised his head and peered over his reading glasses at Saunders, looking at him like he was the densest man he'd ever met. 'I don't know,' he said. 'I can't control where you spend your time off.' His eyes were sharp. 'You went to Harvard, didn't you? Maybe a visit to your alma mater would be just the thing to put you in order.'

Saunders sat back in his chair, looking at his boss. He'd known the man a long time, and he knew how he operated. 'Cambridge is right across the river from Boston.'

'Is it?' Ainsworth shrugged. 'I hadn't given that much thought. Obviously if you wanted to do some other things while you were there visiting your old professors – take in some sights, get some of the local flavor – there's nothing stopping you. Like I said, I can't control what you do when you're on leave. If you don't want to go to Boston, you can always use my family estate in the Berkshires. It's the closest place to heaven I've ever been.'

'I know,' Saunders said. 'I've stayed there before, remember? With Sam.'

'Of course,' Ainsworth said. 'I suppose I'd forgotten.' He put the folder down on top of his desk, close to the edge, and left it open at an angle where the contents were in plain view for Saunders. 'The decision is yours, Jack. Your suspension notice will be in the mail today. You are officially off this case,' the old man said. 'Whether you decide to go to Boston is not my responsibility.'

CHAPTER SEVEN

Kalid Gamol reclined on a set of pillows before a feast table. His house was in the center of Kandahar, in what had once been a wealthy neighborhood, though real wealth had fled the country back when the Russians invaded. Since then, even those with power had to settle for snatches of privilege, like tonight. It was his seventieth birthday, and he would not deny himself this recognition.

The house, like many others in the area, had two stories of rooms and galleries facing onto a central courtyard open to the sky. Nearly one hundred guests had made it to the celebration, each of them submitting to a full search at the door to ensure safety. Even friends were suspect in this country, he knew too well. There had been a time when he'd viewed his native country as a land of honor, but more than three decades of war and subjugation had stripped the nation of any sense of itself. He remembered wistfully the time before, when trade flowed freely, and Afghans took advantage of the nation's location as a cross-road between major commercial centers. He wondered whether the country could ever find that place again, or something resembling that place. He hoped so. Otherwise, it would remain nothing more than a staging area for the battles others wished to fight.

Gamol's table was at one end of the courtyard, and ten of his closest allies and advisors were around him. He would join the rest of his guests shortly, but at the moment there was business to attend to.

'We have confirmation,' Safraz, his primary advisor, was saying. 'The relic has been removed from the country, taken to the United States.'

The faces around the table were grim. 'This is not good,' Gamol said with characteristic understatement.

'Whoever controls it can control the country,' Akhtar Hazara said. 'If the Americans have it . . .' He was still a young man, only twenty-four, but he'd already proved himself to be a leader and a man of substance. He was tall and strong, and living a life without a father had made him hard. Since the death of Gamol's only son, Gamol thought of Akhtar as the closest he would have to an heir.

'You listen too much to your uncle,' Gamol said.

'It has great power.'

'Superstition,' Gamol grunted. 'Nothing more.'

'We live in a superstitious country,' Akhtar countered thoughtfully. 'Even if you do not believe in the power of the relic itself, if it has been stolen by the Americans, it will be blamed on you. It will give Fasil the advantage with the people. Kandahar is your responsibility.'

'Kandahar is Allah's responsibility,' Gamol said quietly. 'Only He could tame this city.'

'It is not much of a campaign slogan,' Akhtar commented, drawing nervous laughs from a few around the table. He was the only one brave enough to risk sarcasm with Gamol.

Gamol reached over to the table and closed his fist on

a bowlful of dates. He sat back and put one in his mouth, frowning. 'Democracy is an American fiction,' he said. 'The people do not want to vote, they want to eat. Whoever takes power and shows that they can provide for the people will stay in power. No one would dare to oppose such a ruler. That is where our focus has been – providing for the people. That is where our focus must stay.'

'Even if it means working with the Americans?' Akhtar asked.

'Even if it means working with the Devil himself,' Gamol responded. 'At least, for a time.' There was a murmur of assent from around the table.

'And what of the relic?' Safraz asked.

'Akhtar is correct,' Gamol responded. 'If it has been taken to America, we will suffer the wrath of Allah, and of the people.'

'What shall we do?' Akhtar asked.

'Your family has always had the honor of protecting it, has it not? You shall go to Boston,' Gamol said, looking at the young man. 'And you shall take it back.'

CHAPTER EIGHT

Cianna Phelan's bleary eyes stared up at the paint peeling off the ceiling in her cramped living room. The dream-faded memory of the young soldier lying on top of her pressed down on her chest as though it had real weight; as though the past were reaching forward to pull her back, heartbeat by heartbeat.

The sofa had shot its springs back in a time before Reagan was President, and it was impossible to get comfortable as the cushions lurched and bucked in uneven spasms with her every movement. She forced herself to take a breath, and was amazed at the effort it required. When she exhaled, the edges of the paint bubbles above her on the ceiling fluttered.

'Morning.'

She looked toward the bedroom. Charlie was standing in the doorway, his short reddish hair riotous from sleep. She ran a hand over her own head and could feel her hair in fits. She supposed they looked alike. They were even around the same size, though that was no doubt a sore subject for her brother. Looking at him now, she could see the sharp bones of his elbow, and the shirt draped over his shoulders as if on a wire hanger. She wondered how he'd ever survived in the Army. Even in the Quartermaster

Corps, where he'd spent his tours overseeing the movement of men, machinery and supplies, he must have stuck out as a target for tyrants and bullies.

'Morning,' Cianna replied. She swung her legs off the couch and rubbed her face.

'Sleep well?' he asked her.

'Sure,' she lied. 'There's instant coffee in the cabinet.'

She stood and went into the bathroom. It took her three minutes to shower, brush her teeth and pull on a pair of cargo pants and a torn sweatshirt. She was used to moving quickly in the morning; extended bathing was permitted neither in the Army nor in the prison. She ran a towel over her hair for fifteen seconds and emerged before the water for the coffee was boiling. Charlie had pulled on some loose jeans and found two mugs.

'So,' she said. 'What now?'

He looked over at her and smiled. She'd always loved his smile. It hadn't changed since he'd been a tiny boy. 'You want some sugar and milk?'

'I don't have either.'

'I could run down to the street. There's still a Tedeschi's on the corner of Mercer and Eighth, right?'

'There is, but black is fine with me.'

'For me, too.' He walked over and handed her one of the mugs, sat in the chair to the side of the sofa. He raised the mug to her, and she lifted hers with less enthusiasm.

'I thought you were going to sign up for another tour,' she said. 'I got your letters when I was . . .' She paused. 'I got your letters.'

'You never wrote me back.'

She looked at her coffee. 'I didn't have much to say.

Besides, I figured it'd be better for you if you weren't getting letters from me. You never know who's looking through your mail over there. Letters from a convict wouldn't have helped you with the brass.'

'Fair enough,' he said. 'It still would've been nice to hear from you, though. Even if just to know you were all right.'

'I know,' she said. 'The thing is, I wasn't all right. What happened over there . . . it's hard to explain. They took away everything I was, and everything I wanted to be. I had it all planned out. Then . . .'

'I understand. But I'm your brother.'

'I'm sorry. I just couldn't talk to anyone. I still don't feel like a real person again, yet.' Neither of them said anything for a moment. She decided to try to change the subject. 'So what happened to re-upping?'

He sipped his coffee. Now he seemed to be avoiding her stare. 'I was done with it,' he said. 'I only joined up to follow you. I didn't know what else to do with my life back then. Once you were gone, it didn't seem to make sense anymore.'

'What are you going to do now?' It was more than an idle question. Her pay barely kept her above the poverty-line; it could never support the two of them.

He sipped his coffee, looking straight ahead. 'I have some leads,' he said.

'What sort of leads?'

He shrugged, and the shadow of a smile appeared on his lips. 'I'll let you know when I figure out whether they're gonna work out.'

She frowned. 'Why not tell me now?' she asked.

61

'Because I don't want to yet.' His tone turned defensive. 'It's something I want to do on my own,' he said. 'But if it works out, I'll be set for a while.' He was no longer smiling. If anything he looked nervous. 'We'll both be set for a while,' he added, looking around the tiny apartment.

Cianna put her coffee down. 'Tell me what this is all about, Charlie,' she said sharply. 'I don't like the sound of it.'

Charlie frowned. 'Tough shit,' he said angrily. He put the mug down and the coffee slopped over the edge onto the crate that served as a table. 'You're not my mother, Cianna,' he said.

'I'm the closest you've got,' she replied sharply.

'I can take care of myself,' he protested.

'Since when?'

'Since two and a half years ago, when you went to prison,' he said.

It stopped the conversation cold. They sat there in silence for a little while. Cianna tried to think of something to say, but nothing came to her. He was right, after all. Any claim she'd had to being the responsible sibling was gone. Any right she had to advise him about how to live his life had been lost.

'I didn't mean that,' he said after a while.

'Yes, you did.'

'I'm sorry, I . . .'

'It's okay. You're right. You've been taking care of yourself for a while now. I'll leave you be.' She stood up and walked over to the front door, took her leather jacket off the peg on the wall. 'I don't have any food in the house,' she said. 'I'm going to go out and get some things. Is there anything you'd like?'

'I have to take care of a few things today,' Charlie said. 'I don't think I'll be here for lunch.'

'If you are, the food will be here.' Cianna opened the door.

'Sis,' he called after her as she stepped out of the apartment. She turned to look at him. 'I'm sorry I said that. I'm a little on edge. Let me take care of a few things and then we can talk. You'll be proud of me. I just don't want you to worry, okay?'

'Me worry?' She gave him a sad smile. 'I'll be here when you want to talk.' She closed the apartment door behind her.

The Southie streets were busy and crowded. In the autumn chill the steam rose in delicate wafts from sewage grates and street vendors' carts. The sounds of kids playing stick hockey on the cement rink down by the highway carried sharply on the crisp air. Hockey was more popular here than basketball, in part because body checking and fighting were built into the rules. Blood was a part of business down in the projects; it was a part of play, too.

Cianna was comfortable here. It had taken some time after her release. She even considered moving someplace new – someplace where no one would know her or care about her past. In the end, though, she knew she could never live anyplace but here. And fortunately for her, a stretch in prison had never been viewed with any particular sense of shame in this neighborhood. It even gave her some credibility in certain quarters.

The Tedeschi's on the corner was like a thousand others across the city. It had narrow aisles filled with low-end staples. Soft, starched-white bread, generic soda, peanut butter and various cheap canned goods were lined along the shelf-space. The store survived, though, on the goods sold behind the counter. Cigarettes and lottery tickets were the items that moved the fastest, most purchased with government-issued EBT food-stamp credit cards.

Cianna picked out some eggs, butter, and bread, and a plastic pack of processed bologna. The girl behind the counter was twenty pounds overweight and in her early-twenties, with bad skin and worse teeth. A look of recognition came over her face when she saw her. 'You're Cianna, right? Cianna Phelan?'

Cianna said nothing.

'I grew up in the building next to you in the Colony. I was about five years younger, but I remember you. You had a brother a little closer to my age. What the fuck was his name, Chucky or something like that, right?'

'Charlie,' Cianna said.

'Right, Charlie. He always got picked on 'cause he was so fuckin' small. You used to stick up for him, but there's only so much you can do, right? How's he doin' now?'

'He's good,' Cianna said. 'He just got out of the Army.' She pulled out her wallet and gave the girl an impatient look in the hope that it would spur her to start scanning her groceries.

The girl took the hint and looked slightly offended as she started ringing up the purchases. 'I heard you went away for a while. And now you're doing that parole-guard shit?' Cianna said nothing. 'Some fuckin' thing that happened last night to Vinnie Bronson at the projects, huh?' she asked knowingly.

Cianna recognized the girl, but had no idea what her name was. She certainly didn't know her enough to make any admissions to her. 'I'm not sure what you're talking about,' she said.

The girl winked like she was in on a secret. 'Uh huh, I'm not surprised. Vinnie's got some friends. Better not to know anything. They say it was a chick that broke his nose. They say he's pissed 'cause he's always been vain about his looks, and now his face is all fucked up. Most people think Vinnie's an asshole, though, so he's not gonna get a whole lot of sympathy, y'know?' She was ringing up the purchases as she talked. Cianna wished she would hurry up.

'Like I said, I don't know anything about it.'

'Yeah,' the girl said, trying to make eye contact. 'Like I said, that's probably better.' She was done ringing up Cianna's purchases, and Cianna ran her debit card through the reader. She held her breath, hoping that she had enough in the account to cover the nine dollars' worth of food. She felt the same worry whenever she was at the store. Living paycheck-to-paycheck caused her more stress than she cared to admit.

'Did your friend find you?' the girl asked as Cianna held her breath waiting for the transaction to clear.

'Sorry?'

'There was a guy here yesterday looking for you. Did he find you?'

'Oh, yeah, that must have been my brother,' Cianna said, giving a polite smile. 'He found me.'

The girl waved her hand at Cianna. 'No, not your brother. Unless your brother grew about two feet, hit the gym and shaved his head.'

Cianna frowned. 'What do you mean?'

'I remember your brother. He was short and skinny. I used to watch the neighborhood kids kick the shit out of him. The guy in here looked more like the kind of guy who does the shit-kickin', if you know what I mean.'

'I don't,' Cianna said.

'He was a fuckin' monster, this one.' The word came out as *monsta*. 'Shoulders like out to here.' She held her hands far apart and over her head. 'Totally bald, too. I don't know, some chicks like that look, but not me.'

'Someone besides my brother was here yesterday?' Cianna frowned again. 'He was asking for me?'

The woman shrugged like it was no big deal. 'Yeah. He was asking if I knew where you lived and where you worked.'

'What did you tell him?'

'I didn't tell him a fuckin' thing.' She looked at Cianna and put a finger on the side of her nose. 'For all I knew he was a cop, and it ain't my business. That's the way it works here. Maybe you should remember that when you bust into people's apartments when they don't want to be found.'

CHAPTER NINE

Charlie Phelan was shaking as he walked into the Iron Cross Tavern in South Boston. It was a dark place where people minded their own business. At ten-thirty Miles Gruden was already sitting in his corner booth, three newspapers spread out in front of him, two plates cluttering the table, and a stained coffee cup in his hand. It looked as though he'd been there for a while. Two men sat a few tables away. They were rough-cut and heavily boned, and they exuded menace. There was no question they were Miles's men.

Charlie walked over to the table. 'Miles,' he said, trying to keep the warble out of his voice.

Gruden glanced up at him like he was looking at a gutter that needed cleaning. He had a weathered, round face, and the pits in his nose testified to fifty-five years of hard living. He was wearing a short-sleeved, button-down shirt, open enough to show a dirty undershirt underneath. He said nothing for a moment, then looked back down at the newspaper in front of him and continued reading.

'It's Charlie,' Charlie said stupidly. 'Charlie Phelan. I grew up in the Old Colony. Chris Connell gave me your number, said you might be able to help me? I called—'

'I know who ya are,' Gruden said, cutting him off. He was still reading the paper. 'Siddown.'

Charlie did as he was told. Behind him he could feel Miles's men move closer, sitting at the table behind him, facing his back.

'You fuckin' believe this?' Gruden grunted. Charlie wasn't sure whether he was talking to himself. 'Economy's still not right and they're talkin' about raising taxes again. Motherfuckers.' Charlie was sure that Gruden had never paid a dollar in taxes in his entire life, but that seemed to be beside the point. 'Gonna bleed the fuckin' country dry.' He shoveled a fork full of cold egg and potatoes off one of the plates into his mouth and looked up at Charlie as he chewed, letting his lips separate enough to give Charlie a view of the semi-masticated breakfast. 'You bring it?' he asked after a moment.

Charlie shook his head. 'I didn't think—'

Gruden put his head back down in the paper without hearing the rest. 'You catch this shit, Joe?' he said into the table. 'Kid asks for my help, and then he doesn't even bring the shit with him.'

'Fucked-up world, Mr Gruden,' said a voice from behind Charlie. Apparently one of the men sitting behind him was Joe. Charlie wasn't sure which, though he supposed it didn't matter. He was guessing he'd have a hard time telling them apart anyway.

'You think I got time to waste, kid?' Gruden said.

'No,' Charlie replied. 'I didn't know whether you could help,' he stammered. 'I thought you wanted to talk—'

Gruden looked up sharply. 'If you didn't know whether I could help, why the fuck you call?'

'I wasn't sure—'

'You weren't sure? Why'd you call, then? You think I'm a fuckin' chump?'

'No, I just . . .' Charlie took a deep breath, tried to relax. Gruden was testing him. Charlie had spent enough time around bullies to recognize the tactic, and he understood that his reaction would set the tone for the negotiation to come. He thought about all the people who had taken advantage of him throughout his life, and he willed himself to appear confident. 'I wanted to talk to you first,' he said slowly. 'I didn't know whether you could help with this. It's an unusual item.'

Gruden picked up a stained napkin and wiped his mouth. 'Is it genuine?' he asked.

'Yeah,' Charlie said. 'It's genuine.'

'Then I can help you move it,' Gruden said. 'But I gotta see it first. I can't do a fuckin' thing one way or another if I can't verify that it's the real article.'

'I understand,' Charlie conceded. 'But I need to know how you plan on moving it.'

'You hear that, Joe?' Gruden said. 'Kid needs to know how I plan on moving it.'

'Unbelievable.'

Gruden narrowed his eyes as he looked back at Charlie. 'You don't need to know shit,' he said. 'If it's genuine, I got people who are interested. You understand, I'm gonna take sixty per cent to move it, though.'

'Going rate is forty,' Charlie said.

'Like you said,' Gruden responded, 'it's an unusual item. Goin' rate don't apply.'

'Maybe,' Charlie shot back, 'but you said you've already

got people interested. If that's true, this is gonna be the easiest sale you've ever made.'

Gruden blew his nose into the dirty napkin. Something escaped and landed on the front of his shirt. Charlie couldn't tell whether it was egg. Gruden either didn't notice or didn't care; it remained on the shirt. 'Maybe the easiest, maybe the most dangerous. I guess we'll wait and fuckin' see,' he said. 'Either way, you need my connections.'

'There are other people with connections in this city,' Charlie said. It was dangerous to try to play a man like Miles Gruden, but Charlie also knew that this was probably the largest fence the gangster would handle all year. It was easy money to him – too easy to pass up.

Gruden looked at Charlie for a long time before he lowered his eyes to his newspaper again. 'Jesus Christ,' he said. 'What do you think, Joe?'

'Like I said, it's a fucked-up world, Mr Gruden.'

Charlie worried that he had over-played his hand. 'Forty-five per cent,' he offered quickly.

Gruden folded up his newspapers one at a time, stacked them in a neat pile on the side of the table. He raised his hand and gestured toward the table and a waitress hurried over to collect the plates in front of him. She came back five seconds later with a pot of coffee and filled his cup. 'I remember you,' Gruden said as he emptied four sugars into the coffee cup. 'From when you were growing up in the neighborhood. Probably seems like a fuckin' lifetime ago to you, but to me it was just yesterday. You were always a scrawny little shit. Scared of your own shadow.'

'The Army changes people,' Charlie said. It was the best he had.

'Yeah?' Gruden sipped his coffee. 'I wouldn't know; I was smart enough to stay out.' He put his coffee cup down. 'But lookin' at you now, it's hard to believe. You still look like the same scrawny little shit from the projects.' He paused for a moment. 'What's your sister doing now? Some kinda fuckin' charity work, I hear. She was always a hot piece of ass.'

Charlie said nothing. He just sat there, staring back at Gruden, trying not to blink.

'If it wasn't for her, growing up you'd have caught an even more serious ass-kicking, you know that? I guess the Army changed her, too, from what I heard, didn't it?' He waited only a beat, and when there was no response, he said, 'Shame, that. I hear she messed up a guy I do some business with occasionally last night. You might want to tell her to be careful who she fucks with. I'll let it pass this time, if we're doin' business here.'

'Fifty per cent,' Charlie said. He folded his arms across his chest, and kept his eyes focused on the man across the table from him.

Gruden stirred his coffee, took another sip. 'You're right, Joe,' he said, looking over Charlie's shoulder. 'It's a fucked-up world.' He looked back at Charlie. 'You know where my shop is?'

Among other things, Gruden owned a barber shop off L Street. Everyone knew where it was. Charlie nodded.

'Good. You bring it by my shop this afternoon. Six o'clock. If it's genuine, I'll move it. Fifty per cent.'

Charlie nodded again. He stood up without saying another word and walked out the front door of the restaurant. He headed around the corner and up the block.

When he came to the first alley, he ducked inside and found a spot where he couldn't be seen from the street. He put his hand against the wall, took a deep breath, and slumped to the pavement as his knees buckled.

CHAPTER TEN

'I never thanked you for Sam,' Ainsworth said. He was leaning against the door to Jack Saunders's office. Saunders was packing a briefcase. 'For what you did for him and the others. It was a violation of every directive you had, but I should still have thanked you.'

'I wasn't looking for thanks,' Saunders said without looking up.

'I know you weren't. Which is why you deserved them more. Thank you. As your boss, I'll tell you that you did a very terrible thing. As Sam's father, though, I want you to know how much I appreciated it.'

Saunders looked up and held Ainsworth's eyes for a moment. He could see at that moment how deeply the death of his son had affected the man. 'He was like a brother to me.'

'I know. You might be the only person who could possibly understand how I felt, because you felt some of the same things. Except you did something about it, while I . . .' His voice trailed off for a moment. 'Well, I suppose that is why I owe you thanks even more. As I sat here and considered all the global political implications, you went out and took revenge.'

'I didn't think of it as revenge.'

'Yes, you did. But in the end, it was only a gesture. The people who were truly behind his murder – and the murders of all the others at Camp Chapman – are still operating with impunity, and they will continue to unless we show the will to oppose them fully. That is why your vacation in Boston is so important.'

Saunders went back to packing his things. 'Any last words of advice, while you're still my boss?'

'Have you ever heard of *The Prophet's Will*?'

'Sure,' Saunders said. 'Jerry Bruckheimer movie, right?'

Ainsworth didn't smile. 'It's the code name for a Taliban operation to remove western influence from Afghanistan once and for all.'

'Yeah, I've heard of it,' Saunders said. 'Don't know much about the details.'

'No one does,' Ainsworth said. 'My guess is there isn't much to know. We get rumors every once in a while. Nibbles of information, really, from the lines we've got out in the water. Nothing more than that.'

'So why bring it up?'

Ainsworth folded his arms. 'Some of the nibbles mention the Heart of Afghanistan.'

'Interesting.'

'Plus, there have been rumors that there could be some people on our side involved.'

Saunders looked at his boss. 'People on our side?'

'In the military.'

'Why would anyone on our side be involved?'

'I have no idea. It's really just ghost stories, probably. I figured you should know, though.'

'Do we know anything about the operation at all?'

Ainsworth shrugged. 'Not much. All the bits and pieces we've got talk about capturing the Heart of Afghanistan – the source of Mohammed's power. The true believers seem to think that if they get their hands on it, it would lead Islam to its final victory over the West.'

'What is it?' Saunders asked as he transferred a couple of pens from his desk to his briefcase.

'We don't know. But whatever it is, they seem to think it's in Boston at the moment.' Saunders looked unperturbed. 'You need to be very careful on this, Jack,' Ainsworth cautioned him. 'Afghanistan is in a very precarious position right now. The American public thinks we've succeeded. The politicians are desperate to pull as many of our troops out as we can; all of them, if possible. That's going to leave a power vacuum in the country, and the civil war that will erupt will be worse than the one that happened after the Soviets pulled out. It's going to be a mess, and everyone over there knows it. You need to understand that the people who are lying in wait, biding their time, are the most dangerous people you will ever deal with, and they will stop at nothing to get power and keep power.' He gave Saunders a hard look to drive home his point.

Saunders considered this for a moment, then went back to his packing. 'Tell me about Phelan,' he said.

Ainsworth opened a leather briefing file. 'Charles Teigan Phelan,' he began.

'Nice Jewish boy, I'm guessing?' Saunders said.

Ainsworth ignored him. 'Born October tenth, 1988, at Metropolitan Hospital in Boston. Grew up in the Old Colony Public Housing Project in South Boston.'

Ainsworth looked up at Saunders. 'You grew up around there, right?'

'Quincy,' Saunders replied. 'We were posers compared to the kids from the Southie projects. They were the real deal.'

'Not Phelan, from what we can tell,' Ainsworth said. 'He was never in trouble as far as we know. Got decent grades in school, but nothing to stand out. He certainly wasn't getting any scholarships to Harvard. Signed up for the Army at eighteen. Passed through Basic, but he wasn't fit enough to get into any of the elite forces he was looking for. Hell, even the infantry didn't really want him. He ended up in the Quartermaster's Corps.'

'Sounds pretty dull,' Saunders said.

'Compared to what you did over there? Sure. He saw some interesting spots, though. Did a tour in Baghdad and was lent out to a unit in Istanbul. Ended up stationed in Kandahar before he mustered out.'

'So, what's his name doing in a Taliban communication to a sleeper cell?'

Ainsworth shrugged. 'Could be nothing. Could be a coincidence.'

'And we've got no address,' Saunders commented.

'No. Like I said, his sister's in Boston. If someone was looking for him, that'd probably be the best starting point.'

'If someone was looking for him.'

'Right,' Ainsworth said. 'Which we both know you're not going to do.'

'Right,' Saunders agreed. He reached into his desk drawer and pulled out his gun, tossed it in his briefcase. 'I'm just doing a little sightseeing.'

CHAPTER ELEVEN

Cianna found herself looking over her shoulder as she walked back to her apartment, the bag of groceries held loosely enough to allow her to defend herself if necessary. Walking up the stairs to her apartment, she peered around the corner at every landing, half-expecting to find someone lying in wait for her.

It was silly, she knew. No one was after her. She'd paid whatever debt she owed to anyone, and then some. Those from her past had neither right nor reason to pursue her. All the same, she turned the deadbolt behind her when she got inside her apartment, and latched the chain.

She put the groceries away, sat on her couch, staring at the wall. She tried to put the thoughts of what had happened years before out of her mind, tried to force herself to think about something else. There was nothing else to think about, though. Her life had once meant something. Now . . .

She looked around her apartment, taking in the stains on the rug and the paint-splashed walls stubbled with the dirt and grime of a long line of the destitute who had preceded her in the tiny abode. How had she come to this?

*

Akhtar Hazara stepped off the plane in Boston with a sense of apprehension and excitement. It felt to him as though every passenger on the plane had regarded him with suspicion and fear, and he was eager to be as far away from the airport as possible. He'd dressed well, in a western suit and collared shirt, but there was no way to conceal his ethnicity, and as he boarded the 747 at London's Heathrow Airport for the last leg of his journey he could tell that his mere presence made many on his flight nervous.

He didn't mind, really. He even understood it at some level. After all the images that had been flashed into the American psyche of young men who looked remarkably like him against the background of destruction from the World Trade Center to the Pentagon to Lockerbie to Luxor, he supposed the fear was unavoidable. Rational though it might be, he would be glad to get away from the airport, where he could more easily blend into the background of America's streets.

He had only one carry-on bag, which contained an empty, ornately adorned wooden box and a change of clothing. The box drew a curious look from the customs official, but only for a moment. Then he was passed through and out into the bustling maul of Logan Airport. From there he headed out to the curb and caught a cab.

The address he gave the driver was for a quiet bar downtown near the TD Banknorth Garden, the enormous arena where two of the local athletic teams played their games. Akhtar had studied briefly in America, at George Washington University in DC. It had cost more money than he could imagine, but his uncle was convinced it was worth it. Gamol had helped out financially, he knew. While there, he'd tried to follow American sports, but he found them pointless and complicated, with their arcane and illogical rules. He preferred European football and cricket.

He went to the bar and ordered a whiskey. He'd developed a taste for booze when he'd lived in the States, and he savored the flavor as he sipped. He didn't drink around his uncle, who still held firm to the Muslim prohibition against alcohol.

The man arrived a few moments later. He was tall, with hair so short the scalp was visible. He wore civilian clothes, but they were clean and pressed and orderly. All that was missing was a rank insignia. He sidled up to Akhtar and put a newspaper on the bar. 'Have you just arrived?' It was a simple code.

'Yes,' Akhtar said. 'The flight from London was very smooth.'

The other man nodded. The bartender was far enough away that they could not be heard. 'He's here in Boston,' he said. 'We've been keeping an eye on him. He's at his sister's place. You'll spot her; she's a real looker.'

'And Stillwell?' Akhtar asked.

'He's here, too.' The man stood up, nodded at the paper folded on the bar. 'There's an address and a map, as well as some additional information that will be helpful for you,' he said. 'We've arranged for a rental car, but we cannot be involved beyond this.'

'I understand,' Akhtar said. 'It is better for both of us this way.'

'Good luck.' The man stood up and turned. Before he walked away, though, he addressed Akhtar once more. 'Stay with the girl,' he said.

Akhtar looked at him, confused. 'The girl?'

'Phelan's sister. Keep your eye on her. The kid's a fuck-up, but she's the real deal. I read her file. If things start to go to shit, stick with her, she'll lead you where you need to be. You understand?'

'I don't think so,' Akhtar said.

'You will.' The man walked away quickly, leaving Akhtar sitting alone at the bar. He picked up the newspaper and tucked it under his arm, threw back the remaining whiskey, put the glass back on the bar, pulled a ten-dollar bill out of his wallet and put it on the bar before he followed the man out.

CHAPTER TWELVE

Jack Saunders sat on the plane, staring out the window. He'd had to go through extra security procedures to get his gun on the plane, but his suspension had not become official, and his position at the Agency still afforded some privileges.

The flight from Washington DC to Boston followed the bend of the eastern seaboard, tracking the north-eastern coastline. It was a crystal-clear autumn day, not a cloud in the sky, and as they passed over the south-eastern corner of New York he gazed down at the island of Manhattan.

For a moment, he found it hard to breathe.

Before Harvard he'd gone to undergraduate school in the city, and had lived just across the Hudson River, in Hoboken. Back then, the New York skyline had been as constant as the sun and the stars. Looking up from the south at Lady Liberty, waving in triumph toward the giant Twin Towers that dominated the horizon, he'd always had a sense of security – of certainty that the nation that was his would continue to rise.

Now, looking down from more than a mile up in the air, he could see the hole at the lower end of the island. Building at the site of the memorial had begun, but progress was slow, like the painful formation of scar tissue at the edge of a wound that refused to heal.

He took it personally now. He took it *all* personally. There had been a time in his life when that wasn't the case. In Bosnia, and Somalia, and Russia, and Chechnya, and Hungary . . . the missions were important because they would give his country a tactical advantage in the crush for global power and influence. And he'd believed the missions usually had the residual benefit of helping the locals try to build their own lives more free from tyranny and violence. He'd taken his role seriously back then, but not personally. The survival of the United States wasn't truly at issue, at least not in a way that was felt to his core. Not in the way he felt it now as he looked down from a plane on a crystal-clear autumn day.

Everything was personal to him now. Perhaps that was his problem.

Saunders walked in the footsteps of his guide, Bashar, a 30-year-old Afghan with better knowledge of the mountains in the far eastern reaches of Afghanistan than any American would ever acquire. Jack had been here before, or near here, at least. It was difficult for him to tell. The terrain was so severe he had to keep his eyes on the ground to be sure of his footing. Without Bashar's aid, he would never survive this far up in the mountains. There were dangers both natural and man-made in the crevasses between the launches of rock that jutted up. A single misstep would be the end of him, he knew, so he placed each foot deliberately. He'd trusted his life to Bashar many times before.

The sun was still behind the highest peaks to the east, and the air was frigid. With each breath a cloud of steam wafted before him. He wore the solid black lungee turban indigenous to the region, and a heavy wool perahan tunban that covered him from his wrists to his ankles. His bushy dark beard helped to keep him warm and gave him the look of a native. The strap of his Kalashnikov dug into his lean shoulder.

They moved inexorably up the mountain, pausing only briefly so that Saunders could consult a map. By his calculations, they were still in Afghanistan, but just barely. In any event, borders mattered little in the Waziri no-man's-land between Afghanistan and Pakistan. Out here, sovereignty extended only as far as a rifle could accurately find its target, and tribal affiliation outweighed any semblance of modern nationalism. His guide nodded up toward the next peak and gave a hand signal that made clear they were close.

'Are you ready, Bashar?' Saunders asked.

'I am.'

'Do you think it'll work?'

Bashar shrugged. 'If Allah wills it.'

Saunders saw the men before he saw the cabin. There were four of them, and they were milling around in a loose, distracted circle 100 meters above the last crest. The flat trodden path along the ridgeline was wider here, perhaps twenty meters between the continuing rise of the mountain to the north, and the sheer drop to the valley to the south. The men on the path reminded Saunders of a klatch of homeless men on the corner of any crumbling US city. They moved in tired, strung out, nervous patterns of boredom, their heads hanging down, shoulders hunched forward.

It was generous to call the dwelling a cabin. It was really more of a lean-to, made of loose flat rocks stacked up against the side of the mountain, held together with mud and straw.

Saunders and Bashar were halfway along the open stretch of wide path toward the cabin before the men outside spotted them. The first to notice them gave a startled, unintelligible grunt to the others, and they turned, watching Saunders and Bashar as they approached. The rifles came off their shoulders, and they held the guns loosely. The demeanor of one of the men changed drastically, though, as Saunders and Bashar drew to within ten meters of the men. His face broke into a wide, crooked-toothed smile. 'Bashar!' he shouted.

Bashar smiled back, put his hand out. 'Symia, my good friend!' he said in his native Pashto. The two men gave each other a vigorous handshake.

The man with the crooked teeth began speaking rapidly to his compatriots. 'This is Bashar!' he said. 'The one I told you of! He works with our allies in the West, and is responsible for the deaths of many infidels!'

'Allah is responsible for all,' Bashar said humbly.

'Yes, yes,' the other man said, waving him off. He was short and slight, with a prominent brow and a wandering eye that, combined with his teeth and his enthusiasm, made him seem slightly mad. 'Have you brought Symia a gift?' he asked in a conspiratorial tone.

'Of course,' Bashar replied. He reached into the folds of his clothing and produced a small paper wrapper. Symia grabbed it greedily, and the other three men shouldered their guns and shuffled in closer.

'Ah!' Symia exclaimed to the other three. 'I told you! Our brothers in the West have the best hashish in the world!' He unwrapped the paper as one of the other three produced a small pipe.

Symia was scraping the pipe across the resin in the paper when Bashar spoke again. 'My friend, this is the one I told you might be coming.' He gestured toward Saunders. 'He is from the north.' Bashar's voice became reverent. 'He is very important, and he has come with a message for Majeed. His name is Timur.'

Symia paused in his effort to load the hashish pipe. 'An honor,' he said, placing a hand over his heart and bowing slightly in traditional greeting. Saunders stood still, fixing the man with a hard stare. The smile disappeared from Symia's face. 'Is he too good to greet me with respect?' he demanded of Bashar.

'He is Tajik,' Bashar said with a shrug. 'He is too good for everything.' That drew a knowing chuckle from the other men, but Symia continued to glower at Saunders.

'He should learn better manners.'

'There are more important things than manners,' Saunders said in unaccented Pashto. It was one of seven languages he'd mastered over the years. 'I was sent here to deal with leaders, not with underlings.'

Symia was holding the hashish and pipe in his left hand now, and his right hand dropped to the pistol grip of his Kalashnikov. His finger toyed with the trigger. 'What makes you think that any leader here would want to talk to you?' he asked.

'Because,' Saunders said, 'I have been sent by Mullah Durrani Rahman.' Saunders could see the man stiffen at the mention of the name. It looked as though Symia was going to say something, then thought better of it. He took two steps back, rapped on the door to the cabin and entered.

He was inside only for a moment, and Saunders could

hear voices, first quiet, then raised, then quiet again. Symia re-emerged. 'Abdur Majeed will see you,' he said. He opened the door and held his hand out to let Saunders pass. As Saunders reached the threshold, Symia began to follow him in.

'I will speak with Majeed alone,' Saunders said.

'I am his bodyguard,' Symia protested.

'I will speak with Majeed alone, or I will not speak with him at all.'

Symia took a step back and nodded reluctantly.

The door closed behind Saunders. Slashes of light cut through the gaps in the tiny building's construction; other than that the place was dark. He could make out the silhouette of a rickety table, a tall, lanky figure bent over it working on some papers. Saunders's eyes were still adjusting and it was a moment before he could make out the man's features. He looked younger than Saunders had anticipated. He had a long, aquiline nose and full lips. He looked up from his papers at Saunders and his eyes were piercing.

'Abdur Majeed,' Saunders said.

'Indeed,' Majeed replied. He looked expectantly at Saunders.

'I am Timur Isthal,' Saunders said. 'I have been sent by Mullah Duranni Rahman.'

'So I have been informed.' Majeed remained seated.

Saunders placed a hand over his heart and bowed. 'Mullah Rahman sends his respects.'

Majeed bowed briefly. 'Mullah Rahman is a man of great influence. It is said that he is the most powerful man on the Quetta Shura,' he said, referring to the Afghan Taliban leadership council established when Mullah Omar, the Supreme

Leader of the Islamic State of Afghanistan, had been chased from power in 2001. It directed the four regional military commands. 'I am surprised that the Mullah would send a message for me directly,' he said. 'I report to Siraj Haqqani, the commander of the Miramshah Regional Military Shura. My orders come from him.'

'And by all reports, you follow those orders well,' Saunders said. 'In fact, our understanding is that you are often the one who gives the orders in the first place.'

'I serve Allah to the best of my abilities.'

'And those abilities are, by all evidence, considerable.'

Majeed was cautious. There were dangerous rivalries within the Taliban. 'Is there something that Mullah Rahman would like from me?' he asked.

Saunders nodded. 'We should speak plainly.' He began to pace slightly. 'The Council is unhappy with the inaction in the Miramshah region.'

'Attacks here are carried out weekly,' Majeed protested.

'The Council believes the attacks could be even more frequent and more effective,' Saunders said. 'The commitment of the American infidels to Afghanistan is weakening. The more we can do now to make clear our resolve, the faster theirs will crumble.'

'Has the Council shared these thoughts with Siraj Haqqani?' Majeed inquired.

'Siraj Haqqani no longer has the faith of the Council,' Saunders said. 'He is without distinction. His only accomplishment in recent days of note has been the attack on the American Camp Chapman.' Camp Chapman was a forward-operating CIA base in the city of Khost. The day before New Year's of 2009, a suicide bomber – a Taliban double agent

working 'with' the CIA – detonated a massive bomb inside the camp, killing eight operatives, including Sam Ainsworth, the son of an influential Assistant Director at the Agency. It was the worst attack in the history of the CIA, and it had shaken the confidence of many of the United States' allies in Afghanistan. The Agency had publicly sworn that it would have its revenge.

Majeed gave a scornful grunt.

'You disagree?'

Majeed's eyes flashed with ambition for the first time. 'I agree that it was a great accomplishment,' he said. 'I question that the accomplishment was Haqqani's.' The man's pride was finally beginning to show.

Saunders regarded him carefully. 'You believe that someone else better deserves the credit?'

'The attack was my operation. It was planned and executed using my strategy and my men.'

Saunders nodded. 'The Council suspected as much.' He stopped pacing. 'Would you accept the role as commander of the Shura here in Miramshah if the Council offered it to you?'

Majeed pulled himself up to his full height. 'It would be an honor to serve Allah and the Council in that position.'

Saunders moved forward. 'It will be done,' he said. He shook hands with Majeed, leaned in to embrace him. As Majeed returned the gesture, Saunders slipped a ten-inch serrated combat knife from his belt. With his lips near the other man's ear, he whispered, 'You deserve this.'

Majeed was still smiling as Saunders drove the knife, in a swift, sure motion, into his chest, just below the breastbone, thrusting upward. As intended, the weapon sliced through the solar plexus and punctured the lungs, robbing Majeed of *his oxygen and preventing him from calling out to his men. His smile twisted into a grimace and his mouth went wide as he tried to suck in a breath to no avail. Blood was pouring from the wound, drenching the earthen floor.*

Saunders held Majeed's gaze as the life ebbed away from him. 'They were my friends,' Saunders said.

Majeed's arms were reaching out now, grasping at Saunders as though holding tight to something might keep him in the world. Saunders twisted the knife once, pulled it out. Majeed fell to his knees, still grasping at Saunders, looking up at him, his expression wild.

Saunders wiped the blade on Majeed's tunic. 'They were my friends,' he repeated. He pulled himself away, and Majeed collapsed on the ground.

The rest of the operation took less than thirty seconds. Saunders walked out of the cabin, his suppressed nine-millimeter drawn. The three militia members were smoking the hashish. Saunders put two rounds into Symia's forehead first. The second soldier was holding the hashish pipe, and he dropped it as he fumbled at his side for his gun. Two rounds to his chest dropped him where he stood. The third was raising his Kalashnikov, shouting curses. Bashar put a single round into the man's temple, then walked over and kicked him in the leg to see whether there was any movement. He put another round into the back of his head just to be sure.

'It is done,' Bashar said.

'It is,' Saunders agreed. He looked around. The sun had warmed the place considerably while he'd been in the hut, but the air was still crisp. The sky was bluer than any Saunders could remember.

'We should pull the bodies inside,' Bashar said.

Saunders nodded and the two of them moved the corpses out of the sunlight.

'I'm going to be leaving,' Saunders said. He was following Bashar as they headed down the mountain trail.

'I know,' Bashar said without turning. 'You are American. Americans always leave.'

'There's going to be hell to pay. My superiors didn't authorize this.'

Bashar said nothing.

'You should leave, too. I can arrange for you to get out of the country.'

'Where would I go?' Bashar asked.

'Wherever you want,' Saunders said.

Bashar shook his head. 'I will stay here. This is my country.'

'It will be dangerous for you.'

'It is Afghanistan,' Bashar said. 'It is dangerous for everyone.'

They continued walking down the mountain in silence for a while. Finally, Saunders said, 'I'll come back.' Bashar said nothing. 'Once I get everything straightened out back in the States, I'll return.'

'I know,' Bashar said quietly. 'You are American. Americans always return.'

CHAPTER THIRTEEN

Charlie got back to the apartment later that afternoon. Cianna had given him a key, and she heard it turn in the lock. The door opened a crack before it caught on the chain. 'What the hell?' he said.

'Coming.' She crossed the room, closed the door, slid the chain off, and opened the door again.

'What's up with the chain?' he asked.

She shrugged, feeling like she'd been silly and paranoid. 'Big city,' she said. 'Can't be too safe.'

He was holding several brown paper bags. 'I've got lunch,' he said, a big smile on his face.

'It's four o'clock,' she said.

'Fine, then I've got dinner. I haven't eaten yet, and I'm starving.' He set the bags on the table and started tearing them open. The aroma of Chinese food filled the apartment. He kept opening the bags until there were seven white cartons spread out before them. The last bag contained a six-pack of Heineken. 'I splurged,' he said.

'I can see that. What's the occasion?'

'Isn't my being back from war enough?'

'You were in the Quartermaster Corps,' she pointed out.

'Fine,' he said, not taking the bait. 'How about us being

together again? I haven't seen my sister in nearly two years.'

She let it go and forced a smile. 'Yeah,' she said. 'That's a good reason to celebrate.'

'Good,' he said, looking satisfied. 'Let's dig in.'

Sirus Stillwell sat in a blue late-model sedan on the corner of Mercer Street. He was tall enough that his bald head brushed against the roof of the car, and there was barely enough room for him to stretch his legs to keep them from falling asleep. He watched Charlie walk into the apartment building carrying something in his right hand. The bag was just about the right size. He picked up the phone and made a call. 'He's back at her apartment,' he said when the call was answered.

'Does he have it with him?'

'I'm not sure,' Sirus said. 'It's possible.'

'Possible? Your time is up.'

'I need another day.'

'No. You've failed. Our friend from Afghanistan will take care of this.'

'One more day. That's all I'm asking.'

'It's too late,' the voice said.

'No!' Sirus yelled into the phone. 'It's not too late! I said I'll handle this!' He clicked off the phone and stepped out of the car. He looked up at the apartment house for a moment, then crossed the street and opened the front door.

Charlie put his fork down. 'I was thinking,' he started hesitantly, looking up at her as if to make sure she was paying attention.

'What?' she asked after a moment.

'I was thinking we should get out of here. Leave Boston. Leave the East Coast, in fact. Maybe go down to Florida.'

'Florida's on the East Coast,' she said with a laugh. He still was a little boy to her in so many ways. Their father had left when their mother was still pregnant with Charlie, and their mother spent most of her energy after that trying to land another husband. She'd burned through a dozen candidates in a few years – in truth they'd burned through her – and always blamed the breakups on the fact that she was saddled with two ungrateful children.

'You know what I mean,' he said. 'We should get out of here. Go someplace else.'

She looked down at her plate and managed to maintain her smile. 'You go,' she said. 'You don't need me weighing you down. Besides, I'm happy here.'

'No you're not,' he said.

'Well, maybe not happy. But there's something good in what I do here. I take some satisfaction from that. It's hard to explain, but I'll be okay.'

'You don't have to just be *okay*,' he said. 'You can be better than *okay*. We both can be.'

She looked at him, and saw in his eyes an intense combination of optimism, excitement and desperation. There was something else underlying it all, too; something she couldn't quite identify. After a moment, she recognized it. She'd seen it all too many times, lining the corners of the eyes and mouths of the men she'd fought with over the years. It was fear.

'What's going on with you, Charlie?' she asked.

He looked away, and his expression changed. The fear

was replaced by shame. 'I'm gonna be coming into money soon,' he said. 'A lot of money.'

She shook her head in confusion. 'What money? From where?'

He still couldn't meet her eyes. 'You don't need to worry about it,' he said quietly.

'I don't need to worry about what?' She heard in her voice the maternal tone she'd taken with him so often when they were younger.

'You don't need to worry about where the money is coming from,' he said. He stood up and went into the tiny kitchen, threw his plate into the garbage. When he turned back to her, his face was bent in anger. 'Look at this goddamned place,' he said, raising his voice. 'I mean, don't you deserve better than this? Haven't you put in your time? Haven't we both? Everybody else out there has spent their lives breaking the rules, but you and me did the right thing. We served our country. And this is where it gets us? You babysitting other people's fuck-ups, and me . . .' His voice trailed off for a moment. 'Isn't it time for us to get a little something for ourselves? Haven't we earned it?' His thin face was bright red, his eyes wide and searching, begging for absolution.

'What did you do?' she asked. She wasn't sure she wanted the answer.

'Nothing!' he shouted back at her.

'What did you do?' she asked again, more quietly this time.

He was breathing hard, staring at her with anger in his eyes, but it wasn't really directed at her; it was aimed inward. 'I stole,' he said. 'You happy? I'm a thief.'

She remained calm. 'What did you steal?'

'An antique,' he responded. 'A very valuable antique.'

'Who did you steal it from?'

He smiled bitterly. 'That's the beautiful thing,' he said. 'I stole it from another thief. A group of thieves, actually; people who were looting the whole damned country of Afghanistan.' He turned and reached into the refrigerator, took out a beer, and opened it. He threw the cap at the garbage and missed.

'Back up,' she said, 'and tell me everything.'

He walked back and sat down on the couch. 'They were running it out of the airbase in Kandahar,' he began. 'A couple of years ago, just after you went away, this guy comes to me and makes me an offer.'

'Who was he?'

'His name was Sirus. Sirus Stillwell. He was a really well-connected officer over there. Huge guy, and known for a dangerous temper. He came to me because I could control the shipping.' He looked up at her. 'In a way, it was flattering – an important guy like that needing me, wanting help from me? No one had ever really needed me for anything. Does that sound fucked up?'

'Go on,' she said.

'Anyways, Sirus comes to me a couple years ago and tells me that he's got a bunch of boxes that need to get back to the States. He tells me that they're labeled "Auto Parts", and he needs to make sure they got through to Ramstein safely. I was in charge of materials transport at the depot. He tells me if I make sure it gets through, and I don't inspect it, he'll take care of me. He slips me a couple hundred bucks, and tells me that was just a taste.

He tells me him and his partners are going to be shipping at least one box a month.'

'What was in the boxes?' Cianna asked.

'I didn't know at first,' Charlie said. 'I didn't look inside them. I figured this was the way the world works, and the extra money was good. But I'm not an idiot, lots of guys talked about shipping stuff home. Hell, in World War Two it was legal. Now it's illegal, but it still happens, so I figured it was no big deal.'

'But eventually you looked?'

'I got curious,' he said. 'So one night when one of the shipments was in the warehouse, I opened one of the boxes and took a look. I figured it would just be some trinkets – you know, the kind of stuff you can get in any bazaar over there.'

'But that's not what you found.'

He shook his head. 'They were moving some serious shit. I mean, there was more gold than I'd ever seen. Plus jewels and little statues – all kinds of stuff. The real stuff; not the crap that most people sneak out of there. This was high-end.'

'Where did they get it?'

'I don't know for sure,' Charlie said. 'But you know the rumors, right? They say that when the Taliban took over in the nineties they looted all of the country's wealth. Some of it was destroyed, but the rumor was that they stashed a lot of it. Relics and gold and jewels. No one knew where for sure.'

'And you think Sirus found the stash?'

'Maybe. Truth is, I don't know and I don't care.'

Cianna sighed. 'So you took some of it,' she said.

'Not right then,' he protested. 'I was so freaked out, I closed the crate right back up and got the hell out of there. I mean, I knew Sirus was seriously connected, and it wasn't gonna do my life any good to mess with him. Besides, he was paying me, so I figured I might as well keep my mouth shut and go along, right?' He took a sip of the beer.

'What happened?'

He took a deep breath. 'You were in prison,' he said. 'Nothing made sense anymore. I got tired of the dust and the heat and the cold and the boredom of every single fuckin' day over there in Afghanistan,' he said. 'I still might have re-upped, just because I couldn't figure out anything else I could do, you know? I couldn't think of any way out. Then it hit me. It was staring me in the face. Sirus was shipping so much stuff out every month, I figured he wouldn't miss a couple of trinkets. And with what I could get from that, I could get a little start. So I decided to muster out and take my chances. After that, every month, when the shipments went out, I took a few things. Not that much; just enough to get some money together.'

'But I thought you said you're coming into a *lot* of money,' Cianna said. 'A few trinkets won't set you up for very long.'

Charlie nodded. 'The last shipment went out the day before I was discharged. And I figured I might as well take one more dip, you know? So I opened up one of the crates, and I was looking around, and I came across this antique knife, wrapped in an old ratty blanket. I mean, I'd never seen anything like it. I almost put it back, because I was afraid this was the sort of thing that someone would notice if it went missing. But then I realized, even if someone did notice it was gone, it would take a week or so – because the crate was being shipped. By then, I'd be long gone. And what was Sirus gonna do then? Go to the police? I don't think so. So I wrapped it back up in the blanket and I took it.'

'Is it here, in the apartment?' Cianna asked.

Charlie shook his head. 'No, I didn't want to carry it around.'

'Where is it, then?'

'The only place I knew it would be safe.' He looked at her, and she stared back, uncomprehending. 'C'mon Sis, you should be able to figure that out.'

She frowned. 'Where?'

'I'll give you a hint: if you wanted to feel safe, where would you go?' She shook her head, and he laughed at her. 'Jesus, it's like we didn't even grow up together. When I show you, you're gonna feel really stupid.' He stood up.

'Can we go there now?'

He looked at his watch. 'Soon.'

She said, 'How do you plan to sell this thing?'

'I've got that all arranged,' Charlie said. 'I'm fencing it through Miles Gruden. I met with him today.'

'Christ, Charlie, are you stupid? Miles Gruden is a psychopath. You remember what he was like growing up? You remember what he did to Davey? This is a bad idea.'

'Yeah, well there aren't many Boy Scouts who have the contacts to fence stolen artifacts from the Middle East. Besides, what's he gonna do? He's making money off this, same as me.'

'Guys like Gruden don't want to make money same as you, Charlie, they want to make all the money.'

'Relax, Cianna, like I told you, it's all gonna be fine.'

As he said the words, there was a pounding at the apartment door. Cianna looked at Charlie. She walked over to the front door and looked out the peephole, but could see no one. 'There's no one there,' she said, turning back to Charlie.

The knocking came again, harder this time. She put her eye to the peephole, but this time it was blocked. 'Who is it?' she called out.

CHAPTER FOURTEEN

Jack Saunders rented a midsized Chevy sedan with a GPS and a full tank of gas from the Hertz at Logan airport. He typed Cianna Phelan's address on the touch screen in the dashboard and a map popped up directing him. He turned the ignition and pulled out of the rental lot.

The airport in Boston was a seven-minute drive from the heart of the city. Saunders took the Ted Williams Tunnel under the harbor over to Southie, exiting near the Convention Center. From there, he turned right and headed into the heart of the residential neighborhood. Southie had managed to maintain its blue-collar feel even as the areas closer in toward Boston proper had become gentrified. Young men dressed in workmen's clothes covered in concrete dust smoked cigarettes on the narrow sidewalks, and cast suspicious glances at his car as it passed. The place smelled of greasy food and salt air.

Saunders looked at his notes and scanned the addresses on the doors. The one he was looking for was easy to spot; it stood out on the street, separated from the rows of townhouses, the numbers writ large in chipped white paint on a black door that looked like it was being held together with rust.

He pulled over to the sidewalk and parked. There were

no signs, and it was difficult to tell whether he was in a legal spot, but he figured he'd take his chances. He didn't expect to be in the building for very long.

One of the apartments on the third floor was apparently rented by Cianna Phelan, Charles Phelan's only known relative. He'd left hers as a forwarding address with the Army when he'd mustered out two weeks before. Since then, he'd not been heard from. A standard check of his accounts revealed no use of his credit or debit cards that might have pinpointed his location.

Saunders got out of the car and walked over to the door and gave it a try. It pulled open without resistance. With luck, he thought, the rest of the visit would go as smoothly.

Cianna had her eye up against the peephole when the door was kicked in with such force that it threw her halfway across the room. She landed hard on the corner of the crate that served as a table. 'What the fuck!' she shouted, as her hand went to her face. She could feel the blood running down her cheek, and the vision in one eye seemed to be gone. She turned and looked through the curtain of blood back at the door. A giant man with a shaved head was standing at the threshold with shoulders broader than any she could remember seeing, and a neck that looked as though it was woven from steel tram cable.

The man looked briefly at Cianna, then dismissed her and addressed her brother. His face was contorted in rage. 'You're a fucking moron, you know that, Charlie,' he shouted. 'You think your sister's place isn't the first place I'd look for you?'

'Sirus.' Charlie's voice was quavering. 'I don't understand; what's wrong?' Cianna could see he was trying to act innocent, but it was a poor performance, and the guilt came through plainly.

Sirus took a step into the tiny living room. 'You want to know what's going on? You want to know, you little shit?' He moved toward Charlie. 'You steal from me, and bad things happen. That's what's going on.' There was nowhere for Charlie to go, and he tripped back against the sofa. Sirus's hand shot out and grabbed him by the throat.

'I didn't steal anything!' Charlie choked out, but it was barely audible. Sirus's hand was crushing his windpipe.

'Where is it?' Sirus demanded. Charlie pulled at the hand, trying to loosen the giant man's grip, but it was useless. He gasped and choked as his thin arms slapped ineffectually. 'Where is it?' Sirus demanded again, but Cianna could see that Charlie was unable to respond with his oxygen cut off.

She was back on her feet now, and she screamed at Sirus. 'Let him go!'

Sirus looked at her briefly, contempt on his face. He grabbed Charlie by the collar and pulled him close, so that he was spitting his words in his face. 'One chance, Phelan,' he said. 'That's all. Tell me where it is!'

Cianna assumed that the discussion was over. Charlie had always been a coward deep down, and there seemed little chance that he would keep up the charade when faced with the seriousness of the physical threat, no matter how valuable the knife was. She was wrong, though. Charlie regarded the bigger man, a look of defiance on his face.

'I don't know what you're talking about,' he choked out.

The words had barely cleared his lips when Sirus's giant fist crashed into Charlie's face. Cianna could hear the snapping sound of what she hoped was cartilage, but feared was bone, and Charlie was thrown back into the wall with a thud that sickened her. Sirus was moving forward again, a look of pure hatred on his face.

She acted before she thought. It was instinctive – primal. The blood was still in her eyes, but she launched herself at the enormous man. He saw her coming, and turned to fend off the attack. Sirus swung lazily and high, assuming she would throw her own weight into the punch. She ducked low and kicked out, catching him on the side of the knee. She heard the popping sound, and felt a rush of satisfaction.

He let out a roar of anger, pain, and surprise, and stumbled as the leg wobbled. It took him a moment to catch his balance, and Cianna knew she had only one chance. Even injured, Sirus was so much bigger and stronger than she, that if she allowed him to recover, the fight would end badly for her.

She moved to her left, forcing him to put weight on his injured leg if he wanted to follow her. He groaned as he moved, keeping his hands up and his eyes on her. Once he was in a position where his body was crossed with his legs, and his balance was back, she kicked out again, this time aiming for his solar plexus.

The blow struck with her heel in exactly the place where she had aimed. To her dismay, however, it had minimal effect. It felt as though her foot had connected with concrete. Sirus gave a grunt, but it sounded more like annoyance than pain. Then he was coming at her. The injury to his leg slowed him, but not nearly as much as Cianna had hoped.

She looked over toward the side of the couch, and saw Charlie stir. That was a relief, at least. From the way he'd been hit, she'd had serious concerns at first that he might have been killed. 'Charlie!' she yelled. 'Charlie, get up!'

Sirus turned and looked over at Charlie slumped in the corner. He was rolling over, his arms reaching out to grab onto something to give him some balance, but he still looked disoriented. Cianna took that opportunity to strike out again. Sirus was too close for a kick, so she swiveled her hips and shoulders to generate as much power and speed behind her clenched fist as possible. She had to find a weak spot, and she knew there would be few, so she focused all her energy on his windpipe. If she could hit him hard enough, she could collapse his air passage, and no matter how strong he was, he would go down. It was her one chance, and she used all her strength.

By turning, he had left his neck exposed for a moment, and his face showed the recognition of his mistake as he snapped his head back to Cianna. It was too late, though, she thought. Time slowed as her fist shot up toward his Adam's apple. For the briefest moment, she thought she would survive the encounter. Just before she connected with his neck, though, his enormous hand swallowed her wrist, holding her firm. She struggled to pull her arm free, but it was useless.

He leaned in toward her, so that his face was close to hers. She swung her other arm, but she had no momentum, and he grabbed her other wrist with his free hand. Now he had both her hands, and he was close enough that she could smell the stench of his breath. His eyes were small and intense. He let go of one of her arms and grabbed her by the throat, held her against the wall. She tried again to swing at him, but his arm was so long that she couldn't reach his face, and when she hit his arm her blows bounced off harmlessly. After a moment, she was having trouble breathing, and her strength began to ebb away.

He let go of her other arm, reached behind his back, and pulled a gun from his waistband. He held it up, showing it to her. Then he held the barrel to her forehead. He stood there for a moment, watching her, reading her eyes. The muscles in his forearm twitched, and she stared into the face of the man who would kill her.

His arm tensed again, and she closed her eyes.

Suddenly, she heard the front door to the apartment bang open, and she looked over to see a man of average height and build standing at the threshold. He was wearing an inexpensive suit, and had neatly trimmed hair, too long for the military, but too short for much else. He had an interested expression, and showed no surprise at the scene into which he had walked. A gun dangled in his right hand. He looked from Charlie to Cianna, to the man holding a gun at her head.

'I'm sorry,' he said. 'Have I come at a bad time?'

CHAPTER FIFTEEN

Jack Saunders's gun hung at the top of his thigh, casually, his finger on the trigger. He'd heard the commotion as he approached the apartment, and seen the door ajar. Coming into the room, he was ready.

Ready for what, though? That was the real question. When he entered the apartment, he took careful stock of the situation. A young man, probably in his mid-twenties, slight and short, was lying in one corner. He was struggling unsuccessfully to get to his feet, and he was bleeding from the head. An enormous man with a shaved head and well-defined features was standing on the other side of the room. He was older, though not quite as old as Saunders, and he was holding a woman by the throat with one hand. She had a cut on the corner of her eye, and was fighting to break free. As Saunders entered, the bald man was raising a gun to the woman's forehead. Saunders noted the make of the gun without active thought.

The woman looked like a trapped animal. If she was scared, she had managed to channel all of her fear into a primal drive for survival. Saunders was tempted to shoot the larger man the instant he walked through the door. It was a natural reaction. Most men instinctively defend a woman in danger. Years of training, though, had molded

Saunders's instincts. He'd been in the game for too long to take any situation at face value. He knew nothing of the players in the violent vignette unfolding before him, and he was unwilling to make a move until he had more information.

He spoke evenly, without threat, and everyone turned to look at him, their eyes full of surprise. He expected that look. It had been his experience that people in the throes of violence this intimate often forget the rest of the world, and, when interrupted, their reaction is one of shock and mortification, not unlike being caught in the midst of a sexual peccadillo.

The giant spoke first. 'Get out of here,' he said. His voice was raised, though not to a yell. He kept the gun pointed at the woman.

'I'm looking for Charles Phelan,' Saunders said, ignoring the warning. 'You him?'

Both the bald man and the woman shot a glance at the young man still struggling to his feet in the corner. *So that's Phelan*, Saunders thought. The woman was likely his sister. The giant's identity was still a mystery. Saunders had little time to ponder the matter.

'I told you to get the fuck out of here!' the bald man yelled. He swung the gun around so that it was pointing at Saunders, and Saunders ducked to his right, raising his own gun. It would have been a simple matter to kill the man. He was too large a target to miss, and Saunders was an expert marksman. But Saunders needed to know more before he started killing people.

'Drop your gun!' Saunders yelled back. 'I'm a cop!' It wasn't exactly true. The Central Intelligence Agency was technically separate from any true law-enforcement agency. Still, it was Saunders's experience that yelling *CIA!* just tended to confuse people. Better to keep it simple. To punctuate his point, Saunders took split-second aim and shot the gun out of the man's hand. The giant roared in surprise as much as pain, as the gun skittered across the floor and hit the wall near Charles Phelan.

It was all the opening the woman needed. She swung her fist at the elbow of the arm that still held her and made solid contact, causing the man's elbow to bend. This allowed her to get in closer to him, and as his head was still turned, she launched her fist out with precision, catching him in the jaw.

The man gave a pained howl, and turned toward her in a fury, swinging his giant arm at her and connecting with the side of her head, sending her sprawling into the coffee table. Saunders heard the loud, dull thud as her head hit the corner and she fell to the floor, unconscious.

The giant seemed to have recovered from the shock of having his gun shot out of his hand, and he dove to his right, grabbing the gun off the floor, aiming at Saunders. It wasn't clear to Saunders that the gun would actually fire, but it seemed foolish to take a chance, so he ducked down behind a chair. In the time it took for him to peer out from behind the chair, the bald man closed the gap with Charles Phelan, who had nearly made it to his feet. He grabbed the smaller man and spun him around, using him as a shield. The gun was pointed over Phelan's shoulder, aimed at Saunders, and he fired off two rounds, sending Saunders diving for cover on the floor.

The man practically lifted Phelan off the ground as he

limped toward the door, using his hostage to prevent a clean shot from Saunders. He slammed the door behind him as they exited the apartment.

Saunders scrambled toward the woman lying on the floor and rolled her over. He reached up to her throat to feel for a pulse and found it. She was unconscious, but he could see her chest moving rhythmically. He figured she would be all right, and he turned his attention back to her brother. He quickly moved toward the door, opening it carefully, his gun drawn. He spun around the threshold, pointing his weapon down the hallway. There was no one there.

'Shit,' he muttered under his breath.

He ran to the stairway and headed down the three flights, careful on each landing to be sure the huge man wasn't waiting to take a shot at him. Saunders came out into the first-floor corridor in time to hear the front door slam shut. He ran the length of the vestibule and emerged onto the street as a dark blue four-door sedan spun its wheels, pulling away from the curb half a block up. Saunders held his gun up and took a shooter's stance. The car was seventy yards away now, and it was moving fast. Still, the street was empty and it was a clean shot, so Saunders focused in on the silhouette behind the wheel. He drew in a breath, held it, and pulled the trigger.

The back window of the sedan exploded, and the driver lurched forward slightly, the car hitching to the left as the driver's hand went up to his shoulder. After a moment, though, the car came back into its lane, and continued to speed away. Saunders looked down the barrel of his gun again, but by then the car was taking a corner hard and fast, and there was no way to get a clear shot.

He looked over at his own rental and considered giving chase, but realized it was pointless. The blue car would already be blocks away, and the chances of picking up the trail on the twisting South Boston streets were low.

He put his gun away and shook his head in frustration as he walked back to the apartment building.

The door to the apartment was still open, and the woman remained on the floor. As he leaned over her, she opened her eyes.

She looked at him in confusion, recoiled, and pushed herself away from him toward the wall.

'Where did he take him?' Saunders demanded.

'What?' she responded, still dazed.

'I need you to tell me where they went. Do you understand? Are you hurt? Are you shot?'

Her hand went to her head, and she pulled away again. He could see a large welt just to the side of her temple. The blood from the cut over her eye had slowed to a trickle, though. 'I hit my head,' she said.

'Are you hurt anywhere else?' Saunders asked. He reached over and touched her shoulder, examining her for wounds. She didn't pull away this time. Other than the bruise on her head, she didn't seem to have any injuries.

She looked around the room. 'Charlie?' she said.

'Your brother, right?' Saunders said. 'The other guy took him. I need to know where. You need to tell me what's going on.'

She looked up at Saunders, her eyes narrowing with suspicion. 'You're a cop?'

Saunders stared back at her. 'Sort of.'

'What does *sort of* mean?'

'It means I work for the government, and I'm one of the good guys. It means you need to cooperate with me, or I can cause problems for you that you can't even imagine.' He was bluffing, but it seemed his only option.

'I've got a hell of an imagination,' she shot back.

'Good,' he said. 'Because your brother's just been taken at gunpoint by a man who is crazy enough to take a shot at a police officer. Imagine what that man is going to do to your brother if we don't find him. You getting a clear picture? Are you going to help me?'

She looked at him. 'Are you going to arrest my brother if I help you find him?'

Saunders shook his head. 'I'm not that kind of cop.'

CHAPTER SIXTEEN

The bullet had shattered the back window of the sedan and passed through the top of the front seat, ricocheting off one of the internal metal supports, before grazing Sirus Stillwell's left shoulder. It had hit no bone, as far as he could tell, but it was causing a significant amount of pain. Not enough to impair his ability to use his arm, but enough to piss him off. He was steering with his left hand as he kept the gun in his right hand aimed at Charlie Phelan.

'I don't understand, Sirus,' Charlie said, his voice quavering. 'What happened?'

Sirus said nothing. He swung the barrel of his gun into Charlie's face. The metal collided with his already mangled nose, and Charlie cried out in pain as fresh blood erupted. 'Aw, fuck!' he screamed. 'I didn't do nothing!'

Sirus swung the gun twice more, hitting Charlie in the side of the head. 'Shut up, Charlie,' he fumed. It made him feel better, even as his right hand sent shivers of pain up through his arm. The shot that struck his gun had not hit his hand, but the force of the impact had jarred the hand badly. He wondered whether it had cracked a bone, but knew he had no time to worry about it. He spent his life in combat, dealing with pain. 'I don't want to hear another fuckin' word from you, understand? Next time I hear a word from you, I'm gonna put this gun in your mouth and blow your tongue through the back of your goddamned throat.'

'Yeah, Sirus,' Charlie said, his hand to his face trying to stop the bleeding. 'I understand.' He pulled his shirt up and held the tail against his nose, which seemed to have some effect.

They rode in silence for several minutes as Sirus steered the car out of Southie and along the edge of the downtown area, down by the Fort Point Channel. From there, he hopped onto Storrow Drive, and took the exit for Memorial out toward Cambridge.

'Where are you taking me?' Charlie asked. Sirus shot him a look, raising his gun slightly. Charlie flinched like he'd been hit, and covered his mouth. Sirus guessed he was thinking about the threat to shoot out his tongue, and Phelan's fear was gratifying. That specific threat was an empty one, though. Sirus needed Charlie to talk.

They pulled off Memorial Drive and onto Massachusetts Avenue, headed north toward the heart of Cambridge, passing the Massachusetts Institute of Technology, with its great dome looking out across the Charles River. From there, they sliced through the residential neighborhoods where the houses of students and teachers and government workers mingled with Title 8 subsidized housing. It was a melting pot like few others in the greater Boston metropolitan area.

The turn was just before Central Square, in a little neighborhood thick with immigrants from India and Pakistan and Iraq. The tensions of the Middle East simmered among the displaced of each ethnic contingent.

Muslims and Hindus warred in café conversations over Kashmir; Sunis and Kurds regularly came to blows over the gassings of the 1990s; Islamic traditionalists and reformers argued over the application of Sharia law. It was, in many ways, a microcosm of those rivalries and hatreds that had plagued the Middle East for centuries.

Sirus guided the car past a bar called The Holy Land, where pierced youths waited on a line for tickets to a concert featuring some indie-alternative rock band scheduled for that evening, and continued two blocks west toward a small brick mosque that looked like a recreational center from the 1970s. He pulled into the driveway of a small house on the far side of the mosque, which led around to a garage in back. The trees and shrubs at the edges of the property had been left to grow wild, providing good cover from the street and neighbors.

Sirus stopped the car and turned off the engine. He looked at Charlie, and said, 'Get out.' Phelan looked even smaller and more pathetic than Sirus remembered, and the dried blood under his nose and on his chin gave him the look of a child who had just finished a raspberry ice-cream cone on a hot summer day. Sirus could see the streaks where tears had been falling from Phelan's eyes.

'What happens now?' Phelan asked.

Sirus stared hard at his hostage. 'That all depends on you, Charlie,' he said.

'I'll handle it.' Jack Saunders was hurrying toward his car, talking on his cell phone with Lawrence Ainsworth. Charlie Phelan's sister was by his side, step by step, the concern evident on her face.

'You really think there's something to this?' his boss asked.

'Phelan's name was on the memory stick, and when I show up here some genetically engineered GI takes a shot at me,' Saunders said. 'Hard to believe that's a coincidence.'

'True,' Ainsworth agreed. 'What are you going to do?'

'I'm going to find him. I've got his sister with me.'

'Is she cooperating?'

Saunders looked briefly at Cianna Phelan. He'd given her a moment to wash the blood from her face, and apply a butterfly bandage to the cut. Even with that triage, though, she was still a mess. 'I think so. She was involved in the dust-up at her apartment and took a couple of good knocks. She's got a nasty bump on her head, and she seems a little disoriented, but I think she'll be cooperative. She's clearly worried about her little brother.'

'Word on the grapevine is she's a looker. That true?'

Saunders glanced at her briefly. 'Tough to tell at the moment. Maybe under different circumstances. What grapevine?'

Ainsworth didn't answer the question. 'Be careful with her.'

'What do you mean?'

'She's more dangerous than you think. That's the report I've gotten from both her commanders in Afghanistan and at Leavenworth.'

'You want to be a little more specific?'

Ainsworth paused. 'I can't.'

Saunders said, 'Thanks, that's helpful.'

'My hands are tied.'

115

'What about other assistance? Any chance we can bring in someone else to help with this?' Saunders asked. 'FBI or the locals?'

'There is no *this*,' Ainsworth said emphatically. 'You're on suspension, remember? You're only in Boston for vacation.'

'Right. That reminds me, I need to pick up some postcards. You like those wide-angle aerial shots, right?'

Ainsworth ignored the sarcasm. 'You need to keep this clean and contained, and make sure there are no fuckups. If you get into real trouble give me a call, and I'll see if I can send in some cavalry.'

'You don't consider getting shot at "real trouble"?'

'He missed, didn't he?'

'You're all heart, Skip. I'll call you when I know more.'

'Jack, I was serious about what I said before,' Ainsworth said. 'Be careful with the girl. I don't care how good-looking she might seem in other circumstances. I don't want to lose you like I lost Sam.'

CHAPTER SEVENTEEN

'Who is he?'

Saunders was sitting in his rented car with Cianna Phelan. He turned the key and the engine came to life. He watched her as she clenched and unclenched her fists. The bruise on her face had darkened to a deep purple, and her clothes were disheveled, but her eyes blazed as they darted back and forth.

'I told you, he's my brother.'

'The other guy,' Saunders said impatiently. He pulled out into the street, and as he gathered speed, he could hear the sound of sirens approaching. He looked into his rear-view mirror and saw two squad cars pull up in front of Phelan's apartment. He kept driving.

'I don't know,' she said.

She was lying; that much was clear. He didn't mind so much when people lied, as long as their lies were obvious. 'Well, let's start with what we can put together,' Saunders said. 'He's in the Army.'

She looked at him. 'How do you know that?'

'His gun was a Walther PK90; standard military issue in active theaters. And the car he was driving was the same blue piece-of-shit four-door sedan the Army uses when it doesn't want to announce its presence openly to the public.

He probably picked it up from the motor-pool at one of the bases around here, which suggests he's still active. Charlie just got out of the Army, right? And you were in the Army, too, at least technically, before your discharge from Leavenworth.'

She looked at him warily. 'You seem to know a lot.'

'I wasn't here by accident. I came here looking for your brother.'

'Why?'

He decided to stick to an abbreviated version of the truth. 'He was mentioned prominently in a communiqué from a terrorist network we intercepted. We figured it was worth looking into so we could find out what his involvement with them is.'

'You think he's involved with terrorists? Charlie?' She rolled her eyes in disbelief. 'That's what your investigation is about?'

'It's not an investigation,' Saunders said. 'Like I said, we thought it was worth checking up on. I wasn't expecting to get shot at.'

'The guy who shot at you isn't a terrorist.' She looked away. 'Not in the way you mean, at least.'

'I thought you didn't know who he was?'

She looked sharply at him for a moment, then lowered her eyes. 'My brother said his name is Sirus Stillwell. He knew him in Afghanistan.'

'Which brings us back to where we were before. Your brother was discharged recently.'

She nodded. 'Two weeks ago. He showed up here yesterday.'

'What's his connection to Mr Clean?'

She hesitated.

Saunders said, 'Like I told you before, I'm not looking to jam him up, but if we're going to find him, you've got to give me some information.'

'Charlie said Stillwell is a thief. He ran a group that was stealing antiquities from Afghanistan. At least, that's what Charlie told me.'

'And Charlie was involved with the group?'

'He wasn't involved. Not really. He said he just looked the other way when some things came through his depot, and made sure they got delivered where they were supposed to.'

'That's it?' Saunders demanded. She nodded, but he shook his head. 'If that was it, none of us would be here. What else is there?'

'Nothing,' she insisted.

He grabbed her by the shoulder and shook her. 'You're not doing him any favors, you know that, right? My guess is that if we don't find him in the next five hours, he'll show up at the morgue. Or worse, they'll never find his body. Either way, the only chance he has to make it through whatever *this* is alive depends on us. So I need to know everything you know. You got that?'

She looked at him, and he could tell she was deciding whether or not to trust him. 'Fine,' she said at last. 'He may have taken something from the last shipment he made for Sirus.'

'What did he take?'

'He said it was an antique knife.'

Saunders considered that. It was possible that what Charlie stole could be the 'Heart of Afghanistan' referred to in the communiqué. If he could find it, it might unravel the mystery of his informant's murder. 'Did he tell you where he stashed it?'

She shook her head.

He looked closely at her, and she stared back. 'It's important,' he said. 'Unless you have some idea where this Stillwell took your brother, we're at a dead end. If we can find whatever he stole, maybe we can use it to get your brother back.'

'You think I don't understand that?' she spat at him. 'He didn't tell me where it was. All he said was that it wasn't in the apartment. He said he would take me to where it was to show it to me, but then Sirus showed up.'

'He didn't say anything else?'

'No, he didn't,' she insisted. She was wearing jeans and a sweatshirt. For the first time Saunders noticed without intention that she was attractive, and he thought about what Ainsworth had said to him. 'Wait, that's not true,' she said. 'He said he put it in a safe place.'

'A safe place,' Saunders repeated. 'Like a bank safe-deposit box?'

'No, wait, that's not exactly what he said,' she said, frowning. 'He didn't say "a safe place". He said "a place where we were always safe".'

'And that's different?'

She nodded.

'Where were you always safe?'

She closed her eyes and frowned. After a moment, she said, 'There's only one place I can think of that makes any sense.'

*

120

Akhtar Hazara pulled up to Cianna Phelan's building as the sun started to set on the backside of South Boston. He looked at his watch; international travel had thrown his sense of time into confusion. It was just after four o'clock. He parked and sat back in the driver's seat, staring at the door to the tiny apartment house, wondering what his next steps should be.

He leaned forward and popped open the glove compartment. A Glock 9mm pistol was tucked under the registration, another gift from his contact at the bar. At least they understood the importance of his being armed.

He sat back again and looked up at the window on the fourth floor.

Suddenly, the door to the apartment house opened and two people walked out. One was an attractive young woman in her late twenties. She was in disarray, and it looked as though she had a large bruise on her face, but she fit the description he had of Charles Phelan's sister. He opened the folder on the passenger seat, flipping through pictures until he came to the one he was looking for. He held it on his lap, looking at the image of the girl in the photo. It was two years old, and the subject in the photo was in military fatigues and handcuffed, but there was no question it was the same woman.

He looked up again. Her companion was a wiry, tense man with black hair and sharp features. Akhtar guessed he was in his late thirties, certainly too old to be Charles Phelan. He was talking on a cell phone, and had his hand through the girl's arm. He was pulling her along with some urgency. They walked across the street, and he led Cianna Phelan around to the passenger side of the red car parked three in front of Akhtar's. He opened the door and deposited her, then walked back around to the driver's side, and got in. The engine came to life, and they pulled out immediately.

Akhtar looked up at the apartment. If Charles Phelan was still there, he was likely alone, and this might be a perfect time to confront him. Something about the demeanor of the sister, though, gave Akhtar the feeling that wasn't the case. There was something in her eyes – fear and anger and desperation – that made him think something had already gone wrong.

He hesitated for only a moment before he turned the key and pulled out after the red car.

CHAPTER EIGHTEEN

Charlie Phelan was on a chair in the basement of the little house in Cambridge. His hands and feet were bound, and a piece of duct tape covered his mouth. The blood clotting in his nose made breathing difficult. It was cold and damp, but Charlie could still feel the sweat dripping down his face, soaking his body.

The basement had an unusual setup. Most of it was unfinished, and moisture stains covered the cement walls. One section, though, had a freshly painted length of drywall propped up against it. A small area of the floor in front of the wall was covered with a run of thin, beige carpet, and two chairs sat facing each other across a knee-high table, like a cheap imitation of the old set for the Dick Cavett Show. Several tin lights hung from the ceiling, aimed at the chairs, and a small camera was set upon a Walmart tripod underneath the lights. It was, Charlie realized, a makeshift television studio. It was unclear, though, what kinds of programs were filmed there.

On the other side of the basement, closer to where Charlie was tied, a massage table stood against a wall with leather straps hanging off it at both ends. There were dark stains running down the side of the table, and on the cement underneath.

Sirus Stillwell had brought Charlie down to the basement as soon as they exited the car. It took a few moments for him to make certain that Charlie was tied tight enough that he couldn't escape, and then he had disappeared up the stairs. Charlie could hear him pacing the floor above him, and heard his voice in the muffled half of a telephone conversation.

A few moments later, Sirus came back down. He was still limping slightly, and he winced as he took off his jacket. Charlie could see the large bloodstain on the man's shirt at the shoulder where he'd been shot. He put his gun down on the massage table and opened a drawer in an ancient wooden cabinet built into the wall. Charlie couldn't see exactly what he took out, but he caught the flash of metal, and he felt his stomach lurch toward his throat. Finally, Sirus turned to Charlie.

'We don't have much time, Charlie,' he said. 'I know you took it. We both know you did. Others know it, too. Some of them are on the way here. If you tell me where it is, I may be able to save you, do you understand? If not, there is nothing anyone will be able to do. If the others get here, and I can't tell them that you've agreed to cooperate, it's over for you. You'll tell them what they want to know eventually, trust me, but you'll suffer very badly first.'

He walked over to Charlie, crouched in front of him, so that he was looking into his eyes. Stillwell's eyes were ice blue, almost clear. They cut through Charlie for a moment. 'I've known you for, what, almost three years, Charlie?'

Charlie nodded.

'You're not someone who is prepared to suffer,' he said. 'Not the way you're going to be made to suffer. I'm going to take off the tape now, and you are going to tell me where it is.' He reached up and tugged at the corner of the duct tape to get a good hold. Then he ripped it off in one clean, quick motion that took several layers of skin off and left Charlie gasping in pain. 'Where is it?' Sirus said after a moment.

It was true that Charlie had known Sirus for three years, but he'd heard of him long before that. Sirus was a legend in military circles in the Middle Eastern theater. His brutality in battle, and his unforgiving nature with respect to those in the allied military forces who crossed him, were legend. Even the illegal activities with which Charlie had helped him were generally regarded as an open secret. The military police were never called in to investigate him. It was as though the command structure was afraid of this man. He had become untouchable. And as Charlie sat tied to the chair, looking back at him, he knew that Sirus Stillwell had no intention of sparing his life if Charlie agreed to talk. It wasn't Sirus's way, and Charlie knew it. He tightened his gut, and tried to brace himself for what was to come.

'I don't know what you're looking for, Sirus,' he said. He tried to sound as scared and honest as he could. He was sure he'd accomplished the scared part, at least.

Sirus nodded, a frown on his face. 'Okay,' he said. He stood up and turned for a moment, and then spun back with force and speed, and his enormous left fist hammered Charlie in the side of his face. Charlie could feel the blood flow from just below his eye, and he was sure that his cheekbone was broken. The pain was more intense than anything he'd ever felt, and he screamed out in agony. Rather than inspiring pity, though, his scream seemed only to inflame Sirus, and he followed his first blow with several more to the exact same spot. Charlie could feel several of his teeth come free in his mouth, and it felt as though the entire left side of his face was sliding off his skull. It was remarkable that Sirus could hit him as hard as he did even with a bullet wound in his shoulder. It was an effective reminder to Charlie of the kind of man Sirus was.

Sirus leaned down close to him again. 'I'm serious about what I said, Charlie,' he said. 'We don't have much time. Tell me what you know.'

Charlie spat blood and shards of teeth. He was crying, and every movement was its own separate eternal agony. He had to hold to his story, though. It was the only chance he had to survive. 'I don't know anything,' he garbled. 'I swear to God.'

Sirus hit him again, this time on the other side of his face and not quite so hard. It was odd, but it felt like a kindness compared to the prior blows. 'You stupid little shit!' Sirus yelled. He sounded more exasperated than angry now.

'I don't know—'

Sirus cut him off. He squatted down in front of Charlie again and grabbed the front of his shirt. 'You need to tell me where it is, do you understand?' Charlie frowned through the pain and shook his head. 'There's a civil war coming in Afghanistan, and our country doesn't give a shit. Those of us still over there need to place our bets, do you understand? I'm not coming home. I've invested too much to walk away. I'm staying there, and that means I need the right people to take charge. It's the only chance I have. It's the only chance we all have.'

Charlie stared blankly back at the man in front of him. Sirus's eyes had grown wide and crazed, and what he was saying made no sense. It was gibberish.

'Do you love your country, Charlie? Do you respect those of us who have bled over there?'

Charlie nodded. There seemed really only one answer.

'Then you need to tell me, now!'

Charlie heard the door open upstairs, and there were footsteps on the floor above them. He could hear them moving toward the top of the stairs that led down to the basement, two or three sets of footsteps moving with direction but without haste.

'They're here!' Sirus hissed. 'Now! Do you understand? You need to tell me now!'

The footsteps were coming closer. They were at the top of the stairs, and beginning their descent.

Charlie choked out, 'I don't know anything.'

Charlie could see the shadows as they crossed from the staircase to the cement floor, and the legs of the newcomers were visible for a moment. Then Sirus hit him again on the side of the face that was most badly injured, and the howling pain began again. Sirus hit him repeatedly. Three, four, five times in a few seconds, and the agony was so complete that Charlie's vision blurred.

The violence stopped, and with his eyes closed Charlie could feel Sirus step away from him. He heard him talking, and his voice sounded distant.

'He hasn't told me anything yet,' Sirus said.

'Are you sure he knows?' The voice sounded kind, almost feminine. It had a light accent that reminded Charlie of his time in the Middle East.

'He knows,' Sirus said, his voice cruel and harsh in contrast.

'And yet he hasn't talked?'

'No.'

Charlie felt someone touch his chin. The hand was soft, and it raised his head up. Charlie opened his eyes and looked into the warmest face he could remember. The man appeared young, and he had a quiet, singular confidence about him that comes only from surety of purpose. A dark brown birthmark in the shape of a teardrop adorned his right cheek under the eye, which made the face appear even more compassionate. He seemed almost to glow, and for just a moment, Charlie felt hope grow in his chest.

Then the man spoke.

'You haven't been persuasive enough,' he said to Sirus. 'Perhaps I can do better.'

CHAPTER NINETEEN

'Where to?'

Cianna Phelan barely heard the question. She was staring out the passenger window, her mind given over to the fear of what might happen to her brother.

'Where to?' Saunders asked again.

She heard him this time, and replied, 'The waterfront.'

He turned his eyes back to the street.

She gave him a sidelong glance. He had an unremarkable appearance that would never be noticed or recalled if passed on the street, or caught out of the corner of an eye at a bar or on a plane. And yet when she focused on his face, she could see a gripping strength. It was in his eyes, and in the set of his mouth – hard and evaluating, intelligent and uncompromising.

'You want to tell me where we're going?' he asked.

'A bar,' she replied.

'Are you thirsty, or just a boozer?'

'Fuck you,' she said. 'We need to get to Spudgie's, down by the water, near the projects. Just drive.'

He leaned forward and tapped the name of the bar into the GPS. A series of options came up on the screen, and he chose the one identified as a bar in South Boston. 'East Ninth Street?'

'That's the one.' Cianna Phelan looked back out of the passenger window.

'It would be helpful if I knew what was at this place.'

'It's just a bar.'

'Then why are we going there?'

She took a deep breath. 'Because it's where we were safe growing up.'

Charlie Phelan no longer felt connected to his body. He was floating above the room, looking down at the awful scene as it flickered inexorably along. At one point, when the pain became too much, he even believed that he'd died and he was no longer suffering. At just that moment, though, he saw the man with the teardrop shaped birthmark reach into a bag and pull out a needle. He measured an amount of liquid from a vial, and stuck the needle into Charlie's arm. Charlie felt himself pulled toward his body. He desperately struggled to stay floating above, away from his body, flailing his phantom arms and legs in an effort to get away as something forced him down, back into the corporeal wreckage.

He opened his eyes slowly. The pain had returned. The teardrop man was standing over him. 'Welcome back, Mr Phelan,' he said. 'You left us for a moment. It is often difficult to find the line where a man can no longer accept the pain. The medicine I have given you should keep you here with us, though . . . for a while. You will feel the pain less, of course. But I do not think it will matter. Your awareness of what is happening to you will be enough.'

Charlie tried to speak, but his lips and tongue wouldn't cooperate. He turned his head and realized that he was no longer in the chair. They had laid him down on the massage table, strapping his arms and legs in the leather – as though he might have the strength to try to escape. The notion almost seemed funny to him.

'Yes, Mr Phelan? You wish to tell us something?'

'Please . . .' Charlie managed to choke out.

'Of course. Tell me what I want to know.'

Charlie looked around the room. He could see Sirus standing behind the teardrop man. Their eyes locked, and it almost seemed as though there was a hint of sympathy in Sirus's expression. There were two others there, watching. Neither of them spoke, and to Charlie they seemed more like ghosts.

'Please . . .' he said again.

'It is within your own power. Tell us where it is.'

'Please, please, please, please, please . . .'

The man frowned. He looked over at Sirus, who gave an exhausted shrug. Looking back at Charlie, the man shook his head. 'It does not have to be this difficult.'

'. . . please, please, please, please . . .' Charlie could feel the sanity leave him as he cackled in a half-laugh, half-cry.

The man nodded, giving a slight smile, as if acknowledging a challenge. He reached into a leather satchel on the floor and pulled out a knife almost as long as a machete. The tip was curved, and the metal gleamed. The man held it up, like he was showing off a new toy. He walked around to Charlie, looking at him.

'You know what you are, Mr Phelan?' he said slowly.

'I'm sorry! Please, I'm sorry!'

'You are a thief.' The man slid the knife up and rested

it on Charlie's neck. 'It is very bad to be a thief where I come from. There are very strict penalties for theft.' Charlie could feel the knife so sharp on his throat that just the weight of it was slicing through the skin. 'Do you know what the penalty is for theft?' the man asked.

Charlie whispered, almost hoping, 'Death?'

The man laughed softly. 'Oh, no. We are not barbarians. You will be spared. But the penalty is still severe.'

'What, then?' Charlie asked.

The man sighed, as though he was loath to even tell Charlie. He reached under the table and pulled out a narrow extension that ran from just below where Charlie's shoulder was. The other men in the room were watching him, and he nodded to one of them now. He approached and untied Charlie's hand.

'What are you doing?' Charlie cried. The man ignored him, and pulled on Charlie's arm so that it was stretched along the extension. 'No!' Charlie screamed. He had no idea what was happening, but he didn't like the look of it. He tried to pull his arm back, but he was too weak, and the man easily overpowered him. He pulled the arm down and strapped it to the extension so that Charlie was now lying on the table with his left arm extended, like a one-winged angel. 'What are you doing?' Charlie sobbed.

The man with the teardrop birthmark stepped forward again. He reached down and took hold of Charlie's hand, just above the point at which the arm was secured to the plank. 'You have such delicate hands,' he said. 'Not unlike my own.' He was caressing Charlie's hand now, almost comforting it. 'There were times when I was younger when

132

the other children mocked me because it was so thin. They assumed it was weakness.' He looked Charlie in the eye. 'They were wrong.'

He picked up the knife again. 'You are a thief, and you must be punished. I take no joy in that,' he said.

'PLEASE! NO! NO! NO! NO! NO! NO! . . .' Charlie was no longer sobbing; he was screaming in terror.

'Shhhh,' the man whispered. 'It will only hurt for a moment.' The man lifted the knife, and in one quick motion swung it in a high arc, bringing it down toward Charlie's wrist. Charlie bucked and pulled at his arm, but it was no use; he was tightly secured to the table. The man brought the knife down with all his weight.

Charlie heard the sound before the pain reached his brain. It was a sickening combination of crunching and popping, like the sound made when tearing a leg off a turkey at Thanksgiving, only much louder. He was screaming so deafeningly now everything was blocked out. When the pain arrived, it was dulled by the anesthetic.

The man reached down and picked the lifeless hand off the table. He held it up, examining it closely as the blood dripped from the severed bones poking from the clean edges of skin. One by one, he wiggled each finger. Charlie watched, his mouth open in a silent scream, as the man toyed with the hand. After a few moments, the man looked at Charlie, and turned the hand to him, moving it up and down in a mock wave at its former owner. Then he let out a long, high-pitched cackle and, with a flick of the wrist, he tossed the hand on Charlie's chest, up by the breastbone, so that it was only inches from his face.

Charlie screamed over and over, wrenching his shoulders

to try to shake the hand off him, but nothing worked. It sat there, oozing from the severed end, tormenting him.

One of the man's silent companions stepped forward and used medical tape as a tourniquet to stop the bleeding at the stump.

'Shhhh,' the man said quietly. 'It is all right. The pain you are enduring today is but a nuisance to the torment Allah is saving for you in return for what you have done. Think of this as . . . what is the word . . . practice?' He leaned down close to Charlie. 'How many pieces of you do you think I could balance on this scrawny goat body?' he asked.

Charlie was no longer screaming. He had no such energy left. All he could muster now was a long, low moan punctuated with his sobs.

'There are many bits that are easy to get at.' He paused, leaning in closer still. 'This is your last chance before I cut them all off. I will not pause again until the job is complete. Do you understand that?'

'Yes,' Charlie sobbed.

'Will you tell me what I want to know?'

Charlie choked as the air rushed too fast into his lungs.

'Will you tell me?'

It took another moment for Charlie to answer. Finally, he managed to choke the word out. 'Yes,' he said. 'Yes, I will.'

CHAPTER TWENTY

Nick 'Spudgie' O'Callaghan was in his early-sixties. His gut hung over his belt more than he cared to acknowledge, but he was still tall and thick through the chest and shoulders, and the veins popped in his wrists when he worked the taps at Spudgie's Seaside Bar and Grill. He'd survived an alcoholic father with a violent temper, two tours in Vietnam, and three ex-wives. He and his bar stood at the edge of Paradise Bay in South Boston, just a few blocks from the Old Colony Public Housing Projects, like a bulwark against time and change.

Nick was pulling the taps at the bar when Miles Gruden walked in with his two fireplug bodyguards. The place was relatively empty. A young couple with well-styled hair and labeled clothing were sitting at the bar, trying to tease conversation from him. Nick had been getting more and more of these types – slum-divers, he called them – ever since Southie started yielding grudgingly to gentrification: adventurous yuppies who thought the trick to fitting in was to poke their moisturized faces into the places the locals held most dear. It was okay with Nick. He kept two versions of his menu behind the bar, one for the locals and one for the well-dressed set with the prices doubled.

He didn't mind them coming, but he'd be damned if he wasn't going to charge them for the privilege.

'Did you ever meet Whitey?' the girl was asking. She whispered the name, as though the mere utterance could conjure up evil.

Gruden took a seat at the bar two away from the couple and stared at Nick.

Nick ignored Gruden. 'Bulger? 'Course. He was in every other week trying to shake me down. Never paid him. He wasn't stupid, though. He knew the neighborhood would back me if it ever came to that. My place was never touched, and we ended up friendly enough.' He set two beers down on the bar in front of the couple. 'That'll be fourteen dollars.'

The young man flipped a twenty on the bar.

'It must have been so exciting,' the girl said. She'd be back in the bar again in the future, Nick guessed. She liked the danger. At least she thought she did. At some point in the near future, she and her thin-hipped euro-boy would break up, and she'd be back in to see what the real life was like. She might even hook up with one of the locals. It wouldn't take her long after that to realize, though, that she had bitten off more than she could chew.

'Spudge, we need to talk,' Gruden said roughly.

The couple looked over at him.

'Always happy to talk, Miles,' Nick said amiably. 'I'm just serving a couple of customers, as you see.'

'Tell them to fuck off.'

'You were raised without manners, Miles. It'll get you in trouble someday. My mother would never have let me use that sort of language around strangers.'

'My mother didn't give a fuck.' Gruden looked at the couple. 'Fuck off.'

The woman looked at Nick nervously. 'Should we leave?' Her boyfriend looked like he was going to throw up.

'Might be best,' Nick said. 'The table in the corner's got a nice view of the street. Miles, here, looks like he's got something to chew over with me, and he's not the most patient man. Let me just get your change.'

'Keep it,' the boyfriend said. 'Please.'

'Nice of you. I'll bring over some popcorn. On the house.'

The couple moved away toward the back of the bar quickly.

'You charge for the fuckin' popcorn?' Gruden asked, shaking his head.

'No,' Nick responded. He cleared a glass from the bar. 'What do you want, Miles? You know I don't like you in my bar; you scare business away.' He picked the glass out of the sink and began wiping it down.

'You seen Charlie Phelan recently?'

'Why do you want to know?'

'I'll take that as a yes.' Gruden stared at Nick for a few seconds. The bar owner went on wiping down glasses without speaking. 'You used to date his mother, didn't you?'

'*Date* would be an exaggeration.'

'Her kid used to hang around here. I remember that. Him and that piece of work of a sister. She was a fuckin' headcase, you remember?'

Nick put down the glass he was cleaning and leaned over the bar. 'What do you want, Miles?'

'The kid, Charlie, was supposed to meet me at my barber shop earlier this afternoon. He didn't show.'

'Maybe he went to Super Cuts instead. I hear they do a hell of a job, and they're only twelve bucks.'

'Funny you say that. He was supposed to bring me some merchandise. A very valuable piece. When we were cutting the deal, he said he had others interested in it. So I'm thinking that maybe he went to one of my competitors.'

Nick shrugged. 'I suppose it's possible. Maybe you should have been more generous.'

'He made the deal with me. We shook hands on it.'

'And your handshake has always meant so much?'

'Don't fuck with me on this, Spudge,' Gruden growled. A narrow line of spittle formed on his lips as his ire was raised. 'The only person the kid knows in town who might be able to refer him to someone else is you. You and I both know that. I want to know what the fuck is going on.'

Nick took a napkin from the tray on the bar and tossed it at Gruden. 'Wipe your goddamned mouth before you spit at me. I don't know anything about your business with Charlie Phelan, and I couldn't give a shit about it. It's time you left my bar.'

Gruden's two bodyguards moved in close behind him. They looked like twin bulldogs, and they flashed identical menacing looks at Nick.

Gruden leaned back in his chair, looking perturbed. 'I've always let you run your business here without any hassle, Spudge. Just about everyone else in the neighborhood pays for the privilege, but not you. You really want to push me on this?'

Nick reached below the bar and pulled out a shotgun. He rested it on the bar, the barrels pointing at Gruden's chest. His movements were calm and relaxed, so that no one not involved in the conversation would even be aware of the confrontation. When he spoke, his voice was quiet. 'Listen here, you scaly little shit. I've never paid a dime of tribute to anyone. Never. And if I didn't pay Whitey and Stevie, I'm sure as shit not going to pay a retard like you. If you've got a problem with that, you send your boys here to talk to me after hours. But don't expect them to come back in mint condition, you understand?'

'You're making a bad mistake, Spudge,' Gruden said. 'You know that, right?'

'Get out, Miles. And don't come back.'

'What do we know of this place? This *Spudgie's*?'

Ahmad Fasil was sitting at the kitchen table in the house in Cambridge. He was freshly showered, and Charlie Phelan's blood had been washed down the bathroom drain. Before him on the table his array of sharp metal implements was laid out on a towel. He was cleaning them one by one, and putting them away in a leather case.

Sirus Stillwell stood at the kitchen window looking out, watching for something. He didn't believe that anyone had called the police. The basement had been sound-proofed, and even the most ear-piercing screams would not have been heard from outside. And yet he was nervous. He couldn't pinpoint the cause of his concern, but he couldn't ignore it either.

'It's a local place,' Stillwell said. 'The owner is ex-military.'

'You are military. So, you can talk to him, yes?'

Stillwell shook his head. 'He's not my military. He fought back in the sixties. Draftee. Got out a long time ago. Word is he knows everyone in the area, both the cops and the criminals.'

'What is his connection to Charles Phelan?'

'There's not much we can find. Phelan's from the same neighborhood, and from what we can tell his sister used to hang out at Spudgie's.' Sirus had taken off his shirt, and was cleaning the wound in his shoulder as he stood in front of the sink. The shoulder was stiffening, and he cursed quietly under his breath.

'Are you going to tell me how you were injured?' Fasil asked. They had been in the basement since Fasil's arrival and had not had a chance to discuss what had happened at Cianna Phelan's apartment.

Sirus hesitated. 'There was some trouble at the girl's apartment,' he said hesitantly.

'I have found that gunshot wounds are rarely suffered without trouble.'

'The police may be involved now. There was a guy who showed up at the girl's apartment claiming to be a cop when I took Charlie. We traded shots. She's probably talking to them right now.'

Fasil turned on Sirus, staring hard into his eyes. 'Tell me about this man,' he said slowly. 'Tell me what he said and what he did.' He listened as Sirus relayed the information, his eyes never leaving Sirus's. When Sirus was done, he said, 'He is not the police.'

'Why do you say that?'

'Because a police officer would have neither the skill nor the presence of mind to shoot your gun out of your hand. If this man was the police, he would have shot you in the chest as soon as you pointed your gun at him. There would have been no hesitation. Police are trained to look after their own safety first in such a situation. This man was able to wound you as you sped away from him in a car.'

'That might have been a lucky shot.'

Fasil shook his head. 'This was not luck. This man you dealt with had special training, and he was trying to keep you alive so that he could gather information from you.'

Sirus frowned. 'If he's not a cop, then who is he?'

'That,' Fasil said, 'is the interesting question, no?'

One of Fasil's men came up from the basement, walked over to the sink and began washing the blood off his hands.

'Is he alive?' Fasil asked.

The man at the sink nodded. 'I stopped the bleeding, and have given him some additional painkillers and a sedative. He should sleep. We will see if he wakes.'

'It would be good to keep him alive,' Fasil said. 'He may be of more use in the future.'

'I will do my best. There is much damage.'

Fasil addressed Stillwell again. 'You were telling me of the tavern owner.'

'Like I said, he's a neighborhood guy. We don't think he's involved in anything illicit, but he definitely hangs out with that crowd. He could move this thing if he wanted to.'

141

Fasil held up the blade he had used to cut off Charles Phelan's hand, examining it to make sure it was clean. 'We will have to convince him that he should not want to move it, then, won't we?'

CHAPTER TWENTY-ONE

Cianna Phelan paused at the door to Spudgie's Bar and Grill. Her heart was beating so fast and hard it was all she could hear. She'd been back in Southie for more than three months, but this was the one place she had taken pains to avoid. Nick was the only person through her tumultuous childhood who had actually cared for her and her brother. He had been the one person she could rely on, and she had let him down. He had been opposed to her going into the military – it was no place for someone as smart as she was, he'd said. She would never be able to conform enough to avoid trouble, he'd predicted. He'd been right about that, and the only time she felt real shame about all she had done was when she thought of facing him. Given how her military career had turned out, he would have every right to throw her out, pretend as though he didn't know her anymore. That possibility struck more fear into her heart than anything she could imagine. It was why she had not returned before now.

He was behind the bar, as always. The hair was a bit greyer, perhaps, and there was a little more fatigue around the eyes, but other than that he looked the same as he had when he'd toasted her deployment with more concern than joy. 'Be careful, and take care of yourself,' he'd said. She was never very good at taking advice.

'Is this the place?' Saunders asked. He was standing behind her, and she was blocking the door as she hesitated at the threshold.

'Yeah,' she said.

'There a problem?'

'There are lots of problems.' She took a step and entered the pub, walking slowly but steadily toward the bar. She realized at that moment she had never been this scared.

Nick O'Callaghan was pouring a drink for a customer, his eyes down, when she reached the bar. 'Can I get you something?' he asked without looking up.

'I don't know,' she said. 'Maybe.'

She could tell that he recognized the voice; his head snapped up, and he took a long look at her. The silence between them was suffocating. 'It's been a long time,' he said finally. More silence. 'I heard you were back in town, but I haven't heard from you.'

'I know,' she said. 'I'm sorry, I was . . .' The words caught in her mouth. 'I was . . .' The collective weight of two and a half years of misery suddenly seemed to come crashing down upon her. She couldn't move, and her arms felt like bags of wet sand hanging from tired shoulders. 'I'm sorry.'

He was still looking at her, his expression inscrutable. He put the drink he was pouring down on the bar slowly. Without a word, he turned and walked in the other direction.

Cianna stood there, watching as he walked away. She felt a single tear running down her stone cheek, and she brushed it away. He had every right to walk away, and it was her responsibility to honor that decision if necessary. When he reached the far end of the bar, he lifted the service top and came out from behind the well. He walked around the outside of the bar, came over and stood in front of her. She scrutinized his face, desperate for some clue as to what he was thinking.

He was looking at the deep bruise on her cheek, frowning. 'You always were a brawler,' he said quietly. 'Some things never change.'

'I've changed,' she said. She fought back more tears, and wondered whether it was true. 'I've changed,' she said again, as though repetition was the same thing as truth.

After a moment, he opened his arms. 'Welcome back,' he said quietly. 'You've been missed.'

She fell against him, letting him take the weight of her troubles as he wrapped his arms around her. She had forgotten how solid and strong he was, how steady and sure he felt. A light sob escaped her lips, and she tried to take it all back. 'I'm so sorry,' was all she could say.

'No need for it here,' he said. 'This is your home.'

Akhtar Hazara sat in the car, parked across the street from Spudgie's Bar and Grill. The windows were small and dark, and he could not see inside. He was beginning to regret his decision to follow Phelan's sister and her companion. For all he knew, they were just out for a night on the town. Something about it didn't seem right, though. They didn't seem like a couple. He'd lived in the US for long enough to see how American couples behaved with each other in public. Unless married, they touched each other almost compulsively, giving all those around them an unseemly insight into the intimacy they shared in private. It was, in his view, overcompensation for the shallow spiritual bond western couples shared.

Phelan's sister and her companion did not behave that way, though. Both as they walked from her apartment to the car, and again when they walked from the car to the tavern, he had held her arm almost as though he was afraid that she might escape his grasp. Inside the car they had barely looked at each other. There was a sense of tension that still convinced him that he had been right to follow them.

Darkness had fallen since they had gone into the bar, and a chilly day had given way to a frigid night. Akhtar was used to the desert cold of Afghanistan, where, during the winters in the mountains and on the desert plains, the cold wind carried with it the wrath of Allah. And yet there was something about the cold of New England that sunk deeper within him. It was a damp cold that saturated his soul, and made him long for the desert.

He looked at his watch. It had been a half-hour since they had gone in to the bar. He would give them another half-hour, and then he would make a move, one way or another.

Nick hugged her for several moments. He could feel her body fighting to retain its composure; to keep everything that was trapped inside from leaking out in some maudlin, self-pitying explication. He understood. It was their way; the way of the streets. When he let her go, he said, 'I heard you've been working with Milo Pratt.'

She nodded. 'It's all I could find.'

He patted her on the shoulder as he glanced warily at Saunders, who was standing a few feet away. 'He does good work. He kept Smitty's son from going back in. Kept him straight through a bad patch. It's good work.'

'You seem to be the only one who thinks so. No one else would hire me. Not after . . .'

He shook his head. 'No need for explanations. The other shit is in the past; you just focus on the future.'

'Thanks. I need you to know the truth, though. Things back in Afghanistan weren't what they seemed. It didn't go down the way people said it did.'

'I never believed it did.' He was silent for a moment. 'Do you want to tell me about it?' was all he said. He'd ask once, and never again.

She shook her head. 'Maybe someday,' she said. 'But there's no time now. Charlie's in trouble.'

Nick glanced again at Saunders but didn't ask to be introduced. 'What kind of trouble?'

'Bad trouble. He crossed a guy he knew in Afghanistan – a very dangerous guy from the looks of it. He came to my apartment and kidnapped Charlie. He had a gun, and when I tried to stop him, he tried to kill me.' She waved at the bruise on her face. 'That's how I got this.'

'Are you okay?'

'Yeah. I was a little shaken up, but I'm fine. I think Charlie stole something from this guy. Did he come here?'

Nick nodded. 'Two days ago.'

'Did he leave anything with you?'

'Yeah. He . . . uh . . .' Nick looked suspiciously at Saunders, and finally asked, 'Who's this?'

'His name is Saunders,' Cianna said. 'He's with—'

'Homeland Security,' Saunders interjected.

Nick examined him. 'CIA?'

Saunders didn't respond.

'He saved my life, Nick. If it wasn't for him, they'd be doing the autopsy on me right now. He's not interested in arresting Charlie, he just needs to know what's going on. And I need his help to find Charlie.'

Nick was still suspicious. 'What were you doing at Cianna's apartment?' he asked Saunders.

'Charlie's name came up in a message we intercepted that was being passed along a terrorist network. The message got one of my informants killed. It piqued my interest.'

'But you're not going to arrest him when this is over?' Nick had trouble believing it. He had never been on the wrong side of the law, but he'd never trusted the law, either. To him, the cops so often seemed like just another faction – another gang, only with the force of law behind them, which often made them all the more dangerous. He knew plenty of good cops, but he'd seen plenty of evil perpetrated in the name of justice.

'If he's not involved in any terrorist activities, he's not my concern,' Saunders said. 'I can't make any commitments on behalf of domestic law enforcement.'

At least he wasn't promising more than he could deliver, Nick thought. That increased his credibility.

'Charlie's got bigger problems right now than the cops, Nick,' Cianna said. 'The guy he was involved with was crazed when he showed up at my apartment. I don't know what's going on, but we've got to get my brother away from him. If you have what Charlie stole, that may give us a bargaining chip.'

Nick nodded.

'Do you still have it?'

'It's up in my office. Give me a minute.' He walked out from behind the bar. The only customers left in the place were the slum-divers, still sitting in the window seats to which Nick had directed them. He went over to them.

'Sorry about this, folks,' he said, 'but I have to close up for the night.'

They looked up at him with hurt and surprise. The boyfriend looked at his watch. 'It's seven o'clock.'

'I know,' Nick said. 'Something has come up of a personal nature. I have to ask you to leave. Your last round is on the house.'

The couple stared for a moment. The girl said, 'We should go.' Her boyfriend shrugged and tossed a ten-dollar bill on the table as a tip.

Once they were gone, Nick locked the door, and flipped the sign facing outward so that it read *Closed*. He walked back to where Cianna and Saunders were standing at the bar.

'You said it was upstairs?' Cianna asked.

'I did. Do you want to see it?' he asked.

Saunders and Cianna both nodded.

'Follow me.'

CHAPTER TWENTY-TWO

Charlie Phelan's eyes fluttered. He sensed movement in the room, but couldn't focus. The place smelled wet and heavy with a peaty fragrance that made his stomach turn. For a blissful moment he was disoriented enough that he couldn't remember where he was. Then it all came rushing back to him with such force he found it impossible to breathe.

He turned his head enough to glance down at the end of his wrist and saw the bandages, soaked through in red. His severed hand had been removed from his chest, at least. It was a small mercy.

'Oh, God,' he moaned. He could feel the tears flowing down the sides of his broken face.

He sensed the movement again. 'Who's there?' he asked quietly. There was no answer. 'Please, can I have water? I'm so thirsty.'

A voice came from across the room, plain and rough. At first Charlie thought the voice was speaking to him, but it was in a language he recognized but didn't understand. Then he heard another voice, this one softer, responding. Charlie turned and looked over, but all he could make out were shapes. Then one of those shapes moved over toward him, coming into focus.

Charlie recognized the man as one of those who had watched his torture. He was short and stocky, and wore a stethoscope around his neck. His eyes were dark and heavily lidded, and there was no sympathy or compassion in them as he bent down to examine Charlie, pulling open his eyelids, shining a light into his pupils, all the while muttering in Farsi. He put on his stethoscope and listened to Charlie's chest.

'Please . . .' Charlie said again. 'Water . . .?'

After a moment, the man looked over toward the other side of the room and nodded. The softer voice said something, and the doctor reached over and poured a cup of water, lowered it to Charlie's mouth.

Charlie was sickened by the overwhelming sense of gratitude he felt for the drink. He lapped and slurped and coughed as the water spilled down around his neck.

'Not so fast,' the man with the stethoscope said in an accent so heavy it was difficult to understand. He pulled the water away.

'Why?' Charlie asked.

'You will choke.'

'No,' Charlie said, shaking his head. He looked down again at the spot where his hand had once been, then back up at the doctor, his eyes pleading for an answer. 'Why are you doing this to me? You are a doctor.'

The man's face hardened even more. 'It is necessary to save my country,' he said. 'A great war is coming, and you are an infidel. You would do the same.'

Saunders followed Cianna and Nick as they headed for the narrow staircase at the back of the bar. The boards groaned under their weight. He looked around for another exit from the second floor, but this was clearly the only way up. It made him tense. He had no reason to distrust the tavern owner, but any space with only one way in or out always felt like a trap to Saunders. He kept his hand on the gun in his pocket.

'You should know there are others interested in it,' Nick said as he continued up the stairs.

'Others?' Saunders said.

'One, at least. Miles Gruden was here earlier. He said he had a deal with Charlie to buy it, but Charlie didn't show. He thinks Charlie got a better offer.'

'Shit,' Cianna muttered.

'Who is Miles Gruden?' Saunders asked.

'Local scumbag,' Nick said. 'Thinks of himself as the heir to the Winter Hill Gang's old business. He hasn't figured out yet that he doesn't have the same muscle. Without muscle, no one in this neighborhood gives a shit about you. Still, he scares enough people to keep himself in business, and he can be vicious when he feels like he's backed into a corner.'

The upstairs housed a small office tucked into a low attic with two dormers. There was a desk and a computer, and two chairs that were losing their upholstery. Books lined the walls of the place, and at first Saunders thought there were built-in shelves. Upon closer examination, though, he realized that the books were just so numerous and neatly stacked that they gave the impression of being supported by shelves. There had to be hundreds, possibly thousands of them, with titles from every genre ranging from political history and warfare to existential fiction.

'I like to read,' Nick said. It sounded like an apology.

He went to the desk and bent down, reaching behind a steel cabinet pushed up against the wall. Standing up, he pulled out something wrapped in a solid length of plain, rough homespun cloth. It was long and thin, and it made a solid noise as Nick laid it down on the desk. Nick stepped back. 'Take a look, if you like,' he said.

Saunders stepped forward and unfolded the heavy cloth. Inside was an ornate dagger around a foot and a half long. He bent down to examine it closely. The handle was fashioned from gold, and decorated with elaborate renderings of animals, both real and fantastic, devouring each other. Turquoise and jade stones adorned the center in the shape of hearts. The edges were festooned with diamonds. The blade was rusted iron, though it still looked as though it could cause damage.

Cianna looked over his shoulder. 'What is it?' she asked.

'I don't know, exactly,' Nick said. 'Charlie didn't really seem to, either. It's clearly very old, but that's about all I can tell.'

'Do you know anything about it?' Cianna asked Saunders.

His face was inches from the handle, and he was squinting to focus on the details. He nodded. 'A little, maybe.' He looked at Nick. 'Do you have a magnifying glass?'

'In the drawer,' Nick replied.

Saunders slid the desk drawer open and pulled out an old magnifying glass. He held it up to the handle, and began his examination over again. Once he had examined the entire handle, he looked closely at the blade.

'Well?' she demanded. 'What is it? Is it old?'

He nodded again. 'More than two thousand years old, most likely.'

'Jesus,' Nick muttered.

'Older than Jesus, actually,' Saunders corrected him. 'From the carvings, it looks like it's from the first century, BC,' Saunders said.

'That's old,' Cianna said flatly. 'Is it worth a lot?'

Saunders looked closer, holding it up to the light, grasping it with the cloth it was wrapped in to keep his fingers off it. 'Its historical value is hard to even estimate. Do you see the images of the animals locked in battle? In the nomadic tribes from the northern region from the Black Sea to Mongolia, these sorts of images were used to suggest aggression and invincibility. This was the dagger of a tribal king.'

'You seem to know a lot about it,' Cianna said.

'Not that much. There are people who spend their lives studying these types of antiquities. I only have enough knowledge to recognize the basics.'

'How did you learn it?'

'It was part of my job, once,' Saunders said. 'Stolen artwork has formed a large part of Afghanistan's underground currency for nearly a decade. The Taliban, Al Qaeda, many of the warlords – they all trade in these things when they are moving arms or drugs. I had to know enough to try to shut it down, or to use it for our own purposes if necessary. Any historian would tell you this piece is priceless.'

'How much does "priceless" go for on the streets?' Nick asked.

Saunders looked at him. 'In the neighborhood of half a million dollars,' he said after some consideration. 'Maybe more.'

'Nice neighborhood,' Nick said.

'I suppose,' Saunders agreed.

'You suppose?'

Saunders frowned. 'You don't understand what I mean. It's a very important piece, and very valuable, but it doesn't make sense that these people would be killing over this.'

'It's worth half a million,' Nick said. 'There are people in this neighborhood who'll kill for a couple grand.'

'Yes, but they wouldn't travel halfway around the world to do it.'

'If you bought the plane ticket, they would,' Nick pointed out.

'Let me put it another way,' Saunders said. 'The people we are dealing with are fanatics. This isn't about money, unless we're talking about enough money to buy a nuclear weapon – and a half-million doesn't get you close. Besides, there are thousands of antiquities that have been stolen from Afghanistan and Iraq that are worth every bit as much as this. I can't see what's so unique about this that it would create some sort of an international conspiracy.'

'Maybe it's got some sort of religious significance,' Cianna suggested. 'That would give it more value for many people.'

'It would,' Saunders agreed. 'But this is from the first century. We intercepted the message about your brother from Jihadis – radical Muslims – who wouldn't care particularly about first-century nomads. Mohammed wasn't born until the sixth century.' Saunders began rewrapping the dagger in the old cloth, then stopped. 'Do you have anything softer? The rag Charlie wrapped this in could scratch the gold.'

'Sure.' O'Callaghan dug around behind his desk and pulled out a soft plaid shirt folded into a drawer. 'I keep an extra here in case I get spilled on.'

Saunders wrapped the dagger in the shirt and left the other cloth on the desk.

'What now?' Cianna asked.

'Now we go back to your apartment,' Saunders said.

'The police may still be there. My neighbors would have heard the gunshots.'

'Maybe, but there's no blood and no bodies. They may ask some questions, but eventually they'll have to give up and go home. Besides, we have to assume that Sirus will try to contact you to see whether you have the dagger. He can't do that unless you're at your apartment.'

Cianna looked at Nick, and he nodded. 'It makes sense.'

Nick looked at Saunders. 'You gonna take care of her?'

'I can take care of myself,' Cianna said.

Nick ignored her. 'I'm serious. I know you've got a job to do, but I need to know that you're looking out for her in all this. Otherwise I'm coming along for the ride.'

'No need,' Saunders said. 'I'll look out for her.'

Nick looked long at Saunders, sizing him up. 'Okay, then,' he said at last. 'I'm here if you need anything.' He nodded and led them down the stairs.

CHAPTER TWENTY-THREE

Lawrence Ainsworth sat at his desk, his wide, bony shoulders hunched forward. In front of him a computer-enhanced map of Afghanistan revealed a mess of divided interests and limited control. Blue borders indicated the various zones where the American military still held sway, but many of them were dotted lines, a nod to the reality of a fully fluid situation. The map was the product of military intelligence enhanced with the information gathered by Agency operatives in the field. There were hundreds of such agents, all under Ainsworth's control. No four of them combined provided the consistency of accurate and useful information that Saunders had when he was active, though. Without Saunders, Ainsworth felt like he was flying blind.

Ainsworth's head was down, but he sensed the door open. It was a part of his training that would never go away. He'd grown accustomed to noticing every aspect of his surroundings, from a shift in a shadow, to the slightest breeze from an opening door.

'Most people knock, Bill,' Ainsworth said.

'Most people have to,' Bill Toney replied.

Ainsworth looked up. The retired colonel was younger than him – in his late fifties, with thick dark hair streaked grey at the temples and a posture that betrayed his military background – but still old enough to remember the Agency's heyday, when the Cold War required that aggression be carried out in secret. Back then, secrecy was the greatest asset the Agency had in the battle for inter-governmental influence, and it had wielded that secrecy effectively to maximize the breadth of its influence and funding. Since the collapse of the Soviet Union there had been far more pressure on the American government to operate in the light of day. The world had little trust for its only superpower, and four successive presidential administrations had bowed remarkably, if not entirely, to a new spirit of transparency. Covert operations were now looked at as unclean – necessary evils to be tolerated only in the most extreme circumstances. As a result, the military's power, and the corresponding power of Toney's NSA, had grown at the expense of the Agency's influence. Toney and Ainsworth were both well aware of their relative positions.

Ainsworth pointed to the chair across from his desk. 'By all means, then. Please sit.'

Toney remained standing. 'Where's your boy, Saunders?'

'On leave,' Ainsworth said. 'I thought it would be best for everyone.'

'I heard a rumor he was up in Boston. That true?'

Ainsworth shrugged. 'I don't keep track of people when they are not on active duty. This job is consuming enough. You've got to allow people a little bit of space in their personal lives, you know?'

'I didn't think Saunders had a personal life.'

'Like I said, I don't keep track.' Ainsworth leaned back

in his chair, looking up across his desk at Toney. 'Is there some reason you care? Are you planning out your next vacation? I could have Saunders give you a call when he gets back, give you a recommendation.'

Toney's face was stone. 'I don't think that will be necessary.'

'Let me know if you change your mind.' Ainsworth leaned forward again and went back to his work. Toney remained where he was. After another moment, Ainsworth looked up again. 'Was there something else, Bill?'

'I've had my people look into this situation involving Charles Phelan,' he said finally.

'That quickly?' Ainsworth sat back in his chair. 'It only took two days.' The sarcasm in his voice was thick. 'You must view this as a high priority.'

'There's nothing to it,' Toney said, ignoring Ainsworth's tone. 'He's a nobody.'

'I thought all our soldiers were heroes.'

'He's hardly a soldier,' Toney continued. 'He was a low-level shipping clerk. And not a very honest one, at that. It looks as though he may have been involved in some activities shipping looted goods out of the country.'

'Not the sort of thing we encourage our people to do, these days, is it?' Ainsworth watched Toney's face closely. 'Still, I suppose it's the same story in every war. It's not exactly surprising.'

'No, it's not,' Toney said. 'But it is embarrassing. And in this war anything that embarrasses the military can have more of an impact than in any other conflict we've dealt with before. We're viewed as marauding Huns over there, set on conquering and pillaging the land. Anything that reinforces that image tends to inflame the passion of the Afghan people and provide recruiting material for the extremists.'

'So,' Ainsworth said slowly, 'perhaps the best thing we can do is to make clear that we will not tolerate this behavior. Arrest him and put him on trial in a very public way.'

Toney shook his head. 'You and I both know that won't work. Look at Abu Ghraib. We couldn't have been any more vehement or public in our disgust over that. Did anyone care? No. All anyone over there could focus on was that it happened. All anyone remembers is those goddamned photographs. It would be the same here. All anyone would focus on is the fact that some assholes in the Army were involved in smuggling antiquities. Christ, by the time the press got done with it, people would think we were paying our soldiers with the ancient treasures of Mohammed.'

'Perhaps we didn't go far enough in our treatment of those responsible for Abu Ghraib,' Ainsworth ventured.

'What are you talking about? They were tried. They are rotting in jail for the rest of their meaningful lives. That's not enough?'

'That's just the people on the ground. Some might argue that nothing happened to those truly responsible. Those farther up the chain of command.' His gaze bore into Toney's eyes as he spoke. 'Perhaps, in this case, if we found the people responsible farther up the chain of command and put them on trial, then people would believe in our commitment.' He could see the muscles in Toney's jaw tense.

'I'm trying to prevent a civil war,' Toney said. 'Maybe you don't comprehend that.'

Ainsworth shook his weary head. 'The civil war has already begun,' he replied. 'Maybe you don't comprehend that.'

CHAPTER TWENTY-FOUR

Saunders followed Nick and Cianna down the stairs into the dimly lit bar. It was clear to Saunders that the place was more Nick's home than a business; more the definition of who he was than what he did.

'Do you think you'll open back up for the rest of the night?' Cianna asked.

It looked as though Nick had just been pondering the same question. It was still relatively early. 'Probably,' Nick said. 'I'm gonna be here anyways, and it shouldn't be that busy a night.'

A voice from over by the doorway startled them all.

'I don't know about that, Spudge,' the voice said. 'It might get busier than you think.'

The light by the front door was flipped on and Saunders saw a short, balding man standing between what looked like three bodyguards. The man's face looked like it had taken the worst of a few fights in the past, and his skin was pitted and veined. He held a gun, as did the two nearly identical men flanking him. The fourth man, taller and leaner than the other three, stood behind them, also armed.

'Gruden,' Nick said in an exasperated tone. Saunders recalled Nick's earlier warning that a low-rent thug was looking for the dagger as well. He saw Nick's gaze go to the tall young man behind the other three. 'You've added to your entourage, I see,' Nick said.

Gruden nodded. 'You know Carlos McSorlly, right, Spudge? He's been makin' a name for himself in the projects. I think you'll find that he's pretty impressive.'

'Too bad he's never learned to read. The sign outside said the place is closed, Miles,' Nick said.

'Sign's wrong. I say you're open,' Gruden replied. He looked Cianna up and down. 'Good to see you back in the neighborhood,' he said to her. 'You still look good, Cianna. Your face is kinda fucked up, but I guess that'll heal.'

'I don't see how you have a say in when my bar is open or not, Miles,' Nick said.

Gruden smiled. He had the pointy, yellow-brown teeth of a goblin. He gestured with his gun. 'I guess I'll have to make that clear, then.'

'I guess so,' Nick said. Saunders thought it was probably not the best strategy to antagonize the man, given the situation, but he respected Nick's refusal to back down to a man like Miles Gruden in his own bar.

Saunders scrutinized each of the four men carefully, looking for weakness. Gruden's was clear: he was the leader, but he oozed overconfidence, and overconfidence was usually a fatal defect. The two twin fireplugs next to him looked as though they were concentrating hard on keeping their drool from running down their chins. They shared their boss's overconfidence, but they lacked even the minimal intellect Gruden displayed. Without his leadership, they would be lost. The younger kid standing behind the three others seemed to be the wildcard. He had a slightly manic look in his eyes, and he was grinding his teeth loud enough for Saunders to hear it from across the room. Saunders's impression was that he was crazy, and therefore would be reckless. That could be both a strength and a weakness, and Saunders would have to watch him most closely.

After his initial assessment, Saunders concluded that the four men posed more of an inconvenience than a genuine threat. If handled properly, they could likely be disarmed without much effort. He just had to wait for his opening.

Nobody moved for several seconds. Gruden nodded, and the three other men with him began spreading out bit by bit, forming a semicircle around Cianna, Saunders and O'Callaghan. 'You're gonna learn some respect tonight, Spudge,' Gruden said.

'I don't think so.' Nick moved back toward the bar. 'You want a drink before the war, Miles?'

Gruden snorted at the question. 'Never a care for you, eh, Spudge?'

'I sleep okay,' Nick said. He was up against the bar, and he put his arm on it, reaching casually to the other side.

'That's far enough, Spudge,' Gruden said, raising his gun and pointing it at Nick's head. 'You think I don't know what's back there?'

Nick's hand was dangling over the inside of the bar, less than a foot from where the shotgun was hanging. Saunders admired the tavern owner's spunk, but it was clear to everyone that he would never get a shot off, even if he managed to get his hands on the shotgun. Nick pulled his hand back and frowned at the mobster. 'What do you want, Miles?' he asked.

'I want to know where the dagger is. Between you and Charlie's big sister, I know you know. You're gonna tell me.'

'I'm not sure what you're talking about,' Nick said.

'No?' Gruden pointed his gun at Cianna. 'Maybe if I shoot her, you'll remember.'

Saunders moved in front of Gruden's gun.

Gruden pulled the hammer back on the revolver. 'Who the fuck are you?' he demanded. He moved forward slowly until he noticed the shirt bundled in Saunders's hand. Saunders shifted the bundle to make it less conspicuous, but it was too late.

'That it?' Gruden asked.

'Is this what?' Saunders responded.

'Charlie's antique golden dagger.'

Saunders squared his shoulders and clutched the dagger to his body. 'I don't know what you're talking about, either.'

The tips of Gruden's ears flushed red. His short forehead crinkled into a malevolent frown, and his smile became a sneer. 'I don't know who you are, but you're gonna learn some fuckin' respect tonight, too. I had a deal with Charlie to buy that, and I'm going to take it. You understand? Hand it over, and we can be on our way while you can still walk.'

'I wouldn't worry about me,' Saunders said. 'I'm pretty sure I'll be walking out of here just fine.' He wanted to draw Gruden in close. He was sure he could make quick work of the man, and that would throw the others into a panic.

Gruden laughed. 'It's four against two. And we've got guns.'

O'Callaghan looked at Saunders and Cianna, counting out the three of them with his finger. 'He's a math whiz.'

'I don't count girls.' He leered at Cianna. 'Besides, I wouldn't hurt this one. I got other plans for her.' To Cianna he said, 'Word is you're spending your time trying to save all the fuck-ups in the world.'

'I haven't reached out to you, so *all* would be an exaggeration,' Cianna replied.

He laughed at that. 'It's a fuckin' shame, you know? You could make a pretty penny for yourself with the right management.' He leaned in closer to examine her face. 'Yeah, that'll heal, all right. A little makeup, and you'll bring some good money even with it. You and I can talk some business. You can make a lot more with me than you can doin' charity work.'

'Fuck you,' Cianna spat.

'Well, yeah sure. For starters. We'll see where it goes from there.'

Nick grunted angrily. 'Get out of my bar,' he said. 'Now.'

Gruden spoke to one of his men. 'Joe, why don't you take the girl over to the side of the bar,' Gruden said. 'No need for her to be in the middle of this. She gets more bruises, and she'll be worth less.'

Nick stepped forward, but Carlos McSorlly raised his gun and pointed it at his chest.

'Keep it up, Spudge,' Gruden said. 'Trust me: Carlos, here, would like nothing better than to put a round into you. It'd only help his reputation.'

Saunders put a hand on Nick's shoulder to hold him back. He didn't want things to get out of control too quickly; the key was to take Gruden out first. Besides, he thought it would not be a bad thing to have Cianna moved from harm's way. In truth he shared some of Gruden's chauvinism, though his flowed from a far more chivalrous vein. He felt he could maneuver more freely if he wasn't worried about Cianna getting caught in a crossfire.

Cianna, too, encouraged Nick to back off, which surprised Saunders somewhat. 'Don't,' she said. 'It's not worth it, Nick. I can take care of myself.'

'Listen to her, Spudge,' Gruden said. 'It's not worth it.'

Nick looked over at Cianna and she nodded. 'It's okay,' she said.

Gruden gave his goblin smile again. 'Joe, take her out of this.'

Saunders watched as one of Gruden's men stepped forward and reached for Cianna's arm. His hand was a ham hock with chubby fingers, at the end of a stubby, short arm. She let him grab her arm and pull her toward him, a resigned look on her face. As he got closer, though, she planted her left foot and spun her body around. The momentum carried her even closer to him, and as she came out of the arc, she swung her right elbow out, putting the force of her shoulder behind it. The sudden, unexpected burst of violence caught everyone by surprise, and even Saunders had no idea how to react.

It was perfectly executed, and the sharp end of her elbow caught the heavy man just below the sternum, in the soft spot right at the solar plexus. He made a noise that was midway between a squeal and a scream, and his body seemed to collapse in on itself, his face going tight, his lips drawn into a tiny circle. He dropped to his knees, grabbing at his chest, gasping for breath, dropping his gun. Cianna rocked back on her heels and swung her leg forward, kicking the man on the ground squarely between the legs. He went blue in the face and keeled over.

Gruden's other bodyguard rushed Cianna, but not before she had managed to kick the gun on the ground over to Nick. He bent down to pick it up, but was warned off by Gruden, who shook the barrel of his pistol at Nick and said, 'I don't think so, Spudge. Kick it to the corner.'

Nick looked at Saunders, who nodded. The last thing Saunders wanted was for the shooting to start before he could get a hold of his gun. Nick nodded back and kicked the gun over to the corner. In the meantime, the second bodyguard had managed to get behind Cianna, and appeared to have her in a solid hold. He wore a determined expression, and he treated her with far more caution than the first man had. With one hand, he twisted her arm behind her back, and he wrapped his other arm around her neck.

'Let her go, Miles!' Nick shouted.

'Give me the dagger, and we'll talk about it,' Gruden said.

'Don't give it to him!' Cianna yelled, breathing hard. 'It's Charlie's only hope!'

Nick shot a nervous look at Saunders. 'They'll hurt her,' he said. Saunders held the bundled dagger high to his chest with his left hand and reached up to it with his right hand, feigning that he was going to give the relic to Gruden. Gruden's eyes watered at the possibility, and his attention was diverted; it was the opening he was looking for. He slipped his hand under the bundle and took hold of the gun in the holster under his jacket.

'I said, don't!' Cianna yelled. She was bending forward, straining against the arm around her throat. She was strong for her size, but Gruden's bodyguard had more than a hundred pounds on her, and he bent slightly forward to keep hold of her. If he'd bent over any further he might have lost his balance, but he was careful to keep his head up. That was his mistake.

Cianna leaned forward with all her strength and then swung her shoulders back, driving her body toward the man. As her torso gained speed, she snapped her head in a perfectly timed strike. The back of her head collided with the bridge of the man's nose, and he screamed in shock, his face erupting in blood. His grip on her loosened, and she lifted her boot and brought it back down hard on top of the man's foot, driving the heavy heel into the bone, drawing a fresh howl.

He'd released her completely now, and his hands were at his face, wiping away the blood that streamed into his eyes. Cianna squared herself and launched a straight shot with her fist that connected with his throat. There was an awful popping noise, and the man's expression went from pained to panicked as his hands flew to his throat and he struggled to breathe. Cianna stepped back and kicked him in the abdomen hard enough to send him reeling back into a table against the wall. He collided with the table, his head catching the edge and splitting open as he collapsed to the floor.

The men in the room were frozen. Everyone's attention was on Cianna as she turned and regarded Gruden and Carlos, her face twisted in rage.

'Holy fuckin' shit,' Gruden said. 'This bitch is crazy. Shoot her, Carlos.'

Saunders didn't hesitate. His hand was already inside his jacket, gripping his gun. The world slowed as he watched the scene play out, matching his actions to the rhythm of the violence around him. He pulled the gun out and stepped toward Gruden and McSorlly. Cianna rushed Gruden, and Carlos McSorlly raised his gun, taking aim at Cianna's chest. Cianna never hesitated, though. Carlos smiled slightly as he pulled the trigger.

A shot rang out, deafening in the small bar. 'No!' Nick yelled in anguish.

Cianna heard the shot, and waited for the impact to carry her off her feet. It didn't happen, though, and in her rage, she kept moving forward, rushing Gruden.

'Shoot her again!' she heard Gruden shout to Carlos. There was no answer, and out of the corner of her eye, she saw Carlos lying with his arm at an impossible angle, his shoulder looked as though it had been torn apart, and blood was pooling underneath him.

'What the fuck?' Gruden said.

Glancing to her left, Cianna saw Saunders with his gun standing over McSorlly's prostrate figure. As Gruden raised his gun toward Saunders, Cianna lowered her shoulder, and drove it hard into Gruden's chest, throwing him back. She heard his gun hit the floor as the two of them tumbled to the ground.

He landed on his back, and she was on top of him.

She saw him struggling to find his weapon, and she raised her fist and drove it hard into him. It caught him just under the ribs, hard and sharp, taking his breath away. Before he could turn and focus she unleashed a second punch, this one just under his eye, tearing the skin open. She could see the blood as it flowed, close enough for her to smell the iron in it. His face was inches away, and she could see the terror in his eyes. She lost track as she continued to swing at him, each blow with the power of a jackhammer. She felt his collarbone snap at one point, and he curled into the fetal position to try to protect himself. Rational thought had deserted her, and she was driven now by forces more primal than anything she could recall in the past two years.

The screaming in the background continued, and through her fog she realized that it was not just she who was yelling.

'Cianna! Stop!' Saunders shouted, pulling at her arms. 'Cianna! You'll kill him! Get her off him!' She fought to keep throwing punches.

Then she heard Nick's voice. 'Cianna, it's me! It's Nick! Stop! You've got to get out of here!'

Slowly the fog lifted. She looked around at Nick and Saunders, and saw the worry in their faces. Looking down at Gruden, she could see the blood pouring from his head. She thought he was still breathing, but couldn't be sure.

She surveyed the bar, and saw Carlos lying in a dark puddle of his own blood, unconscious. At the far end of the room, one of Gruden's bodyguards was in a ball under a table. The only one of the four who seemed conscious was the first bodyguard who had grabbed her, but he was curled into a fetal position, gasping for breath, and Nick had a gun loosely pointed at him.

Cianna looked down at Gruden and spat in what was left of his face. She saw Nick and Saunders exchange a glance.

'You need to get her out of here,' Nick said to Saunders.

Saunders nodded. 'You'll be all right dealing with these people?'

'I'll call the cops,' he said. 'It's a little much for a Wednesday night, but it's nothing they haven't seen before in this neighborhood. Gruden and his boys will keep their mouths shut. It's our way. Besides, you think they want to admit that a girl did this to them?'

'*I* shot that guy,' Saunders pointed out. He reached down and picked up the gun that had fallen from Carlos McSorlly's hand, slipped it into his jacket pocket.

'Fair enough. The point still stands. I'll be fine. You get moving before anyone shows up.'

Cianna stood up, but her legs felt weak as the massive rush of adrenaline deserted her. Nick held her by the shoulders. 'You take care of yourself, got it?' he ordered her. 'And get your brother out of this.'

She nodded weakly. Nick kissed her on the forehead, then let go of her.

'Off with you now.'

Saunders put an arm around her shoulder and started leading her toward the door. At the threshold, she gave one last look at the destruction wrought behind her and shuddered.

CHAPTER TWENTY-FIVE

Saunders said nothing for a while as they drove back toward Cianna's apartment. South Boston rolled by, its clapboard houses flush to the street, its residents shuffling along the narrow sidewalks. Halfway up the hill from the water, they passed The L Street Pub, and they could hear the subdued revelry from inside. Saunders marveled at the way the world continued to march on for most of those in it, even as events that could alter the course of nations unfolded within earshot.

He looked over at Cianna, leaning back in the passenger seat. Her shoulders were square, thrown back into the seat. Her head was up, and though her eyes focused straight ahead, her face had a look of defiance.

'You want to tell me what happened back there?' Saunders probed.

She didn't look at him. 'What do you mean?'

'You know what I mean. You did a lot of damage.'

'You'd rather it turned out differently?'

'No,' Saunders said. 'But I'm still wondering where that came from. You incapacitated three armed men. Some would consider that impressive.'

She looked at him. He was sure it was the first time she had met his eyes without evasion, and he saw a fire

173

in them that was magnetic. After a moment, she turned back toward the front windshield and closed her eyes again. 'That's just training,' she said.

'What exactly did you do when you were in the service?'

She didn't open her eyes. 'It's classified.'

'I have clearance,' he said.

'If you had clearance, you would have been told more about me before they sent you out to find my brother.'

She was right about that, though he was loath to admit it to her. 'I didn't ask the questions,' he lied. 'Maybe I should have.'

'Maybe.' It was clear she was saying nothing more on the subject.

After a moment, he said, 'I have one more question.'

'Feel free to ask,' she said. 'I don't know whether I can answer it.'

'There was something more than training working for you at the bar.'

'Yeah? Like what?'

He thought for a moment. 'Rage,' he said.

She looked at him again. 'This is my brother's life,' she said. She gestured toward the dagger wrapped in Nick's shirt. 'That dagger may be the only thing keeping him alive, and Gruden didn't give a shit about what would happen to Charlie if he took it. That pissed me off.'

'Remind me not to piss you off,' Saunders said.

'Just don't mess with anyone I care about,' she said. She looked away from him, out her window, as the new buildings along the waterfront rolled by.

CHAPTER TWENTY-SIX

Boston Police Detective Harvey Morrell was exhausted and annoyed. At fifty-nine years old, he wondered for how much longer he could put up with his job. It probably would have been for longer if he wasn't carrying more than 250 pounds on his five-foot, ten inch frame. He should have taken early retirement as soon as he hit his twenty years back in his forties, lived off his pension. More to the point, he should have stayed married to his first wife. Or his second. Without alimony and child support, he could have gotten by on a bartender's salary. That ship had sailed, though, and there was little that he could do to escape the daily grind now.

Few days recently had ground as painfully as this one. He'd spent the first half of it chasing down leads on a case involving the disappearance of Sal Decanta, a wise guy in Boston's North End. 'Sal the Fish', as he was known, had gone missing a week earlier. Well, most of him had gone missing. An ear had been found in his apartment by his landlady, and DNA testing had identified it as Decanta's. Morrell's best guess was that, wherever Decanta's remaining body parts were, they weren't breathing.

By all accounts, Decanta had been high up in Boston's La Cosa Nostra, which meant that no one would ever admit to knowing anything about his whereabouts. So many doors had been slammed in Morrell's face throughout the day that he was beginning to think *Vaffanculo* was Italian for 'watch your toes'. The investigation had gone nowhere, which would surprise no one. And yet his name was the one that would be on the report, so when the press and public and politicians came with their outcry, his would be the phone line they would call, and his would be the name mentioned in the newspapers.

As if that was not injustice enough for one day, he was now stuck on a call in Southie after dark, chasing down a phantom shooting. He had two uniforms with him, going door to door, rousting people to see whether they had any information. Information about what, exactly, Morrell wasn't sure. The emergency lines had received three calls late that afternoon, jabbering away unintelligibly about a shooting. As usual, no one was willing to give their names, or even their exact locations, lest they be identified. All three calls left the impression, though, that the area near the Old Colony projects was under siege. Uniforms had been dispatched to the block in question, but when they arrived all was quiet. No bodies lay in the streets, and no shop windows had been smashed. The officers had been unable to locate the people who had called in. In more rational times, the matter would have been closed. But it was an election year, and those whose employment depended on the electoral whims of the public insisted that the BPD feign concern for the special interests within the under-privileged communities. As a result, here he was in the middle of the evening, knocking on doors. The absurdity of it all soured the phlegm in the back of Morrell's throat.

He was contemplating his misery when he saw Ayden McMurphy walking towards him, shaking his head. In almost all respects, it was hard to imagine a police officer better cut for the job than McMurphy. He was tall and well-built, with a mellow way about him that put people on the streets at ease, even in difficult situations. He was ethically straight enough to avoid trouble, but flexible enough to be trusted in a department that still had the old way of doing things in its DNA. And then there was the name. Few names belonged so readily on a force that traced more of its roots to County Kerry than to any borough in Massachusetts; a nominal fit made ironic only by the fact that Ayden McMurphy was black and had grown up in Roxbury. *Who knows,* Morrell thought, *maybe that just makes him the perfect police officer for the modern force.*

He didn't mind. For all his old-school ways, Morrell's view was that a good cop was a good cop. And Ayden McMurphy was that if nothing else.

'We learn anything?' Morrell asked him as the officer approached.

'Yeah,' McMurphy responded. 'We learned the Irish are deaf, dumb and blind when it comes to anything that reeks of local crime.'

'I thought you were Irish.'

'I kept trying to point that out to the townies,' McMurphy said in an exaggerated brogue. 'I even showed them my name tag, but they seem to think I'm taking black-Irish too far. It's not hard to see why bussing never really caught on here.'

'You can't expect everyone to be as enlightened as me,' Morrell said.

'I can't?' McMurphy shook his head. 'Fuck me then, I guess.'

'Got that right.' Morrell chuckled in spite of himself. 'You find out anything useful?'

'Depends on your definition. Three people were willing to talk to me for long enough to say they heard gunshots. All of them agreed it came from the other side of the street. Two of them thought they came from that building.' McMurphy pointed toward a rundown three-story building with a narrow front, set off from the two rows of town-houses on either side of it. 'The third thought they came from farther up the street. None of them saw anything, and no one is sure what actually happened. A couple of them thought maybe it was fireworks.'

'That falls short of my definition of useful,' Morrell said.

McMurphy pointed to the large stain on the front of the shirt struggling to contain Morrell's prodigious gut. 'Yeah, but you're a perfectionist, Detective.'

'Only in the ways that matter.' Morrell took a deep breath, and caught a whiff of the hardscrabble mixture of soot and salt and fish that linger in Southie like the hint of open revolt. 'Probably nothing more than fireworks,' he said with a sigh. After another deep breath, he said, 'Okay, we'll do a quick door-to-door in that building and call it a day.'

As he spoke the words, a car pulled up ten yards in front of the building and parked on the street. Morrell watched it without particular interest, noticing it only in the way that cops who have been around for long enough tend to notice everything. It wasn't until the driver and passenger exited the car that his instincts truly perked up.

He would have zeroed in on the girl under any circumstances. Her appearance commanded male attention. She was fit and attractive, and had the look of a wild animal in her eyes.

The man looked in all respects her opposite. He was of average height and build, and he wore the nondescript suit of an accountant. His hair was short enough that it didn't need a brush. Notwithstanding the rigidity of his appearance, though, he moved fluidly as he and the girl headed through the door of the clapboard building across the street.

Morrell and McMurphy shared a look.

'Make sure we talk to them,' Morrell said.

'You got a feeling?' McMurphy asked.

Morrell nodded. 'Yeah,' he said. 'I got a feeling.'

Ahmad Fasil was on his knees in the little house in Cambridge. He brought his hands to his cheeks and raised his face in supplication, then bent forward, letting his forehead touch the prayer mat. He stayed in that position for several moments, beseeching Allah; begging for the patience to carry through with what he had started, and for the strength to suffer the incompetence that surrounded him.

When he felt that he had conveyed his supplication sufficiently, he rose and went to his black bag. Reaching in, he pulled out a satellite phone. He had been told that the line was secure, and that the transmissions were untraceable. He didn't fully believe it, but then again, he wasn't really the one at risk.

He dialed the number and waited. The line rang twice before it was picked up.

'Do you have it?' the man on the other end of the line asked as soon as the call was connected.

'Not yet,' Fasil said, working to keep the contempt out of his tone.

'Why not?'

'Because,' Fasil said slowly, 'my assets are inadequate. I was told that you were in control of the situation. That does not appear to be the case. I was told that the relic would already have been recovered before I arrived.'

'That was supposed to be the case,' the man said. 'Sirus failed us.'

'He did. And now there is another party involved.'

'Another party?' The voice on the other end of the line sounded calm. 'Who?'

'I do not know. That is what I need for you to find out. He claimed to Sirus that he was with the police, but I suspect that was a lie. Do you know who this person is?'

The line was silent for a moment. 'You don't need to worry. I can take care of him if necessary.'

'It is necessary now,' Fasil said. 'You will take care of him now, or I will. I assume I do not need to remind you what would happen if people were to discover your role in this. It would cause great damage. For everyone.'

'Is that a threat?' the man on the other end of the line demanded. 'Are you threatening me?'

Fasil remained calm. He was used to American bullying. 'I am merely reminding you of the information I have, and the consequences for all of us if I fail.'

'No one understands that better than I do,' the man said. 'But you should remember that we're not friends and we're not allies. Our short-term interests are complementary, but we will always be enemies, and in the end I will destroy you. Do you understand that?'

Fasil clicked off the satellite phone and put it back into his bag. 'I understand that, too, better than anyone.'

CHAPTER TWENTY-SEVEN

They were on the third floor. Going door to door starting from the ground, Detective Morrell had begun to wonder whether the couple he'd seen earlier had slipped out the back. They hadn't, though. When the door to apartment 3B opened, he was standing face to face with the girl he'd seen entering the building fifteen minutes before. There was something familiar about her, but he couldn't place what it was. She had an older, weathered version of a face that echoed in his memory.

He observed her for a moment before saying anything. 'Can I help you?' she said at last. She sounded annoyed.

He reached into his jacket pocket and pulled out his shield. 'Police, ma'am,' he said, holding it up. 'Detective Morrell.' He watched her closely, saying nothing more.

The change was instant. She straightened, pulled her shoulders back, and retreated ever so slightly from the threshold, adopting a defensive posture. The door, which had been opened a foot, closed to half that. The reaction wasn't entirely unusual, even for an innocent person, but it was universal from those who were hiding something from the authorities. It reinforced Morrell's hunch.

After a moment's tension, she said, 'What do you want?' The encounter had officially become confrontational, which was fine with him. Often he could tell more about someone when they felt their backs were against the wall.

'We've had a report of a shooting,' he said. He let the silence set in briefly again.

'And . . .?' she said. 'What do you want from me?'

That was the tip-off. The natural reaction of someone told there had been a shooting in the vicinity was almost uniformly to seek information. *Who was shot? Where did it happen? When? Was anyone hurt?* There were a thousand natural questions that came into the heads of most people. This woman wasn't looking for any of this kind of information. That meant, in all likelihood, that she already knew something about it.

'Can I come in?' Morrell asked, moving toward the door as though there was no question that he could, in fact, come in.

The door opening went from six inches to three. 'I'm busy,' the woman said. 'Is there something that you need from me?'

Morrell stepped back. 'The first thing you can give me is your name.'

She rolled her eyes, looking put out. For a moment he thought she wasn't even going to give him that. 'Cianna,' she said at last. 'Cianna Phelan.'

He squinted at her. The name didn't mean anything to him, but he couldn't shake the feeling that he'd seen her before. 'Have we met?' he asked. 'You look familiar.'

'You hitting on me?' she said sarcastically. If he seemed familiar to her, she was concealing it brilliantly. He decided to move on.

'Can you tell me whether you heard anything.'

183

'No,' she said. 'I didn't.'

'Don't you want to know when?'

Her eyes narrowed, but she didn't flinch. 'I didn't hear any gunshots at all,' she said. 'So I guess it doesn't matter when it happened. I've been out for most of the day.'

He nodded. 'I saw you coming back. You were with a man. Is he here? I'd like to talk to him, too.'

'He doesn't live here,' she said.

'Is he here now?'

'He wouldn't have heard anything either,' she said. 'He was with me for most of the day.'

'Can I talk to him?'

She seemed to hesitate, turning her head as though listening to someone from behind her. 'I'm very busy now. I don't have any information, and I have to be going.' She started to close the door.

Morrell's phone started buzzing, but he ignored it for the moment. 'I could get a warrant,' he said. 'Or take you down to the station.' That often softened people up.

The door was little more than a crack now, but it was enough for her to look out at him. 'You could,' she said. 'But you would need to swear out an affidavit saying you've got probable cause to believe I've committed a crime. Because I haven't committed any crime, I seriously doubt that you could truthfully say that you have any kind of cause.'

He stared at her. She was right, of course, and it made him angry. 'You'd be surprised how easy it is to get a warrant,' he said. It was a bluff. Unless he was willing to lie, he'd never get a warrant, and there was nothing here worth lying about. Still, he hated the notion that she could get the best of him. His phone continued to buzz.

'Maybe,' she said. 'I guess we'll see.'

He frowned, considering his next move. To buy time, he grabbed his phone. 'Gimme a sec,' he said to her. Into the phone, he said, 'Morrell, here.'

'Morrell, it's Scotty.' He recognized the voice of Sergeant Will Scott.

'Yeah,' Morrell said. 'What is it?'

'We got a mess down here at the waterfront,' Scott said. 'Someone fucked up Miles Gruden and a couple of his boys pretty badly.'

'Anyone dead?' Morrell asked.

'No. One shot, though. And Gruden and two others are gonna end up spending some time in the hospital. We could use your help.'

'I'm a little busy,' Morrell said. 'Can you get someone else?'

'Yeah, I could, but I figured you'd want to be called,' Scotty said.

'Why? I gotta pull the sheet every time these morons fuck each other up?'

'No, but this happened at Spudgie's. I figured . . . you know. I figured I'd give you a call on it.'

Morrell looked at the girl through the crack in the door. She was still staring back at him, her eyes sharp. 'Anyone else hurt other than Gruden and his boys?'

'No. Just them.'

'Okay, I'll be there in about two minutes.' He turned off the phone, put it back into his pocket. 'I may be back,' he said to the girl.

'I may be here,' she snapped back.

She had balls; he had to give her that. 'You should

consider being a little more cooperative with the police,' he said. 'It'll keep you out of trouble.'

'I'll keep that in mind,' she said. Then the door was closed, and Morrell was standing there like an idiot. He shouldn't care, he knew. It was a bullshit call to begin with. In all likelihood McMurphy was probably right; it was probably fireworks. Still, he couldn't help but feel the anger at having been ignored.

'Fuck it,' he said at last. He turned and headed back down to his car.

Cianna leaned her forehead against the door, and eye to the peephole, watching as the cop walked away from the door. 'He's gone,' she said. It didn't make her feel any better. 'What now?'

'We wait,' Saunders said.

She turned to look at him. He was over by the window, looking out on the street below. He opened the window a little, stuck his head out, looked down both sides of the building. 'Is there a fire escape?'

'At the end of the hall,' she said. 'But I'm not sure I would trust it.'

He went to the door to the apartment, looked through the peephole. Once he was satisfied there was no one out in the hallway, he opened the door and looked down toward the fire escape, then pulled his head back in.

'Is there any other way up or down from here, other than the stairs or the fire escape?'

'I periodically think about jumping,' she said.

'I'm serious.'

'I'm not?'

He looked sharply at her. 'You think this is a game?'

'No, I don't. My brother's the one who is out there being held by that giant psycho – which is why I have a hard time just sitting here and waiting.'

'Sirus Stillwell is the least of your brother's problems,' Saunders said.

'What the fuck does that mean?' Cianna demanded. 'What is going on?'

'I don't know yet,' Saunders said. 'But whatever it is, Stillwell is only a small part of it. According to the information we got from the terrorist communiqué, the Taliban believe your brother has stolen the "Heart of Afghanistan".'

'What's that?'

Saunders shook his head. 'We've never known for sure, but my guess is that it's this dagger. All we know is that it is a relic that the Afghan people believe controls their destiny. They believe it has great power.'

Cianna nodded to the dagger. 'That knife has great power?'

Saunders walked over and unwrapped the shirt protecting the dagger. 'It's possible that's what people believe. I don't know why. I've been trying to decipher the markings along the edge; trying to figure out whether there is some significance I'm missing. I haven't pieced it together yet. But I can guarantee you that there are people far crazier than Sirus Stillwell involved in this. And they are likely to show up here; so I need to know how many ways there are to get up and down from here. Do you understand?'

She stared at him. 'Just the staircase and the fire escape,' she said. 'There's no other way in or out.'

'Good. Do you have a phone?'

She nodded.

'Is your number listed in the phone book?'

Another nod.

'Good. The only question, then, is whether they'll call, or just show up here. One way or another, though, once they realize Charlie can no longer help them, they'll reach out to you.'

'Are you sure?'

Saunders nodded. 'Are you ready to deal with people like this?'

'Yeah,' Cianna said. 'I've dealt with them before.'

CHAPTER TWENTY-EIGHT

Detective Harvey Morrell chewed on the inside of his cheek as he surveyed the wreckage inside the bar. Blood-covered broken tables and chairs, knocked to the floor. 'Jesus Christ,' he said. 'Looks like the 99 in Charlestown back in 1995.'

'The Luisi hit?' McMurphy said. 'You were there?'

Morrell nodded. 'I was low man on the organized-crime squad going after the Winter Hill Gang back then. I coordinated with the Charlestown force. I'm telling you, it didn't look any worse than this.'

'Except the bodies weren't moving,' McMurphy said. 'You gonna talk to Spudgie?'

'Yeah, in a minute. I want to talk to Gruden, first.'

Two of the wounded men had already been loaded into ambulances and driven to the hospital. Carlos McSorlly had lost around a gallon of blood from the gunshot wound and had gone into shock even before the paramedics got there. He was rushed to the emergency room, but the suspicion was that he would recover. One of Miles Gruden's regular bodyguards had also been taken away unconscious. His head had hit the corner of a table so hard it had split open. His prospects for recovery were less rosy.

Miles Gruden was sitting on a chair, attended by a

189

paramedic. His head looked like it had been stuffed in a blender, and his arm was hanging at an odd angle. He was being checked out before they moved him. Morrell made his way over.

'Miles,' he said. 'How's things going for you?'

Gruden looked up. 'Morrell. You still on the job? I'd have thought you'd be dead by now.'

'Says the guy without a face.' He leaned down to get a closer look at the wound. 'Holy shit, Miles, what the fuck happened to you?'

'I was shaving,' Gruden said. 'I slipped.'

'You were shaving your eyelids?' Morrell pulled over a chair and sat down in front of Gruden. 'C'mon, Miles, you're really gonna protect the guys who did this to you? Jimmy's in the hospital, and from what they say, if he ever gets out, he's gonna have to have someone spoon-feed him strained carrots for the rest of his life.'

Gruden winced as the paramedic touched his face, shining a light into his eye. 'Jimmy always liked carrots.'

The paramedic stood up. 'He needs to get more fully checked out at the hospital,' he said. 'He's got at least three broken ribs and a mild concussion. The rest of it is superficial.'

'You call that superficial?' Morrell said, pointing to the carnage of Gruden's face.

The paramedic shrugged. 'It's not going to kill him.'

'Maybe not, but it'll make it hard to get a fuckin' date, eh Miles?' Morrell chuckled at his own joke.

'Fuck off, Morrell.'

'Look, Miles, not for nothing, but the way I see it, your guys are the victims here. You let us know who did this to you, and we can go get 'em. Why not let us take care of this for you?'

'We can take care of ourselves.'

'Doesn't look that way tonight,' Morrell said. 'You really want a war over this? That's not gonna help Jimmy. He worked for you, what, fifteen years? You're gonna let that go?'

Gruden looked away. 'I ain't letting shit go.'

At first Morrell thought Gruden was just looking off into space, but after a moment, he realized that the man's attention was focused. Morrell followed his gaze and saw Nick O'Callaghan off in a corner talking with one of the officers on the scene. 'Spudgie got something to do with this?' Morrell asked.

Gruden's eyes snapped back to the floor. 'No,' he said. 'Spudgie didn't have nothin' to do with this.'

'You sure? It looked like—'

Gruden cut him off. 'Spudgie didn't have nothin' to do with this,' he said adamantly.

'Okay, okay,' Morrell said. 'But just so you understand, you say Spudgie doesn't have anything to do with this, and then he turns up dead or missing next week, I'm coming after you, and it won't be for an arrest. You get it? I'm not kidding about that.'

'I get it, Morrell. Spudgie's got nothing to worry about. This ain't about Spudgie.'

'What's it about, then?'

Gruden just shook his head. The paramedic wheeled a gurney into the bar and stopped it in front of the man. 'I gotta take him to the hospital now. You can ask him any more questions there.'

DAVID HOSP

'You gonna talk to me at the hospital, Miles?' Morrell asked.

Gruden looked at him as he settled onto the gurney. After a moment he looked away. 'No,' he said.

The paramedic wheeled Gruden away, and Morrell watched him go. He hadn't expected to get any information from the man. That wasn't the Southie way. You didn't talk to the cops in this neighborhood; that had always been the rule. But there was something in Gruden's manner that was unusual. Walking into the scene, Morrell had assumed that he was dealing with a fairly simple gang rivalry. After his chat with Morrell, though, he was beginning to suspect that was wrong. There was only one gunshot fired, and most of the damage was inflicted by hand. It seemed there was something more at play. As Morrell walked over to talk with Nick O'Callaghan, he wondered what it was.

Sirus Stillwell sat in the car two blocks up from the little bar down by the water in South Boston. He was behind the wheel; Ahmad Fasil was in the passenger seat next to him. One of Fasil's men was in the back seat. They all looked out at the lightshow down the street. It had died down a little; there were now only two police cars and one ambulance parked out front, the blue of the police lights tinged by the red of the ambulance lights. When they had first pulled up, there had been at least six emergency vehicles, and it had reminded Sirus of the Fourth of July fireworks displays they used to have in his hometown. It was his favorite holiday, and the celebrations of

192

the American spirit every year had instilled in him a deep unconditional love for his country.

Now, though, the lights angered him. They were so close to completing their mission, and yet at every turn it seemed that fate was against them. He could feel Fasil seething in the seat next to him. Under different circumstances, the man's displeasure might frighten even Sirus. Sirus had seen what the man was capable of when displeased. At the moment, though, Fasil needed Sirus, and they both knew it.

'Maybe Phelan was lying,' Sirus offered, to break the silence that seemed to suffocate them all.

'He was not lying,' Fasil said. 'The relic is there.'

'Maybe. Maybe not. Even if it was there at one point, though, chances are it's not anymore. Not with all that activity.'

'We will wait,' Fasil said. 'And then we will see.'

'How are we going to see?'

'The tavern owner. He will tell us.'

Sirus was doubtful. 'That's not his reputation.'

Fasil looked over at Sirus. His eyes were so black, they seemed bottomless. Sirus wondered what had happened in the man's life to drive the hatred to such a depth. 'He will tell us,' Fasil said slowly. His voice was deep and clear and powerful, and Sirus didn't doubt him for an instant. 'Trust me.'

Sirus said nothing more. Theirs was a partnership of convenience and necessity. In truth, he hated Fasil, and he couldn't wait to be done with him. If he wanted to waste time sitting on the street, that was his call; it had been made clear to Sirus that Fasil was in charge of this portion of the mission. But that didn't mean that Sirus had to be polite about it.

Morrell approached Nick O'Callaghan the way one would a stray dog, slowly and with caution. Nick was sitting on a barstool, looking out on the street. Morrell sat next to him, staring out in the same direction. 'How's business, Nick?'

'Knocking 'em dead, can't you tell?'

'Funny.' They sat in silence for a moment. 'You wanna tell me what went down?'

'I already gave my statement. I was upstairs when it happened; I didn't see anything. Check with your boys.'

'I checked with them. I was just wondering whether you'd tell me what really happened. It's me, Nick.'

O'Callaghan took a deep breath. 'Yeah, it's you. I figured somehow you'd catch this case.'

'You surprised? You're my brother. You think no one's gonna call?'

'Half-brother,' O'Callaghan reminded him.

'True. But Ma's the better half of both of us.'

'Ma was never up for Mother of the Year, God rest her soul,' O'Callaghan pointed out. 'You were just a little too young to see what was going on.'

'You protected me from that. You both did, probably.'

'You were always her favorite. You were her baby.'

O'Callaghan looked down at the bar, his brow drawn tight. The resentment had always been there, just under the surface. It was amazing to him that, at times of stress, it could still break the surface. 'Nick, I'm trying to help here. I could see the way Gruden was lookin' at you, like he wanted to put a fuckin' slug in your eye. If you're involved here, you need to tell me so we can provide a little protection.'

O'Callaghan looked over at Morrell. 'From Gruden? Gruden's a punk. He's always been a punk.'

'No disagreement, but punks can do a lot of damage when their backs are up against the wall. I don't want to see him using you to make a point to the neighborhood.'

O'Callaghan let out a clipped guffaw. 'Shoe's on the other foot. You trying to protect your big brother now?'

'Yeah, maybe.'

It took another moment for O'Callaghan to talk, and it looked like he was wrestling with something inside. 'It's okay,' he said at last. 'What happened here is over, and it had nothing to do with me. I appreciate the thought, though.'

'You sure?'

'Yeah, I'm sure.'

Morrell took in a deep breath and let it out slowly. 'We're both gettin' too old for our jobs, you know that, right?'

'Speak for yourself.'

Morrell stood up off the stool and put a hand on O'Callaghan's back. 'You change your mind – either about your statement or taking some help – let me know, okay?'

'Yeah, okay.' Morrell started to walk away. O'Callaghan looked over his shoulder at him. 'Hey, Harvey!' he called out. Morrell turned around. 'Don't be such a stranger. Popcorn's on the house for relatives, you know?'

Morrell nodded at him. 'I'll keep that in mind.'

CHAPTER TWENTY-NINE

The waiting was the worst of it. Minutes passed like days, and the quiet allowed Cianna's mind to wander to the darkest possibilities. She knew that dwelling on the worst that could have already befallen her brother served no purpose, but there was no way to avoid it. She was his big sister. She was his protector. She had failed.

'Stay sharp,' Saunders snapped, shaking her from her torment. For a split second, she thought she was back in the Army, and she felt good. She looked up at him and saw that he was looking back. It was clear he had been watching her for a while.

'What if they don't try to contact me?' she asked. She still couldn't stomach the notion of sitting still while Charlie was out there somewhere in danger.

'They'll contact you,' Saunders said. 'You have this.' He held up the dagger. 'True believers don't travel halfway around the world for something just to give up after a few days. They'll chase down every lead until they get what they are looking for.'

She stood up and walked over to the window, glanced down at the street.

'You spent time over there,' Saunders said. It wasn't a question. 'Afghanistan.'

'Yeah,' she said. 'So did you.'

He nodded at her. 'You see action?'

'Yeah,' she said. 'You wanna compare scars?' Her tone was aggressive, but she couldn't help it.

He shrugged. 'I was just curious. There aren't that many women who have seen active combat up close.'

'More than you think.'

'True, but most can't fight like you. Hell, there aren't many men who can fight like you. I watched you at the bar. I'd heard that you weren't the standard GI grunt, but still . . .'

She said nothing.

'So what happened?'

She turned away from the window and looked back at him. Her eyes felt like they were burning. 'You Oprah? You want me to sit on the couch with you while I pour out my troubles? Is that going to help protect Charlie?'

He was still looking at her. Most men backed down with her when she went on the offensive. They turned away or apologized or blinked. She noticed that his eyes were steady, though. 'I'd like to know. I gather things didn't work out. I know about Leavenworth, but I don't have the details.'

'You think I'm a liability?'

'I don't have enough information to be much of a judge on that.'

'Fuck off.' She turned away.

'That's your choice,' he said. 'I can't make you talk about it. But whatever it was, you made it through. The instinct to make it through the worst – that's what your brother needs from you right now. I saw some of it here

197

earlier when Sirus was attacking you. I saw more of it back at the bar. You're gonna need that if you're gonna help your brother. I just need to know that you can control it when necessary, because this is going to get ugly. Knowing what happened to you over there would help me figure out how useful you're really going to be.'

She looked back at him, and all of a sudden she felt more tired than she'd been in a long time. 'What's the worst thing you've ever done?' she asked him.

His eyes held hers, and she could feel the connection between them. 'I guess that would depend on who you asked.'

Nick O'Callaghan took his time with the cleaning. To him, scrubbing the bar floor was a labor of love and a sign of devotion. Besides, years of cleaning up after fights had taught him that blood required special attention. If you didn't get it all up the first time, the stains would set in and become permanent.

Cleaning also relaxed him after his encounter with his brother. To this day Nick had trouble fully coming to terms with Harvey. They were several years apart, and Nick could remember the trauma of his mother's divorce. In a way, the time after the split had been heaven for him, as his mother lavished attention on him as a young boy. Eventually, though, she had fallen in love again, or, at least, found someone suitable enough to help in the daily struggle for economic survival in exchange for a portion of her affections. Even that had been okay with Nick. It was clear that she never really loved the man, and her devotion to him never felt challenged. The marriage lasted less than three years and produced nothing but divorce lawyers' expenses . . . and Harvey.

Harvey represented the first legitimate challenger for Nick's mother's affections, and given the fact that he was the baby, it often seemed an unfair fight. All Harvey had to do was cry and their mother was there for him, scooping him up to provide comforting kisses. Nick tried crying once, but he was eight, and at that age it was apparently far less endearing. His mother had slapped him lightly on the face and told him he was too old for that. It was the last time he could remember crying.

Nick and his half-brother had carved out a relationship through obligation and sheer force of will. They would never be best friends, but Nick had come to respect Harvey over the years, and even had some affection for him. Harvey, for his part, was always there whenever Nick would allow it, almost as if he was still the little kid trying to tag along with his big brother. For whatever reason, Harvey would do anything for Nick, and Nick knew it. He felt a pang of guilt for keeping his brother at a distance.

One guilt led to another, and as he scrubbed the blood from the floor, Nick wondered whether he had done the right thing in letting Cianna leave with Saunders. He felt the guilt gnaw at him. For no rational reason other than that he was a decent man deep down, he had come to view her as his responsibility. His dalliance with her mother had not lasted long, and his feelings for her had been admittedly shallow. Back in the day, though, he'd had no problem letting her children hang out in the bar if it meant that he'd get laid later in the evening. It never occurred to him that they would be far more effective at worming their way into his heart than their mother would be.

That was how it happened, though. He could remember Cianna there, a little kid helping with the dishes at the scalding hot sink when not even asked, sweeping up broken glass that wasn't hers, doing anything she could to gain the attention of her mother, to make her happy – an unachievable goal, Nick could tell early on. Kate Phelan was not a woman born to be happy. She was a woman made to carry the weight of slights and injustices, most imagined, nearly all self-imposed, on her narrow, defensive shoulders. She was a woman who saw the world and everyone in it as owing her something. Nick realized within a few weeks of seeing her that she was auditioning for the role of ex-wife number four, and he wanted none of that. He continued to see her because he had grown attached to her children, particularly Cianna. Charlie was easy to like because he was her shadow, but in Cianna he saw real genius for survival. It inspired in him a paternal streak he'd never known before. When the melodramatic end came for his relationship with Kate, his only regret was that he would lose his relationship with Cianna and Charlie. He couldn't have been happier the next evening when the two of them wandered into the bar by themselves and took up their normal positions near Nick.

'Your mother coming in?' he'd asked her.

She'd shaken her head. 'She's out on a date.' He didn't think she'd said it to try to make Nick jealous; he thought her more perceptive than that. His impression was that she wanted to make clear that Kate's break with Nick was permanent, but that it wouldn't keep Cianna and Charlie from hanging around. He could still see her face, watching him, waiting for a reaction, probably terrified that he would toss them out.

'She leave you at home?' he asked.

'Yeah. I'm not sure when she'll be back.'

He served two customers without saying anything. He'd long heeded the dangers of caring for others too much, particularly in situations where they might come to depend on him. Finally he spoke again. Without looking at her, he said, 'You wanna do me a favor?'

'Sure,' she'd said.

'There's a rack of glasses in the dishwasher. You wanna pull them out for me?'

'Sure.'

That was how it had started. Perhaps it was the shared understanding of maternal abandonment that had created the bond. She was eleven at the time. Now, seventeen years later, he could see that she still needed him. And what had become clearer to him since seeing her again was that he needed her, too.

'Do you have a gun?'

Cianna turned and looked at Saunders. He was sitting on the couch, cleaning his semi-automatic, pulling it apart and putting it back together to make sure that all the moving pieces were well-lubricated and that it wouldn't jam up on him at an inopportune moment. She remembered what it felt like to clean a weapon. It felt good. It felt right.

'I'm an ex-con,' she said.

'Lots of ex-cons have guns,' Saunders said. 'I'd be willing

to bet that a higher percentage of ex-cons have guns than the general population.'

'You could be right. But, no, I don't have a gun. It would violate my parole, and I have no interest in getting myself violated and going back on the inside.'

He considered that for a moment. After a brief internal debate, he reached into his jacket pocket and pulled out the gun he'd taken off of Carlos McSorlly, put it on the table and nodded to her.

She walked over slowly. 'You sure?'

'These aren't local thugs we're dealing with. These people are well-trained and fanatical. We're a lot better off with two guns if we're going to be thinking seriously about dealing with them.'

She picked up the revolver and opened the cylinder. It was loaded; six shots. She closed it and held it up, feeling the weight and finding the balance.

'You know how to handle one of those, I assume?' Saunders said.

'Yeah,' she replied. 'But how do you know that you can trust me?'

'I don't. But I don't have any reason to *dis*trust you, and I can't say the same for the people who will be coming for the dagger.' Saunders finished reassembling his gun, pulled the release back. 'Besides, if I think for a minute that you're going to cross me, I'll kill you.'

She looked off her aim and over toward him, the gun still pointed at the wall. 'That's not really fair,' she said. 'I've only got six shots, and you've got sixteen.'

He shook his head. 'It wouldn't matter.'

'Why not?'

'Because, you'd be dead with my first shot.'

The noise came from the back of the bar, outside by the dumpster. It was a loud, dull thud against the back door, followed by an ear-piercing *meow*. At first Nick O'Callaghan figured it was a cat chasing after a large rat. Normally he would go out to make sure that the cat was successful in its chase; rats were bad for business, even at the water's edge in Southie. It had been a long enough evening that night, though, that he wasn't even going to bother with it. The dumpster had a solid lid, and it had been emptied two days before, so there wasn't enough trash to worry about the mess if an animal got in. He could take care of it in the morning.

When the noise came again, though, it made his hair stand on end. It was the same sound, but this time it continued in a slow, steady rhythm.

Thud . . . meow . . . thud . . . meow . . . thud . . . meow . . . thud . . .

The bar was dark, and he was alone. He had just finished cleaning the floors, and was about to wash down the bar before heading back to his nearby apartment. He had a rag in his hand, and as the noise continued, he could feel the muscles in his hands tighten on the cloth.

For a moment he thought about calling the police. Then he remembered his conversation with his brother. He put the rag down and picked up the shotgun he kept behind the bar. No one was going to scare him out of his place.

The noise continued as he walked toward the back door, growing louder as he drew close. There was a tiny window just at eye level in the center of the dark green steel, but it was caked over with years of smoke and grime. It was dark outside, and when he flipped the switch to turn on the back light, nothing happened. He thought he remembered the light working the night before, but he couldn't be sure.

It was quiet now; the banging had stopped. When he listened closely, though, he could still hear the cat, alternating between a satisfied purr and an angry growl.

He stood next to the door, the gun at his side, rubbing at the tiny window, trying to see. Realizing the futility, he finally pushed the door open a crack, sticking the barrel of the gun out first.

The light from inside the bar illuminated a sliver of ground in the alley out back, narrow and bright in close, spreading out in a diffuse fan further from the entryway. He narrowed his eyes, searching at the edge of the darkness. 'Anyone there?' he called out.

His voice drew a response from the cat. She hissed angrily from six feet away, over near the bar's brick siding. Her back was to Nick, but she was looking over her shoulder, baring her fangs. Nick had seen the cat before. She was one of the thousands that wandered the streets of Boston, fighting for any available scrap of sustenance. Her eyes were bright and threatening, but her coat was mangy and insect-ridden; half an ear was gone, and ribs showed through her fur. After a moment's territorial display, she went back to the prize hidden from view. She bent down, head facing away from Nick now, sinking her teeth into something tough enough to require several pulls to dislodge a small chunk of stringy meat.

'What you got there?' Nick asked the cat, opening the door a bit wider. The light and the sound of his voice drew a renewed protest from the cat, and she turned more fully to face him, adopting a pathetic battle-stance. Nick knew the cat would back down; he'd been dealing with strays his entire life.

'Get outta here,' he said, lowering the barrel of the gun toward the cat. He'd never been more tempted to shoot an animal than he was at that moment. Something stopped him, though; threw him back into the doorway, his mouth hanging open.

As the cat turned to face him, she'd moved enough that he could see what she was chewing on. And even in the dim light, he could make out the knuckles of a hand. At first, he assumed that it was some sort of a sick rubber toy, but then the cat went back at it with her teeth, tearing a patch of skin from just below the thumb, and a fresh patch of red muscle appeared. 'Oh, God!' he exclaimed.

At that moment, the hand moved, jumping and bouncing of its own accord. The cat let out an angry roar as the hand skittered across the alley, pausing in the middle, as if to look at him, then continued on. Nick was so stunned he couldn't move.

When the severed hand made it to the far side of the alley, it flew into the air, spun around in a circle. At that moment, Nick could make out the silhouette of a man standing just at the edge of the light cast by the doorway. He realized that the man was holding a string that was tied to the hand, and was swinging the hand around on the string like a lasso. After a moment, he slung the hand hard across the alley, and the hand collided with the clapboards just to the side of the doorway, only a few feet from where Nick stood. The cat screamed and pounced on the hand as it hit the ground. The man pulled the hand back toward him, the cat nipping at the flesh along the way.

'You have something of ours,' the man at the edge of the alley said. He spoke with a soft voice and a slight accent Nick couldn't place.

'Get out of here!' Nick yelled numbly. He watched as the hand flew again across the alley, mesmerized by the grotesque display. It hit against the bricks even closer to Nick this time, and landed so close to his feet, he could have reached down and picked it up.

'Don't you want to know what has become of Mr Phelan? My understanding was that he is an acquaintance of yours.'

The cat screamed again and pounced on the hand, grabbing it by the stump near the wrist, where the bones protruded, and the flesh was so worn that the grey-white skin flapped raggedly.

He could feel the man staring at him, but Nick couldn't pull his eyes away from the hand as the cat continued to gnaw on it.

The man said, 'Don't you want to know what we will do to his sister?'

Sense overtook horror within Nick at last and he raised the gun, aiming at the man. 'Where is he?' he called. 'What the fuck did you do to Charlie!'

At that moment, Nick felt a blade against his throat. Turning to his left, he realized that he'd left the front door open. Another man was standing behind him in the door, holding a combat knife hard against his neck. He was a bald giant, with massive shoulders. 'Put the gun down, Mr O'Callaghan,' he said. Nick did as he was told, and the gun clattered against the cement alley.

The man from the alley walked toward them. As he came into view, Nick could see a soft, kind face with a birthmark in the shape of a tear on his cheek. The man wound the string attached to the hand as he walked, and once he was next to Nick, he pulled the string up, so that the hand dangled at thigh height. The cat batted jealously at it, letting out a long, frustrated cry as it swung just barely in reach.

The man watched the hand for a moment as the three of them stood there in silence. Then he looked into Nick's eyes. 'We have much to discuss, Mr O'Callaghan, no?'

CHAPTER THIRTY

There is no accounting for a cop's intuition. It comes with years of experience and careful attention to detail. The good ones become experts in the way people behave and interact, and the best seem to have a window into the minds of those with whom they come into contact. It was that intuition that drove Detective Morrell to the street in front of the girl's apartment on Ninth Street early the next morning.

In Morrell's case, it wasn't just intuition; it was a touch of obsessive compulsiveness – another common attribute among detectives. He couldn't shake the feeling that he had seen her before. In addition, something about her behavior had bothered him the previous day. No, that would be an understatement. Something about her behavior had angered him the day before. The nervous arrogance in her voice and the defiance in her posture sent warning flares shooting off in his head. The bloody mess down at his brother's bar had taken precedence, but he'd been unable to shake the feeling that something was terribly off about her.

As a result, Morrell found himself sitting in his car for an hour before his shift, sipping coffee, staring up at the apartment windows. It wasn't a hardship to him; his job was all he had now. The wives, thankfully, were gone. He had a daughter, but he hadn't heard from her in more than two years, and her last words had been unkind. Not unfair, perhaps, but unkind nonetheless. As for friends . . . well, he had long since determined that, for most, friendship was a convenience based on shifting self-interest. After a long list of petty betrayals, he no longer had the strength to feign friendship. He was probably closest to Nick, but there was a distance to their relationship that seemed difficult to fully bridge. He supposed that was natural among half-siblings. As a result, for the moment, the job, and those in whom he placed his temporary trust, were all he had.

At least the coffee's good, he thought as he sat there. The area was honeycombed with corner bodegas and delis and donut shops that opened early to sell egg-and-cheese sandwiches and beers to road crews just coming home off the night shift. There was nothing better to Morrell than a cup of coffee from the first pot brewed. It made even the most boring parts of his job bearable.

The morning hadn't been a total waste on the investigative side, either. He'd discovered that he wasn't the only person watching the girl's apartment. Parked a half-block ahead of him a man sat in a dull tan rented car, looking up at the windows that were the subject of their mutual attention. Morrell knew instinctively that the man was watching for the same girl.

From what Morrell could tell, he was a young man, perhaps in his early-twenties, with dark skin and a thin beard covering his face unevenly. He didn't behave nervously, but his focus on the apartment was unwavering.

Given the gunshots that had been reported the day before, it was enough to cause Morrell to act.

He opened the door to his car, got out, and started walking slowly up the street toward the car.

Akhtar Hazara didn't see the man until he was standing directly beside his car window, rapping on the glass with a heavy ring. He'd been too caught up in his own thoughts and worries to pay attention to anything other than the girl's apartment.

The night before had been agony for him. He'd been sitting outside the bar by the waterfront, watching as it closed down, waiting for them to come out. He'd watched as four armed men entered the place, and had listened to the sounds of the altercation – with the shattering of glass and the crashing of tables – followed by the sharp crack of a single gunshot.

The girl and her companion had emerged moments later and hurried to the man's car, speeding away even as the sound of sirens approaching began off in the distance. Wanting no involvement with the authorities, Akhtar had followed them back to her apartment, but there had still been no sign of Charles Phelan.

And so he'd sat in his car all night, drinking coffee to stay awake in case Phelan showed up, or the girl left. Now he was running on pure adrenaline, and he knew that was in short supply at this point. He was raw and anxious, and he wondered whether he even had the courage to do what needed to be done anymore.

The knocking at the car window made him jump, and

he considered reaching for the gun in the glove compartment. Fortunately he recovered his composure quickly.

He rolled down the window and looked up at a round, middle-aged man with more chins than hair. 'Yes?' Akhtar said. He tried to keep his tone polite but short; he wanted no involvement with anyone.

'You don't have a sticker,' the man said. The words made no sense, and for a moment, Akhtar thought his English had gone stale.

'Pardon me?' Akhtar said.

'A parking sticker,' the man said. 'This street is for resident parking only. You need a zone sticker to park here.'

Akhtar was relieved that he understood. 'Ah, yes,' he said. 'I am not parking, I am waiting.'

'Waiting for what?'

Akhtar began to get annoyed. 'That is not your business,' he said. He glanced up and down the street, and took note of the fact that there were very few cars and plenty of parking spaces. 'I am bothering no one,' Akhtar said. 'Please, leave me alone.'

He rolled up his window and faced forward, thinking that if he ignored the man, he would go away. It didn't work, though, and the tapping came again on the window. It was a different sound this time, though; heavier. And when he turned to roll down the window, ready to be more aggressive in his tone, he noticed that the man was tapping with a badge now.

Akhtar's heart began to beat with greater violence, and he willed his hands not to shake as he rolled down the window again.

'Yes?' he said. His voice was back to polite.

'It *is* my business. What are you waiting for?'

'A friend.' It was the best Akhtar could come up with.

The policeman pulled out a small notebook and a pen, and for a moment Akhtar thought that he was going to write him a parking ticket. That would have been a relief, as it likely would have meant an end to the interaction. He didn't write a ticket, though.

'Who is your friend?'

Akhtar's mind raced. He had not prepared himself for an interrogation. 'David,' he said. 'His name is David.' It was the first western name that popped into his head.

'David what?'

'I . . .' Akhtar stumbled for a moment before recovering. 'I don't know his last name. That is why I am waiting for him. He lives nearby, and I am hoping to see him.'

'Why do you need to see him?'

'It is because of a woman,' Akhtar said. It was an easy story. Americans lived in such a sex-driven culture that they believed there was a woman at the core of any obsession. 'He knows a woman I wish to see.'

The older man frowned. 'You're sitting on a street waiting to see a guy about a girl you want to date?'

'She is a very beautiful woman.'

'What is her name?'

'I don't know. That is why I am waiting for this man.' For a moment, Akhtar thought that he had pulled it off. He thought the cop was going to let him go.

'License and registration,' the police officer said.

'I'm sorry?' Akhtar said. He did not understand.

'I want to see your driver's license and your registration for the car.'

212

That presented a problem. Akhtar had a valid international driver's license, which would suffice. But he knew the registration for the car was in the glove compartment. Right under the gun. He took his license out of his wallet and handed it to the policeman.

'Registration, too,' the man said.

'It is a rented car,' Akhtar replied.

'Registration and rental papers should be in the glove box.'

Akhtar looked over at the glove compartment. It was narrow and shallow; he knew that, because he'd had to work to fit the gun in the tiny space. Looking back at the policeman, he gave a nervous smile.

'Is there a problem, sir?'

'I have done nothing wrong,' Akhtar replied. 'This is not right.'

The police officer took a step back and pulled out his gun. 'Step out of the car, sir,' he said. 'Now, please.'

'I tell you, I have done nothing wrong!'

'That may be, but I want you out of that car, now.'

Akhtar opened the door and slowly pulled himself out of the driver's seat.

'Face the car, hands on the roof, please. Feet behind your hips, shoulder-width apart.'

Akhtar did as he was told. 'Are you arresting me?'

'I don't know. Depends on what you're hiding in the car.' He performed a thorough frisk and found nothing. 'Stay right in that position,' he ordered. He kept an eye on Akhtar as he walked around to the passenger side. It was early enough that there were few people on the street, but those who passed by stopped a short way away to watch what was happening. 'Move along, people,' the cop said. No one listened, though, and a small crowd began to grow.

The officer opened the passenger door, reached in and opened the glove compartment. When he saw the gun, he pulled back and looked sharply up at Akhtar. 'What are you planning to do with that?'

Patrolman Ayden McMurphy was on the scene five minutes later. Detective Morrell had called in for uniformed support, and McMurphy had been dispatched. Whenever possible, McMurphy was dispatched when a call came in from Morrell. He was one of the few people in the department who could deal with the crotchety old cop. When the uniformed officer arrived, Morrell couldn't help but notice that McMurphy was treating his superior with an odd deference and solemnity. Morrell chose to ignore it, though, and focus on his job.

'He says it's not his,' Morrell told him. The young man was sitting in the back of Morrell's car, his hands cuffed behind his back. The semi-automatic pistol was in a plastic evidence bag on the hood. 'He says he doesn't know anything about it. It's a rental car, and he says he never looked in the glove compartment.'

'Where was his rental agreement?'

'In the glove compartment.'

'There you go.'

'He says someone at the rental place put the agreement in there.' Morrell looked around the street. There was more foot traffic now, but the small crowd that had gathered before was gone. People were moving around, too engrossed in their own troubles to concern themselves with the young man in the police car.

'What is it?' McMurphy asked. Again, Morrell noticed that the patrolman was having difficulty meeting his eyes.

'I don't know,' Morrell said. 'Something about this doesn't feel right. What was he here for? And what was he planning on doing with the gun?'

'You think it's gang related?'

Morrell shook his head. 'He's got an international license. Issued out of Pakistan. Says his name is Mohmad Hadid. I haven't heard anything about the Crips or the Bloods recruiting out of the Middle East, have you?'

'So, what are you thinking?'

'I don't know.' Morrell ran his palm across his face. 'I guess I'm thinking maybe we'll get some answers from him down at the station.'

'You never know,' McMurphy said.

'You never do,' Morrell agreed. There was an awkward silence between the men. McMurphy finally said, 'I really admire that you're out here doing the job. I think it's a good thing.'

Morrell gave McMurphy a curious look. 'You're not goin' gay on me, are you?'

'No, I just mean under the circumstances, it probably is the best way to handle things.'

'What circumstances?'

'You know, with what happened over at Spudgie's.'

'Last night?' Morrell grunted. 'It was a mess, but my brother can take care of himself.'

'Not last night,' McMurphy said. 'I mean what they found this morning.'

Morrell's voice became serious as a feeling of foreboding crept through his chest. 'What did they find this morning?'

McMurphy gave Morrell a frightened, incredulous look. 'You haven't heard?'

'Heard what?'

'I thought you knew. I guess you didn't go into the station yet this morning, did you? It's your brother. They found him this morning. I'm sorry, man. I know you weren't that close, but still, he was family, right? Apparently Miles Gruden has a little more juice than people thought.'

Morrell stared blankly at McMurphy. 'I gotta go over there,' he said. He opened the door and pulled the young man out of his car and pushed him over toward McMurphy. 'Can you take this guy down to the station and book him? I'll deal with him when I get back.'

'Sure,' McMurphy said. He grabbed the man by the elbow and picked the gun in the bag off the car. 'He'll be waiting for you.'

Morrell hardly heard what the patrol officer was saying. He put his police light on the roof of the car and pulled out at speed. Whatever concern he'd had about the young man with the gun was gone for the moment. He had warned Nick about possible retaliation, but he'd never thought it would come this fast.

CHAPTER THIRTY-ONE

Cianna didn't sleep. She put her head down on the arm of the sofa at one point, even closed her eyes for a moment, but the images running through her mind were torture, and she spent most of the night staring at the wall.

Saunders slept like a soldier on patrol, she noted. He sat on a chair next to the phone, and for two hours straight he didn't move. His eyes were closed, though she thought a few times she could see a slit through which he might have some vision. Combat veterans learned to capture what sleep they could in stressful situations, but to keep one foot in the conscious world so that they could react instantly if necessary.

She'd learned the skill herself while on active duty, and she'd perfected it during her time in prison, where constant alertness was necessary for survival. At least in combat theaters there were bases, which provided an occasional sense of security. There was no such respite in prison; there, the threats were constant.

She thought about her brother as she sat in the silent squalor that had become her life. The dagger he had stolen was on the makeshift coffee table in front of her. She wondered about his decision to steal it, and wondered whether the uncertainty created by her arrest had led to that decision. He'd depended on her for so long, it must have been devastating when she was taken away.

'He's alive.'

She looked up. Saunders's eyes were open now, and he was looking at her. She had the sense that he could see through her skin, into her thoughts. It was at once disconcerting and comforting.

'Maybe,' she said.

'The people who are behind this don't have what they are looking for yet. Until they do, he is worth more to them alive than dead. They'll call.'

She looked at the phone for a moment, then back at him. 'Where did you serve before you joined the Agency?'

'Who said I was in the military?' he responded. It was the first time she had heard his voice defensive.

'No one,' she said. 'It shows.'

He didn't answer immediately.

'You don't have to tell me,' she said. 'I was bored. That's all.'

'Kuwait,' he said. 'First Gulf War.'

'The easy war,' she said.

'Yeah,' he said quietly. 'Easy.'

'I didn't mean—' she started. He cut her off, though.

'It's okay, you're right. We got in, we got out. We chased Saddam Hussein and his men right back to the Iraqi border and stopped on the line. Then we stood there and watched as he slaughtered those in the Iraqi resistance who had helped us gather the information and had laid the groundwork for our victory. We stood there and watched as all the goodwill we had built up with those who supported freedom in the Middle East was pissed away.'

'You think we should have gone in?'

He shrugged. 'I wasn't a politician or a diplomat. I was a soldier. I didn't believe in leaving people behind, and I didn't believe wars could be fought halfway.'

'And now?'

'Now,' he said slowly. 'Now, I suppose I'm still a soldier. I still don't believe in fighting wars halfway.'

The words had barely left his lips when the phone rang.

Akhtar had heard stories of prison. As the Imam of one of the most important mosques in Afghanistan, his father had been an important and influential figure. Prominence in Afghanistan brings with it great danger, though. Loyalties and political allegiances are mercurial enough that influence can be of dubious advantage. Relatives of his had spent time in the custody of the various regimes that had drifted through control of Afghanistan, and they had told him what to expect.

The Russians had been cruel, but more out of bureaucratic habit than anything else. After the Russians came the Taliban. Their prisons were by far the most terrifying. Fear had been the only unifying principle under the Taliban's rule. The stories of random torture, mutilations and killings without any apparent justification or purpose were widespread. Tongues were often cut out, and limbs removed, all in professed loyalty to Allah and the Koran. For the vast majority of Afghans, the day the Taliban fled was a day for celebration.

The American military prisons were a riddle. On the one hand, the Americans were institutionally organized and humane. It was clear that there were rules about the treatment of prisoners that were taken seriously. Those in custody were identified and catalogued and tracked. They were given decent food, and allotted time for prayer. Notwithstanding the order that was imposed by the Americans, though, rumors of random acts of perverse cruelty spread throughout the prison population. The American military guards came to be seen as smiling serpents, waiting for the right moment to pick out anyone who let their guard down to torture them in unspeakable ways. That uncertain fear was more debilitating than anything else.

And so, when Akhtar entered the police station in the Back Bay, the fear ate at him. The large black uniformed police officer called McMurphy walked him through the booking process, then snapped handcuffs on Akhtar and led him down a hallway to a plain room with a mirror on one side, and a wooden table with three chairs in the middle.

'Sit,' McMurphy said.

Akhtar did as he was told. He understood this was the place where the beatings would be administered. That was acceptable; there were beatings in every prison. It was the right of the strong to test their prisoners.

'You want some coffee?' the police officer asked.

Akhtar said nothing.

'Coffee,' McMurphy repeated. 'You want some? Or maybe some water?'

Akhtar refused to fall for the ruse.

'You speak English, right?'

Akhtar looked carefully at the man. Finally, he said, 'Yes.'

'Good. That makes all of this easier. Do you want some coffee?'

It was disorienting to have a captor offer simple kindness. 'Yes,' Akhtar said. 'I would drink some coffee.'

McMurphy walked over and stuck his head out the door, calling to someone, 'Hey, Kenny! You wanna bring me a couple cups of coffee in room four?' His head came back in, and McMurphy walked over and sat in the chair opposite Akhtar. The coffee was brought in a moment later.

'There was a shooting reported in Southie yesterday, just around where you were parked this morning. Did you know that?'

Akhtar shook his head.

'Three people called it in. We knocked on some doors, but couldn't find anything. You know anything about this?'

'No,' Akhtar responded honestly. He could feel McMurphy probing his eyes, searching for any sign of prevarication. There was none there yet.

'You understand why we're asking, right? Shots are reported on that street last night, and then this morning, you're sitting there in your car, waiting for someone, gun in the glove compartment. You can see how this looks, right?'

'I was waiting for a friend,' Akhtar said quickly. 'And it is not my gun.'

'Right, your friend. What was his name again?'

'David.'

McMurphy's eyes were probing again, and this time Akhtar felt less confident. Neither man spoke for a few moments, and Akhtar was convinced that the beatings would begin then.

They didn't, though. There was a knock on the door, and another officer brought in two cups of coffee. McMurphy took one and took a sip. He handed the other to Akhtar and Akhtar looked at it suspiciously.

'Detective Morrell will be back in a little while. He's gonna want to talk to you,' McMurphy said. 'You get one call; is there anyone you want to tell you're here?'

Akhtar's eyes widened. 'A call?'

'A telephone call. You don't have to use it now, but if there is someone you want to notify that you're here, you can do it.'

'I can call anyone?' It made no sense.

'Yes. You want me to bring you out to the phone?'

Akhtar assumed again it was a ploy, but on the chance that it wasn't he didn't hesitate. 'Yes. Please take me.'

'Hello?'

Cianna would have expected her voice to have been more unsteady. She understood the danger her brother was in; understood the consequences of any mistake. And yet her voice sounded confident. Serious and concerned, but strong.

'Cianna.'

'Yes?'

'My name is Sirus.'

She drew in a quick breath and nodded to Saunders, who was leaning in close, listening as best he could to the earpiece, which she held just inches from her ear. 'You were at my apartment,' she said. 'You took my brother.'

'I did.'

'Where is he?'

'He's here. You can talk to him in a moment if you'd like.'

'Now.'

'It's not that simple, Cianna,' Sirus said. 'You should know that it never is. There is someone here who wants to talk to you, first.'

'Let me talk to Charlie!' she screamed into the phone.

A new voice came over the line, quiet and soothing. 'All in good time, Ms Phelan,' he said. She caught the slight accent from the Middle East. 'You have something of mine. Something of great importance. I want it back.'

'I don't know what you're talking about.' It was the answer that she and Saunders had agreed on. She would eventually admit that they had the dagger, but Saunders wanted to draw more information out of them first.

'Your brother will be disappointed to hear that,' the man said. There was a pause, and then an anguished scream in the background that she recognized as coming from Charlie. It sucked the strength from Cianna's resolve to play the game.

'Okay!' she screamed. 'I have it!'

The screaming in the background settled into a whimper. 'Good,' the man on the phone said. 'Very good. I was certain that this was the case, but Mr O'Callaghan refused to confirm it.'

'Nick?' Cianna felt like she was going to throw up. 'What does he have to do with this?'

'I think you know,' the man said. 'Charlie left my property with Mr O'Callaghan. If you have it now, you must have received it from him. We paid him a visit last night;

but his resolve to keep his secrets was remarkable. It is refreshing to know that you are more reasonable.'

'What did you do to Nick?'

'Nothing that was undeserved. And in the end, he told us very little. He was very strong, and he clearly cared for you very much.'

'Oh, God, Nick,' Cianna moaned. 'Is he alive?'

'If I was in your position, I would worry now more about your brother. You can save him, you know. All I want is my property. As I said, Mr O'Callaghan told me very little, but he did say that you have a man with you – the man who claimed to Sirus that he was the police, is he still with you?'

Cianna looked up at Saunders, and he nodded back to her. 'He is,' she said.

'Good. By all means, make sure that he is with you when you come to me. I want to meet this man. If you do everything that I tell you to, and if you bring to me what was stolen, you and your brother can go free. Do you understand?'

'Let me talk to him,' Cianna demanded. 'I need to know that he's all right, before I agree to give you anything.'

'Of course,' the man said. 'He is right here.'

There was a rustling on the phone, and then she could hear his voice. It sounded confused and distant. 'Cianna?' he said. He was still whimpering, and it broke her heart. A flood of memories of him as a child swept over her, from the days when she was still able to protect him.

'It's me, Charlie,' she said soothingly. 'I'm here. I'm going to come get you. Everything is going to be all right.'

She could hear him sob. 'No,' he said. 'It's not.'

'Shhhh,' she tried to quiet him. 'Shhhh, it will. I promise.'

'You can't!' he screamed through his sobs. The anger in his voice frightened her. 'You can't promise, because you don't know!' He wasn't making any sense.

'It's okay, Charlie,' she tried again. 'I don't know what?'

'You don't know what they did!'

Cianna had trouble breathing. She closed her eyes. 'What did they do?' she asked. He tried to answer her, but she could barely understand him, he was crying so hard. 'Tell me, Charlie, what did they do?'

'They took my hand!'

Cianna didn't understand. 'What do you mean? How did they take your hand?'

He was sobbing uncontrollably now. 'They took it! They cut it off and they fucking took it!'

It took a moment for that to sink in, and she couldn't speak. The phone on the other end was pulled away from her little brother, and his anguish faded again into the background. The man with the accent was speaking again. He was telling her where to bring the dagger. She listened, and memorized the information, still unable to speak.

'Are you still there?' he asked.

Her breathing was shallow. 'You cut off his hand,' she said.

'He is a thief. I left him one, which is more charity than he deserved. That is justice. That is what the Koran teaches. You will bring my property back to me.'

'I will kill you,' she said. It came out without thought.

'No you won't,' he replied without emotion. 'You will do what I tell you to do.'

'Or what?' she challenged.

'Or your brother will share Mr O'Callaghan's fate.'

The squad cars were thick around Spudgie's as Morrell pulled up. It wasn't unusual for a sense of excitement to surround a crime scene. Crime was the police force's business, and as in any business, when important things are happening, those involved are infused with an energy that can sometimes approach giddiness. Macabre jokes are common. Rumor and speculation are rampant. The scene often takes on a feel that is somewhere between beehive and fraternity party.

That was not the case that morning at Spudgie's. There was energy at the crime scene, but it was muted, serious. Faces were drawn into dark frowns. Shoulders were hunched over, and people moved about without comment or wisecrack.

Morrell understood it. Most of those there knew or had heard by now that the victim was the brother of a cop. Attacks on the relatives of police officers were treated with a special seriousness. In addition, Nick O'Callaghan was respected, even admired among those on the force. He was a military man who'd survived more than his fair share of dangers both on and off the battlefield. Most of those working the scene had been in the bar on happier occasions, and O'Callaghan had always treated them well. He was one of the world's few faithful arbiters of right and wrong, and he provided a touchstone in a neighborhood that often seemed lost. It was right that people treat his misfortune with a certain reverence.

Morrell realized quickly, though, that there was something more to the way people were acting. The shock in their eyes went beyond losing a good man. The frowns were lined with horror and disbelief. Morrell sought out the detective in charge of the scene, Reggie Halloway, ten years his junior, but well-liked within the department.

'Reggie,' Morrell said upon approaching him.

The detective looked up. 'Morrell,' he said. The silence stretched painfully for a moment. 'I'm sorry,' Halloway said, putting a hand on the man's shoulder.

'How bad?' Morrell asked. Halloway didn't reply, and after a moment Morrell nodded in understanding.

'I'm sorry,' Halloway said again. After a brief moment, he took a deep breath and moved on. Like many on the force, Morrell included, Halloway lacked sentiment when it came to matters of death. 'You were here last night?'

Morrell steeled his jaw. He was on the job now. 'I was.'

'I've seen the reports. You want to add a little color?'

'Not much to add. According to everyone involved, it was an altercation between Miles Gruden's boys and another group. The Gruden faction got the worst of it.'

Halloway nodded. 'Any idea who the other group was?'

Morrell shook his head, looking straight ahead. Around him, he could feel the stares, but he ignored them. 'No one was talking. Least of all my brother. I'd assume it was Sully's boys from over in Charlestown, but it could have been the South Americans, too. No way to tell.'

'It wasn't any locals,' Halloway said with certainty.

'No? How do you know?'

'Locals don't do what was done to your brother.'

Morrell shot the other detective a sharp look of inquiry. 'What the fuck does that mean?' he demanded.

Halloway rubbed his forehead. 'You don't need to deal with this, Morrell,' he said. 'Why don't you go on back to the station house, and I can interview you there a little later.'

'What the fuck are you saying?' Morrell demanded. 'What did they do to him?'

Halloway shook his head.

'Where is he?' Morrell asked quietly.

'He's still in the backroom. On a table.' Morrell moved toward the backroom, but Halloway grabbed him by the arm. 'You don't want to go back there. It's like nothing I've ever seen.'

Morrell gave an offended grunt. 'I've been doing this for thirty-five years.'

'So has the coroner. He threw up out in the alley.'

For a moment, Morrell thought the other detective was kidding. A look in the man's eyes told him he wasn't. 'What happened?'

'You don't want to know.'

'Tell me.'

'They used a power drill,' Halloway said. His eyes went to the floor.

'A power drill?' Morrell was confused. 'Where?'

'Everywhere. They . . .' He paused, looking pained at relaying the information. 'They drilled out his eyeballs. They took out his intestines while he was still alive, Doc says. It's fuckin' medieval.'

Morrell stood there for a moment, his mouth hanging open. 'No,' he said at last. 'Not medieval. Mid-Eastern.'

'What do you mean?'

'Afghanistan. I read an article about a series of dungeons

228

they found over there. Hundreds of people locked up, chained to the walls, tortured over time. They used power drills.'

'You think there's some connection?'

Morrell shook his head. 'I can't see how.' He thought about the young man he'd arrested earlier in the morning. He was from that area of the world, but his passport was from Pakistan, not Afghanistan. Besides, there was no power drill in his car. There was no reason to connect him to the atrocities committed here. And yet Morrell felt the itch of intuition. He set it aside. 'I want to see my brother,' he said.

Halloway nodded. 'It's up to you. You've been warned.'

'I have been. I need to see him for myself, though.'

'Why?'

Morrell shrugged. 'Because he was my brother. And maybe just so I know what we're dealing with.'

Halloway looked at Morrell. 'We're dealing with something I've never seen before.'

CHAPTER THIRTY-TWO

'Tonight,' Cianna said. 'Ten o'clock.'

Saunders had to ask the question three times before he got a response. He was sitting right next to her, and yet she seemed a thousand miles away.

'Where?' he asked.

'Cambridge,' she replied after a moment. Her voice was quiet, calm. 'The Gardner College Boathouse along the Charles River, up past Massachusetts Avenue.'

'You know it?'

'I know where it is. There won't be anyone there at night.' She was staring off into space.

'You okay?' he asked.

She shook her head. 'They cut off his hand.'

He thought for a moment that she was going to slip away. 'He's alive,' he said, trying to reassure her. He still needed her help, and there was a strength about her that he admired. He didn't want to see her crack.

'He's alive,' she repeated. She didn't sound enthusiastic.

'We'll get him back.'

She didn't respond to that.

He stood up and walked over to the window, pulled out his phone.

'Who are you calling?' she asked.
'The cavalry,' he replied.

Cianna went into the bathroom to let Saunders talk to his people alone. She turned on the shower and got undressed. She'd been wearing the same clothes for more than a day, and it had been longer than that since she'd bathed. She was working on no sleep, her nerves were raw, and her heart was broken by the news of what had already been done to her brother. And yet, somehow, she felt better physically than she had in years.

She let the hot water run down her body. When she finally turned off the water and stepped out of the tub, her mind was focused.

She wrapped a towel around her and slipped into her bedroom, pulled on her underwear and a grey T-shirt. She went to her closet, and rooted around on the floor in the back. The foot locker was still there. She hadn't opened it since she'd gotten out of Leavenworth, and the clothes were still inside, neatly folded the way regulations required.

She pulled out a pair of khaki cargo pants and put them on. Tugging the boots on over the military-issue socks brought back a flood of memories, but she brushed them away and kept her attention on the present. There was too much to do to allow that indulgence. Her brother needed her, and she couldn't let him down. She'd let too many people down in her life.

She was about to close the lid of the locker when she saw the leather case. It was in a side pocket, like some forgotten foot-care set. She pulled it out, opened up the case and looked at it.

For gallantry in action against an enemy of the United States.

She closed the case and put it back, latched the foot locker and slid it to the back of the closet. She stood up, and as she turned to head to the door, she caught a glimpse of her reflection in the mirror. What she saw shocked her. It was like looking at an image from the past. It was as though two years had been washed away.

'I'm coming for you, Charlie,' she said quietly. 'Just hang on for me.'

'You're on your own.'

Jack Saunders heard the words and took a deep breath before responding. 'Did you hear what I said?' he asked. 'They cut off Phelan's hand.'

'I heard you,' Ainsworth said. 'And just to let you know I'm not keeping anything from you, they killed O'Callaghan as well. Quite gruesomely, from what I understand.'

'That's one dead that we know about. And this freak Sirus Stillwell took a shot at me and tried to kill the girl. Add to that the mutilation of Charlie Phelan, and you're telling me that isn't enough to get others involved?'

'I told you at the outset that we were off the reservation on this,' Ainsworth said.

'You said you would send in reinforcements if things turned bad.'

'I've got my orders, and my orders are that we are not going after Charles Phelan. Bill Toney was very specific about that. If you pursue this any further, you are on your own.'

'Toney again?' Saunders felt the anger and frustration

boil up in him. 'Jesus, you'd think he was working for the other side.'

The line was silent for a moment before Ainsworth's voice came back, quiet and serious. 'You need to be careful with accusations like that, Jack,' he said. 'Toney is a very powerful man; you never know how he would react.'

'What do you suggest I do?'

'Leave the relic at the boathouse and get yourself back here. That's your only option.'

Saunders could feel his fist tightening on his cell phone. 'You're kidding me, right, Lawrence? Tell me that this is a fucking joke. Give me the goddamned punchline.'

'Sorry, Jack, there is no punchline.'

'We still don't know what this is all about!'

'No, we don't. And apparently that's the way it's going to stay. I don't make policy.'

'What about Charlie Phelan? He served his country, doesn't that count for anything?'

'He is a thief. He got himself into this mess.'

'And the girl?'

For the first time, Ainsworth raised his voice. 'What about the girl? She's a convicted killer, for Christ sakes! She's mentally unstable and a liability.'

'She needs my help,' Saunders said evenly.

'Oh Jesus, Jack. You're not losing your objectivity over a girl are you? Please tell me I'm not dealing with some romantic twenty-two-year-old just out of training.'

'You're not,' Saunders said firmly. 'There's something more to all this. Something important. All I'm asking for is the backup you promised me.'

There was a long pause on the line. 'I'm sorry, Jack,' came the response. 'There's nothing I can do.'

CHAPTER THIRTY-THREE

Detective Morrell arrived back at the station house feeling like he'd aged a decade since the morning. He'd been on the police force for more than twenty-five years, but he'd never seen the kind of sadistic violence that had been inflicted on his brother. The thought of it sapped his strength.

He nodded to several officers as he made his way through the public area of the precinct house and they nodded back, looking at him with that awful halting expression of pity, uncertain whether to express their condolences or keep quiet. He crossed through the swinging door back into the restricted area where most of the work was done and headed back to his desk and checked his messages. There were several tips on the whereabouts of Sal Decanta's corpse, but it all seemed so pointless now.

He went to the men's room to relieve himself, and to splash some water on his face. Looking in the mirror, he realized that he might have to retire soon. His stomach for the job seemed to grow weaker every day, and even on days better than this, he wondered how he even dragged himself to work. And yet, he didn't know what he would do if he retired. His work was all he had, and for his brother's sake he resolved to throw himself into it now.

He took a deep breath, straightened his tie, and headed back out to the Desk Sergeant's station. The sergeant on duty was busy helping a tourist who'd been robbed earlier in the day, so Morrell went behind the desk and started flipping through the booking sheets. He was looking to find out where they were holding the Middle Eastern kid he'd arrested that morning near the projects in Southie. He wanted to ask the young man some questions. The use of a power drill to torture Nick O'Callaghan was distinctive, and the only other place he'd heard of anything similar was in the part of the world from which the kid had come. It might mean nothing, but he had to satisfy himself that there was no connection.

He flipped through the list of holding cells, looking for Hadid, the name on the young man's license, but came up with nothing. He closed that book, and picked up another that had the specifics on each arrest that was kept updated. It took a moment for him to find the entry McMurphy had made when booking the kid in. He'd been processed and printed and placed in holding. Then, at the end of the final column, Morrell saw an entry that made no sense. It read 'Released'.

He looked around, confused. 'Hey, Joe!' he shouted.

The Desk Sergeant held up his hand and kept talking to the distraught tourist.

'Joe!' Morrell said, more insistent.

The Desk Sergeant turned toward him, annoyed. When he saw that it was Morrell, though, he looked instantly apologetic. 'Morrell. Sorry about your brother. He was a good man.'

Morrell ignored the condolences. 'McMurphy brought

in a kid this morning. Name was Hadid. What happened to him?'

The Desk Sergeant looked confused for a moment and glanced at the booking record. After a moment he nodded, 'Oh, yeah. Junior towelhead, right? He must've had some juice. Maybe he was a diplomat's son or something.'

'What do you mean?'

'I mean we were told to cut him loose.'

Morrell was dumbstruck. 'Who gave that order?'

The Desk Sergeant shrugged. 'How do I know? The kid got his one phone call, and fifteen minutes later, the word came down from upstairs to let him go. So we let him go. Damnedest thing I've seen in a while, but there wasn't anything we could do but follow orders, right?'

'And you have no idea why?'

'No, like I said. But the word around the house is that the feds got involved. That's why I'm guessing he's a diplomat's son.'

Morrell shook his head. 'He didn't strike me as a diplomat's son.'

It was dark when they arrived at the boathouse on the Cambridge-side shore of the Charles River, several hundred yards northeast of the Massachusetts Avenue Bridge. It was a great Victorian structure with gabled roofs and angled bay windows. Twin towers at the corners framed the building, making it appear as though the structure loomed out over the river. In the darkness it looked like a haunted house, leering at Saunders.

The parking lot was empty as Saunders guided the car through the gates and parked at the side of the building.

The two of them got out and came together at the front of the car. They paused there, staring at the building. Saunders carried the dagger wrapped in O'Callaghan's old shirt. He checked his watch; it was just before ten.

'You sure about the meeting time?' Saunders asked.

'I'm sure,' she said. Neither of them moved. 'You sure your people aren't sending backup?'

'I'm sure,' he said.

'I guess there's no point in waiting, then,' she said. Her determination seemed only to have hardened since he'd told her that Nick was dead.

He nodded and walked toward the front door. She fell into step with him. The only sound was the crunching of the gravel under their feet. His head swiveled, keen for any movement, but he sensed none.

The door was a heavy institutional portal with thick glass over wire mesh in the window. He peered through, but it was dark inside and he saw nothing. Reaching out, he tried the knob, and it turned without resistance. He pushed the door open and stepped into the building.

They stood there in the darkness for a moment, waiting. There was no sound, no movement within the building. He looked at her. 'What's supposed to happen now?' he asked.

She looked at a loss. 'I don't know. He just said to meet here.'

'It's a big place. Did he say where?' She shook her head. His eyes had adjusted enough for him to see the interior better. They were on the ground floor in a vestibule with an archway in front of them. There were two sets of stairs off to their left, one leading up and the other down. He nodded to her, and they moved slowly further into the building, through the archway into the main room where the sculls were kept. It was an enormous space with fifteen-foot ceilings, taking up most of the building's footprint. There were racks forming aisles running parallel to each other throughout the place, on which were stacked the long boats, upside down, their hulls shining like oddly thin coffins in a crypt. Along the far wall a series of over-sized glass doors, large enough to allow the boats to be carried out to the water, looked out to the riverfront and the docks. Long sharp oars stood in racks near the doors. The place smelled of old wood and sweat and mildewed leather. 'Keep close,' Saunders whispered to Cianna.

They walked up and down the aisles slowly, quietly, peering around the boats that partially blocked their view.

'Nothing,' he said, after they'd made their way through the place.

She frowned. 'The stairs,' she suggested after a moment. He nodded and they headed back out toward the entryway. They looked up the staircase that led to the upper floor, and down the one that led to the basement. 'Which way?' she asked.

Saunders gave it a moment's consideration. 'Up,' he said.

'Why?'

'No reason. It's gotta be one or the other.'

He took his gun out and started up, the stairs creaking with his weight. At the top of the stairs was a large room that looked like it hadn't been touched since World War II. The overstuffed chairs were covered in soft, cracked leather, and the walls fluttered with ancient posters and news clippings with pictures of thin, muscular, short-haired young men in boats, the headlines announcing victories from days long passed. A rug that looked as though it might once have been a nice oriental lay tattered and worn on the floor. A hill of pewter cups and trophies stood in a corner of the room, the patina of age making them appear at once forgotten and revered.

Saunders moved quickly through the room to two doors at the far end, opened them, turned to look at Cianna. He shook his head. 'Office and bathroom,' he said. 'No one's here.'

'Downstairs?'

He nodded. 'Looks like that's all that's left.'

He led the way, retracing their steps back down to the ground floor, stepping as lightly as he could to ease the creaking. It was useless, and he knew that each step was announcing their approach like an entourage of trumpeters.

The staircase wrapped around the landing on the ground floor and continued to a basement. As they started down, he could smell the heavy, damp odor of chlorine and wet cement. His fingers tightened on his gun and he slowed his pace, taking each step carefully. He motioned again for Cianna to keep close to him.

When they reached the bottom of the stairs, Saunders was surprised at how light it was. He'd been expecting a basement with no windows allowing the wan moonlight in. He hadn't realized that the building was built on a rise, and that the land on the northern side of the structure fell away so that there were more glass doors leading out to a lawn. The moon was nearly full, and it shone low in the sky, directly behind the windows, casting blue shadows throughout the place.

The basement was a training facility. The smell of chlorine came from two large indoor rowing tanks, both of which had sculls set in the middle of them, oars slung over the side, hanging over the water. A spit of cement roughly five feet wide ran between the two tanks. The windows were at the far end from where they were standing. Set off to the side was an elaborate set of fitness equipment including weight machines, stationary bicycles, and treadmills. Saunders had tried crew briefly as a freshman in college, and discovered it was a test of physical endurance that pushed most bodies to the limits of their tolerance. He'd dropped the sport and taken up rugby, far preferring the head-to-head physical brutality of the scrum to the slow, steady self-torture of the sculls.

He saw them as soon as they turned to face the far wall: two silhouettes set against the moonlight coming through the windows, standing across the room from them on the other side of the two rowing tanks. One of them was recognizable, even in outline. He was huge, set with square shoulders, the moonlight shining off a gleaming bald pate. 'Sirus,' Saunders said quietly to Cianna. He raised his gun slightly. Not so much that it was aimed directly at either of the figures, but enough so that it would be noticed.

The other dark figure was the first to talk. He was much smaller than Sirus, and there was something softer about him, even in the way he stood. His voice, too, was gentle and assuring as it floated in echoes across the enormous expanse of the basement.

'Ms Phelan,' he said. 'Do you have my property?'

She replied, 'Do you have my brother?'

From across the darkened room, Saunders could see the man smile, his teeth large and white. 'In due time,' he said. 'In due time.'

CHAPTER THIRTY-FOUR

Saunders raised his gun so that it was aimed at the man's chest. He was tempted to pull the trigger. The man stood there without any trace of fear in his eyes. He had a fanatic's confidence, and Saunders was generally of the view that fanatics made the world a more dangerous place. He wanted to shoot, but he knew that it would mean the end of Cianna's brother's life. Besides, Saunders still didn't have enough information about the conspiracy that had brought the soft-spoken sociopath to Boston. He wouldn't get that information if the man died.

Slowly he lowered the gun again so that it was pointed at the man's feet, keeping it in a position that would enable him to react instantly if necessary.

'Who are you?' Saunders asked.

The man replied with a dismissive wave of his hand. 'If you must call me something, Fasil will suffice.'

Saunders frowned. 'Fasil,' he said. He knew the name from when he was in Afghanistan, and understood the reputation for cruelty that came with it. 'I've heard of you.'

'Good,' the man said. 'Then you will understand that I am a man of some resources.' He moved along the far wall slowly, keeping his attention on Saunders. The two rowing tanks separated them. 'I am well aware of your history also, Mr Saunders.' Saunders tried not to flinch, but the realization that the man knew his identity felt like a shot in the stomach. 'Your reputation is impressive. It is good to work with a professional. I hope that it will make this meeting go more smoothly.'

'How did you—?'

Fasil cut Saunders off. 'That, too, is unimportant. What is important is that I am no longer delayed in my mission.'

'What is your mission?' Saunders asked bluntly.

Fasil smiled slightly. 'I will ask the question again: Do you have my property?'

'Where is my brother?' Cianna demanded sharply.

Fasil looked with forbearance at Cianna. 'In my country, we are not nearly as permissive with our women. I would prefer if we dealt with each other as men.'

Saunders could feel Cianna's anger radiating from her, but spoke quickly to keep the situation under control. 'This was supposed to be an exchange,' he said.

'And it is,' Fasil said. 'I will exchange your lives for my property.'

Saunders felt the movement behind him. Before he could turn, he felt the barrel of a gun pressed into the base of his skull. He eased his head around slowly, carefully, until he could see out of the corner of his eye the man holding the pistol. He was bearded and thick-set, with dark hair and eyes. Saunders turned slightly in the other direction, toward Cianna, to see whether there was anyone else there with a gun to her head. There wasn't; there was just one man behind them. He turned back and faced Fasil. 'If you do it this way, people will die,' he said.

Fasil smiled again. 'I think that is inevitable, no?'

'And you would go back on your word?'

'A promise to a liar and an infidel is no promise,' Fasil replied.

'I think you'll find I rarely lie,' Saunders said.

'Give me my property!' Any patience was gone from Fasil's voice. The man behind Saunders pressed the barrel of the gun with greater force into the base of Saunders's neck.

'Okay, okay,' Saunders said. He held the knife still wrapped in the shirt up over his shoulder to where the man behind him could grab hold of it. He saw the man's arm come forward, the fingers closing on it. At that moment, when he was sure that the man's attention was focused on taking possession of the dagger, Saunders ducked and spun to his right, bringing his shoulder up to knock the man's gun up.

A shot rang out, ricocheting off the tiling that lined the ceiling, and everyone in the room ducked. Saunders grabbed hold of the man's arm at the wrist and swung it down, bringing his knee up at the same time. When the elbow connected with the knee it snapped, shattering the joint with a sickening pop that echoed throughout the place. The man screamed in pain and fell to his knees as the gun fell from the uselessly dangling arm. He dropped the shirt with the dagger in his other hand and reached out for his weapon, but it was no use. Saunders turned his gun on the man and pointed it at his forehead.

'No!' the man screamed. 'Don't shoot!'

Saunders pulled the trigger and a spray of blood and brains coated the cement behind the man. His lifeless body toppled back. Saunders turned and aimed the gun at Fasil. Sirus raised his gun and pointed it at Saunders. For a moment no one moved. 'Shall we try this again?' Saunders said. 'Where is Charles Phelan?'

For the first time since they had arrived, Saunders could see a shadow of concern in Fasil's eyes. 'You exceed your reputation,' he said.

'If we don't see Phelan in the next thirty seconds, the next shot is between your eyes.'

'And the one after that will come from Captain Stillwell's gun,' Fasil said.

'At least we'll see which of us is a better shot,' Saunders said. 'Now, where is Phelan?'

Fasil slowly reached into his jacket pocket and took out a cell phone. He hit a button and put it to his ear. He gave an order in Farsi, then put the phone back into his pocket. 'It will be just a moment.'

'Good. That's all you've got.'

'Do you really believe that you have the upper hand, Mr Saunders?'

'Ask your friend,' Saunders said, nodding to the corpse lying near his feet.

'He was not my friend,' Fasil scoffed. 'He was a warrior, and he is proud to have given his life in our cause. He has his reward now.'

Saunders nodded. 'We agree on something, at least.' He held the gun aimed at Fasil's head. 'What is your cause, by the way?'

'My cause is my country! My cause is Allah! My cause is Afghanistan!' Fasil's voice was raised, but he stopped speaking when the door to the locker room off to the side of the windows opened and one of his men stepped through, holding Charles Phelan by the arm, half pushing him and half holding him up.

'Charlie!' Cianna shouted. She took two quick steps toward him, but Saunders caught her by the arm, holding her back. As he did, the Afghan standing next to her brother raised his gun at her.

'Cianna?' It was clear from his voice that Cianna's brother was heavily drugged. He was disoriented, and his eyes whirled as though trying to find something on which to focus. Saunders could see the bandages at the end of Charlie's arm where his hand had once been.

Fasil had composed himself after his outburst, and seemed calm again. 'You see?' he said. 'I am a man of my word. Now, give me my property.'

Saunders reached down and picked up the dagger, still wrapped in the shirt. 'Let him go, and I will leave it on this side of the tanks.'

Fasil laughed derisively. 'Americans believe all Afghans are stupid. Walk to the point between the two water tanks,' he ordered. 'Put it on the floor, and then back away. I will bring Mr Phelan to the same place to ensure that there has been no deceit. Once I am satisfied that it is real, I will walk back to this side alone, and Mr Phelan is free to make his way to you.'

Saunders didn't like it. There were too many ways Fasil could go back on his word once he had the dagger. He had few choices, though. Besides, both he and Cianna were armed, and having seen her in combat, he suspected they would have an even chance against Fasil and his men. He nodded and walked around the tank closest to the stairs and out onto the narrow spit of concrete that separated the two tanks. As he got nearer, he could see Fasil's expression change. It was as though the man was approaching rapture. His eyes grew wide, and a light perspiration broke out on his face.

Saunders reached the center of the concrete isthmus and set the dagger wrapped in Nick O'Callaghan's shirt on the floor, then backed away. Once he was back on the other side of the tank, Fasil took Phelan by the arm and moved around the second tank, toward the center. As he drew close to the dagger, he let go of Phelan, leaving him standing there, swaying unsteadily. Fasil knelt as though approaching an altar, reached out and took hold of the fabric. A look of confusion swept across his face. He began pulling at the shirt, the confusion quickly turning to panic and then to anger. He held the shirt up, and the dagger clattered to the floor. Fasil looked at the ancient weapon and then up at Saunders. He picked the dagger off the floor and stood.

'What is this?' he demanded.

Saunders looked from Cianna to Charlie, then back to Fasil. 'I don't understand,' he said.

'What *is* this?!' Fasil demanded again, more urgently this time.

Saunders frowned. 'It is the dagger Phelan stole from you. We got it from Nick O'Callaghan.'

Fasil held the dagger up, displaying it for Saunders and Cianna. Then he threw it at them. It was a poor toss, and it hit the water in the first tank, short of Saunders and Cianna. 'A bauble!' he screamed. 'You think I have come for a trifle such as this? Where is the Cloak?'

Saunders looked at Cianna, and she returned his blank expression. 'I don't know what you're talking about,' Saunders said to Fasil.

Fasil now appeared to be on the edge of insanity. 'The Cloak of Mohammed! Where is it? Give it to me now!'

Saunders shook his head. He opened his mouth to speak, but could think of nothing to say that might appease the madman.

Fasil took two steps back over to Charlie, who still appeared to be only marginally aware of what was happening. He pulled a Glock out of his pocket and slid the release back to chamber a round. He held the gun up to the side of Charlie's head.

'Charlie!' Cianna screamed. She pulled out her own gun and aimed it at Fasil. 'Let him go!' Stillwell and the Afghan who had brought Phelan pointed their guns at Cianna and Saunders.

'Tell me now! Where is the Cloak?' Fasil screamed back.

Phelan started sobbing. 'I told you!' he wailed. 'I don't know! I told you!'

'Charlie!' Cianna cried again.

'Tell me where the Cloak is now!' Fasil ordered. 'Or he dies!' He pushed the gun hard into Charlie's temple, forcing his head back as Charlie continued crying.

Saunders had few choices. It was clear that Fasil was no longer rational enough to be bargained with, and Saunders had no idea what the man was talking about. He kept his gun aimed at Fasil's head. There was a risk that the bullet could fragment and kill Charlie even if the shot was successful. There was also a risk that Fasil could pull the trigger in a death spasm, and the result would be the same for Cianna's brother. But neither of those risks was as certain as the fact that Fasil would kill Charlie if Saunders did nothing.

He took careful aim and increased the pressure slightly on the trigger to steady his hand.

The explosion did not come from his weapon, though. It came from the rear of the boathouse, as the glass in the windows out toward the back shattered. Fasil was spun around by the force of the shot that hit his left arm, and his gun fired, missing Charlie's head. Charlie, no longer supported, fell to his knees. Saunders turned to look over at the window and saw a young man standing there. His gun was still pointing at Fasil. 'Allahu Akubar!' he shouted.

Suddenly, the room erupted in gunfire. Sirus and the Afghan were shooting at the back window, and the young man there pulled his head back and disappeared. Sirus took aim at Cianna, and Saunders threw himself at her, knocking her to the ground. 'Who the hell started shooting?' Cianna shouted to Saunders. He shrugged in return.

As they scrambled to their knees, shots came again from the window, and Fasil dove to the ground. Sirus and the remaining Afghan scurried back toward the door to the locker room from which Phelan had been led.

'Come on!' Saunders yelled at Cianna. 'We've got to get out of here!'

They crawled toward the stairs, staying in a low military crawl to avoid the shots that still rang out.

'Wait!' Cianna screamed. 'Charlie!'

They both looked back. Charlie was now lying on the narrow strip of cement, just a few steps from Fasil. He was struggling to get back to his knees, his eyes still spinning wildly. 'Cianna!' he called out.

Cianna started back, but Saunders grabbed her by the leg. 'No!' he said. 'You can't!'

'I have to!' she shouted at him. She shook free from his grasp and started toward her brother again. As she did, Fasil crouched behind Charlie, using him as a shield. There was a bloodstain on his left sleeve, but his back was straight, unwavering. He had a look of hatred on his face, and his eyes went back and forth from Cianna to Saunders.

'I am a man of my word!' he shouted to them.

Charlie was still struggling to get to his knees, only feet in front of Fasil. It was difficult for him. The drugs had robbed him of whatever equilibrium he would otherwise have had. After a moment, though, he managed to make it to a kneeling position, and he raised his arms up, reaching out in the direction of his sister. 'Cianna!' he called. For just a moment, he sounded almost hopeful.

'I'm coming, Charlie!' Cianna called back desperately. She was still moving toward him.

'I am a man of my word!' Fasil yelled again. He raised his gun and aimed at the center of Charlie's back.

'No!' Saunders cried. He raised his gun and started firing. Cianna did the same, and the cacophony was deafening.

Fasil pulled the trigger once, rose, and sprinted along the spit of concrete toward the locker room.

CHAPTER THIRTY-FIVE

Cianna saw the bullet rip through her brother's body. He was kneeling, his arms stretched forward, his eyes meeting hers. And then he lurched forward, and his chest exploded out in a fountain of red that polluted the water in the tank before him.

'No!' she screamed.

He looked down at the gaping hole in the front of his shirt, and back up at her, his face a mask of confusion and fear. He opened his mouth and it looked as though he wanted to say something, but before he could, gravity overtook him, and he fell forward into the water.

She dropped her gun and dove into the water taking short, panicked strokes to the other side. She had to dive under the scull suspended in the center of the tank to get to her brother, and that slowed her down. Even in the dark, she could see the cloud of blood in the water. He was face-down in the water, and she grabbed his shoulders and rolled him over, speaking in a desperate voice. 'It's okay, Charlie. It's going to be okay.' She could feel Saunders behind her, reaching into the tank and pulling Charlie onto the cement. She climbed out and knelt over the body, feeling Saunders's hand on her shoulder, pulling her away. They were still in danger. 'It's going to be okay,' she mumbled again to her brother's lifeless body.

'We have to get out of here,' Saunders said to her. 'We can't stay out in the open like this.'

'I've got to bring Charlie!' she yelled, struggling to lift him.

Saunders grabbed her and pulled her away. 'No!' he pleaded.

'I have to!'

'Where are you going to take him? The police will be here soon. They will take care of his body.' He pulled harder at her.

She knew her brother was dead, but her heart wasn't quite ready to acknowledge it. 'No! I have to save him!' She struggled harder against Saunders's grip.

It was remarkable how strong Saunders was, given his size. His arm held her around the neck and under the armpit, and would not give at all. If anything, he tightened his grip, immobilizing her. 'He's dead!' he yelled. 'And we will be, too, if we don't get out of here!'

As he said the words, the gunfire came from the door to the room where Fasil and his men still were, strafing the ground around them. 'We have to go! Now!' Saunders said. With that, he stood and lifted her off the ground as though she were a child. He started running toward the stairs. Looking back, Cianna could see Fasil and his bodyguard giving chase. Sirus was nowhere to be seen.

'Charlie!' she called. But she had given up the fight to get back to his body. She let herself be carried.

Saunders hit the stairs at a full sprint, and a moment later they reached the front door and slipped outside.

Saunders paused there, setting Cianna down and scanning the parking lot for danger. He took her by the shoulders and looked her in the eyes. 'Are you okay? Are you with me, or do I need to carry you?'

'I'm okay,' she said vacantly. 'I can make it on my own.'

He continued to look at her, and she could tell that he was skeptical. Finally he nodded. 'We need to make a run for the car,' he said. 'I'll go first and get your door open. You follow right behind me, got it?'

She nodded.

She watched as Saunders tucked himself into a sprinter's posture, took a deep breath, and ran into the parking lot.

The gunshots rang out as soon as Saunders got out from under the portico. They were coming from the side of the building, and Cianna realized that Sirus had slipped out the glass doors in the basement and taken up a position from where he could easily pick them off. Saunders dove to the ground and slid behind a tree, which provided little cover. Cianna could hear the footsteps inside the building as the others approached the door. She looked down at the spent revolver in her hand, and realized that there was little she could do. Looking around desperately, she put her back to the exterior wall, just outside the door hinges, to give her some chance to surprise the first through the door. If she could wrestle his gun away quickly, she and Saunders might stand a chance. It was a long shot, but it was all she had.

As she readied herself for close combat, she saw a beige sedan tear into the parking lot, wheels screeching. It pulled to a stop in between Cianna and Saunders, and the passenger side door opened. Sitting behind the wheel was the young man who had opened fire through the glass doors earlier. He motioned to her. 'Please!' he called. 'Come with me, now!'

As he called, gunshots plunked the side of the car. The young man put his arm out his window, and returned fire toward Sirus at the side of the building. 'Please!' the young man said again, this time to both Cianna and Saunders. 'There is no time!'

Cianna looked over at Saunders. He hesitated for only a moment, and then scrabbled over to the rear door and climbed in. Cianna was moving next, sprinting from the building just as the door opened and Fasil emerged.

The young man threw the engine into gear before Cianna reached the door. She could hear the shots firing off behind her, but she didn't look back. Her legs were pumping hard, and once she drew within a few feet of the car, she launched herself at the open door.

The momentum of the moving car had already begun to swing the door closed. Her head and shoulders made it through the opening, but the door slammed against her hip, and her feet dragged along the pavement. Her hands slipped from the seat, and for a moment, she thought she was going to fall out. As she grasped for something to hold onto, though, a hand reached out and grabbed her wrist. She looked up and saw the young man at the wheel pulling her toward him as he steered the car wildly toward the street. After a moment, her fingers found the seatbelt, and she was able to pull herself the rest of the way into the car.

She slammed the door behind her as the car fishtailed into the street and sped away. The gunshots behind them faded quickly into the distance, and for a moment all Cianna could hear was her own breathing as she gasped for air.

She looked over at the young man in the driver's seat, and he looked back at her. He gave a shy smile and a slight nod. 'I am Akhtar,' he said. 'I am pleased to meet you.'

CHAPTER THIRTY-SIX

Lawrence Ainsworth was in a meeting with Mark Humallah, the chief liaison officer to the Kabul station. They were in one of the large steel-paneled conference rooms on the third floor. The table in front of them was illuminated with an interactive map of Afghanistan and the surrounding countries. With a touch of his finger, Ainsworth was able to zoom in on particular cities or villages. The map was a compilation of satellite images that could be focused in on to reveal detail down to the larger grains of sand. There were intelligence reports spread out in front of them, and the two men were deep in strategic discussions regarding an upcoming operation.

There was no knock; the door swung open with just enough force to slam off the wall. Bill Toney stormed into the room, his face red, his lips quivering in anger. 'Ainsworth!' he yelled.

Lawrence Ainsworth didn't look up. He continued his discussion with Humallah as though Toney wasn't there.

Toney walked over and put his fists down on the table, and the map of Afghanistan sucked itself up into a dot in the center of the table and disappeared. 'You had to do it, didn't you?'

'I'm in a meeting, Bill,' Ainsworth said calmly. 'We can talk later.'

'We'll talk now!' Toney bellowed.

Ainsworth looked at Humallah with the embarrassment a host might show if a badly trained dog urinated on his guest's leg at a cocktail party. 'I'm sorry, Mark. Can we take a break for a few minutes? Apparently Bill has something he feels is pressing that he needs to discuss with me.'

'That's Colonel Toney,' the NSA Director snapped.

'Retired,' Ainsworth said.

'I'm still entitled to the rank.'

Ainsworth rolled his eyes again. 'Mark? A few minutes?'

Mark Humallah nodded and left the room without a word.

'Now, Bill,' Ainsworth said once they were alone. 'What is it that seems to have disturbed you?'

'You know goddamned well. I gave you a direct order that you were not to get involved in the Charles Phelan matter in Boston. You couldn't resist, though, could you? You had to keep your finger in it.'

'I have no idea what you're talking about.'

Toney's face reddened even further. 'Then I suppose it's just a coincidence that I'm getting reports that Jack Saunders is in Boston, and that he has been accompanying Phelan's sister around the city?'

'Saunders is on vacation,' Ainsworth said. 'What he does on vacation is his business.'

'I told you to stay out of this!' Toney hollered.

Ainsworth leaned back and folded his hand across his lap. 'You know, Bill, you're not technically my superior. I don't know that you have the authority to give me orders.'

Toney smirked. 'You really want to play it that way, Lawrence?' He walked around the table so that he was behind Ainsworth. 'I am more than happy to turn this into an official inter-Agency complaint.' He leaned in so that he was speaking quietly into Ainsworth's ear. 'Who do you think will come out on top in that event?'

'I don't know, Bill,' Ainsworth said. 'You've certainly kissed more asses in the administration, so I guess I'd give you the better odds.'

The smirk disappeared from Toney's face. 'I'm serious, Lawrence. No more interference.'

'Of course, Bill,' Ainsworth said, relenting. 'Like I said, Saunders is on vacation. I just have one question. You told me the other day that there was nothing to this Phelan issue.'

'I did,' Toney agreed.

'So who do you have in the field who is giving you these reports?'

Toney's face was stone. He walked to the door. 'Tell Saunders to get out of this,' he said. 'As far as I'm concerned, he's a civilian in Boston. He will get hurt if he stays out there, and it will not be on my head.'

CHAPTER THIRTY-SEVEN

'My name is Akhtar Hazara.'

The young man was sitting on the edge of the bed in a motel on Dorchester Street in South Boston. It was the kind of place where few questions would be asked, and memories would be short. Saunders was sitting on a battered faux-wooden desk chair. Cianna sat on the sofa facing him, her eyes vacant, staring through the floor as though she could see into the depths of hell.

'My father was Mohmar Hazara,' he continued. Seeing Saunders's reaction, he said, 'You remember him, yes?'

Saunders nodded. 'I didn't know him, but I knew of him. And I remember when he was killed.'

'I was with him,' Akhtar said. 'I was thirteen, and it was right after the Taliban fled. The Americans had not yet reached Kandahar, but we knew they were coming. Everyone knew it, and everyone was wondering what would happen. Many assumed that it would be the start of a new way of life for my country; that it would be the dawning of a new golden age for Afghanistan and its people, when we would be able to control our own destiny. There were those who welcomed the fall of the Taliban, and the possibility of a genuine democracy. My father was one such man.'

Saunders nodded, remembering. 'I was one of the first into the country,' he said. 'Even before the invasion, twelve of us were sent in to begin the process of separating the good guys from the bad. Your father was on my list of good guys. I'm sorry I never had the chance to meet him.'

'Thank you,' Akhtar said. 'My father always said that his individual life was meaningless, though. What was important to him was that everything was done for the good of the country. If his death had sparked a movement toward all that he had hoped for, he would have been happy to die a martyr.'

'But that isn't what happened,' Saunders said.

'No,' Akhtar agreed. 'Instead, my country sank deeper into tribal squabbles that still set the tone for what is happening there today. Local chieftains and tribal leaders sell their loyalties to the highest bidder for whatever they can get, and those loyalties last only as long as whatever advantage has been gained. Until someone emerges who can unite the country, it will remain so. That is why I am here. That is why I need your help.'

'I don't understand,' Saunders said.

'For four centuries, my family has guarded the Sacred Cloak of Mohammed from within the center mosque in Kandahar. It is one of the three most sacred relics in all of Islam, and it has great power. Three weeks ago it was stolen. I need your help in finding it.'

'That's why my brother was killed?' Cianna demanded, her voice so loud that it startled Saunders. From the look on his face it appeared that Akhtar had forgotten that she was in the room. She hadn't said a word since the three of them arrived at the motel. Now her eyes were wide and burning furiously, and she stood, leaning over, putting her face right up to the young man's, spitting her words out with contempt and outrage. 'For some shitty piece of cloth—!'

'It is far more than cloth!' Akhtar protested, clearly offended. 'It is the Heart of Afghanistan. The Prophet Mohammed himself wore the Cloak into battle. It was brought to the sacred mosque in Kandahar by Ahmad Shah Durrani, the first king of Afghanistan, four hundred years ago. Since that time, my family has guarded it with our lives!'

'And my brother paid for it with his! Why? For what purpose?' Cianna waved her arms in the air as she screamed at Akhtar.

Saunders reached a hand out and put it on her shoulder to calm her. 'It's not his fault,' he said. 'He didn't kill your brother.' She looked at him, and for a moment he thought she might punch him for taking the young man's side. After a brief pause, though, she reluctantly sat back down. 'Akhtar is right, it isn't just a piece of cloth,' Saunders said in an even voice. 'For a Christian, it would be the equivalent of the robe that Christ wore at the last supper.'

'Christians don't kill for relics,' Cianna pointed out.

'No?' Akhtar replied. 'I must have misread the tales of the Crusades, then.'

'This isn't the fucking Middle Ages!' Cianna screamed back. 'This is the twenty-first century, and my brother is lying dead in a boathouse with one hand! So don't talk to me about the injustices of five centuries ago, okay?'

'This isn't about what happened five centuries ago,' Saunders said to Cianna. 'This is about right now. This is about who will succeed in taking power in Afghanistan.'

'What the hell does some cloak have to do with that?' Cianna demanded.

'The Sacred Cloak has everything to do with that,' Akhtar said. 'It is said that the Cloak will only sit on the shoulders of those chosen by Mohammed himself to lead my nation. He who can show that he holds the Cloak without tragedy befalling him will be able to unite all of the tribes of Afghanistan.'

Cianna shook her head in disbelief and looked at Saunders. 'Are you listening to this superstitious crap?'

'It's not just superstition,' Saunders said quietly.

'You really believe this?'

'It doesn't matter whether I believe it.' Saunders walked to the window and looked out toward the highway onramp. 'Many of the people of Afghanistan believe it.'

'It is not just that they believe it,' Akhtar said. 'It has been proved in the past. The Cloak has only been seen in public three times in the past four centuries. In 1760, Ahmad Shah, the founder of Afghanistan, displayed the Cloak around his shoulders as he announced jihad against his rival Pashtun and Marathan tribal leaders. He swiftly defeated his enemies and created the first united nation of Afghanistan, which his family ruled for generations. In the 1930s, a deadly outbreak of cholera threatened to lay waste to the city of Kandahar. The Cloak was taken out and held aloft from the roof of the mosque over the city. The disease disappeared within a week.'

'And the last time it was displayed?' Cianna asked skeptically.

Saunders looked at Akhtar, and the young man bowed

his head. Akhtar spoke penitently. 'The last time was in 1996, after the Soviets fled from my country. A civil war erupted and it seemed as though it might never end. One of the strongest leaders in the country came to my father, and asked to see the Cloak – to give him inspiration, he said. My father allowed it, against his better judgment, and the leader stole the Cloak and took it with him to a rally of his people outside of the mosque. He held it aloft and claimed his legitimacy based on the touch of Mohammed. He later returned the Cloak to the mosque, but his brief display was enough. Two days later, inspired by the stories of the Cloak, his forces were able to finally take Kabul. He was installed as the leader of Afghanistan.'

'Who was he?' Cianna asked.

'Mullah Omar,' Akhtar replied. 'The leader of the Taliban. The dark age that swallowed my country for the next five years was in large part due to my father's mistake. Now there are only two people who can possibly lead Afghanistan, and they are both searching for the Cloak to provide the legitimacy they need to take power. I must make sure that the better of these two succeeds, and that the worst fails.'

'Who are the two?' Saunders asked.

'One is a man I work for in Kandahar named Gamol. He is the better of the two. He is older, and he remembers the days, even before the Soviets, when Afghanistan was a land of hope. He is a politician – in all that means, both good and bad – but he would at least take the country forward, and that is what is needed.'

'And the second man?'

'The second man you met at the river tonight.'

'Fasil,' Saunders said.

Akhtar nodded. 'Fasil. He is the only other who stands a chance of uniting my country.'

'Who is he?'

'He is a fanatic. A rising star in the Taliban before the invasion, he has stayed true to their principles. Even more, his view is that the Taliban was too lenient against non-Muslims, and those Muslims who strayed from what he believes is the true path. He believes it was that weakness that led to the fall of the Taliban. For several years, he has been consolidating power among those who believe that the true glory for Afghanistan is a return to the ways of the Taliban. The Sacred Cloak of Mohammed is the only thing that could draw him out of hiding in the mountains. Twice before he has tried to capture it, but he has failed. My father was the mullah of the mosque where the Cloak has been kept for centuries. For generations, my family has had the great honor of protecting the Cloak from harm, guarding it with our lives. We had been successful throughout history. Now it would seem that we – I – have failed. That is why I am asking for your help. I am trying to save my country.'

Cianna stood up and looked at the young man. 'I don't give a shit about your country,' she said. 'I cared about my brother, and now he's *dead*! He didn't take your goddamned relic; he took a dagger. Maybe that was wrong, but he did it for me, and he never meant to hurt anyone. You may not have pulled the trigger, but it's people like you who killed him. You and your whole goddamned country can go to hell!'

She walked toward the door to the motel room. Akhtar stood up and went after her. 'Where are you going?'

She spun on him. 'I am going to kill the man who murdered my brother.' She held his gaze for a moment before she turned and reached for the doorknob.

'Wait!' he said. She turned to look at him once more, and again it looked to Saunders as though she might strike out at him. The young man seemed unintimidated. 'I share your rage,' he said. 'I am not like Fasil, though. He wants a return to the darkness. He wants to kill all those who do not believe as he does. I understand your hatred, but I want only peace for my country.'

Cianna stepped toward him and put a finger in his chest. 'You cannot possibly understand my hatred after what I saw today,' she said in a slow-burning rage.

'No?' he replied. 'When I was thirteen, just after the Americans invaded my country, the Taliban sent a messenger to my father. He reached my father as I was walking with him in the center of the city. This messenger demanded that he release the Cloak to the Taliban so that they could inspire confidence in their supporters once again. My father refused. He had seen what the years of Mullah Omar's rule had wrought on my country. He would not make that mistake twice. The messenger smiled as though he knew my father's answer even before he gave it. It was almost as though it was the answer he had wanted. Then he pulled a long knife from under his robe, and sliced through my father's throat. I was standing there, and I watched as the life poured out of his body. I held him as he died.'

'I don't care,' Cianna said coldly. 'Don't you get it?' She

turned and started back toward the door, but Akhtar grabbed her by the arm and spun her back around.

'The Taliban messenger who killed my father? He is the same man who killed your brother today.'

She looked at him. 'Fasil,' she said.

'That is correct. So do not think that I misunderstand your hatred. That is why I am asking for your help. It is not just for my country; it is to avenge my father. To avenge your brother. Otherwise, all is lost.'

She stared at him for a moment before answering. 'All is lost already.'

CHAPTER THIRTY-EIGHT

Detective Morrell made his way through the parking lot at the boathouse along the Charles River. The place was a maze of police cars and uniforms, with crime-scene tape draped across stakes hammered into the ground at regular intervals across the lot. He held his badge up, and met every curious glance with a look that made clear he would not be deterred. This was Cambridge, and he was outside of his jurisdiction. He wouldn't be prevented from looking around, but the local authorities would be wary of the outside intrusion, particularly from a Boston detective. The two forces worked well together when necessary, but the Cambridge cops felt the condescension occasionally directed their way by police officers from the neighboring big city. Under normal circumstances he would try to be sensitive to that dynamic. These were not normal circumstances, however.

After a moment, Morrell caught sight of Peter Amano, a detective with whom he'd worked in the past, and made his way toward him. The expression of recognition on the man's face when he looked up and saw Morrell soured quickly.

'Pete,' Morrell said as he drew close. He didn't offer his hand. He touched people in a familiar way as little as possible.

'Detective Morrell.' Amano forced a smile. 'What brings you out to our little suburb?'

'My brother was murdered last night.'

The smile faded from Amano's face. 'I heard. I'm sorry about that.'

'Fuckers used a power drill on him. It wasn't pretty.' Morrell spoke evenly, letting each word fall like lead.

'Yeah,' Amano said. 'I heard that, too. Like I said, I'm really sorry.'

'I hear you got a nasty one out here, too.'

Amano nodded. 'It is that. There are some very sick people sharing our world with us.'

'And you haven't even met any of my ex-wives.' Amano looked curiously at Morrell, as though he couldn't tell whether the older detective was making a joke or not. *Most humor springs from truth*, Morrell thought. He kept the notion to himself, though. 'What happened?'

'We're still not sure. It's remote over here; no houses or other buildings for a few hundred yards in any direction. A few people taking a night stroll along the river, though, heard what sounded like a full-on shoot-out in there. Unfortunately, they didn't have their cell phones with them. It was twenty minutes before we even got the call; by then, whatever happened out here was over. It sure as hell left a mark, though.' Amano turned toward the east wall. 'We've pulled twenty shells out of the plaster in this wall alone. We're still finding more. Military-issue. Looks like one hell of a battle.'

'Two dead?' Morrell asked.

Amano nodded. 'Two dead. One shot in the forehead at close range. Looks like he was executed. Same with the second except he was shot in the back. But he wasn't involved in the shoot-out.'

'How do you know?'

'It'd be hard to pull a trigger with no hand.'

Morrell looked at him. 'No hand?'

'Yeah. Like I said, there're some fucked up people in this world.'

'You know anything about the vic?'

'We're learning. Ex-military. Just got back from Afghanistan. Grew up over in Southie, but no present address we've been able to identify yet. Apparently he has a sister who lives over in Boston, but we haven't been able to track her down. I've got people over there waiting to see if she makes it home. This can't be the kind of news she's looking for today.'

Morrell's eyes narrowed. 'Where does she live?'

'Over on Mercer.'

'In Southie,' Morrell commented quietly.

Amano's face curled into a frown. 'Yeah, in Southie. That mean something to you?'

'Maybe.' His memory went back to the little apartment near the projects, and the girl there who had seemed so familiar. His heart was pounding. 'You got a name?'

Amano now looked suspicious. Morrell knew what the man was thinking. The last thing he needed was for a Boston Detective to come over to his town and solve a high-profile case like this. 'Phelan,' he said at last. 'Charles Phelan.'

Phelan. It all came swarming back on him in an instant. *Charlie Phelan. Cianna Phelan.* He'd met them the few times he'd been by Nick's bar years ago. They were kids

– like mascots in the place – who did dishes and waited the occasional table. It was a long time ago, but it was too much of a coincidence. Morrell felt a rage welling up within him. He had to find the girl. He was so lost in his thoughts, he didn't notice Amano studying him carefully.

'Is there something I should know?' Amano asked.

Morrell looked at the Cambridge detective. The man had shared information with him, and he knew that Amano was expecting Morrell to return the favor. It was fair, after all, and in any other situation Morrell would have honored the code and reciprocated. But this situation was different. It wasn't some addict or unidentified gang-banger lying in the morgue with his guts drilled out, it was Morrell's brother, and he'd be damned if someone else was going to get to the girl to question her before he did.

'No,' Morrell said, his jaw stiff. 'There's nothing you should know, Detective.'

'She cannot leave. We need her help.'

Akhtar's voice was quiet and calm, but determined. Saunders frowned as he studied the young man's face. He agreed that their chances of locating the Cloak seemed far greater if Cianna helped them. She had known both her brother and Nick O'Callaghan better than anyone else. If either of them had ever had possession of the Cloak and had hidden it, she would be the person best able to puzzle out its location. But Saunders had also seen the look in Cianna's eyes, and he understood her need for revenge. It was a powerful human drive, and it fueled so many of the world's conflicts. He knew that if they pushed her too hard, they would lose her to that drive.

'Let me reason with her,' Saunders said. 'I can convince her.'

Akhtar nodded. 'I hope so.'

She was in the bathroom. Earlier she had started to leave the motel room, but Saunders had prevailed upon her to stay. 'Where are you going to go?' he'd asked. 'Are you going to walk the streets blindly, hoping that you will run into him?' She hadn't had an answer to that. 'Maybe we can help each other.'

Her face remained hard. 'You don't care about Charlie,' she said. 'To you this is some sort of geopolitical chess match. I don't see it that way.'

'Maybe,' he'd admitted. 'But at the moment, it seems to me that our interests are aligned, even if our motivations aren't.'

Her eyes had blazed back at him and he could feel her hatred. It wasn't directed at him; it was directed at the entire world. It made her dangerous, and that might make her useful. Her clothes were wet and disheveled, and a single tear cut a track through the dirt and grime on her face from the boathouse. There was a smear of her brother's blood on her neck. 'Clean yourself off,' he'd said. 'Then we can talk.'

Without a word she'd walked past him and into the bathroom. She'd been in there for several minutes.

'She'll stay,' Saunders said to Akhtar. He didn't feel as confident as he sounded, though.

'She must.'

'Or what?' Saunders asked sharply.

Akhtar said nothing for a moment. 'Do you not understand how important this is?' he asked at last. 'Do you understand what is at stake? If Fasil finds the Cloak, Afghanistan could fall. All of the work that my people have done in the last ten years, all the sacrifice will be for nothing.'

'Americans have been dying in your country for a decade, too,' Saunders reminded him.

'Yes, they have,' Akhtar agreed. 'Nearly two thousand. And for every one of them, more than twenty Afghans have died. If Fasil is permitted to take control of the country back for the Taliban, all of that will be for nothing. More than that, the conflict could spread. People throughout the region will believe that democracy is not the way, and that the United States is nothing more than a paper tiger, unwilling to stand by those who stand with you. It cannot be allowed.'

Saunders said nothing. He knew Akhtar was right; he just prayed that Cianna would come to the correct decision on her own.

The door to the bathroom opened a moment later. She stood there, her clothes straightened, her face cleaned, her hair slicked down and parted. Her eyes had turned dark and her face had drawn tight. In so many ways she seemed like a completely different person.

'I'm going after him,' she said.

Saunders took a deep breath. 'So are we. If we work together, we have a better chance of finding him.'

'You don't care about finding him,' she said. 'You care about finding the Cloak.'

He shrugged in admission. 'It's one and the same thing, isn't it? That's what he is after. If we find the Cloak, we'll find him. Either that or he'll find us.'

She looked back and forth between Saunders and Akhtar. 'We're going to kill him, right? This isn't about capturing the man to interrogate him, or just scaring him back into his hole in the mountains?'

'We will kill him, yes,' Akhtar readily agreed.

Saunders nodded slowly.

'Fine,' she said. 'I'm in. On one condition.'

Saunders waited to hear what it was. He suspected he would not like it.

'What is it?' Akhtar asked.

She looked Saunders straight in the eye, fixing him with cold eyes. 'I want to be the one who pulls the trigger.'

CHAPTER THIRTY-NINE

'Is there anyone else your brother trusted?'

Saunders paced as he asked the question. It had been over an hour, and they seemed to be plowing the same ground over and over. Cianna was sitting on the chair, leaning over, her head hanging between her knees. Akhtar sat at the edge of the bed, watching the other two. He'd had little to add since the process had begun.

'No,' Cianna replied, the frustration coming through in her tone. 'We've been through this. There was just me and Nick, no one else.'

'How about your mother?' Saunders asked.

Her head shot up, and she glared at Saunders as though he'd just insulted her. 'No,' she said. It was definitive.

'How can you be sure?'

Saunders could sense the tension as her shoulders drew in close to her ears and her expression hardened. 'He hated my mother,' she said. 'With good reason. She left us and never looked back. Charlie and me were on our own even before she walked away. Plus, she disappeared. Neither one of us had any idea where she was.'

'Maybe he found her,' Saunders suggested.

She shook her head. 'No.'

'How can you be so sure? You were out of contact with

him for two years. Maybe he started looking for her when you went away.'

She put her head down again. 'He wouldn't have done that,' she said. There was an element of defeat in her voice.

Saunders watched her for a moment and then abandoned the line of questioning. It wasn't getting them anywhere. 'Okay,' he said with a sigh. 'What are we missing?'

'I don't think he took it,' Cianna said quietly. 'I think this is all just a huge fucking mistake.'

Saunders shook his head. 'People like Fasil don't travel halfway across the globe unless they're certain. He's taken a huge risk coming here.'

'Did you see Charlie's face just before Fasil killed him?' Cianna asked. 'My brother was a terrible liar. Always was. Before Fasil killed him, he was screaming at him, asking him where the Cloak was. If he'd known where this thing was, he would have said. I saw his eyes, and he was terrified. I don't think he had any idea.'

Saunders considered that for a moment. He'd had the same sense at the time. 'He didn't bring anything else to your apartment with him?'

'Not that I noticed,' Cianna said. 'I assume I would have spotted something as spectacular as an 800-year-old cloak.'

Saunders admitted, 'I'd assume that, too. I was just checking.'

'What does it look like, anyway?' Cianna asked. 'Maybe I missed it. Is it gold? Embroidered? What?'

The question brought Saunders up short for a moment.

'I'm not sure, actually. It's never shown to the public. I suppose I've always assumed it was silk. That would have been the common luxury of the time.' He looked at Akhtar, who was shaking his head.

'Such an American perspective,' he said with a touch of superiority. 'The Cloak is not powerful because of what it is made out of. It is a relic of the Great Prophet. Its power flows from his spirit, not the fabric. Luxury has nothing to do with it.'

'So, what does it look like?' Cianna asked.

'It is homespun,' Akhtar said.

'Homespun?' Cianna said.

'Yes,' Akhtar replied. 'A simple fabric woven by peasants, course and gray, but very practical. This is what Mohammed wore into battle.'

'So it would have just looked like a length of regular cloth,' Saunders said.

'Yes.'

Cianna shook her head. 'Charlie didn't bring anything like that to my apartment,' Cianna said. 'I suppose it could be in his duffle bag. We could go look.'

'No,' Saunders said. 'It's not there.' He was staring off into space as he worked his memory. Something Akhtar had said sparked a recollection. 'Charlie wasn't a student of Islam or of Afghan history, was he?'

'Not that I know of,' Cianna said.

'So if it looks like a simple piece of fabric, Charlie wouldn't have had any reason to take it. Unless he was using it for something else.'

Akhtar frowned. 'I am not following you.'

'I am,' Cianna said. She looked at Saunders, her eyes wide. 'We know where the Cloak is.'

He nodded back at her. 'Yes, we do.'

Morrell ran a finger over the handwritten name next to the buzzer on the first floor of the apartment house in Southie. *C. Phelan.* It was her. He'd been nearly certain when he heard the name, but he needed to be positive. The dead man who was missing a hand at the Cambridge boathouse was the brother of the young woman he'd talked with the day before. She was the same woman his brother had befriended years before. She was the same woman being stalked by the young Middle Eastern man who managed to get himself released from police custody with nothing but a phone call. And that was the morning after someone had taken a Black & Decker to Nick O'Callaghan in a manner strangely reminiscent of the kinds of torture used in dank buildings in Afghanistan.

Even if he'd believed in coincidences, those connections would be too many for Morrell. The girl was involved somehow in all of this. What *this* was and how she was involved were still beyond his comprehension. He intended to find out, however. It was now his singular focus.

He had to pause twice on the climb up to her apartment. His gut was hanging so far over his belt that it almost touched his crotch, and sweat was pouring down his face by the time he reached her door. Standing there, panting, he took a moment to catch his breath before he knocked. There was no answer, so he knocked harder. 'Ms Phelan, it's Detective Morrell, Boston Police Department! Open up!'

There was still no answer, so Morrell put his ear up to the door to listen to the silence from within for a moment. Once he was reasonably sure there was no one moving inside, he slipped a leather case out of his pocket and pulled out a pick. It took him less than thirty seconds to turn the locks and let himself in. If he found anything useful, he'd leave it there and go for a warrant, inventing a pretext for the search. It wouldn't be the first time. Nor would it be the last, unless his heart gave up on the hike back down the stairs – a scenario he was becoming acutely aware was a growing possibility with each inch he added to his waistline.

He cracked the door open. 'Ms Phelan?' he said once more, just in case. 'Police, Ms Phelan.' He stepped into the empty apartment and pulled the door behind him.

CHAPTER FORTY

Police tape was draped around Spudgie's Bar and Grill at the edge of Boston Harbor like toilet paper hanging from a pranked house after Halloween, fluttering carelessly in the breeze. The windows were dark, and the front door, normally lit up in the evenings, was lost in the night shadows of the peaked overhang. Even the streetlight on the corner was out, as though in deference to the aura of death that seemed to have swallowed the place whole.

Jack Saunders leaned against the corner of the building across the street from the bar. He'd been keeping an eye on the place for two hours, making sure that there were no police there. He suspected that there would not be. It was past midnight and Nick O'Callaghan's body had been discovered early in the morning. The crime scene had been picked apart for hours by all manner of specialists. Fingerprints had been collected, blood and tissue samples scraped into plastic evidence tins, and scraps of body parts that had been removed bit by bit, undoubtedly while O'Callaghan was still alive and watching in horror and agony, had been bagged and tagged and loaded into the coroner's truck. They would be kept with the primary remnant of O'Callaghan's body, which had been left on a table like the picked-over remains of a Thanksgiving turkey.

Eventually, though, a decision had been made that all the evidence of possible use had been located, photographed, and removed. Notwithstanding the precision with which television shows and movies portrayed the investigative sciences, the process remained one of trial and error, where guesswork and instinct were as important as DNA samples. Often more so.

Once the decision had been made that nothing else that might provide investigative insight remained, the crime scene had been wrapped in yellow tape and deserted until further notice. All that remained was the ghost of the dead and the echoes of his suffering.

Saunders contemplated O'Callaghan's ordeal as he watched the building. As part of his training, Saunders had been schooled in the brutal art of interrogation – both in how to apply torture and how to resist it. As part of his work in the field, he'd been on both sides of real-life interrogations. He, better than most, had a genuine understanding of what Nick O'Callaghan had endured in the final hours of his life. As a result, his respect for him had grown, and the desire to avenge an honorable man was added to his list of motivations to unravel the mystery of the international conspiracy upon which he'd stumbled.

Once he was satisfied that the bar was deserted, he called Akhtar's cell phone. 'It's clear,' he said.

'Are you sure?'

'As sure as I'm going to be. I'm going in.'

'No,' Akhtar said. 'You must wait. I will meet you there. I must retrieve the Cloak myself.'

'I don't like it,' Saunders said. 'Two of us will slow the process.'

'You must not touch the Cloak,' Akhtar said. 'Its power cannot be underestimated. My family has had the responsibility of guarding it. I alone must handle it.'

'No offense, Akhtar,' Saunders said, 'but the Cloak's power is symbolic, not literal. I don't believe that those who are not pure of purpose who handle the Cloak are doomed.'

'You mean people like Mr Phelan and Mr O'Callaghan?'

'That's different,' Saunders said. 'They weren't killed by a curse; they were killed by a psychopath.'

'The instrument of Allah's will,' Akhtar said. 'Besides, even if you believe the power of the Cloak is symbolic, you must respect that symbolism if you seek to harness its power. I am very nearby. It will take little time.'

Saunders looked at his watch. 'I'll give you five minutes. No more. I don't like the possibility that someone else might figure this out.'

'I will be there.'

The rental car pulled up three minutes later, and parked on the side street around the corner from where Saunders was standing. Akhtar got out of the car on the driver's side. He was carrying an ornate wooden box. Cianna Phelan emerged from the passenger's side. Saunders cursed under his breath.

'No,' he said.

'What?' Cianna responded.

'Three of us are not going in.'

'My brother was murdered for this thing,' Cianna said. 'I'm going in.'

Saunders shook his head. 'You're waiting here. No discussion. Three of us will draw more attention than a carnival.

I don't have time to argue,' Saunders said. 'You're staying here.' He looked at Akhtar. 'What's the box for?'

'The Cloak has been kept in this box for 300 years,' he said. 'I must return it in the box so that the people know that it has been treated with respect.'

Saunders nodded. 'If you say so. Are you ready?'

'I am,' Akhtar said.

'I'm coming with you,' Cianna insisted again.

'Don't make me shoot you,' Saunders retorted. Then to Akhtar, he said, 'Let's go.'

The back door was off an alley that ran from the street toward the water. There was a permanence to the heavy stench of mildew and garbage, and the cracked cement was puddled even though it hadn't rained for days. Saunders moved silently along the brick wall at the back of the bar, slipping through the shadows cast by the dumpsters lined up in the wan moonlight. Akhtar was behind him – every bit as quiet, Saunders noted thankfully – the wooden box cradled under his arm. Cianna Phelan was back at the car, waiting.

As he expected, the door was locked, and another roll of crime-scene tape had been used to cover the door like a giant yellow spider web waiting to trap the unwary. Saunders used a knife to slice through the tape and get to the doorknob, and it took him only a moment to have the door opened. He slit through a few more pieces of the police tape and then slipped through the opening he'd made. Akhtar followed.

The back hallway was pitch black, and Saunders had to feel his way along the wall until he came to the swinging door to the kitchen. He pushed it open just a crack and listened.

Nothing.

He continued moving forward and came to the small room at the back of the place that had been used for private functions. There was no door; just a brick archway topped with cedar beaming. He poked his head through, and the smell of death made him pull back sharply. It took him a moment to chase the thoughts of O'Callaghan's ordeal from his head and keep going.

At last they came to the large open bar space at the front of the building. Here the light from the moon through the windows was enough for them to see shapes and navigate their way to the far side, where the staircase to the second floor stood. Saunders nodded to Akhtar, and made his way over.

Saunders went up first, and he could feel the young man behind him, pressing him on. For the first time, he could hear Akhtar's breathing becoming heavy with excitement, but Saunders kept his pace deliberate, his gun drawn, his ears tuned for any sound.

The office upstairs looked as though it had been ransacked, and for the first time Saunders worried that someone had gotten there before them. After a moment, though, he concluded that the police had clumsily knocked over O'Callaghan's books as they had been looking for clues to the man's gruesome killing. The police had had no idea what they were looking for.

It was there.

He saw it almost immediately, lying casually over the back of the chair behind the desk, exactly where he'd left it a day before. To anyone else it would look like nothing – a spare rag, useful, but insignificant. That was what Charlie Phelan must have thought of it when he used it to conceal the dagger he'd stolen. How was he to know that the length of coarse homespun was far more valuable than any of the bejeweled items in the crate he'd opened on the day before he'd left Afghanistan? To him it had been merely a convenient piece of cloth that could cover the dagger – the true object of his theft.

Saunders moved toward the desk, but Akhtar stepped in front of him. Saunders did nothing to hold him back. He watched as the young man approached the piece of cloth like it was a living thing, moving forward bowed down, his head bent forward, the wooden box held open in front of him, like an offering.

Akhtar reached the desk chair and knelt before the piece of cloth. He bowed his head, averting his eyes as he lifted the Cloak off the back of the chair and slowly, with deft hands and great care, folded it neatly. The box was open on the floor, and Akhtar lifted the Cloak and laid it inside. He closed the box gently, as though afraid of disturbing the Cloak in its newfound comfort, and latched it closed. Then he stood, holding the box in front of him. He looked up at Saunders, and Saunders could see the tears flowing from hard-set eyes, bearing witness to Akhtar's anger and grief at the manner in which the relic had been treated.

Saunders nodded at Akhtar. 'We have to leave.'

Akhtar took a deep breath, and Saunders could see him release some of the hatred. 'Yes,' he said. 'We must leave.'

It was only then that Saunders felt a third presence within the room. Behind them, nearer to the staircase, he felt the waft of another person moving, and the sickly-sweet mixture of stale aftershave and chewing gum.

'Oh, I don't think you boys are going anywhere just yet,' the voice said.

CHAPTER FORTY-ONE

Cianna Phelan was livid. What right did Jack Saunders have to dictate to her where she could go and where she couldn't? He couldn't even manage to get his people to provide support at the boathouse where Charlie had been killed. Come to think of it, she'd never had any definitive proof that he worked for the CIA at all; for all she knew, he was lying to her all along.

And yet, she knew that he wasn't lying. She'd spent enough time around men who knew what they were doing in combat, and those who didn't, to be able to recognize a fake. Saunders wasn't that. He was the real deal.

She'd known an older man like him when she was serving in Afghanistan. They'd been together for nearly a month. Like Saunders, he wasn't much to look at; no one would ever pick him out of a crowd as being attractive. And yet there was something about him that Cianna had been drawn to. Some of it was the way that others had treated him. He was left alone, like a ghost others were afraid to acknowledge because it would come too close to an admission of their own fears. It was as though he was there and not there at the same time. Someone described him as a man for whom the term 'fearless' was inadequate. He operated on principle, outside of the formal system of team warfare, and he relied primarily on his own abilities to stay alive. As he told her in the quiet of one blissful night, he understood that if everything went wrong on one of his missions, no one would acknowledge his existence, and no one would come to try to rescue him.

She still remembered the look in his eyes, the last time she saw him. He was boarding a helicopter that had been stripped of all identifiable markings. She had no idea where he was going. As he stepped up into the copter, he'd turned, and caught her eye. She could see the look he had; a look that said he would sacrifice everything he had and everything he was for those things he truly cared about.

Saunders had that look about him. She'd seen it the first time she really looked in his eyes. She hadn't been able to place what it was about him that seemed so familiar until just now, and it explained, in part, why it was she'd obeyed his order.

Cianna also recognized that Saunders was right. Retrieving the Cloak was a task that required stealth above all else. The mission was made more dangerous with more people. If she had been in combat and been in charge of such a mission, she would have given the same orders Saunders had given. She couldn't deny that.

And yet the notion of accepting anyone's orders, no matter how rational or correct, clawed at her, almost more so because she now recognized the attraction she felt toward him.

She looked at her watch. She'd give them two more minutes. After that, she was going in, whether it made rational sense or not.

*

Saunders turned slowly. He'd seen the police detective before, standing outside Cianna's apartment. He'd watched him through the peephole as Cianna talked to him through the cracked door, shooing him away like a gnat. Saunders thought at the time that it was a dangerous tactic. Men with badges didn't react well to disrespect.

Now this same man was standing at the top of the staircase with the same badge in one hand and a gun in the other. He glanced at Saunders, but most of his focus was on Akhtar, and his face was twisted with rage. Even in the dark, Saunders could see the sweat running down the man's jowly face, soaking his collar. He was breathing heavily, and Saunders wondered how it was possible that he'd allowed a specimen like this to sneak up on him. 'Up against the wall,' he said to them. 'Both of you.' Saunders could see that Akhtar was loath to set the box with the Cloak down. 'Now!' the cop said.

Akhtar carefully set the box down on the ground, then took up a position next to Saunders, both of them with their hands against the wall, legs spread. Still holding his own gun pointed at the two men, he used his other hand to frisk them. He pulled Saunders's gun and knife out of his pocket and put them in his own. He removed Akhtar's gun from him, as well, and stepped back from the two of them. 'Okay, turn around,' he said.

The cop spoke to Akhtar. 'Mohmad, right?' he said. 'Mohmad Hadid? That's what it said on the license you gave me.'

Saunders turned and gave Akhtar a quick glance. He reminded himself that he had no real idea who the young Afghan was. All he knew was what he'd been told. Saunders trusted no one. Even those who saved your life in the field might have reasons for doing so that had nothing to do with a unity of ultimate purpose. In Saunders's world, an ally could turn quickly, and a savior on one day could turn into a killer the next. Akhtar saw the look that Saunders was giving him and shook his head.

'No,' the cop said. 'Not your real name. I figured. I had an idea that you were involved in all of this when I got back to the station house after my brother was pulled apart piece by piece in the back of his bar with a power drill, and you'd been mysteriously released.'

'Nick O'Callaghan,' Saunders said quietly, looking at the cop with new eyes. 'He was your brother?'

The cop turned his anger toward Saunders. 'You knew him?'

'I met him,' Saunders said.

'Did he still have his eyes when you met him?'

Saunders nodded slowly. 'He did. We had nothing to do with his death.'

'No?' The cop's tone was acerbic. 'Nothing? I find that very hard to believe.'

'Why?'

'Because I arrested "Mohmad" yesterday morning outside the house of a girl who used to be friends with Nick. Then I got the call about Nick's murder. When I got back to the station house he had been released. Just like that. No one knew how. No one knew why. All anyone knew is that someone made a call to someone at the top. The word came down without any explanation, and he was gone. Then a day later a body shows up in Cambridge missing a hand. Turns out it's the girl's kid brother.' He shook his head at Saunders. 'You believe the shit they do in this kid's part of the world. Cutting off fuckin' hands? Killing people with power tools? I mean, we've got some sick fucks here, but at least they're not running the country, am I right?'

'Not all of it, at least,' Saunders replied slowly.

The cop looked more closely at Saunders. 'Do I know you?'

Saunders shook his head. 'No.'

'No?' The cop put the badge away and pointed the gun at Saunders's chest. 'That's okay, I guess, 'cause we're gonna get to know each other real well now. I wanna know everything about you two, and everything about what the fuck's going on in all this. You understand?' He was seething, and Saunders looked at Akhtar. Neither of them spoke. The cop pushed the gun hard into Saunders's ribs. 'You say that you two had nothing to do with Nick's death? You better explain that to me, because I got a charitable nature for the most part,' he said. 'But not so charitable that I'm gonna believe that this is all a big coincidence. So somebody better start talking.'

'Are you going to arrest us?' Saunders asked.

The cop pulled the gun out of his ribs and pushed it up under his chin. 'He was my fucking brother!' he screamed in Saunders's ear. 'I'm way past arresting you, you get it?'

'Yeah, I get it,' Saunders said. The cop relented a little and pulled the gun out of his chin. 'It's complicated, though,' Saunders offered.

'Yeah? Well, good thing I got time.'

Akhtar looked expectantly at Saunders. Saunders decided

to start with a version of the truth. 'I can't tell you every-thing,' he said.

'No?' the cop said. 'Why not?'

'It has to do with an issue of national security.'

'National security, huh?' The cop pursed his lips in a mocking way. 'I guess that would explain how your little friend here got his get-out-of-jail-free card.'

'That's right,' Saunders said. 'That's why I can't tell you everything.' He moved ever so slightly forward, testing the waters.

The cop raised his gun at him, motioning him to stay back. 'You got any identification?'

'I don't carry any official identification,' Saunders said. 'I'm a field operative. It wouldn't make much sense for a field operative to carry business cards, now, would it?'

That stumped the fat officer for a moment. After a second, though, he shook his head slowly. 'I don't buy it,' he said. 'You killed my brother for national security? You wanna tell me how he was a threat?'

'I told you, we didn't kill him,' Saunders said. 'Someone else did.'

'Yeah? Who?'

'A man named Fasil.'

'Who's he?'

'He's from Afghanistan.'

'How can I find him?'

'Look for the guy with the teardrop birthmark. Other than that, there's nothing I can tell you.'

'Oh, well, if that's all you can tell me, I guess I'll have to be satisfied with that, right?'

'In this case, that's right,' Saunders said. He could sense

the cop struggling with his conflicting doubts. 'You don't want to know anything more.'

'Oh, but I do.' The cop looked over at the table. 'What's in the box?'

Akhtar looked panicked. 'It's nothing,' Saunders said.

'Nothing?' the cop said doubtfully. 'Your friend was cradling it like it was the baby Jesus. You want me to believe it's nothing?'

'It's nothing that concerns you,' Saunders said.

'If it has anything to do with my brother's murder, then it has everything to do with me.' The cop moved toward the desk, his hand outstretched toward the box that held the Cloak. Saunders realized too late that Akhtar was moving to stop him. The young man crossed the short distance between him and the cop in an instant, grabbing the cop's heavy arm before it touched the box. 'No!' he screamed, yanking the arm back as he tried to tackle the huge man. 'You mustn't!'

It was pointless, Saunders knew. The man, though fat, was enormous, and powerfully built. With the first swing of his arm, Akhtar flopped off him onto the floor. With the second swing, the gun cracked across Akhtar's face and sent him sprawling into the corner of the room. The cop swung and pointed his gun at Saunders to make sure he wasn't joining the fray. Saunders raised his hands to show that he wasn't moving. Lying against the wall, Akhtar raised a hand to his stunned head.

'Either one of you moves again, and I swear to Christ, I'll kill you both!' the cop yelled at them. 'You understand?'

Saunders nodded.

The cop turned his attention back to the box. 'What's in it?' he asked.

'It's nothing, I told you. It's a piece of old cloth.'

The cop shook his head doubtfully. He reached out and unlatched the lid of the box.

'No!' Akhtar yelled from the floor. 'Don't touch it!' he demanded, though he didn't move.

The cop opened the box and leaned over it to peer in. He looked at Saunders in confusion. 'I don't get it,' he said.

'That's the point,' Saunders said. The cop looked at him for a moment, the confusion deepening.

'Please,' Akhtar said, quietly this time. 'Don't touch it.'

The cop looked back and forth between the two men, then shook his head and closed the box, re-latching the top. 'This whole thing is too fucked up.'

'It is,' Saunders agreed. 'That's why you have to let us go.'

The cop looked at him and gave a short, bitter laugh. 'Just like that?' he asked. 'My brother's guts are drilled out, and you want me to just let you go?'

Saunders nodded.

The cop shook his head. 'Not gonna happen. If you are who you say you are, we'll get it all straightened out at the station house. If not . . .' he shrugged, 'I guess we'll get that figured out, too.'

Saunders shook his head. 'You take us to the station house, and there will be too many problems. None of this can become public.'

'That's too bad,' the cop said. 'Because that's what's going to have to happen here.' He looked at Akhtar. 'You can pick up the box,' he said.

Akhtar got to his feet and grasped the box in both hands. 'Are you going to arrest us, officer?' Akhtar asked. He was still holding the box out in front of him.

The cop shrugged. 'Maybe not,' he said. 'Maybe I got me a Black & Decker downstairs.'

No one said anything for a moment. Then the cop stepped aside, and pointed toward the staircase with his gun. 'You two first,' he said.

Akhtar looked at Saunders. Saunders nodded. 'I'll go after you,' he said.

Akhtar looked ashen as he started down the stairs with Saunders and the cop following close behind. Saunders could hear the wooden staircase groan as the cop shifted his weight from step to step. The man was still breathing heavily, wheezing and huffing with each step. Saunders looked around the bar as they came down, searching for anything that might give him an advantage if he chose to jump the cop and try to disarm him, but nothing presented itself.

At the bottom of the staircase, Akhtar turned to the right to head down the hallway toward the front of the bar. As Saunders passed the door off the hallway leading to the kitchen, he thought he saw movement in the little circular window. He kept walking and looked over his shoulder at the cop. 'Is your car out there on the street?' he asked, nodding to the door.

The cop was just passing the door to the kitchen. 'Yeah, why?'

''Cause it looks like someone's trying to steal it.'

Saunders's body was blocking the detective's line of vision to the street, so the cop had to lean his body forward and

round Saunders to see his car through the window. 'What
he fuck are you talking about?' he demanded.

Just at that moment, the kitchen door swung open.
aunders glanced back and ducked as he saw something
irge and black and heavy taking a wide arc near his head.
moment later he heard the sound of iron colliding with
one and looked over his shoulder to watch the cop fall
the ground. Looking up, he saw Cianna Phelan standing
ver him with a large frying pan in her hand. The cop
roaned once and rolled over, unconscious.

Saunders moved over to him and felt for a pulse. It
asn't easy through all the fat on the man's neck, but after
moment he satisfied himself that the man was alive.
esus, you could have killed him,' he said.

'You think I should have shot him, instead?' she replied.

'Fair point,' he admitted. Then he frowned. 'I told you
o stay out on the street.'

'You did,' she agreed. 'And if I was still there, you'd be
n the way to the police station.'

'I would have found a way out of this,' he said seri-
usly.

'Right,' she said. 'I could see you were about to make
our move.'

'I'm just saying—' he started.

'Just say thank you,' she said. She looked over at Akhtar
nd the box in his hands. 'Is that it?' she asked.

'Yes,' he said. 'This is the sacred Cloak of Mohammed.'

'Great,' she said. She looked at Saunders. 'Now what?'

CHAPTER FORTY-TWO

It took all three of them to drag Morrell's enormous boc
into the kitchen. Cianna, who was familiar with whe
Nick O'Callaghan kept things from the years she'd spe
helping in the bar, found a roll of duct tape, and Saunde
bound the cop's hands and feet to a table. The huge ma
regained consciousness just as Saunders was getting read
to put duct tape over his mouth.

'What are you doing?' the cop mumbled in a disor
ented haze.

'We're leaving you here,' Saunders said. 'You'll be fin
We'll call your buddies in a few hours to come get you

The cop looked around and saw Cianna. 'You . .
he said.

'I'm sorry about Nick,' she said to him. 'He was th
closest thing I ever had to a father.'

'He was the closest thing I had to a brother,' the co
garbled. He squinted up at Saunders. 'You didn't kill hin
then?'

'If I'd killed him, would I leave you alive?' Saunde
put the tape over the man's mouth. He nodded to the bo
containing the Cloak. 'That is going to lead us to the ma
who killed your brother. Either that, or it will lead hir
to us. Believe me,' he said, 'if there is any way we car

296

we will kill him for you.' He nodded to the others and they left the cop in the kitchen and headed out to the bar.

'What kind of resources do you have?' Saunders asked Akhtar. 'We have to find a place to stay, and a way to get you out of the country and back to Afghanistan. It's only a matter of time before Fasil retraces his steps and figures some of this out.'

'What do you mean, what kind of resources do *I* have?' You have the American government behind you.'

'I wouldn't say the *entire* government is behind me on this,' Saunders admitted.

Cianna gave him a sharp look. 'How much of it would you say is behind you?'

'A small bit of it.' She continued to stare at him. 'One man,' he said. 'But he's very highly placed, and he has resources. He just may not be able to move quickly.' Saunders looked at Akhtar. 'How about it? What kind of help can you get us?'

Akhtar frowned. 'I have only a phone number where I can leave a coded message, and I am sent a contact, but it takes time.'

'How long?'

'To get me out of a Boston jail, a few hours; to get me out of the country,' Akhtar shrugged. 'Who knows?'

Saunders thought about this for a moment. 'You have no idea who your contact is?'

Akhtar shook his head. 'I assume he is CIA. That is all.'

'Do you know what he looks like?'

'I met him once, in Afghanistan, but he was wearing robes and a headscarf, so I only saw part of his face.'

'Was he tall, with a thin face and receding hair?'

Akhtar shrugged. 'As I say, I saw only a part of his face, and to me your white faces all look similar, but yes, that is generally what I remember.'

Cianna said, 'What are you thinking?'

Saunders shook his head. 'Nothing.' He walked out of the kitchen and the other two followed him. The moon was high in the evening sky now, and it cast a broad light on the street. 'We need to get out of here, that's the first issue. This place draws too much attention.' He looked at Akhtar. 'Go get your car. Pull it behind into the alley by the back door, and we can leave here.'

'To go where?' Cianna asked.

'We can figure that out once we're on the road. The most important thing is to keep moving right now.'

Akhtar nodded and started out toward the back door. He was still holding the box in his hands. 'Akhtar,' Saunders said. Akhtar turned to look at him. 'Leave the Cloak.'

Akhtar looked down at the box, and Saunders could see the dread in his eyes at the notion of giving up possession of it. 'Why?' he asked.

'Because,' Saunders said, 'I don't want you out on the street alone with it.'

Akhtar stared hard at Saunders.

'You're going to have to decide at some point whether or not you really trust us,' Saunders said. 'It's that simple.'

Akhtar nodded and set the box down on a table, turned and headed out back to the alley so he could slip out and bring his car around. Saunders and Cianna watched him go. When the door closed behind him, she turned to Saunders and said, 'You wanted him to leave.'

He nodded. 'I did.'

'Why?'

'I have a suspicion, but I couldn't do anything to confirm it in front of him.' He pulled out his cell phone and dialed. He considered asking Cianna to go into another room, but decided that she would not be able to decipher anything he was saying in a way that could cause any problems.

The phone rang twice before it was answered. 'Lawrence Ainsworth's office,' Agnes Shoals's melodious voice sang out.

He took a deep breath. 'Agnes, it's Jack,' he said. It felt as though the phone line had frozen. 'I need to talk to him.'

She cleared her throat over the line. 'Jack,' she said. 'You've been suspended. I can't let you—'

'Cut the shit, Agnes, I know he trusts you. You know he's still in contact with me. I need to talk to him. Now.'

'I have no idea what you are talking about,' she said icily.

'Agnes, it's vital. I wouldn't call the office otherwise. Please put me through to him.'

There was a pause, and then the line clicked over. For a moment he thought she'd hung up on him, but then there was another noise on the line, and Ainsworth picked up the phone. His voice was tense. 'You shouldn't call my office,' he said. 'You know that.'

'I had no choice, Lawrence,' Saunders said. 'We're in a tight spot.'

'We?'

'Yes, we,' Saunders said. 'I am still with the girl. I'm also with a young man. His first name is Akhtar. Do you know his last name?' Saunders was making a guess, but it was an educated one. There was silence on the other end of the line for a moment.

'Hazara,' Ainsworth said at last.

'You win the blue ribbon,' Saunders said. 'You always were the wily one.' He smiled to himself. As soon as Akhtar had said that he was working with someone in the government, he'd suspected it was Ainsworth, who always seemed to have all the angles covered. 'We need your help, Lawrence,' he said. 'We're at Spudgie's Bar and Grill in Southie. We need transportation and protection. How soon can you—?' Saunders didn't get another word out as Ainsworth cut him off.

'Don't say anything else,' he said. 'You need to get out of there, and get out of there now.'

'I don't understand,' Saunders said.

'Then I didn't train you well enough,' Ainsworth replied. 'You called my office. I'll figure out a way to help you if I can, but you need to get moving without another word. Don't call me here.' The line went dead.

Saunders turned his phone off and put it in his pocket. 'What happened?' Cianna asked.

He didn't look at her as he cursed his stupidity. 'Someone was listening,' he said. 'We need to get moving.'

Bill Toney was pacing in his office when the call came from the communications room. He'd given explicit instructions that he be contacted at once. The voice on the other end of the phone was excited. 'He's made contact with Ainsworth,' it said.

'When?'

'Just now.'

'What was said?'

'Very little that we can use. Only that they have the
loak, and that they are at someplace called Spudgie's Bar
d Grill in South Boston. Does that mean anything to
ou?'

Toney controlled his breathing. 'Thank you, Lieutenant.
hat's of more assistance than you know.'

'Yes, sir. Do you want us to consider monitoring the
ne?'

'Yes, Lieutenant. Now it is more important than ever.'

Toney hung up. He considered his options for a moment.
nce his decision was made, he picked up the phone and
ialed the number.

CHAPTER FORTY-THREE

Cianna could see Akhtar pulling into the alley behind t[...]
bar as she and Saunders exited through the back do[...]
They were hurrying, and he barely managed to get t[...]
vehicle stopped before they'd opened the doors and pil[...]
in. Cianna was in the front seat, and Saunders, holdi[...]
the box with the Cloak, was in the back seat. Glanci[...]
over his shoulder, Akhtar winced when Saunders put t[...]
box roughly on the seat beside him.

'What's going on?' Akhtar asked.

'Drive,' Saunders ordered.

Akhtar threw the car into reverse and started to ba[...]
out of the alley. It was a narrow lane with dumpsters lin[...]
on one side, running the length of the block. Spudgi[...]
was on the water-side, and the alley opened there on[...]
Columbia Avenue, but a stack of crates and an old rust[...]
fence blocked the alley's exit at that end, so Akhtar h[...]
to back all the way out.

'Faster,' Saunders said. His voice was calm on the su[...]
face, but insistent enough to convey the urgency of t[...]
situation.

'What happened?' Akhtar asked again.

'Hopefully nothing,' Saunders replied.

As they neared the street, though, another car pull[...]

up at the end of the alley and screeched to a halt, blocking their way. Fasil, Sirus Stillwell and the Afghan bodyguard jumped out and started toward them. They all had military-issue machine pistols drawn, and both Sirus and Fasil leveled them at the back of Akhtar's car and squeezed off shots. The pistols fired ten rounds per second, and both volleys struck the back window, which exploded. Saunders ducked down and hoped that the metal in the car's body would be sufficient to stop the shells. Akhtar hit the brake, and the car skidded to a stop fifteen yards from the three men.

'Drive!' Saunders shouted, slamming his fist against the back of the front seat. 'Forward!'

Akhtar put the car in gear and stepped on the gas. The car lurched ahead with a squeal just as another round of gunfire slammed into its rear, knocking the bumper off and causing the back of the car to skid into the building to the left. Akhtar ducked down to avoid being shot. The car lurched back to the right and slammed into a dumpster. Fortunately the giant steel container caromed off the building and spun out into the alley, providing a partial shield from the next volley of gunshots. One ricocheted off the dumpster and smashed the window next to Cianna's head.

'Fuck this!' she said, as she pulled out her pistol, spun on the front seat, and took aim out the shattered back window. She squeezed off three quick shots and saw all three of the men in the alley dive out of the way. It would buy them a moment, but not much more. Fasil was yelling to the other two, and he and Sirus ran back to the car. They got in and spun it around so that it was headed into the alley. The third man stood back up and continued firing, stopping only when the car pulled alongside him to let him in.

'They're coming this way!' Cianna shouted. She fired two more shots, leaving her with only one more.

'Keep going!' Saunders shouted to Akhtar.

'There is nowhere to go!' Akhtar shouted back.

Cianna and Saunders looked up to see the crates and fence at the end of the alley coming up fast. Akhtar seemed to hesitate just for a moment, and Cianna sensed the indecision. She turned back around in the passenger seat and swung her left leg over so that she was straddling the center console. She stepped down hard on Akhtar's foot, pushing the accelerator down to the floor. The car lurched forward as Akhtar screamed, his fingers digging into the steering wheel, trying to keep the car under control.

'Duck!' Cianna shouted.

The car hit the crates first, and they were all relieved when they realized they were empty. The wood shattered, and splinters flew across the car and into the alley behind them.

The fence, however, was more solid. Notwithstanding its wretched appearance, it was well-constructed, and the car jolted as it hit. Cianna saw the hood buckle near the right headlight. For a moment she thought they were not going to make it through, but after the initial impact, the gate snapped and the metal pole that held the fence in the ground broke off. The car burst through and onto Columbia Avenue, a quiet two-lane street that followed the contours of the harbor's shore, separated from it only by Day Boulevard, a larger four-lane thoroughfare directly on the shore, and a greenway of grass and trees that ran between the two roads.

Cianna was thrown back into the passenger seat, and her foot came off the accelerator. Akhtar strained to keep control of the steering wheel as the car bounced and jostled on Columbia, but managed to turn the wheels sufficiently to keep the car from slamming into a tree. Cianna's relief at the near miss was short-lived, though, as she heard the car behind them burst through what was left of the fence and crates.

'They're still on our tail!' Saunders yelled, as he leaned over the back of the rear seat and squeezed off several rounds. Cianna saw the car behind them swerve, but it, too, stayed on the road.

'Faster!' she hollered at Akhtar. He hit the gas again, and the car gathered speed. Cianna looked behind them and saw that the other car was gaining, nevertheless. 'Can't this thing go any faster?' she demanded.

'Not with that on it,' Akhtar responded, nodding toward the front of the vehicle.

Cianna looked out the front windshield and understood instantly. The pole that had held the fence in place had sliced through the front bumper and become lodged in the grill. She could hear it dragging on the street as the car struggled against it. 'Can you get it off?' she asked.

Akhtar had no time to respond before the pursuing car slammed into the back of the rental, snapping her head back. She heard Saunders fire off two more rounds, and then recognized the sound of automatic gunfire. She ducked her head down and grabbed the wheel, yanking it to the right.

The front wheels collided with the curb and the car jumped onto the greenway, mowing down carefully land-scaped shrubs as it cut over toward the more heavily traf-ficked boulevard. Horns blared as the car skidded into two oncoming headlights before quickly finding the right side of the road. Cianna looked over and saw the other car weaving through an intersection to get over onto the highway after them. There was a loud popping sound, and Cianna looked at the hood to see the pole come free and disappear beneath the speeding car.

'That should be better,' she said.

'Not much,' Akhtar said, nodding at the hood. The pole was gone, but now there was steam coming out of the front of the car where it had been only a moment before. 'We will not outrun them with that,' Akhtar said. He looked at her, then in the rear-view mirror at Saunders. His expression was one of defeat. 'They cannot be allowed to have the Cloak,' he said. 'That is of the greatest impor-tance.'

'I agree,' she said. 'If you have any suggestions, we're all ears.' As she said this, the other car swerved into the lane behind them and accelerated into them. Akhtar main-tained control.

'You two must get out,' he said after a moment, his face serious.

'As tempting as that is,' Cianna said, 'I don't think it's going to happen. This car's not going that slow.'

'We're not leaving the Cloak,' Saunders shouted from the back seat just before firing two more shots.

'No, I agree,' Akhtar said. 'You are taking it with you.'

Cianna looked at him in disbelief. 'What are you talking about?' she demanded.

'You said it yourself, Mr Saunders,' Akhtar said. 'I must choose whether or not I will trust you. I have decided that I will.'

'I'm not sure that will help us at this point,' Saunders said, 'but it's a nice gesture.'

They were approaching an intersection, and Akhtar spun the wheel hard to his left. The car cut through the intersection, leaving a long thick trail of rubber as the tires screamed. He held onto the wheel and guided the car back onto Columbia, headed in the other direction. Cianna could see that the other car was still following them, but it had lost ground.

'I will find a way,' Akhtar said. 'A moment is all it will take. Just long enough to slow down in a place where they cannot see you. You two jump out and take the Cloak with you. I will drive on, and they will follow me.' Cianna turned back to him, still incredulous. 'It is the only way the Cloak will be safe.'

Cianna looked behind her at Saunders. He nodded. 'It's the best chance we have to keep the Cloak out of their hands,' he admitted.

'There is a place up ahead,' Akhtar said, 'where there are thick trees and bushes between the two roads. I will cross onto the grass just before that. We should have enough space that they will not be able to see us for several seconds. That is when you must jump. I will slow down as much as I can, and then try to outrun them.'

'You'll never outrun them with the car in this condition,' Cianna said.

He nodded. 'I will give you as much time as I can, but it will not be long. You must get out of here quickly. They will come back when they realize you are no longer in the car.'

'What will you do when they catch you?' Cianna asked.

Neither Saunders nor Akhtar said anything for a moment. 'I took the policeman's gun,' Akhtar said after a while. 'I will use that.'

'They have machine pistols, and there are three of them,' Cianna said. 'You have a much better chance of surviving this if we stick together.'

'But the chances of protecting the Cloak are better if we split up,' he said. 'I have known my whole life that I have one task in this world, and one alone. That is to protect the Cloak. It has been the great honor of my family for three hundred years. If I am martyred for that cause, I will die a happy man.'

'No martyr really dies happy,' Cianna insisted. 'It's a myth.'

He smiled bravely at her. 'You have not heard the descriptions of the afterlife for martyrs in my religion?'

'You don't really believe all that, do you?'

His smile disappeared. 'I believe that my country will be better off if Fasil is prevented from returning with the Cloak. My country will not survive another reign of the Taliban. You must jump when I tell you to?'

Cianna looked back again at Saunders. 'We have to,' he said. He turned back around to spot Sirus's car. It was gaining ground again. Saunders took aim and fired off a shot, and the pursuing car shimmied as one of its headlights exploded. It kept coming, though.

'The trees are coming up here!' Akhtar advised them. 'Get the Cloak and be ready.'

Saunders picked up the sturdy box and held it under one arm. Both he and Cianna put their hands on the door handles. The car hopped and shook violently as Akhtar guided it over the median curb once again, and it slowed naturally on the soft grass. Akhtar spun the wheel so that the car followed the tree-line on the Day Boulevard side of the divider, and the lights from Sirus's car disappeared behind the tree. The car was in a skid as it made the turn, slowing it even more, and Akhtar had only to tap on the brakes to get their speed under twenty miles an hour. 'Now!' he shouted.

Cianna opened the passenger side door and dove out of the car, careful to keep her knees and elbows bent in a classic paratrooper's landing position. Even at under twenty miles an hour, the ground came rushing up at her, and her limbs readied for impact. As soon as she felt herself hit, she allowed her body to roll with its momentum, not trying to stop it, but letting the energy of the fall spend itself as she tumbled toward the trees. As soon as she felt the momentum abating, she dug her knees in to stop the roll.

She looked around and spotted Saunders just a few feet off. He still had the box under his arm, and had managed to protect it through his fall. 'Quick!' he called to her.

They both scrambled toward the trees and threw themselves under the surrounding shrubs. Just at that moment, Sirus's car roared by, directly in Akhtar's tire tracks. The right fender passed within a few feet of Cianna's face concealed under the bushes, and for a moment she had a terrible feeling that they had not moved fast enough. If anyone in the car had seen them dive from the car, they would surely stop and the final battle would be waged here by the highway. She looked around and considered their defensive options if that were to come to pass. It was unnecessary, however. Sirus's car kept moving, and picked up speed as it came out of its turn.

Cianna waited for a few seconds before getting to her feet. She looked around the trees and saw the chase continuing, and even from her distance it was clear that it wouldn't last long.

'He's not going to make it,' she said quietly.

'No, he's not,' Saunders agreed.

'They'll kill him.'

The cars disappeared around the curve of the road. A moment later the sound of metal tearing on concrete ripped through the air. There was yelling and gunfire, and an explosion rocked the waterfront. Just over the trees, they could see the orange-yellow fireball rise into the sky. There was more shouting and gunfire.

Cianna took a step toward the mayhem. 'We need to help him.'

Saunders shook his head. 'No one can help him now.'

'You're just going to let him die?'

Saunders had no response. 'We need to find someplace safe.'

Now it was her turn to say nothing.

'Cianna!' he said. She looked at him. 'Unless we want his sacrifice to be in vain, we need to get off the street. Is there anyplace we can go? Anyplace they wouldn't know about or wouldn't think of?'

She thought about it for a moment. 'Yeah,' she said. 'There is one person left in the world I can call. He'll help me.'

CHAPTER FORTY-FOUR

The James J. Curley Community Center stood like a gargantuan balustrade along the shoreline on Day Boulevard. Built by Boston's legendary four-term mayor during the height of the depression, at a cost of over $400,000, it was a monument to the power of persistence. Curley was first elected to public office as an alderman while he was serving a prison term for fraud, and spent over a year of his final term in prison for influence-peddling, before President Truman issued a full presidential pardon and returned him to office. The community center that bears his name and shelters the beach along the Old Harbor in Southie now offers yoga, Pilates, and classes on first-time home ownership.

That night, it also offered brief shelter for Cianna and Saunders. They stood in the shadows of its broad columns as Cianna made a phone call. She knew the number by heart, and she knew what emotional buttons to push to achieve the desired result. Appeals for assistance were particularly persuasive to some people, and none more than Milo Pratt. She might even have felt guilty about her manipulation if it hadn't been for the fact that she did, in fact, need help. Desperately.

Seven minutes after she clicked off her cell phone, the

dented Nissan Sentra pulled up in front of the community center. Cianna and Saunders hurried from their cover and slid into the car, Cianna in front and Saunders in back once again. She turned as soon as she was in the car and gave the driver a tense smile. 'Thanks, Milo,' she said. 'You're a lifesaver. Literally.'

His concern showed on his face. 'Is everything okay?'

'No,' she replied. 'It's not.'

'What's going on?'

'I can't tell you. I know that's a shitty thing to say when you came out to help us, but believe me, you don't want to know anyway, okay? Can you trust me on this?'

He looked skeptical, but he didn't argue. 'What do you need?' he asked simply. That was why she had called him. She knew that, when pushed, he would ask no questions. That was his strength and his weakness. Milo Pratt believed implicitly in the goodness of others, particularly those for whom he felt some responsibility. Notwithstanding the deceit he witnessed every day, he remained trusting. She supposed it was the one thing that kept him going in his work.

'We need a place to stay.' As she said the word *we*, she could see Milo glance in his rear-view mirror at Saunders. 'This is—'

Saunders cut her off. 'Just call me John,' he said. She turned to look at him. 'It's easier that way,' he said simply.

'Okay, this is John,' she said to Milo. 'We need to get out of sight for a little while. Can we use your apartment?'

'Of course,' he said. He paused a beat, and said, 'Just let me get this straight: you need a place to take your John for the night? Do I have that right?' She shot him a look, and he gave her an impish smile that almost made it look as though he had a chin. 'Are you moonlighting? If you need cash, I could have loaned you money.'

'Shut up, and drive,' she said.

'I'm just saying . . .'

She rolled her eyes and looked out the window as the shoreline ran past them. Inside, though, she was grateful to him. It was the closest to a smile she'd managed in two days.

Milo drove them to his apartment on H Street, up the hill, away from the water, toward Boston. The houses were packed tight on narrow streets in this section of town, and that made Saunders nervous. He would have preferred to be away from people. And yet he knew that hiding in plain sight was often the best strategy at times like this.

Milo's apartment was a second-story one-bedroom with an efficiency kitchen. He kept it neat, and it was comfortable for its size. Saunders catalogued six other units in the house, taking note of where their entrances were.

'Can I get you anything?' Milo asked them, playing the perfect host. 'I have water and OJ. Or I can whip up some tea?'

'You have any Scotch?' Saunders asked as he parted the shades on the bow window that hung over the street. It was quiet out there, and he pulled the shades.

'Milo doesn't drink,' Cianna replied for the host, a little defensively.

'No, Milo doesn't,' Milo said. 'But Milo has friends who sometimes forget that.' He dug into a cabinet under the sink and produced a liter bottle of Jack Daniel's Sour

Mash. 'A gift from one such forgetful friend,' Milo said and he showed off the bottle. 'I meant to get rid of it, but haven't gotten around to it.'

Saunders crossed to the kitchenette and opened the cabinet above the sink to get a glass.

'Right on the first guess,' Milo commented.

'Not too many places to keep glasses,' Saunders said. He pulled out two and put them on the table. The seal wasn't cracked on the bottle, and he opened it and poured some into both glasses.

'Does it bother you to have booze in the house?' Cianna asked Milo. She knew more about his past than she let on.

'No,' he said. 'It bothers me to have useless clutter in the apartment. By all means, have at it. Just get rid of the bottle when you're done, okay?'

'No problem.' She looked at Milo, and Saunders could tell she was waiting for him to leave. Saunders took his gun out of his pocket and laid it on the table next to the glass, picked up the glass and took a sip. He could see Milo's eyes go wide at the gun.

'Do you have someplace you can go?' Cianna asked.

Milo gave a dismissive wave. 'Of course,' he said. 'I'm a resourceful guy.'

'It's better for you if you're not here,' Cianna explained.

'So I can see,' he said. 'Someday you'll have to tell me what this is all about.'

'Probably not.'

'Right. Let me just get my things.' He disappeared into the bedroom for a moment, came out with a jacket. 'It's supposed to be cold tomorrow,' he said. He walked to the

315

door and turned back to them. She went over and gave him a hug.

'Thanks so much,' she said.

'Like I said, no problem. Will you be back at work tomorrow?'

She looked at Saunders and he took another sip of the Jack. 'Not likely,' she said.

'Ever?' Milo asked. His voice sounded small.

'Keep a good thought,' was all she would say.

He hugged her again, more tightly this time. 'I need you around to help with the kids,' he said to her. 'You know that, right?'

'You did what you do before I started working with you,' she replied, touching his face.

He shook his head. 'Not very well. Now we're actually making a difference. I need you to come back. The kids need you.'

She nodded and leaned in and kissed his cheek. 'We'll see. But you'll be fine either way. You have more strength than you know.'

'And less than you think.' Saunders thought Milo was going to cry, but he didn't. He sucked it up and turned the doorknob. Over his shoulder, he said, 'John, it was nothing but a pleasure meeting you. Take care of her, okay?'

Then he was gone.

CHAPTER FORTY-FIVE

'He likes you,' Saunders said.

'He does,' she agreed. 'Not in that way, though,' she added. She was walking around the apartment, looking at the pictures on the walls. They were all generic prints of boats and seascapes. 'He's gay.'

'Is he?'

'Do you have a problem with gays?' she asked. There was the hint of an accusation in her tone.

He shook his head. 'Gays serve in the military. I have no problem with anyone who serves in the military.' He slid the second glass of Jack over to her, tipped his own up in toast. 'Hooah,' he said.

She picked up the glass and raised it. 'Hooah,' she replied. She picked the glass up and took a long pull. It felt good, and for the first time that day she felt the exhaustion creep up on her. 'What's the plan now?'

'We wait,' Saunders said. 'My boss has my cell number. He's been helping Akhtar all along, so he must have had a plan to get the Cloak out of the country from the start. He'll get things organized and contact us soon.'

'How will he feel about Akhtar's death?' she asked. 'About the fact that we didn't do more to save him?'

Saunders shook his head slowly, took another sip, and poured some more. 'He was an asset. Nothing more.'

'*An asset . . . nothing more,*' she repeated quietly.

He shrugged. 'It's one of the first things you learn on the job. Never get attached to an asset. Eventually they all get burned. That's the nature of the business.'

'And me?' she said. He looked up sharply at her. 'I'm just an asset, too, right? You used me to find my brother. To find the Cloak. I'm *an asset . . . nothing more.*'

He looked at her silently as he took another sip of the bourbon. 'You're an asset,' he agreed. She was glad he didn't lie to her. She would have lost respect for him if he'd done that. 'But you have skills. You'd make a good agent.'

She shook her head. 'No, I wouldn't.'

Neither of them said anything for a little while. They both just sat there at the table, waiting. 'Where will he go?' Saunders asked finally. She looked at him, an eyebrow raised. 'Milo,' he explained his question. 'Where will he go?'

She understood. 'He has another apartment,' she said.

'Another apartment?'

She nodded. 'He doesn't know I know about it. It's over in the South End in Boston. Nice place. I followed him when I'd just started working with him. I wanted to know a little bit about him, figure out who I was dealing with. There seemed something off about him; like there was something he was hiding. Turned out he's been hiding something for most of his life. I'm not sure he's come to grips with it yet, so he keeps that part of his life separate. I think that's why he's so dedicated to the kids he helps.

318

's like it's some kind of penance for what he still, deep own, thinks of as his sins.' She took another drink. 'He's good person.'

Saunders gave a skeptical smile. 'There's no such thing,' e said.

She looked at him. 'You believe that?'

The smile faded. 'Maybe not. Maybe I just don't know hat it means. *A good person.* If you do bad things, but ou have a good motive for doing them, where do ou fall?'

'Is that how you see yourself?'

He shook his head. 'I don't see myself.'

'Must be nice.'

'It is,' he agreed. 'It makes things easier. How about you?'

'How about me?'

'Who is the real Cianna Phelan? Soldier . . .? War hero . .? Guardian of wayward children . . .?' he paused, atching her. 'Murderer . . .?'

She could feel her face fall with his last pronounce- ment. She poured some more bourbon, picked up her lass and stepped away from the table. She couldn't bring erself to look at him. 'You read my record,' she said. 'Of ourse. You were looking for Charlie, you would have. So ou think you know me.'

'I know your file. I also know that files contain only he information others put into them.' He walked over to er. The apartment was small enough that it was difficult ot to stand close. 'I've read about the medals and the issions, and the remarkable things you've done in the ervice of your country. I've read the accounts of you illing a man in cold blood. I know what it is that you

do now, and I've seen what you're capable of when t
shit hits the fan. None of it fits. None of it makes sen.
So, no, I don't think for a second that I have any id
who the hell you really are. You remain a mystery, if i
any consolation.'

'Very little,' she said. 'What would solve the myste
for you?'

'I want to hear it from you. In your words.'

'What happened over there? You want me to tell you

'If you want to.'

'And you think that will matter?'

'I don't think anything really matters.'

She turned and looked up at him. She hadn't been th
close to anyone without a fight in two years. 'Yes, you d
You know that some things do matter.'

*In early August the heat in Kandahar was at its peak. Outsi
the madrasa the temperature was pushing 110 degrees, a
it wasn't noon yet. Sergeant Cianna Phelan squinted up in
the punishing Asian sun and wondered how hot it might g
One-twenty at least was her guess. Under the full uniform
including the Kevlar vest and helmet – a body could be ov
come in this kind of heat without any warning.*

*She was there with an elite Delta Force unit that speci
ized in anti-terrorism tactics. Radicals were recruiting m
and more women to carry out terror attacks, and in order
combat this phenomenon, the Army recognized that De
Force needed women in anti-terror roles. Afghan society u
still so segregated that men alone could not adequately inv
tigate, search and identify those women who might be prepari
an attack.*

Few were surprised when Cianna was one of three women chosen for the training. She was the most decorated woman serving in Afghanistan, with a silver star, two bronze stars, and two purple hearts; she'd already seen more active combat than most of her male counterparts. Even for all that, there was some concern that those within the Delta Force unit would only see the tits under the medals. She'd found acceptance, though, and the training was beyond anything that any women had undergone in the US military to date.

On August 11, her unit had been called up to support the local military police to make sure that a series of demonstrations and counter-demonstrations did not get out of control. 'Control' was a difficult concept to define in a place like Kandahar, where most men carried weapons, and the area just outside the city was rife with poppy fields fought over by the Taliban, the territorial militias and the Federal Government forces. Often the best the US military could do was limit chaos, rather than exert control.

The demonstrations that day were likely to get ugly. Five days before, a young Shia woman had refused her husband's sexual demands in violation of a Federal Law. The woman, who was pregnant and sick when she'd dared to rebuff her husband, was dragged to the center of the local square in her village outside the city. There she had been tied to a boulder and whipped mercilessly as a warning to other women in the village. When she was finally released, she had to be taken to the hospital, where it was discovered that she had miscarried. That news had driven her husband to beat her again, right in the hospital. It was no longer clear that she would survive.

News of the attack had spread throughout the nation. The

Karzai government was under intense pressure from the UN and its allies to take the law off the books, but he needed the support of the Shia Mullahs in the upcoming election, so he was walking a middle line, promising to review the law without making any commitments about taking it off the books. Others within the country, though, were not being as passive.

The demonstration in Kandahar that day had been organized by the Revolutionary Association of the Women of Afghanistan – RAWA – an independent group that had been struggling for women's rights for more than three decades. Many of the organization's leaders had been executed in front of the crowds at local football stadiums during the Taliban rule, but the organization was gaining strength again. There were expected to be as many as seventy young women joining the protest that day, walking three blocks, from the madrasa run by an influential Shia cleric to the city center. It would be the first protest for women's rights in the city of Kandahar since 1973.

The demonstration wasn't the danger, as far as the police and Delta Force were concerned. The danger would come from the counter-demonstrations. The challenge to the law recognizing male supremacy within the household was viewed by many in the community as an attack on the Muslim faith as a whole. Worse, it was viewed as an attack organized by foreign interests. They were expecting as many as a thousand counter-demonstrators to confront the women marching. Those numbers made physical confrontation a virtual inevitability, and the Delta Force anti-terrorism unit, thirty-strong including the three women, was sent in to support two hundred Afghan police officers in trying to prevent a massacre.

The protest began as expected. A bus pulled up in front of the madrasa at 11.30 a.m. and stopped. No one was moving on the street except the police and military. The rest of the city seemed deserted. The faded-grey school bus blended in with the cement buildings and the chalky road. It was as if the place could hold no color – the entire area had given up the battle against the dust that had covered it since the beginning of time. The street was eerily quiet as Cianna sweated under her gear, her assault rifle hooked in the crook of her arm.

The women came off the bus in silence, like spirits, single-file, eyes fixed straight ahead of them. Most of them wore western-style dresses or jeans and blouses. By and large they were in their twenties and thirties, and they held their heads up high. There were even a few young girls with them, holding hands with their mothers as they took up the fight to change their world at an early age.

Cianna looked around the small square where the madrasa was located. It was near the center of the city, and a narrow tin arch marked its entrance. A series of billboards in multiple languages pictured wanted men alongside smiling faces hawking commercial products Cianna couldn't identify from the context. The archway resembled the ticket gate of a decrepit southwestern drive-in theater in a Stephen King novel. In the distance, the 100-foot Ferris wheel at the old fairground in the center of the city stood rusted and motionless, like the skeletal remains of a city that had once held promise. The air seemed to buzz around them as the women lined up, and all of the tension of the city seemed concentrated on the one tiny area.

Then it began.

The doors to the madrasa opened and the men poured out, screaming and chanting and shouting foul oaths. Cianna swiveled her head back and forth, trying to comprehend what was happening. They were coming from the front door, but also from side doors, and from around back of the building; swarming the square like ants from a giant anthill. It hardly seemed possible that they had all fit within the madrasa itself.

The Afghan police hesitated, overwhelmed by the sheer numbers. There were two hundred police, but five times that many counter-demonstrators, and those organizing the men had effectively surprised the police with an instant show of force. Cianna had only just begun learning Pashto, but she understood enough. They were shouting at the women, calling them western whores and telling them to go home to fuck their fathers. For a moment, Cianna thought the women would actually get back onto the bus. Who in their right mind would stay to face such a bloodthirsty mob?

The captain in charge of the Delta Force was the first to react, barking out orders to his own unit, as well as to the Afghan police. The Delta team split up and surrounded the line of women, fifteen soldiers on each side, establishing a barrier to protect them from the crowd. They stood there, facing out, using their training to try to spot any specific threat that might surpass an acceptable level. The Afghan police milled around outside the line of military, forming a looser barrier between the women and the mob. Cianna questioned their resolve. She knew that many of them actually sympathized with the mob and agreed that the women should not be demonstrating in the first place.

She had taken up position near the front of the line of women, and out of the corner of her eye she could see a

oman close by her turn to address her compatriots. A young
rl who looked to be around nine or ten years old was at
r side.

'Women of Afghanistan!' she said in Pashto. In spite of
emselves, those in the mob grew quiet at the power of her
ice. 'We will no longer live in a country where we are
eated as property! We will no longer submit as non-persons
rapes and to beatings and to those indignities that only
ose without rights and a voice can understand!' The square
d grown very quiet now, and only her voice could be heard.
stand here, and I pledge to my daughter,' she looked down
the girl by her side, 'that she will not have to live in a
nd where she does not have the chance to stand up for
rself and be judged on her merits as all human beings
ust be!'

She finished her speech, and no one said anything. The
at continued to press down on them. Cianna looked around
the faces in the mob. They were still and inscrutable, and
r a moment she actually believed that they had been won
er by the force and simple dignity of the words that had
en spoken.

Then the cheer went up from the mob. Angry and violent,
ey screamed as one, and the force nearly knocked Cianna
f her feet. 'Whores!' they shouted. 'Allah shall punish you!
nemies of the true faith!'

The crowd began closing in as the women started marching
ward the city center where the local government offices were
cated. The mob pursued them, still screaming. They had
ne no more than twenty feet when Cianna felt the first
ray hit her face. She looked around and saw that those in
e mob closest to the column of women were spitting at them.

It rained down on them in heavy wads from angry faces w
bulging eyes. She lowered her head and took shelter un
her helmet. At one point she noticed that even some of
Afghan police were spitting. The crowd continued to p
closer and closer, and pushing started to break out betw
the mob and those Afghan police who were still trying to k
order. The Delta team had their guns at the ready, and
suspected that their presence was all that was warding o
full attack from the crowd.

The rocks came next. She saw one of the women in
column recoil and stumble, and at first she thought the wom
had fainted from the heat. Then she saw the blood runn
down her face. The other women marching put their ha
over their heads to try to protect themselves, but there
little they could do, and the barrage kept coming. Cian
finger tightened on the trigger of her assault rifle, and
looked around for the lieutenant, hoping that he would g
the order to fire off a few rounds in the air to at least dispe
the crowds.

'Delta Force, hold your fire!' he said instead. 'We are
to engage the crowd unless the situation is life-threateni
Keep eyes peeled for explosives!'

A rock pounded off her helmet and set her ears ringi
and she had to fight the urge to retaliate.

At that moment, a scuffle broke out just to her right,
the mob tried to break through the mass of Afghan poli
The police were beating people back with sticks, but they u
badly outnumbered and two policemen went down as t
were pelted with rocks. The sight of their blood inflamed
crowd, and they pushed forward with even more vigor. T
two policemen on the ground were now being beaten a

326

kicked as some of their colleagues made an effort to get them to their feet and out of harm's way.

'Lieutenant!' Cianna shouted. 'We've got a situation over here!'

'Stand firm, Delta!' he shouted back. For just a moment she felt the pride of being acknowledged as a Delta Force member. They were the elite of the elite, and she had stuck through the training step-for-step with the men, in some cases a step ahead, because she knew that if she wasn't near the top of the class she would never really be accepted. And now she stood in heavy armor before a mob determined to kill a small group of women just for wanting to learn to read, and to have jobs, and to choose when to give up their bodies. The irony was almost as thick as the heat.

The scuffle had cleared out an area near Cianna, which was a relief for the moment. Just then, though, two men broke through the crowd and rushed the protesters right near Cianna. They both had scarves covering their faces and carried large cups in their hands. She froze for just a moment, and as they reached her, they threw something over Cianna's shoulder toward the woman leading the march. Cianna understood instantly what it was.

Acid.

It was a common tactic used against women in Afghanistan: throwing acid on their faces to disfigure them. It served the multiple purposes of causing incredible pain and disfigurement, branding them as whores, destroying their self-esteem, and scaring other women from stepping out of line.

As they let loose the acid, they both screamed out 'Qatala armad zaniya!' *The high-pitched screams were instantly locked into her consciousness. They came over and over again, and the crowd joined in, chanting, 'Qatala armad zaniya!'*

Cianna swung her rifle butt around and caught one of the men in the stomach and he toppled to the street. She swung for the other assailant, but he ducked, screamed again, and disappeared into the crowd. Looking over her shoulder at the woman for whom the acid had been intended, she was relieved to see that she was unharmed. The acid had apparently missed her completely.

Cianna turned back to the man on the ground. She pointed her rifle at him, and made as though she was going to shoot him. She knew he probably wouldn't even be arrested for attempting to burn the woman, and even if he was, the religious courts would probably let him off with a warning. In the eyes of Afghan law, throwing acid on a woman challenging societal order was entirely justified. Still, at least Cianna figured she could put a good scare in him. She hiked the butt of her gun up to her shoulder and looked down the barrel, aiming at his head. She kept the safety on, though.

She waited to see the fear in his eyes, but instead he just stared at her with smug hate.

Then she heard the sound.

Even through the cacophony, the wailing was distinct in its horror and anguish. Cianna turned to see that it was coming from the woman leading the march. At first Cianna thought perhaps the acid had hit her after all. It took a moment for her to realize that the reality was much worse. It had flown by her and hit her daughter square in the face.

There was blood everywhere. The little girl was trying to scream, but the acid had already eaten through the skin on her lips. Her eyelids were gone, and her eyeballs swirled wildly as her mother held her, trying to wipe the acid from her daughter's face.

'God! Please no!' the mother screamed. 'Get me some water!'

Two of the soldiers dug their canteens frantically from their belts and offered them. Everyone knew that it was too late to do much, though. The acid had worked its evil instantly.

The lieutenant saw what was happening and decided it was time to take matters into his own hands. 'Deltas!' he shouted. 'Disperse the crowd!' He fired three shots into the air. Two other soldiers did the same, as the others held their arms at the ready in case the tactic was unsuccessful.

The effort was effective, and the mob turned and fled immediately. They went screaming and swarming back into the building and up the street in genuine terror.

Cianna looked down at the little girl again, and the rage welled within her. The attacker was still on the ground, and she pointed her gun at him again. 'On your feet!' she screamed at him. 'Now! Up! Up!'

He got to his feet and she kept her gun pointed into his chest. It was all she could do to keep herself from beating him with her gun. That wasn't her role, she knew, but she couldn't bear the thought that he wouldn't pay for what he had done to the little girl. She pushed the barrel of her gun into his chest. 'Hands behind your head!' she ordered. She reached up and ripped the scarf away, revealing the face of a man who would use such obscene tactics against those who were fighting only to be recognized as human beings.

He just stood there, staring at her. He was an average-looking man, in his early-twenties, and he had a thin beard on a pocked face. His clothes suggested that he was from a family of some wealth.

'Now!' she shouted again. 'Hands behind your head!'

He didn't move for a moment. Then he smiled malevolently. 'Whore,' he said in English. 'I take no orders from a woman.' He stared at her for another moment. Suddenly his face became serious and he moved his hands quickly to his abdomen, under his robes. Cianna had learned in her training that it was a move that often preceded the detonation of a suicide bomb. Cianna had no time to debate.

'Bomb!' she yelled as she pulled the trigger.

Everyone in the area ducked as the bullet ripped through the young man's chest. He staggered backwards a few feet and fell to his knees. He pulled his hands out from under his robes and held something up to her. It was a Koran, she could see. A trickle of blood ran from the corner of his mouth. The only sound now was the wailing of the woman whose child lay mutilated in her arms. The man raised up the Koran to Cianna, holding it almost as though it was a shield. 'It is better . . .' he choked out unevenly, gasping for breath. 'It is better . . . for the girl to die . . .' He paused, struggling for breath. 'Than for her to be a whore.' He seemed relieved once the words were out, and he looked to the sky. 'It is what Allah—'

He never finished the sentence. Another gunshot rang out and caught him in the throat. He toppled back into the street and lay there squirming for a moment. Then he was still. Cianna could still hear the wailing behind her, but she was aware of little else. The world seemed to close in around her.

She looked down at the gun in her hands and saw the thin trail of fresh smoke coming from the end of the barrel.

CHAPTER FORTY-SIX

'Everything was by the book,' Saunders said quietly. 'Except the second shot.'

She nodded. 'Turns out the young man was the son of a mullah who was a highly placed local government official. There were witnesses in the crowd who saw that I shot him the second time when he was already wounded and lying on the ground holding a Koran, so the Afghan government demanded that I be prosecuted. I think the panel at my court martial was feeling the pressure. They initially convicted me of voluntary manslaughter. The charges were reduced after I got back to the States, down to involuntary. I was paroled early. I think everyone understood.'

'Except you.'

She looked at him. 'Except me,' she admitted. She turned away and stared at the wall. 'I don't remember pulling the trigger the second time. I never meant to. It wasn't a conscious thought. Maybe I was just holding on too tightly. Maybe there was a noise that startled me. Maybe . . .' she searched for some explanation that would make sense. 'Maybe . . .'

He put a hand on her shoulder. 'Maybe you saw a little girl dying in agony in front of you, and you wanted justice for her.'

'Maybe,' she admitted. The hand on her shoulder felt so good. 'It all happened so quickly. I don't even remember. The only thing that sticks with me is the way the two men screamed with such hatred as they threw the acid. '*Qatala armad zaniya!*' I had someone translate it for me later. It means "Death to the dirty whores!" And they were screaming it at their own women.' She let her head drop to her chest. 'I suppose it doesn't matter. There are some moments you just can't get back, no matter what you do.'

'Do you regret what you did?'

She sighed. 'I regret what I lost.'

'That's not the same thing.'

'No, I guess it's not.' She wiped a single tear from her cheek, turned and looked up at him. His hand was still on her shoulder, and he was so close. 'So,' she said. 'Am I still a mystery?'

He nodded. 'Even more so,' he said.

He leaned in slowly, and she felt his body, warm and hard against hers. She wondered whether she would pull away. She didn't, though, and then his lips were against hers, soft and firm and gentle. She parted her lips slightly, and she could feel his tongue on her lips. Her body was still for a moment, and she wondered whether she'd lost the ability to love, just as she knew she'd lost the ability to be loved.

And then something turned within her. She could feel a burst within her chest, and the warmth spreading out from there to the rest of her body. It was like coming alive again, and her hands moved against Saunders's body, exploring. She responded to his touch, welcoming it, riding a wave of pleasure with every move of his hands.

She could feel the tears pouring down her cheeks, mixing with their kisses, and she had no idea whether they were tears of joy or pain. At the moment, joy and pain seemed inextricably intertwined, both desperately screaming to get out from the places deep within her where they'd been trapped for years.

Saunders paused and looked at her. 'Are you okay?' he asked.

She had trouble finding her voice as the tears continued to fall. She merely nodded and kissed him again. *I will be*, she thought. *Tonight, I will be.*

They were both awake when his cell phone rang. It was just after 5.30 the next morning, and her legs were draped languidly over his, her head on his shoulder as they touched each other idly, running fingertips over arms and legs and chests in a silent, comfortable post-coital dance. She was still trying to adjust to the thought of being a complete person once more. She didn't love him, certainly, but he'd opened up possibilities for her again. In many ways, the notion frightened her.

He reached over the side of the bed, found his pants on the floor and dug the cell phone out of the pocket. 'Yeah,' he said. He listened to the person on the other end of the line. 'Yeah, I know it.' More silence. 'Okay, when?'

He clicked off the phone and put it on the bedside table. He lay back down and maneuvered himself into a position that approximated the one he'd abandoned to answer the phone.

'Do we have a plan?' she asked.

He nodded. 'That was my boss. He's flying up, and he's going to meet us. He can get the Cloak to Akhtar's people and make sure it's safe.'

'Is he coming here?'

He shook his head. 'Castle Island in three hours.'

'You spooks do like your drama, don't you?'

'It's a public area. Plenty of cops around if anything happens. My boss thought it made sense. He thinks there are people on the inside who are helping Fasil.'

'Plus, it's right around the corner,' she noted. 'Which means we have two and a half hours before we need to leave here.'

'Sounds about right,' he agreed.

'Hmmm,' she mused. 'How will we pass all that time?'

He looked into her eyes as his fingers traced the outer edges of her arm. The sensation of being touched by another human being again was exquisite, and it sent a ripple of pleasure through her entire body. She was tempted to look away, but managed to hold his gaze. He smiled. 'I'm sure we can find something productive to do.'

At 7.45 that morning, Detective Harvey Morrell pulled up to the curb a half-block down H Street from Milo's apartment in Southie. His joints ached from having been left curled around the table in Spudgie's kitchen, and the skin on his cheeks and around his lips was raw where the uniformed officer had pulled the duct tape off. The man who claimed to be a spook had been good to his word, at least insofar as he had called and left an anonymous tip as to where Morrell could be found. At three o'clock, two patrolmen had been dispatched to investigate, and had found Morrell there, hogtied and gagged.

It wasn't the humiliation of having been found in such a state that angered Morrell; he had long since relinquished the last shreds of concern over what others thought about him. Being left out of the search for his brother's killer, though, was an insult he could not abide. When he'd arrived back at the station house, he'd typed up a cursory report of what had happened, leaving most of the details out, and then started researching Cianna Phelan's background. For all he knew, they could have already fled the city, but that seemed unlikely to him. Besides, if that were the case, there was really nothing he could do to track them down, so he was forced to start from the assumption that they were still nearby. It seemed unlikely that they would go back to her apartment; that would be too easy. He had to figure out what other options they had.

After an hour, he came to the conclusion that, unless the CIA spook or the towelhead had someplace for them to go, there were very few of her contacts they could rely on. She had no family, and no serious attachments that he could uncover. The only thing she appeared to have in her life was her job, and that was at a tiny non-profit with only one other employee. It was a long shot, but it was the only information he had, so he decided to take a chance. He owed at least that much to himself and his brother.

As he sat in the car, looking down the street at the little apartment building, he considered different plans of action. He could march up to the front door and knock – see what would happen. The chances that they would simply open the door to him, assuming they were there, were roughly zero, though. He could bust in the door, but in all likelihood they would see him coming and be prepared for such a frontal attack. Besides, he had looked into the spook's eyes when he was being tied up, and he believed that they had not killed his brother. The spook would have killed him if he'd been involved in his brother's death; he was sure of that. Morrell also believed that the piece of cloth in the box was at the heart of whatever nefarious plot had caused his brother's death. What he wanted more than anything was to find out who was responsible and take them down. He couldn't do that by confronting Cianna Phelan and the other two directly.

His only option was to wait, and pray against prayer that he'd gotten lucky. If they were there, he would watch them as they left, and follow them. It was the only way he could think of that might provide answers.

CHAPTER FORTY-SEVEN

It was still early when Cianna and Saunders headed out to Castle Island. The place was, in fact, no longer an island, but was connected to the mainland by a causeway that jutted east from South Boston out into Boston Harbor. The causeway looped in an even curve that enclosed Pleasure Bay, a protected inlet that formed the primary recreational beach in the area. At the end of the causeway, the land opened into a large bell-shaped protuberance on which Fort Independence was built. Covering ten acres, Fort Independence had been the main military installation that protected the mouth of Boston Harbor since before the Revolutionary War. It was the final spot from which the British redcoats were driven following the siege of Boston in 1778, and it had served its watchful role until 1962, when it was officially decommissioned. It now served as a place of historical and recreational interest. The walkway around the thirty-foot-high stone and earthwork pentagon was a near-perfect-half-mile track, and joggers and strollers were thick there except in the worst weather.

Ainsworth had told them to walk around the fort and meet him on the far side. Under different circumstances, the walk would have been delightful, Saunders thought, as they headed out. It was a beautiful autumn day, cool enough to be comfortable, but with biting sunlight that radiated off the water. As he walked, he could feel Cianna close to him, and he wondered what she was thinking. She was, in all respects, a remarkable woman; remarkable enough that, even now, he had yet to figure out who she was. He supposed it didn't matter at the moment. All that mattered for now was getting the Cloak back into the hands of Akhtar's people.

He realized to his chagrin that his idle musings had allowed his focus to wane. There were dozens of people on the walkway, and each one was a potential threat. Joggers and roller-bladers and old men with bags of day-old bread to feed the birds: any one of them could be waiting to make a move.

Saunders tightened his grip on the box under his arm.

He saw Ainsworth when they were still fifty yards away from him, out at the edge of the pier on the easternmost edge of the land, leaning against the railing, looking out at the water and the islands that crept their way down south, lining Boston's outer harbor. He had a bag of peanuts in one hand, and he was dipping into it with his other hand, cracking the shells deftly and letting them fall to the water fifteen feet below as he popped the nuts into his mouth. When they were twenty feet away, Saunders turned to Cianna. 'Wait here,' he said. 'I have to talk to him alone.'

She nodded. 'Don't take too long,' she said.

Ainsworth didn't turn to greet Saunders as he approached. Saunders sidled up to him, and leaned against the railing. 'Taking in the harbor sights?' he said.

'I am,' Ainsworth said.

Saunders looked out at the water with his boss. 'It's nice, I suppose.'

'It is, depending on your perspective,' Ainsworth said. 'You see Deer Island out there, with the giant holding tanks?' Saunders nodded. 'Back in the 1600s, it was used as an internment camp for the native Americans. They were left there, stranded on an island without any trees or shelter, through the brutal winters. Several hundred of them. They were all dead within two years. I wonder if they found the view as pleasant then as we do now.'

'Everything in life is a matter of perspective,' Saunders said. 'You taught me that, Lawrence.'

'I did,' Ainsworth said. 'And I taught you better than I taught anyone else.' He looked over at the box in Saunders's hands. 'You got it.' It wasn't a question, but a statement. 'I never doubted that you would.'

'You knew,' Saunders said. 'You were working with Akhtar the entire time. You knew what I was after.'

Ainsworth nodded. 'I considered telling you, but I couldn't.'

'Why not?'

'First of all, because I'd given Akhtar my word. And second, because I didn't know where you stood in all of this. There are people in our own government working against us. For all I knew . . .'

'Bullshit,' Saunders said. 'You know me. You trained me. You know exactly where I stand. Always.'

'I should have trusted you,' Ainsworth acknowledged. 'That was my mistake. I still had faith that you would come through in the end.'

'No thanks to you.'

'Admittedly. But I knew you'd come through nonetheless.'

'And what about Akhtar? Did you know that he wouldn't make it through? Did you consider him expendable?'

Ainsworth looked stung. 'If there was anything I could have done—' His voice was full of an uncharacteristic protest. He stopped himself and cleared his throat. 'Akhtar died for a cause he believed was just,' he said, changing course. 'It is the way he would have wanted it.'

'I'm not sure,' Saunders said.

The two of them stood in silence for a moment.

'I knew his father,' Ainsworth said. 'A lifetime ago, when I was working with the Mujahedin to fight the Soviets in Afghanistan. I worked with his father. He was a good man; a moderate. He had great hopes for his country if he could just get the Russians out. Then came the Taliban. Now we're there. It's safe to say Akhtar's father would be disappointed in the progress we've made since he was murdered.' He shook his head.

'You can't compare us to the Taliban,' Saunders said.

'I don't.' He finished the peanuts, crumpled the bag and put it in his pocket. 'But I'm not so blind that I can't see that we are all products of our beliefs. And subject to the limitations they impose.' Looking up, he said, 'Is that the girl? Phelan's sister?'

Saunders nodded.

Ainsworth stared at her for a moment. 'The reports of her beauty seem not to have been exaggerated.' He shifted his gaze to Saunders, left it there for a moment before a slight smile crossed his lips. 'You'll never change.'

'Who amongst us will?' Saunders took the box out from

under his arm. 'How do you plan to get it back to Kandahar?' he asked, handing it over.

'It's arranged,' Ainsworth said. 'I have a plane lined up, and the right people in place. Akhtar's uncle has already been alerted. He'll be waiting for it.'

'All for a thirteen-hundred-year-old piece of homespun,' Saunders said, raising his eyebrows. 'Superstition,' he muttered.

'Are we any different?'

'I thought so.'

Ainsworth laughed. 'Think again.' He straightened up. 'You'll be reinstated. Of that I'm sure, at least.'

'What about Toney?'

'Toney's an asshole. He has problems of his own. I don't think he'll be paying too much attention to you.'

'What does that mean?'

Ainsworth gave a sphinx-like smile. 'You needn't concern yourself with that right now, my boy. You've done well. Lay low for a few days, and then meet me back at the office. I'll make sure everything is straightened out.'

'Just like that?'

Ainsworth nodded. 'Just like that,' he said. 'You didn't think I'd really let them put the best field agent we've got in mothballs, did you?'

'I was beginning to wonder, honestly,' Saunders said.

Ainsworth gestured to Cianna. 'I'd like to meet her, if that's okay. Convey my appreciation, and my condolences.'

'Sure,' Saunders said.

The two of them walked over to where she was standing. Ainsworth was carrying the box under his left arm. He extended his right hand to Cianna. 'Ms Phelan, my name is Lawrence Ainsworth. I asked Jack to introduce you to me so that I can express my great sympathy regarding your brother. I wanted to tell you that he and Mr Hazara did not die in vain, I will see to that. I'm sure that is of little consolation to you at the moment, but I wanted to say it anyway.'

'Thank you,' Cianna said. 'It would mean more to me if you could tell me that the man who killed them would be brought to justice.'

'If I have anything to do with it, I promise you with all my heart that he will be dealt with. I'll promise you more than that, even. I will promise you that I will not rest until all those who harbor similar hatreds have been as well. As for justice . . .' He hesitated. 'I would have thought that you would have a certain amount of skepticism toward the notion, given all that you've been through.'

'It's not justice I question,' Cianna said. 'It's just sometimes the people who administer it.'

'Fair point,' Ainsworth said. 'I've read your file carefully. I can say without question that in your case both justice and those who administered it were flawed. You did not deserve to be treated the way you were by the country you served so well. For that, also, you have my deepest sympathies.'

'Thank you,' Cianna said. 'That means a lot to me.'

'If I may suggest it,' Ainsworth said, 'when all of this is over, I would be interested in talking to you about coming to work for me.'

Cianna didn't respond for a moment. 'At the CIA?'

'Why not?' He smiled. 'We are not all as rough around the edges as my friend Jack, here. Based on your record, you might find that you are well-suited to it. And you certainly have the skills and much of the training already.'

'I'd need to think about it,' Cianna said.

'I wouldn't have any interest in you if you didn't,' Ainsworth said. 'You and Jack need to stay out of sight for a little while anyway. Think about it. We can talk later.' He turned to Saunders. 'Jack, my boy, thank you again.' He gestured to the box under his arm. 'This will have more of an impact than even you know.'

'I hope so,' Saunders said.

Ainsworth put his hand out and Jack shook it. Then he turned and started walking around Fort Independence, toward the parking lot. They watched him go.

'He cares about you,' Cianna said.

'Maybe.' Saunders shrugged. 'It's a hard business in which to let yourself care about anyone.'

'Maybe,' she said. 'But he does. I can see it in his eyes.'

CHAPTER FORTY-EIGHT

They went to breakfast at a diner not too far from Fort Independence, down on Columbia Avenue, only a mile or so from where they'd stood watching Akhtar's car explode over the tree-line. She ate well, he noticed. An order of blueberry pancakes and bacon, with a side of hash browns. For dessert she had a small plate of scrambled eggs.

He had coffee.

'You want waffles with that?' he said, as she dug into her eggs.

'I'm hungry,' she said.

'No apology needed,' he replied. 'I just hope there's enough left in Boston for the school breakfasts when you're done.'

'I haven't eaten since before . . .' She hesitated as the realization hit her. 'Since before they took Charlie,' she finished. 'He got us Chinese food. He was so full of hope. Just before Sirus kicked the door in, he was nervous, but it was the closest I've seen him to being happy since when we were kids.'

'I'm sorry,' he said. 'There was nothing you could have done. You know that.'

'In the last two days? Probably not. I'm wondering more about the first nineteen years. I could have done a better

344

job back then. I was so focused on myself sometimes, I'd forget that he was a little kid, and he had no one.'

'He had you.'

'Sometimes. When I could give him the time. I used to think of myself as his mother – like I'd done such a great job of raising him. I used to actually take pride in that. Now I'm not so sure. I mean, I tried to make sure he was getting food to eat, and that he had a warm place to sleep, but I don't think I ever really spent the time I needed to listening to him. I think I let him be lonely because I didn't know how to deal with it sometimes.'

'You were a kid,' he pointed out.

'I was older than he was. He was my responsibility.'

'You're being a little hard on yourself.'

She ate another mouthful of eggs, her eyes down on the plate, an expression of exhaustion on her face. 'I think it still hasn't hit me fully. The fact that he's really gone.'

'That's natural,' Saunders said. 'It takes time.'

'Time when I'm not running for my life,' she added. 'This is the first moment we've had to breathe since this all began.'

'We were breathing last night.'

Looking up at him, she thought of giving him a smile. She knew that was what he wanted, and maybe it was what she needed, but she was still thinking about Charlie, and she just couldn't bring herself to grin. Instead she reached out and put her hand on top of his. 'Last night was important to me,' she said.

'But . . .?'

'No buts.'

He took his hand off the table. 'What did you think about what Lawrence said?' he asked.

She looked away from him, not wanting him to see her eyes. 'About working with the Agency?' she said, choking out a half-laugh. 'It's not going to happen. I'm an ex-con. You really think that's going to wash with the CIA brass?'

'If they understand the context of your conviction, maybe,' Saunders said. 'Hell, you'd be surprised at what Lawrence Ainsworth can accomplish when he puts his mind to it. He may even be able to get your record expunged. It would be like the conviction never happened. Like you never spent a day in prison.'

She shook her head. 'It will never be like I didn't go to prison. That will be with me no matter what I do or where I go. It's a part of me.'

'I understand, but it doesn't have to be a part of your record. If the brass at the Agency sign off on it, and you can get the record expunged, you should consider it. You've got the skills, there's no question about that. You'd be a natural.'

'Maybe,' she said.

She looked up and through the window. Outside, a young girl passed by the door. She couldn't have been more than three, and she had greasy blond hair and an angelic, dirt-smudged face. She turned to smile at someone behind her, calling out 'Mamma!' excitedly.

The little girl's mother came into view a moment later, and Cianna recognized Jenny, from the Old Colonial Projects – the girl she and Milo had saved from a drug-crazed rape-train in that dreary apartment two days before. She looked healthier, somehow. She was still skinny, but there was color in her face, and she was smiling. She had a nice smile, Cianna thought. Far nicer than she would have suspected.

'I don't know,' Cianna said. 'Sometimes I think I can do more good in the world right here in this little neighborhood.'

She looked up again. Jenny and her little girl were passing out of view, but just before she lost sight of her, Cianna noticed Jenny looking behind her, giving a smile to someone behind them. Cianna's heart sank, and a moment later, as she knew he would, Vin passed into view. He had two black eyes and a bandage on the nose she had broken with the butt of his gun. 'I'll think about it,' she said with a heavy sigh.

'That's all I'm asking.'

She lowered her head as the weight of the past two days came crashing down upon her. 'Right now, I just want to rest.'

Cianna turned her face to the sun on the walk back to her apartment. The air was crisp and clean, the way autumn gets in New England, when it seems like you could see forever out on the water if only you could get up high enough on the hills of South Boston. Notwithstanding what the calendars said, the fall always felt like the beginning of the year to Cianna. Children hurried off to school, excited to meet their new teachers and test the new kids; a fresh wave of college freshmen descended on the most over-Universitied city on the face of the planet; people came back from vacations tanned, rested, and ready to pick up their jobs with renewed vigor. For Cianna, an autumn day like this one usually held the promise of opportunity. Today, though, all she felt was loss.

They walked along Columbia Avenue all the way around Pleasure Bay, down toward the southwesternmost end of

South Boston, where the housing projects blended over into Dorchester, a town that had become even more renowned for its grit than Southie.

They cut up Old Harbor Street and over a block to her apartment house. In days long ago it might have been referred to as a tenement house. Laundry hung from clotheslines sticking out from several windows, and the stairs creaked as they made their way up. She hadn't asked Saunders to come to her apartment, at least not specifically, but Lawrence Ainsworth had instructed them to make themselves scarce for a few days. She assumed that meant together. Saunders clearly had the same notion.

She wondered whether they would make love again. It had certainly been the most alive she'd felt in years when they'd been together the night before. But that was when the adrenaline was still flowing, and before the enormity of the events of the past days had truly set in. She decided she would let herself be carried along by whatever happened between the two of them for the moment. She no longer had the energy to try to direct events.

The sound of the lock turning as she opened the door brought some comfort. It was familiar, and that was what she needed right now. She was desperate for a quiet moment to start digesting all that had happened.

She took two steps into the apartment before she realized that something was wrong. An old wing-backed chair at the far side of the room was turned around at an awkward angle so that it was looking out onto the street, rather than back toward the rest of the room. She could see a head just over the top of the chair. She turned to warn Saunders, but never got the chance.

A gun was pointed directly at her face.

A man grabbed her and threw her against the wall, pulling her hands up high, palms down; kicking her legs out and apart as he frisked her. He seemed to be taking his time with it.

She looked to her left briefly and saw that Saunders was getting the same treatment. A hand slapped at her face. 'Eyes forward!' a voice ordered.

As the searching continued, the man sitting in the chair spoke. 'Be careful with both of them. They are both exceptionally well-trained.' The hands kept moving over her body. They found the gun tucked in her pocket and pulled it out. Out of the corner of her eye, she could see that they had taken Saunders's gun and knife as well. After a moment the man was done and he stepped back. She remained facing the wall.

'You may turn around,' the voice from the chair said.

She and Saunders turned slowly, keeping their backs to the wall. There were two men standing in front of them. They were both tall and powerfully built, with short hair and thin lips that looked like they would tear if a smile was forced onto them.

The man in the chair stood up, still facing away. 'You two are in a lot of trouble,' he said. He turned. 'And I am the only hope you have to make things right.'

She didn't recognize the man, but Saunders clearly did. His expression telegraphed his hatred. 'Toney,' he said. 'I should have known.'

The man nodded. 'Yes, Jack. You should have.'

CHAPTER FORTY-NINE

Saunders's mind was racing. The men with Toney were too big to be overpowered, and he had little doubt they had been warned to watch Saunders very closely. They never let their eyes leave his face.

'Where is it?' Toney asked.

'What's the matter? Government work not paying enough?' Perhaps he could goad the man into making a mistake, Saunders thought.

'The government pays me exactly what I need,' Toney said, calmly. He walked over to Cianna. 'I'm being rude,' he said. 'Ms Phelan, I presume? My name is Bill Toney. I am the Director of the National Security Agency.'

'Wow,' Cianna said flatly.

'Indeed. I need to know where the Cloak of Mohammed is, and I need to know now. Do you understand?'

'I'm not sure what you are talking about,' Cianna replied.

He stepped toward her, so close that she had to push her head back against the wall to prevent him from touching her. He was taller than her by several inches and he loomed over her, bending his neck so that his face was right in hers. 'I don't have time for these games,' he said in a slow, menacing voice. 'I need to know where it is, now.'

'How much is Fasil paying you?' Saunders asked. 'Whatever it is, is it worth betraying your country for?'

Toney kept staring at Cianna, though an angry smile crossed his lips. 'You truly don't understand anything that is happening here, do you Jack? It's amazing that someone with your reputation for field skills could be this clueless.' He still hadn't looked directly at Saunders. 'You see, Ms Phelan, while Mr Saunders may be charming, he is operating with less than perfect information. I am not the traitor, he is.' Finally, Toney turned his head and looked at Saunders. 'He just doesn't know it yet.'

The room was silent for a moment, and Saunders could hear a huge fly, sleepy from the gathering cold, banging off a window pane out in the tiny living room. 'You're lying,' Cianna said. Saunders was glad she had said it before he'd had to. 'He's not working with Fasil. They have been trying to kill each other for the past two days.'

'Yes, that's true,' Toney said. 'He is not working with Fasil. But he is a traitor, nonetheless.'

Saunders said nothing. He knew that Toney was trying to draw him out; trying to get a reaction out of him so that he could move him off balance. That's when an interrogation subject gives up useful information. Saunders wouldn't give Toney that satisfaction.

'How is he a traitor, then?' Cianna demanded. Saunders shot her a look, trying to signal her to stop talking; it was exactly what Toney was looking for.

'Someone who works with a traitor is a traitor,' Toney said. 'Even if he doesn't know it.'

'Jack works with the CIA,' Cianna said.

Toney shook his head. 'He was suspended two days ago. Didn't he tell you?' He looked back at her, and Saunders could see the shock in Cianna's face. Toney laughed. 'Of course not,' he said.

'He's still working with them, though,' she protested. Her voice was thin now, though. 'I know he is, I met his boss.'

Toney's expression went deadly serious. 'Ainsworth?' he demanded. 'You met him? He was here?'

'Yes,' Cianna said quietly.

'When?'

'This morning.' It was clear from her tone that she had lost all confidence. She looked over at Saunders and he could see the doubt in her eyes. 'We gave him the Cloak,' she said.

The reaction was instantaneous. Toney whirled on Saunders, grabbing him by his shirt and pushing him up against the wall. Saunders was surprised at the man's strength. He was taller than Saunders, but Saunders expected him to be skin and bones and ego, and nothing more. But Toney had real power in his body. 'You fool!' he yelled. 'You gave the Cloak to Ainsworth?'

Saunders kept his silence.

'Where did he take it?'

In spite of himself and all his training, Saunders couldn't help responding. 'He's taking it back to its rightful owners. He's taking it back to the mosque where it belongs, and to the people who have guarded it for hundreds of years.'

Toney was shaking his head violently. 'No, he's not,' he said. 'He's going to give the Cloak to Fasil. Don't you understand that?'

Saunders shook his head reflexively. 'No, he's not. Lawrence isn't working with Fasil,' Saunders said. 'You are.'

'No, I'm not, you fool!' Toney said. 'Ainsworth is working

with Fasil. And if we don't figure out a way to stop him, he will give the Cloak to the enemies of Afghanistan.'

'That's a lie.'

'It's not. Think about it, for Christ's sake! Who knew where and when you were meeting Hassan Mustafa on the night he was killed down in Virginia?'

'No one,' Saunders said. 'Just me.'

'No? Only you and . . .?'

Saunders blinked twice. 'Me and Lawrence,' he admitted.

'And who gave you the information you needed to track down Charles Phelan?'

'Ainsworth,' Saunders said grudgingly. 'But he got that information from the memory stick we took off the doctor during the raid in Alexandria.'

Toney shook his head. 'There was some useful information on the drive, but Phelan's name wasn't on it. If Ainsworth gave you his name, he had to have gotten it from somewhere else.'

'You're lying.'

'Am I? Did he actually show you the data from the drive? Or did he just show you some dummy report he had thrown in a file?'

Saunders didn't answer. 'Why would I trust you – you had me suspended from the Agency? You started all this.'

'No. Ainsworth suspended you. And he did that so he could cut off all contact you had with anyone on the inside. Once you were on your own, the only way you could get any information was through him. And you let him know where you were every step of the way. Did you not notice that Fasil has been able to track your every move? How do you think that was possible?'

'Lawrence was helping me.' Saunders was beginning to wonder, though.

'Was he?' Toney shook his head. 'Did he bring in anyone to actually help you? Or was he just following your progress so he would know if you got your hands on the Cloak?'

The ground continued to slip away from Saunders, and he reached for anything that might allow him to keep his sanity. 'You're wrong,' he said. 'Ainsworth was working with the son of Mohmar Hazara. They have been trying to get the Cloak back to the mosque in Kandahar. Hazara was killed, but Lawrence is going to finish the mission.'

'How do you know that Ainsworth was working with Hazara?'

'Akhtar told me.'

'Who told you?' Toney demanded. 'Think carefully. Was it Hazara himself, or was it just Ainsworth?'

Saunders thought hard. 'Hazara told us he was working with an American; someone in our intelligence branch, but he didn't have a name. Ainsworth confirmed he was the one.'

'So you never heard it directly from Hazara.'

'No. He died before he had the chance to contact Ainsworth again.'

Toney shook his head as though he was looking at one of the most pathetic souls he'd ever had to deal with. 'You really believed it, didn't you? You trusted Ainsworth that much.'

'Of course I trust him. Why wouldn't I? And for all your bullshit, you still haven't given me any proof that Lawrence wasn't working with Hazara. Why would I trust you more than him?'

Toney let go of Saunders's shirt and backed away a little bit. 'I'm not asking you to trust me.' He turned and walked across the room, over toward the closed door to the bedroom. He turned the doorknob and pushed the door in.

There was a man there, visible only in silhouette, the sun streaming in behind him. Saunders squinted at the figure, trying to make out the features of the face. Then Akhtar Hazara stepped into the living room. Saunders felt the ground give way completely underneath him, and the sensation of falling was dizzying. 'You died,' Jack whispered. 'We saw it.'

'No,' Akhtar replied. 'Mr Toney's men saved me. Jack, he is the contact I have been working with. He received my message last night, and was on the way to help us when Fasil was chasing us. I was lucky; his men were on the way to the tavern when they saw me crash on the street. I would have died, but his men engaged Fasil in a gunfight, and got me out of there.'

'We thought . . .' Saunders didn't finish the sentence.

'I do not know Mr Ainsworth, but I do believe Mr Toney. Mr Ainsworth is the one who is working with Fasil. Will you help us?'

Saunders looked over at Cianna. She was standing there, gaping at Akhtar like he was a ghost. 'How is it possible?' she whispered.

Saunders slid down the wall until he was sitting on the floor, his head in his hands. 'Oh God,' he said. 'What have I done?'

CHAPTER FIFTY

The wind cut into Lawrence Ainsworth's skin as he walked along the mountain trail. The trees had lost most of their leaves, and the evergreens that dominated the hillside below grew sparse as he climbed higher, approaching the tree-line. He'd hiked these trails a thousand times since he was a boy, and he felt a connection to the past as he moved along the mountainside – a past when the world was less complicated, and considerably less dangerous. People could say what they wanted about the Soviets, but at least they were relatively stable and predictable. They provided a steady wind against which those in his profession could set their sails. There was a tacit understanding of what the rules were back then, and a general comprehension that, ideology aside, both sides needed each other.

Now all that was gone, and the United States sat rudderless in the water, assaulted from all sides by unpredictable gales that blew and died faster than anyone could predict. It could not go on this way, Ainsworth knew. The country could not survive it.

The tiny schoolhouse was up ahead now, in a clearing near the top of the mountain. He looked down at the wooden box cradled under his arm. He hadn't looked inside of it; hadn't touched the sacred relic within. He cared little for such superstitions. His was a mission grounded in the cold hard facts of the real world.

The door opened and Fasil stepped out. His gun was in his hand, gripped sure, pointed at the ground. His one remaining bodyguard came out and stood next to him. Sirus Stillwell was there as well, and as he exited and separated from the other two, he walked over and stood next to Ainsworth, facing Fasil.

'You have the Cloak,' Fasil said, nodding at the box under Ainsworth's arm.

'I do.' Ainsworth stepped forward and held the box out. Fasil took it and set it on a stump near the front of the tiny building. Slowly he unlatched the top and opened it just enough to see inside. Then he closed the box back up and re-latched it, turned and handed it to his man.

He looked back at Ainsworth. 'The plane is still ready to get us back to my country?'

Ainsworth nodded. 'It will be at the airstrip at nine to take you to Canada. From there, I have a jet waiting. You will leave this evening. I will come to get you. If I'm not here by nine o'clock, it means something has gone wrong, and you need to get moving.'

Fasil nodded. 'Good.'

Ainsworth looked at Sirus. 'You need to come with me.'

'Yes sir,' Sirus responded with a half-hearted salute. He looked at Fasil with distain, clearly glad to be rid of him.

As Ainsworth turned and headed back down the trail, Sirus followed him. 'Is there a problem?' he asked.

'I don't know yet,' Ainsworth said. 'We'll have to wait and see.'

They were only twenty feet down the path when Fasil called after them. 'Perhaps we shall meet again, Mr Ainsworth!'

Ainsworth turned and looked at him, the hatred clear in his eyes. 'If we ever meet again,' he said, 'I will kill you.'

Fasil laughed derisively. 'I have no doubt!' he called.

Ainsworth walked away. As he followed the path down from the mountain peak, it seemed as though the wind had never blown so cold.

Saunders could hear Toney pacing as Jack stared out the window onto the narrow street in South Boston. 'Did he say anything specific about how he was getting the Cloak out of the country?' Toney was asking.

Jack didn't respond.

'He said he had arranged for a plane,' Cianna answered.

'Did he say out of what airport?' Toney asked.

'No,' Cianna said. 'Not unless he told Jack.'

Saunders could feel the eyes on him as he stood there, motionless. He shook his head without turning around. It felt as though his entire world had collapsed. Nothing made sense anymore.

'Call down to Langley, and have them run a check to see whether Ainsworth used any of our people to arrange a flight,' Toney ordered one of his men. 'It's a long shot, but it's worth a try. In all likelihood he's got someone to freelance. No records. The question is, where would he fly out of?'

Saunders turned and looked at them. 'It won't be an airport.'

'How do you know?'

'I know him.'

'All evidence to the contrary.'

Saunders winced. 'Fair enough,' he conceded. 'At an airport there will be too many questions, and too many flight records. He'll fly out of an area that's fairly rural, to draw less attention.'

'Any specific thoughts?' Toney demanded. 'Anything that might actually be helpful?' Saunders shook his head again. The two men stared at each other for a few moments, until Saunders averted his eyes. It was his fault that Ainsworth had the Cloak, and there was no way to deny it.

Cianna's phone rang, startling everyone in the room. They all looked at her. 'It must be Milo,' she said. 'He's the only one who would call me.' She crossed the room and glanced at the receiver as she picked it up. 'Blocked number,' she commented. She pressed the button and held the handset up to her ear. 'Milo?' she said. Her face darkened, and she looked at Saunders in confusion. 'How did you . . .?' she said into the phone. 'Okay.' She held the phone out to Saunders. 'It's for you,' she said.

'Who?'

She shook her head and handed him the phone. He held it up to his ear. 'Who is this?' he asked.

'Detective Morrell,' a gravelly voice responded.

'Who?'

'Nick O'Callaghan's brother. We met last night, remember?'

Saunders's heart felt like it had exploded in his chest, and he wondered whether there would be an end to his screw-ups. The notion that he had allowed the cop to track him down this easily was pathetic. 'How did you find me?'

'Not too hard to look up the girl's number. I tried her friend Milo's place, first, but no one answered. I figured I'd take a chance that you'd gone back to her apartment. It was the only other place I knew about, so I played the odds.'

Fair enough, Saunders thought. 'What do you want?'

'I want answers.'

'I can't give them to you.'

'I think you can.' There was silence on the other end of the line for a few seconds. Then Morrell continued. 'Why didn't you kill me, last night? You killed my brother.'

'No, I didn't,' Saunders said. 'I told you that last night, and it was the truth.'

'Then the people you were working with did,' Morrell growled. 'So you knew about it. The rest is semantics.'

'No, I didn't know anything about your brother's death. I had nothing to do with that.'

'Right, you told me. That was the man with the teardrop birthmark.'

'That's right.' Saunders could hear the cop breathing hard into the phone. 'I'm telling you the truth,' Saunders said.

If it wasn't for the breathing, Saunders would have assumed that the connection had been broken. Everyone in the room was staring at him quizzically. He waved them off. Finally Morrell spoke again. 'Who was the man you gave the box to?'

Saunders's heart stopped. He said nothing for a moment,

as he tried to gather his thoughts. 'How do you know I gave the box to someone?'

'I was there at Castle Island,' Morrell said. 'I saw you.'

Saunders felt as though he'd stuck his hand in an electrical outlet. His entire body tensed. 'You followed me,' he said slowly.

'I did.'

'Where are you now?' Saunders held his breath as he waited for the answer.

'You told me to follow the box, and it would lead me to my brother's killer,' Morrell said at last. 'Now, tell me what's going on.'

They were headed north on Interstate 93, through the mountains of New Hampshire, toward the village of Glencliff, set in the heart of the Green Mountain Range. It was an area unconquered by mankind, where towers of granite carved by glaciers more than a million years before jutted up from the ground like living things reaching for the heavens. The populace, much like the land itself, had resisted domination since its split from Massachusetts in 1679. The state motto, *Live Free Or Die*, was a credo most residents held close to their heart.

One of Toney's men was driving the conspicuous black suburban, a vehicle that was difficult to mistake for anything other than what it was. He was pushing the giant car to its limit; at one point Saunders glanced at the speedometer and saw that they were travelling at more than 110 mph, weaving in and out of the sparse traffic.

There were six of them in the car. Toney's other man was riding shotgun; Toney and Saunders were in the second-row captain's chairs; Akhtar and Cianna sat on the bench that was the last row of seats. Saunders stared out the window at the passing landscape, cataloguing all the mistakes he'd made. It was a daunting task.

'Morrell was following me and Cianna this morning,' Saunders said. 'When we handed the Cloak over to Lawrence, he followed the box. Lawrence took it up to his family compound in New Hampshire.'

'Why did he call you?' Toney asked.

'Because I could have killed him last night, and I didn't. He also believed me when I said that I wanted to kill the man who murdered his brother. But then Fasil showed up at Lawrence's house, and it looked like they were working together. He wanted answers, and he figured he didn't have to tell me where he was unless he was satisfied with what I said.'

'And he was,' Toney noted.

'Apparently. He said he would watch the house and wait for us. It's up at the next exit, and then a half-hour out into the mountains,' Saunders said. 'Down Route 25.'

'You've been there?'

Saunders nodded.

'What's the house like?' Toney asked.

'It's big and old,' Saunders replied. 'Two floors, several bedrooms. There's a large living room and a study on the first floor, along with the kitchen. A two-sided fireplace separates the living room and the kitchen, so when there's a fire going, it warms both rooms.'

Toney asked, 'Why so much space?'

'It used to be a state-run sanatorium. They treated more than a thousand tuberculosis patients there through the first half of the twentieth century. There used to be a patients' dormitory, but it was torn down. It was built close to the top of the mountain so the patients could get as much fresh air as possible. The state sold it off in the sixties, and Ainsworth's family has owned it ever since.'

'A sanatorium? Creepy. What's the approach like?'

'Treacherous,' Saunders said. 'It's set on the edge of the mountain. The driveway is cut out of the side of the hill. It has a cliff wall on one side, and falls off down a steep slope on the other side. The house itself backs up against the mountainside on the western side, and there are thick woods to the south with a wide open field between the tree-line and the house.'

'Security?'

Saunders nodded. 'Less than you might expect. Motion sensors in the yard are linked to an internal silent alarm and floods. The doors and windows on the first floor are wired, but the house is pretty remote. The security was set up to keep burglars and vagrants out, not to protect state secrets.'

'Anything else?' Toney asked sarcastically.

'Not that I know of,' Saunders replied. 'Unless it's been updated since I was there last. There weren't any motion sensors on the interior when I was there.'

'Great,' Toney said. 'So he can't track us inside the house. But how do we go in?'

'*We* don't. I do.'

'How?'

'I ring the doorbell.'

Toney gave Saunders a sharp look. 'No.'

'That's crazy,' Cianna agreed.

'It's the only way,' Saunders said. 'Any approach to the

house is protected. He won't shoot me. If anything, I think he'll welcome the chance to explain this all to me.'

'What makes you say that?' Cianna demanded.

'You said it yourself; he cares about me. I'm the closest thing to a son he has left.'

Cianna shook her head. 'What if Fasil and his people are there? They'll kill you on sight.'

'Morrell says they're not there,' Saunders said. 'It's only Lawrence and Stillwell in the house. Lawrence won't let Stillwell kill me.'

'How do you know?'

'I don't.'

Toney stared distrustfully at Saunders. 'If you're playing me, I promise you, I will burn you.'

'Yeah, I know it,' Saunders responded, without looking at the National Security Advisor.

'I don't like the idea of you going in by yourself. You're too close to him.'

'Maybe. But it's our only option. There's no way to mount an assault against the place. There's only one route down the mountain, so you can wait where you can see the house. I'll deal with Lawrence and get the information we need.'

'How?'

Saunders stared out the window again. They were passing through a wooded ravine, the road following the curve of a narrow rushing river. 'I'm not sure yet,' he admitted. 'I'll figure that out once I'm inside.'

Glencliff was a tiny hamlet of fewer than 100 living souls and forty man-made structures spread out over twenty square miles of mountainous terrain. The town center was set in a small glen nestled in between two mountainous outcroppings. Ainsworth's family house was on the mountain a few miles from the town center.

The sun was setting as Saunders and the others drove up the road that led to Ainsworth's house. As they approached, Morrell stepped out of the woods along the edge of the drive and pointed to a small turn-around shielded from view of the house, where his car was parked. Toney's driver steered the car in and parked behind Morrell's car.

Perched at the edge of the cliff, the house looked as though it might topple over the precipice with a strong wind. It wouldn't, Saunders knew. It was solidly built, and had been renovated several times over the years so that it had all the customary modern conveniences while retaining the old Yankee feel of the place. In that respect, it reminded Saunders of Ainsworth's personality. At least, it reminded him of the personality of the Lawrence Ainsworth he'd thought he'd known for two decades.

Saunders got out of the car and walked toward Morrell. The cop had his gun in his hand, and a wary look on his face. Saunders nodded to him. 'You did the right thing,' he said. Morrell didn't respond. 'This is Bill Toney,' Saunders said. 'These are his men. You met Cianna Phelan at her apartment the other day.'

Morrell didn't offer to shake hands; that would have involved letting go of the gun, and it didn't look as though he planned to do that anytime soon. 'He got here a few hours ago. I watched him from the woods, and just after he arrived, he walked farther up the mountain to a little building near the top.'

Saunders nodded. 'There's a deserted schoolhouse up there from the first half of the last century.'

'On the top of the mountain?' Toney asked.

Saunders shrugged. 'It's New Hampshire.'

'The man with the teardrop birthmark was there. Your boss gave him the box, and then came back to the house. He's been there ever since.'

'Any movement?' Saunders asked.

Morrell shook his head. 'There was another guy there briefly. Tall, bald. He went back up the mountain, though.'

'Did he come back?'

'Not that I saw.'

Saunders nodded. 'Okay. I'm going in.'

Morrell stared at him. 'Just like that?'

'Yeah, just like that.' Morrell looked at the others in the group, the doubt clear in his eyes. 'Don't worry,' Saunders reassured him. 'Everything I told you was the truth. I'm not working with the man who killed your brother, and I'll die before I let him get out of this with the Cloak.'

The driveway was a narrow dirt rut carved into the edge of the mountain. An old wooden fence that looked as though it would snap over if a bicycle bumped into it guarded the cliff on the right. Shards of uneven rock jutted out from the cliff on the left, interspersed with thick woods. It was narrow enough that only one car could pass at a time. Saunders glanced over the right side as he approached and saw that there was a hundred-foot drop to the next flat area.

The first alarm was tripped as the drive opened up fifty

yards from the house. He knew when it happened because flood lights popped on automatically, shining in his eyes and blinding him momentarily, casting shadows in the waning light.

He paused when the lights came on, looking straight ahead and raising his hands slightly to show that he wasn't holding a weapon. He had a gun in a shoulder holster under his jacket, but he knew that if he was to have a hope of getting inside, he had to appear as friendly as possible.

He continued, walking straight and steady toward the front door. His breath was ragged as he considered the possibility that Stillwell would take a shot at him, even if Ainsworth told him not to. It seemed unlikely; the logic he'd laid out for Toney had been sound. He couldn't know for sure, though, and if he was wrong, in all likelihood he'd be dead before he ever knew it.

Another set of lights set on the peak of the roof came on when he left the yard and started on the cobbled walkway that led to the door. They fired down on him as though he was the star of a Broadway show. He was, at that moment, the perfect target for anyone within the house who might want him dead. He kept his eyes straight ahead as he walked, accepting his fate. When he reached the front door, he swung the brass knocker and waited for a moment.

Nothing.

He knocked again, more forcefully this time.

The door was pulled open on the third knock. Ainsworth stood in the doorway, a fresh drink in one hand, a semi-automatic pistol in the other. 'Jack,' he said in a friendly tone. 'It's good to see you.' He held out the drink. 'Here, I just poured this. I haven't even taken a sip yet. I'll make another for myself.'

CHAPTER FIFTY-ONE

'He's at the door.'

One of Toney's men was perched on a rock, peering through the scope of a sharpshooter's rifle. 'Ainsworth is there. I have a clean shot. Do you want me to take it?'

'He didn't kill my brother,' Morrell said.

Toney looked at him before responding to his agent.

'Can you see anyone else?' he asked.

'No. Just Ainsworth. He has a gun. What do you want me to do?'

Cianna waited to hear Toney's response. There was a part of her that wanted him to tell his man to take the shot, if only to remove Saunders from danger. She knew that it didn't make any sense, though. They had no idea where the Cloak was, and without Ainsworth, they were far less likely to find out.

'Don't take the shot,' Toney said. She could hear the frustration in his voice. 'Keep him sighted for as long as possible, though. I may change my mind.'

Saunders took the drink, saying nothing. He stared at his boss.

'Come in, come in!' Ainsworth bade him. He stepped back to let Saunders pass. 'Just, please, close the door. You never know up here what may lurk in the woods.' He gave Saunders a knowing look. 'I saw a mountain lion the last time I was up here.' He looked out the window. 'And they're not even the most dangerous animal out there, am I right?'

'Lawrence . . .' Saunders began. He had no idea where to start the conversation. Ainsworth seemed strange, almost manic. He had never seen his boss in such a state before.

'You're armed, I assume?' Ainsworth asked.

'I have my sidearm in a shoulder holster, if that's what you mean.'

Ainsworth scrutinized his protégé, his brow furrowed, and Saunders had the feeling that he was considering whether to take the gun away. After a moment, his expression cleared. He continued holding his gun in his hand, though. Without warning, he exclaimed, 'Bears!'

Saunders was startled, and had to work hard not to reach for his gun. 'What?'

'Bears,' Ainsworth repeated. 'Bears are far more dangerous than mountain lions. Mountain lions are afraid of people. A good-sized man is far larger than the average mountain lion, and we don't make very good prey for them. All they really want is to be left alone, so they're not particularly dangerous. But a bear is a different story. You get a bear that is hungry?' He whistled as he shook his head. 'You've got a real problem. A motivated bear isn't afraid of anything. They're huge; they can weigh up to a ton. They're strong, and deceptively fast . . .'

Saunders eyed the gun that was still in Ainsworth's hand. Ainsworth walked over to the island in the kitchen and poured himself another drink. 'Lawrence, what are you doing up here?'

'I'm taking a few days off. I haven't been up here in a while. Since Sam died, actually. Remember? Four years ago when the three of us came up?' It took him another moment to get his next thought out. 'I'd forgotten how beautiful it is up here. Come look.' He walked over to the far side of the house. There was a deck off the back. It hung out over the edge of the mountain cliff, facing due west. The sun was just disappearing over Webster Slide Mountain and the Owl's Head Cliff, a sheer eight-hundred-foot wall of granite that was a perennial draw for rock climbers. 'It's as close to heaven as you can get. I should have come here sooner. I realize now that I feel closer to Sam here than anywhere else in the world.' He gave Saunders an embarrassed smile. 'I don't believe it is a matter of actual proximity, Jack. Don't worry, I haven't completely taken leave of my senses.'

'I didn't think you had, Lawrence. Is that why you came here? To be closer to Sam?'

Ainsworth shook his head. 'The opposite, actually. I figured as long as I was up in Boston, I could come up here, see the old place. Maybe clear out some of Sam's things, and make a fresh start.'

'We need to talk, Lawrence,' Saunders said evenly.

'You know the funny thing?' Ainsworth continued as though he hadn't heard Saunders. 'I can't tell Sam's things from mine.' He laughed and it came out as a bit of a cackle. 'We were the same size, you see? He had my build. Same size feet, too. I started digging through the shoes in the closets and I couldn't for the life of me remember which were his and which were mine.'

'I miss him, too,' Saunders said. 'He was like a brother to me.'

'He was,' Ainsworth agreed. 'When he died, you were the closest thing I had to a son left. It's just the two of us now. You understand that, don't you?'

'I think so, Lawrence.'

'Good,' Ainsworth said. He seemed to be staring past Saunders. 'Now more than ever this country needs people who understand.'

'It's been too long,' Cianna said to Akhtar. They were crouched at the edge of the woods that crept up the slope from the drive leading to the mountain house. Toney was standing nearby, his three men spread out at the edge of the tree-line to increase the chances that one of them might catch a glimpse of something happening inside. They had seen and heard nothing, though, since Saunders had entered.

'Do you think he is in trouble?' Akhtar asked.

'Maybe,' Cianna said. 'You never know what Ainsworth may do if he really has turned.'

'We don't know what either of them will do,' Toney said quietly.

'What is that supposed to mean?' Cianna demanded.

'It means exactly what I said,' Toney replied. 'The two of them have worked together for decades. They've been in contact with each other throughout the past three days. We have no way of knowing whether they've been on the same page the entire time.'

'Bullshit,' Cianna said.

'Yes,' Akhtar said to Toney. 'I agree. What you say is bullshit.'

'How can you say that?' Toney demanded of Akhtar. 'You know nothing of this man.'

'I know what I saw of him. That is enough.'

Toney shook his head. 'What's taking so long, then?'

'Perhaps Mr Ainsworth has not been welcoming.' He was silent for a moment. 'Or, perhaps Mr Saunders was not correct. Perhaps Fasil and his men were with Mr Ainsworth all along.'

Cianna took a step toward the house. 'I'm going in,' she said.

'How?' Toney demanded.

'Through the front door,' she said. 'I'll shoot my way through, if necessary.'

'No, you won't,' Toney said, moving toward her and holding out a hand to restrain her. She grabbed him by the thumb and twisted the hand around so that he was forced to bend over to keep the thumb from breaking. He grunted in pain.

'You'll never make it across the open field,' he said, still bent over and puffing against the pain in his hand. 'Now let me go.'

'Why?'

'Because if you don't, I'm going to have you shot.' One of his men pointed his gun at her. She let go of his hand, and he stood up, rubbing his thumb and wrist. He looked at her with a combination of anger and respect. 'I read your file,' he said.

'Good for you,' she said.

'Interesting material.'

'Fiction usually is.'

'I'm not talking about the incident that put you away,' he said. 'I'm talking about your training record.'

She scowled at him. 'What about it?'

'You were chosen for one of the toughest units in the military, and received some of the most extensive combat training there is. Weapons, anti-terrorism, self-defense, all under brutal mountain conditions in the heat and cold of Afghanistan. No women had been given the training you had before. There was a debate among the heads of the military as to whether or not it was wise. Some believed women weren't suited to what they were asking you to do. Many still believe it.'

'I did everything they asked of me,' Cianna said. 'I was just as good as most of the men in the training.'

'No,' Toney said. 'Not according to your training reports.'

She looked at him with contempt. It took a significant amount of self-control not to put him on the ground with one swing. She knew she could, but she also knew that it wouldn't help Saunders. She decided to ignore the baiting and turned back to the house, looking for the best approach.

'According to your training reports, you weren't just as good as most of the men,' he continued. 'You were better.'

She shot him another hostile look, unsure whether he was still trying to goad her. 'What are you saying?' she demanded.

'It was never brought up at your court martial. They figured it wouldn't look very good. But it's true. According to your fitness reports, you were among the three best trainees in the unit.'

'Why are you telling me this?'

'Because I want you to understand that I have nothing against you. Personally, I think you got screwed. But that doesn't change the fact that I am in charge here, and you will do exactly as I say. I've had enough of people who think they can freelance US security policy. Do you understand that?'

She stared at him for a moment. 'Yeah,' she said finally. 'I understand that.' She looked back at the house. There still had not been any noise or movement that they could see since Saunders had gone in. 'So, what do we do now?' she asked impatiently.

Toney looked at the house. 'Now, we see how much of your training stuck.'

CHAPTER FIFTY-TWO

'Where is the Cloak, Lawrence?'

'I've taken care of it. It's safe.'

'Who did you give it to?'

Ainsworth looked out the window. 'They say once they have eaten human flesh, there's no choice but to hunt them down and kill them. It gets into their blood, and they will keep coming back for more. Again and again. There's no way to stop them but to kill them.'

'Who?' Jack asked. 'Kill who, Lawrence?'

Ainsworth looked at Saunders as though the younger man was crazy. 'Bears, of course.' He frowned. 'Maneaters. They will forever pose a lethal danger to all people, and they must be put down. For everyone's safety.'

Saunders frowned. 'Who did you give the Cloak to, Lawrence? Where is it? I need to know.'

'People aren't so different from bears in that respect, I suppose,' Ainsworth continued, ignoring the question. 'Once they get the taste for human blood, there is no way to get it out of their system. So often we search for the reasons for the wars that we have, but in reality there doesn't need to be a reason beyond the war itself. For those who have a taste for blood, they can use any excuse.' He looked up at Saunders. 'You know that better than anyone, no doubt. You've been out in the field. You've seen it with your own eyes.'

Saunders nodded. 'I have.' He breathed slowly. 'Is that why you're doing what you're doing?'

Ainsworth looked sharply at him. 'What am I doing?'

'You're working with Fasil, aren't you? Is it because you've got a taste for blood? Or is it all about money?'

'It's neither of those, I assure you, Jack. You know me better than that.'

'Why, then? Why would you do this?'

'Because I'm tired, Jack.'

'You're tired?'

'Yes, I'm tired. I'm tired of seeing this country's commitment to its ideals flutter like a flag in the breeze. I've seen it too many times. I saw it as a young man in Vietnam and Laos and Cambodia. From the 1950s the Agency worked to keep those nations free from the scourge of Communism. We had the plan and the people in place to get the job done, but those on the home front didn't have the will. Three million people died when we pulled out. Three million people who had trusted us. I saw it again in Somalia, and in Bosnia. I watched as they ordered us to stand at the Iraqi border in the first Gulf War. And we stayed there and listened on the radio to the screams of those who had opposed Saddam Hussein from within. Countless good men and women who had risked their lives to help us, and we sacrificed them – giving away an intelligence network we had spent decades building.'

'I was there.'

'I know you were. You and Sam, and thousands of others with the commitment to do a job that needed to be done. And we left it for another time. Even after we went back in, even after the Towers fell, we refused to stay the course. We refused to do what needed to be done. We went in with half-measures, and fucked the place up for years, and then we declared victory, turned tail and left. Now we try to pretend that the Iranians won't run the place within a matter of a few years.'

'What does that have to do with all this?' Saunders demanded.

'Because it's happening again, this time in Afghanistan. We've already declared a 30 per cent reduction in forces by the end of this year. The plans are to have all combat forces out of the country within two years from that. What is needed is an all-out war on our part, and instead we're going to walk out of there and leave it to crumble.' Ainsworth took a deep breath. 'I won't let that happen, Jack. Not in the land where Sam gave his life. Not when there is something I can do about it.' Just then, a faint noise came from somewhere near the back of the house. Both men turned in that direction. It could just have been the ancient house settling, but it occurred to Saunders that he might be able to use it to his advantage.

'How can you do something about it?' Saunders asked thoughtfully. 'You won't even be able to get off this mountain.'

'No?' Ainsworth walked over to the front door and peered out. 'You came with others,' he said. 'I thought you might. Who is out there?'

'Toney,' Saunders responded. 'And he has others with him.'

'The biggest asshole of them all,' Ainsworth muttered.

'Good for you. Still, they won't be able to make it to the house. There's too much open ground, and the alarms will alert us. They'll test it, but they'll stay away. He's an asshole, but he's not stupid.'

'You're still trapped,' Saunders pointed out.

'Am I?' Ainsworth asked. He smiled. 'You might be surprised.'

Cianna was moving on quickly but with care. Hand over hand, she shimmied her way along the steep slope on the other side of the road, moving her way around the side of the mountain toward the house at the edge of the cliff. It was difficult going, but the creases on the granite were pronounced enough that it wasn't impossible. Judging from her speed, she figured she was more than halfway to the house. Looking ahead, she could see that the slope became steep from here. That would add some challenge. She was more concerned, though, that she was running out of time.

She dug her boot into a crag and pushed herself on, remembering the training she'd had in the chalky mountains of Afghanistan. It all came back to her with little effort. If she could make it to the back side of the house, she could avoid the security systems and get close enough to see what was happening without alerting those within to her presence. That was the plan, at least. Whether it would work was another matter. She wouldn't let herself become distracted with doubts, though. That was another thing that her training had taught her: focus on the immediate task at hand, and trust your instincts to pull you through the challenges that lay ahead.

She put her head down and kept moving along the mountainside.

'Even if everything you say is true, I still don't understand,' Saunders said. 'Why work with Fasil? He is the enemy. How does that advance any of the ideals you claim to stand for?'

'It seems to make little sense, I know,' Ainsworth said.

'He is the sworn enemy of the United States. He makes no attempt to hide that.'

'He is,' Ainsworth admitted. 'But he is the means to an end.'

'What end?'

'He will bring the Taliban back in power,' Ainsworth said.

Saunders shook his head. 'It's insane. You want the Cloak to give Fasil the legitimacy he needs to lead the country back to Taliban rule?'

'Not just that,' Ainsworth said. 'Not only will Fasil have the Cloak, but he will be able to say that he has saved it from the Americans. He will be a hero.'

'And America will be reviled.'

'It will be. These people riot when Danish newspapers print cartoons of Mohammed. Can you imagine how the Afghan faithful will react in the area when it is revealed that Americans have defiled one of the three most sacred relics in all of Islam?'

'Even those few who support us now will turn against us.'

'Exactly. It will drive the populace, including those who still cling to our protection, away from any association with us. It will result in an unexpurgated war against the US forces in the country.'

'How will that help us?'

'Don't you see?' Ainsworth prodded. 'We will have no option but to declare a complete war in Afghanistan. Finally, the gloves will come off. America needs to be pushed to realize that we need to fight for real in Afghanistan. If the population turns against the troops, we will give up the notion that we can win a war and still win the people's hearts and minds. For all its faults, the US population will not stand for attacks on its military. If this happens now, when we still have the combat muscle committed over there, it will give us the best chance to succeed.'

'And if Pakistan gets involved?' Saunders demanded. 'What happens then? They have nukes, and if there is a feeling that the US has dishonored Mohammed in this way, you never know what could happen. Even if they couldn't reach the US, they could attack Israel.'

'It is a risk, but a small one – and an acceptable one. We have intelligence that maps Pakistan's nuclear weapons. If they fire one, we will respond with fifty.'

'And what of the people who are killed?'

'The losses in Israel would be tragic, but in the long run, the Israelis will be better off if the other countries in the region understand that we are committed to their defense. The losses in Afghanistan and Pakistan are necessary. They are our enemies, and if they could, they would bring down every highrise in America. We've known that for a long time; we just didn't know what to do about it. I realized I could fix this when I learned of Captain Stillwell's ring of thieves. It has been operating for some time, quite profitably. Profitably enough that our industrious captain had managed to buy off all the brass he thought he needed. I made it clear to him that if he didn't cooperate with me, I would bring them all down. He was fairly easy to convince when I explained it to him, and his people have developed an expertise in thievery that proved quite useful. It would have been simple were it not for a dim-witted corporal named Charles Phelan. The Cloak was to be shipped to Kabul and make its way to Fasil through intermediaries. I can't tell you the consternation that was caused when it did not arrive. Once that happened, word seeped out slowly and the race to find Mr Phelan was on. When you came to me with the tip from your informant in Virginia, I saw that you could be very useful.'

'You used me. Like an asset.'

'No,' Ainsworth insisted. 'Like a professional. I knew no one was better than you, and that if I had you on our side, we would surely get to the Cloak before anyone else. I would have told you the whole plan, but I couldn't risk it at that point. I knew it would be far easier if you thought Fasil was the enemy.'

'He is the enemy!'

'Ultimately, yes,' Ainsworth agreed. 'But not in this. In this, he is an asset like any other.'

'Just an asset,' Saunders said quietly.

Ainsworth nodded. 'Just an asset.'

Saunders looked at his boss, the man he had repeatedly trusted with his life, with fresh horror. 'You must stop this, Lawrence. You know that, don't you? Otherwise you will be betraying every principle you've ever held dear.'

Ainsworth shook his head. 'No! That's not true! I am

standing up for everything I've fought for my entire life! I'm standing up for Murphy and Desouza and Keller and Schmidt and Jeffs and Klein, and the rest of them! Just like you did up in those mountains. You of all people must understand!' As he shouted, he spilled his drink, and his gun was raised, waving about.

'That was different,' Saunders said.

'No it wasn't!' Ainsworth yelled. 'It was the same. Just on a smaller scale. But the principle was the same. If nothing is done, we will pull out of Afghanistan, and everything we as a nation have fought for over the last decade will be lost. The country will eventually be run by the Taliban one way or the other, but if it happens five years from now, there will be nothing we can do about it.'

'No, you're wrong.'

Ainsworth had stopped waving his arms now. He stood very still, looking at Saunders with new distrust. 'How can you say that?' he demanded. 'You must be with me on this, you must.'

Saunders shook his head. 'I'm not.'

Ainsworth seemed to consider this for a moment. Then he pointed the gun at Saunders's head. 'I really think you should reconsider, Jack. It would be best for both of us.'

CHAPTER FIFTY-THREE

The last fifty yards were the worst of it. Behind the house the slope was at its steepest, the rock wall its most sheer, bereft of vegetation. The only handholds and footholds were clefts in the surface, often only inches deep. The fall was over a hundred feet to a brief shelf twenty feet wide, with a few shrubs and grasses. From there, it was another two hundred feet before the slope leveled off.

Cianna dug her fingers in and moved along the mountain face, pulling herself along until she could see the deck from the back of the house hanging over the edge above her. Slowly, carefully, she made her way up. Twice the holds to which she clung pulled free, small portions of the mountain plunging to the plateau below, almost taking her with them. She cursed as she struggled to stabilize herself.

It took several minutes before she reached the top of the cliff and hauled herself up there, panting as she caught her breath. After a moment she got to her feet and crept along the foundation underneath the deck that hung out over the cliff, looking for a way in.

The foundation was stonework built into the mountain granite. At times she had trouble distinguishing that which had been put there by man, and that which was a part of the land itself. On one side, though, she found a narrow wooden window sealed into the rockwork. Spider webs covered the outside, thick as cotton candy, and she had to push them away, angering the arachnids, which scurried for cover.

She thought back to Saunders's description of the security system: the windows and door on the first floor were wired into the alarm. It seemed less likely, though, that the small window in the foundation would be alarmed, as well. It was so narrow it wasn't clear that she would be able to get her small frame through it, and the paint made it look as though the window hadn't been opened in decades. It was a risk, but an acceptable one. She worked her fingers around the edges to see whether the ancient wood had been sealed in such a way as to allow an alarm wire to function. It looked as though the wood there was far older than any of the other doors and windows she had seen from the drive. As she dug her fingers along the sides, she could tell that it had weakened enough over time that it might come loose with reasonable effort. She pushed and pulled, trying to get her fingers far enough into the gap to gain leverage. It took a few minutes, each of which seemed an eternity, but eventually the wood gave enough that her fingers could get behind it. With one final pull, the piece of wood came free, and she was able to prize the narrow opening further apart.

She hesitated, waiting for some sign that an alarm had been tripped. There was nothing but silence, however, and after a moment, she felt sure that she was still undetected.

She got down on her belly and shimmied her way

through the low gap, letting herself down onto the damp and uneven basement floor.

It was even darker inside than she'd expected. She crouched on the ground, waiting for her eyes to adjust. After a moment, she was able to make out charcoal-toned shapes. The basement was little more than a glorified crawl space, with a low ceiling of exposed beams and rotted insulation dripping from in between the joists. It ran the length and breadth of the house, except that in the easternmost section, away from the cliff, the natural rock ledge grew from beneath and ran up to meet a low span of foundation on the far side. In the center of the area, a rough but sturdy tower of stone rose up through the flooring above. She guessed that it was the foundation for the chimney. In between that tower and the north side of the house, a ladder was built into a support.

Cianna crept over to the ladder and looked up. There was a hatch cut in between two joists, hinged on one side. She put a foot on the bottom rung and put her hand up to push on the hatch. It moved, but reluctantly. Climbing up another rung, she pushed harder, and the hatch rose higher. She snaked a hand into the gap to see what was causing the resistance and felt the bottom of a piece of rug. With a little effort, she was able to move it to the side and raise the hatch enough that she would be able to slip through onto the first floor.

It was dangerous; perhaps even foolish. She had no idea what part of the house she was emerging into, and whether it was in a spot where Ainsworth could see her and pick her off as she pulled herself out. But she had few options, so she climbed the ladder as quickly and quietly as she could.

The hatch opened into a large pantry. The door was closed, and the lights were off, but there was enough light coming from the wide gap underneath the door for her to see. She let the trapdoor down quietly and stood at the door, listening for any movement. Hearing none, she opened the door slowly, and followed the barrel of her gun out into the house.

'Your gun,' Ainsworth said. His voice was cold, and it was clear that any sentimentality that had kept him from viewing Saunders as a threat was gone.

'My gun?' Saunders could only play for time now.

'You said it was in a shoulder holster.' Ainsworth gestured with the barrel of his gun. 'Open your jacket slowly, please.'

'Lawrence, I don't understand . . .'

'Yes, you do. Do it now, Jack. You know me well enough that you have little doubt that I will shoot you if I need to. Open your coat, now.'

It was true. He'd been behind a desk for several years, but before that, Ainsworth had been known as one of the most ruthless men in the Agency. He had taught Jack everything he knew, and there was little question that he was prepared to kill even Saunders if he thought it necessary to ensure the success of a mission he'd set in motion. Saunders did as he'd been instructed.

'With your right hand, unsnap the holster,' Ainsworth instructed.

'It's unsnapped,' Saunders replied.

Ainsworth looked offended. 'Did you come in here

expecting to be able to reach for your gun? Did you really think that I would allow that to happen?'

'You always taught me to be ready for anything. I figured it couldn't hurt. You never know what kind of dangerous creatures there are up here in the mountains.'

'Ah yes,' Ainsworth said. 'The bears.'

'The bears,' Saunders agreed.

Ainsworth advanced toward Saunders, his gun now pointed at the man's head. He was close enough that a shot couldn't miss. 'If I see either of your hands move, I'll kill you.'

'Understood.'

Ainsworth reached out with his left hand and grabbed Saunders's gun by the butt. He pulled on it, his eyes still on Saunders. It caught, and Ainsworth gave it a harder tug. It still didn't come free. Ainsworth looked down at it for the first time, and saw that the holster was snapped shut. He was confused for a moment, as he pulled at the strap to free the gun. 'The holster is snapped,' he said in an annoyed voice. 'You told me—'

He realized his mistake even as the words came out of his mouth. He'd taken his eyes off Saunders only for a split second, but he understood instantly that it was enough of a mistake to be fatal. He squeezed the trigger on his own gun even before he looked up, hoping that he'd get lucky.

He didn't.

At the moment Ainsworth's eyes went to Saunders's gun, Saunders ducked to the left and swung his right arm upward. His fist connected with Ainsworth's arm just as the gun went off, and Saunders could hear the bullet whistle by his ear. Ainsworth was thrown off balance, and Saunders grabbed the older man's gun with his right hand and locked him in a headlock with his left. The two of them struggled as Ainsworth tried to maneuver the gun around to aim it at Saunders. Saunders tightened his choke hold on his mentor, cutting off his breath bit by bit. He could feel Ainsworth losing strength. For a moment, he thought the fight was won. Ainsworth had only his left hand free, and it was unlikely that he could generate any strength in a punch, or would be able to grab hold of anything he could use as a weapon.

Saunders realized he'd underestimated the old man when he felt the tightening on his testicles. Ainsworth had reached around behind him and sought out a weak spot. There was little Saunders could do; he couldn't let go of the gun, and the headlock was the only way he saw to put the man down at the moment. He screamed out in pain, and tightened the choke hold. His reaction only encouraged Ainsworth, who tightened his grip.

Saunders hung on as long as he could, but the pain was too great, and he released his grip on Ainsworth's neck, swung his fist at the back of the man's head, and pushed off to separate himself from the left-handed grip. At the same time, he clung to the gun to prevent Ainsworth from getting a shot off. The move might have succeeded, but Ainsworth's fingers were wrapped so tightly around Saunders's gonads that when he pulled away, it sent a wave of blinding pain and nausea through him so powerful that he collapsed.

Ainsworth stumbled, choking as he tried to catch his breath. As Saunders released the gun, Ainsworth swung it around and lost control, and it fell to the floor. Saunders saw it and made a move toward it, but he was doubled over in pain; there was no chance for him to grasp it first. Ainsworth dove and grabbed it, still coughing. 'I always told you during your training to remember, Jack,' he sputtered, 'that old men fight dirty.' He raised the gun to shoot.

Before he could get the shot off, though, there was an explosion from the far side of the room. Ainsworth was knocked off his feet, and fell backwards into the wall. There was a splatter of blood on the floral wallpaper that smeared as he slid to the floor; the gun dangled loosely in his lap.

Saunders, still doubled over, looked up and saw Cianna at the door in a shooting stance. He looked over at Ainsworth. His eyes were still open, and he still held the gun, though it lolled impotently. Saunders crawled over to him.

The gunshot had taken him in the chest. Cianna was carrying a military-issue 9 mm loaded with shredders that spread on impact to maximize internal damage. Saunders could tell immediately that the wound was fatal. Ainsworth was sweating and there was a heavy bubbling sound with every breath. Saunders leaned in close. 'Where are they going?' he asked. 'How are Fasil and his men getting out of here?'

Ainsworth looked at Saunders and seemed surprised that he was there. 'Jack,' he said. 'It's better this way.'

'Tell me, Lawrence. I need to know how they plan to get the Cloak back to Afghanistan.'

'They're gone already,' Ainsworth said. He smiled, and

Saunders could see the blood seeping between the older man's teeth. 'They heard the gunshots, I'm sure.' He coughed up some blood. 'You won't catch them.'

'Tell me how,' Saunders demanded. He took Ainsworth by the shoulders and shook him. 'This is your one chance to set things right, don't you understand? You can't let this be your legacy.'

Ainsworth shook his head. 'My legacy is a ghost.' He was struggling with each word. 'That's what we do, Jack. We take all of the risk, all of the blame, and none of the credit. That is what we signed up for.'

'I didn't sign up to start a holy war!' Saunders screamed at Ainsworth, shaking him again.

'I'm glad it was you and the girl, Jack,' Ainsworth said, choking on a sad smile. 'Toney's an asshole. I would have been very unhappy if he'd been the one to take me down.' His eyes rolled into the back of his head and his body convulsed.

'Tell me, goddammit! Tell me now!' Saunders was shaking Ainsworth more violently, but it was too late. He was dead.

'Shit,' Saunders said, releasing Ainsworth's body and letting it slump to the floor.

'What now?' Cianna asked.

'We try to catch them. Morrell said they were up at the abandoned schoolhouse. Even if they've left, they can't be too far ahead of us. There's a trail that leads up the mountain from here; maybe we can catch up to them. It's our only chance.'

'Do you know where the trail is?'

He nodded and pulled out his gun. 'I'll show you.' He

started to head toward the door, but turned and said to her, 'Thanks. If it wasn't for you, I'd be the one dead on the floor.'

'Don't mention it,' she said. 'You're better-looking when you're breathing.'

The words had barely left her mouth when his chest exploded, splattering blood and tissue all over the front of her shirt. She didn't understand what was happening as his expression went blank and he fell to his knees. As he went down, she saw Sirus Stillwell standing in the door, his gun pointed at her.

CHAPTER FIFTY-FOUR

Saunders had no understanding of what was happening; that was the strangest thing about it. In his mind he was still on his feet, turning to give chase to Fasil and his men. And yet, somehow, the images flashing before his eyes didn't match what his brain believed he was doing. His optical screen, which should have been shifting to the front of the house, to images of running down the hallway and out the door, instead remained static, teetering on some unknown precipice, looking at Cianna Phelan as a spray of red covered her blouse. The image tilted, slowly at first, but with gathering speed, crashing to the floor – as though someone had dropped a video camera but left it on.

There was no pain. Perhaps that was the disconnect that barred rational comprehension of what had happened. Stillwell's round, a shredder not unlike the one Cianna had fired into Lawrence Ainsworth, struck Saunders in the ribs and ricocheted toward the center of his body, narrowly missing his heart, causing immediate trauma to his spinal cord. It had continued through his body and exited out his side and smashed into the wall as a mangled hunk of lead with three times the diameter it had had as a projectile. The feeling to most of his body had been instantly snuffed. He could move his hands a bit, but it felt as though they were caught in semi-congealed Jell-O.

Cianna was moving even before Saunders hit the ground, rolling to her left, nimble and balanced, like some acrobatic dancer whose every muscle had been trained to adhere to set choreography. She was a vision, and from his vantage he appreciated the full range of her beauty for the first time. Her face was determined, her reddish hair untamed, her body taut and athletic. As she rolled, the hardwood floor exploded within inches of her, two rounds from Sirus's gun throwing up splinters and smoke. It was as though the rounds couldn't catch up to her; she transcended physical threats.

With much effort, he pulled one hand closer to his face. It was dark and sticky and smelled of wet iron. He could hear a gurgle, and he wondered whether Ainsworth had come back to life, his lungs making one final effort to absorb the air through the pools of blood. He knew it was impossible, but then everything that was playing out before him seemed impossible.

He put the thought out of his head.

She came out of her roll firing her gun, the weapon sighted even before she was vertical. Three shots – though, judging from the precision of her movements and the clarity in her eyes, one would have been sufficient. At the edge of the movie playing out before him, Saunders saw an enormous bald figure collapse.

He felt an inexplicable proprietary pride in her. She was not his, he knew, and she never would be. And yet it felt as though he could take some credit for some part of her. It was probably wishful thinking, but he thought it anyway.

She remained in a crouched shooting position for a moment, the gun pointing at the tumbled mass at the other end of the room. Then, finally, she turned and looked Saunders in the eye.

He smiled at her. At least, he tried to smile. He had no idea that the muscles in his face were no longer responding to the nerve impulses his brain continued to send out, like a castaway cut off from the rest of the world, sending an emergency message that no one could hear. She didn't smile back.

She came to him, and he could see her lips moving, but he couldn't understand the words. It was as though she was talking under water. That was okay with him, they didn't have any time for conversation at the moment anyway; they needed to get going to chase down Fasil. They could talk about whatever seemed to have her concerned later. He expressed these thoughts to her, though they never emerged as words that could be understood.

She was kneeling over him now, a senseless gesture. They should be moving, and yet she hovered there, her lips still moving, a look of panic on her face. Then the image began to dim and narrow. The film he'd been watching was coming to a close. That was okay with him, too. He had no more desire to be a mere spectator. If he couldn't be a participant, what was the point of being there at all?

The screen had gone black now, and he waited for the credits that would never come.

CHAPTER FIFTY-FIVE

'Holy shit! What the hell happened?'

Cianna heard Toney's voice from the door. Ainsworth's lifeless body lay in a pool of blood against one wall, and Stillwell's enormous frame was just inside the doorway. Her first shot had taken him just under the left eye on an upward trajectory and had blown the back of his skull off. In between the two dead bodies, she knelt over Saunders, blowing into his mouth, desperately trying to keep him alive. She paused only long enough to shout at Toney, 'Help me!' He hung at the threshold for a moment, still gaping. 'I said, help me!' she shouted again.

He moved toward her. 'Is he all right?'

She blew three quick breaths into Saunders and paused. 'Does he look all right? Do something!'

He was by her now, leaning over Saunders from the other side. She could see him looking at her dubiously. She went back to giving mouth-to-mouth. She would have performed CPR, as well, but there was not enough of Saunders's chest left to push down on. 'I think he's gone,' Toney said.

'No he's not!' Cianna replied. She redoubled her effort, blowing harder. With each breath Saunders's chest rose and fell, giving her hope despite the wheeze of wet air that escaped from the wound in exactly the same rhythm and strength with which she blew. She heard one of Toney's men enter the room.

'Holy fuck,' he said.

'Get on the phone and get a medevac up here, now!' Toney shouted. 'Use my clearance identification, and tell them to hurry!'

Cianna could hear the man on the phone, shouting orders. He returned a few moments later. 'Are they coming?' she demanded in between breaths.

'They are,' the man said. He touched her shoulder. 'I don't think he can survive,' he said. 'I was a medic in the Gulf before this.'

She turned on him. 'You were a medic?' He nodded. 'Good, take over for me.'

He shook his head. 'You don't understand. I didn't mean—'

She cut him off. 'I don't give a shit what you meant!' she screamed at him. 'You keep working on him until they get here, do you understand?'

The man looked at Toney, who nodded, and then he bent over Saunders and began administering CPR, while also applying pressure to the wound to try to stem the bleeding.

Toney grabbed Cianna and looked her in the eyes. 'Did he say anything? Did you find out how they are getting out of here?'

'No,' she said. She bent down to try to help with Saunders, but Toney grabbed her by the shoulder and pushed her to try to get her to focus on his question. Her reaction was swift and violent. Her fist shot up and caught him in the nose, knocking him back and drawing blood. She flew at him over Saunders's body, grabbing for his throat with one hand as the other battered away at him. He covered his head with his arms.

'You bastard!' she screamed. 'You fucking bastard! You did this!'

'What the hell are you talking about?' he yelled back, still protecting himself as best he could.

'It's your fault!' She continued to attack, praying with each blow that she might find relief. It was not coming, though.

'Get off me!' he shouted.

The cadence of his plea caught in her consciousness, and she was transported once more to her youth, kneeling on her little brother, torturing him as he called out to be released. She recoiled, horrified. For a moment she was frozen, her mind incapable of grasping all that had happened in such a short time. She looked around the room, taking it all in. The stench of blood and gunshot and death brought her back to the battlefields of Afghanistan: the streets and the mountains and the desert, each one splattered with the lives of those with whom she'd served, and those she'd sought to protect. 'Oh, Jesus,' she said softly.

'Cianna!'

She looked at Toney. He still had one arm over his face, as though afraid she might attack again. She sat back in despair.

'We know where they were,' Toney said, standing. 'The cop saw them, and he knows how to get up there.' He was moving toward the door. 'I'm going up; it's our only chance.'

She sat there, watching Toney's man work to keep Saunders alive, her head feeling as though someone had filled it with gravel. Then she got to her knees, leaned forward and kissed Saunders's forehead. She hovered there for just a moment before she got to her feet and followed Toney outside.

They found the path easily with Morrell's help. It sliced like a wound off the northeast corner of the property, through a roll of tall grass at the edge of the trees. Even in the gathering darkness, it was difficult to miss. Cianna, Akhtar, Morrell, Toney and his last man sprinted up the mountain, ignoring the branches that clawed at their faces as they went.

The schoolhouse was a quarter of a mile away, its foundation drilled into an expansive slab of granite at the peak. Cianna wondered who could have conceived of such a spot for the local center of education. It was a tiny rundown structure with an abbreviated steeple over a doorway where a bell had once sent its clarion call over the valley below. The bell was gone now, the steeple's wood shingles had partially pulled away revealing the wood skeleton underneath.

They approached quietly but without hesitation, all with guns drawn, hoping for a confrontation. They were disappointed, though. As Ainsworth had predicted, the place was deserted. All that remained was a scattering of food wrappers and empty water bottles.

'They were here,' Akhtar said.

'This trash could have been here for months,' Toney grumbled in frustration, kicking an empty bag of pita chips. 'It could have been left by campers for all we know.'

Akhtar picked up a bottle of water near the center of the one-room structure. The top was off, and it was still half full. 'The air is dry up here,' he said. 'The water would evaporate quickly, as in the mountains back home. Whoever left this was here recently.'

'So, campers could have left this here days ago. What does it matter? We would have seen them come through Ainsworth's property if they had been here tonight. We were right there.'

'There must be another way down,' Cianna suggested. They all looked at her. 'It's the only thing that makes sense,' she said.

They headed outside and spread out, walking the perimeter of the granite slab, moving east from the path by which they'd come, looking for another way down. In the dark the search was treacherous. Twice Cianna stumbled and almost pitched down the mountain. She saw the path the second time she lost her balance close to the edge. She would have missed it were she not looking straight down the narrow ledge, but it was there, snaking down the east side of the mountain through the sparse, low brush.

They headed down the mountain, their pace hindered by the steep slope and the darkness, until they came to a high valley between two peaks, running like a river of green for a half-mile before climbing on the other side, back up the second rise of granite. They were two hundred yards into the lush vegetation when they heard the plane. It started as a low drone, like a dull ringing in the ears.

Cianna at first thought it was the buzz of dehydration she had experienced so many times before on the humps through the arid Afghan mountains. The noise continued to grow in volume, though, and she noticed the others with her looking up in the sky, searching for the source.

At that moment the valley seemed to ignite with bright spotlights and a trail of tracers that ran in two parallel lines along the valley floor. It startled the group so badly that they all dove for cover.

'What the hell?' Toney barked.

'Airfield,' Cianna said, picking her head up and looking over the valley.

'Up here?' Toney sounded incredulous, but it was true. A narrow strip of land had been cleared, paved and lined with lights. It wasn't elaborate, and it would service only small prop planes with limited range, but it was functional. At one end there was a little weather-beaten shingled hut with a windsock hanging off the top. Several of the lights along the runway were out, but there were enough to give a good sense of the landing strip's parameters. It looked as though the strip had been there for years, but had fallen into disrepair. 'Ainsworth must have put this in so he could fly up from Virginia when he used to use the house more often,' Toney said.

The plane had circled back and was now coming in on approach. The lights were on in the small cabin, and Cianna could see through a large window that there were two men in the building, moving about and getting ready to exit. 'We've got to stop them,' she said. Everyone looked at Toney, but he faltered. He dropped his head, and the other men looked back at Cianna.

She glanced around at the terrain, assessing their situation. The path cut through scattered waist-high shrubs. The rest of the vegetation looked to be wispy mountain grass. 'Okay,' she said. 'We have to split up. If we all come down the path, they'll be able to pick us off one by one as soon as we hit the runway.' She looked at Morrell and Toney's man. 'You two, split off here to the west, and make your way off-path toward the building. Make sure that they don't get back in once they come out. We don't want to be dealing with a siege.' She motioned to Toney and Akhtar. 'You two split off to the east and head to the far end of the runway. The plane is going to have to turn around to take off again. Get there before that happens and take the plane out. Everyone move fast and stay low; try not to be spotted until the last second possible. They heard the gunfire from before, so they'll be looking for us, but the more we can surprise them, the better off we'll be.'

'What are you going to do?' Toney demanded.

'I'm going straight down the middle of the path.'

'They'll see you,' Akhtar protested.

'I certainly hope so.'

'A diversion,' Morrell commented, catching her plan.

She nodded. 'Like I said, they'll be looking for us, so let's give them something to focus on. If they're dealing with me, they'll be less likely to see you until it's too late.'

'But you'll be out in the open,' Akhtar said. 'You'll be an easy target.'

'Maybe,' she said. 'But it's the only way. I'll be fine, you just worry about getting to the plane before it takes off, you got it?'

He nodded reluctantly. She looked at the rest of them, and they nodded as well. 'I'll wait thirty seconds. Get moving.'

CHAPTER FIFTY-SIX

Fasil looked down at the wooden box on the table next to him. He felt nothing; no sense of awe or reverence, and it angered him. Here he was, inches from one of the great relics of Islam – the very Cloak that the Prophet Mohammed wore into battle – and yet still he felt totally unconnected to God. He wished he was more surprised.

The truth was, this was consistent with the experiences of his entire life. He'd attended the madrasa near his home as a young man under Taliban rule. He had learned the Koran backwards and forwards, and spent the better part of three years rocking back and forth, chanting the verses, waiting for the hand of God to reach down and touch him. It never happened, though.

Others in the madrasa claimed that it had happened to them – that they had reached a point of divine inspiration through the repetition of the sacred words; that God had come down and laid his hand upon them with his blessing. He doubted many of the stories, but the mullahs seemed pleased by every report that confirmed their methods, no matter how implausible. And so eventually Fasil too gave in. He claimed the privilege of rapture one day after an exceptionally long prayer. In reality, nothing had happened to him.

The authenticity of his claim had never been questioned. Indeed, the mullahs seemed even more pleased than usual. They had recognized that Fasil was a gifted young man from the outset, and had great plans for him. Fasil went along with their desires willingly, even as he felt the blackness of the hole within him. Perhaps it was this emptiness that allowed him to do the things he had done throughout the Taliban reign and thereafter. He was not tainted with a truly God-given sense of morality, and was therefore willing to go to extreme lengths to enforce the orthodoxy that others told him was essential to God's desires. That was an enormous asset in uncertain times.

And now he had the Cloak. It would give him great earthly power, he knew. When it became known that he had saved the relic from the Americans, the support he already had would increase. In short order, much of the country – and particularly the fundamentalist elements – would coalesce around him. He intended to use that power to enforce the will of Mohammed. Perhaps then he would truly be given the gift of divine inspiration.

The plane was on its approach and, in less than an hour, he would be out of American airspace. Then he would breathe easily again. Until then . . .

He looked across the airstrip at the path that led back toward Ainsworth's house. Ainsworth and Stillwell would be able to fight off any assault for hours. The chances that anyone would be able to storm the house and get enough information to come after him and his bodyguard seemed remote. And yet there was always a chance, and he intended to stay vigilant.

He saw the movement on the path before his bodyguard did. At first he thought it was a shadow playing tricks on his eyes, but then a gunshot echoed in the distance, and the window of the little hut exploded.

'They are coming!' he shouted in Farsi. He and his bodyguard took up positions along the bottom edge of the shattered window. He expected that their attackers would have taken cover in the brush, but it was not the case. Instead, the woman – Phelan's sister – was coming down the path at full speed. She took loose aim and set off another shot at the little cabin. This one went well high and wide, though, and Fasil could hear it ricochet off the roof. She wasn't even keeping low to the ground as she ran, and so she made a generous target. He strained to see whether there was anyone following her, but the path seemed empty. 'She may be alone,' he said to his man. 'Take her out.'

His man squared himself in the window and carefully sighted down the barrel of his pistol. Time stood still for just a moment. Then he pulled the trigger, giving off a deafening report in the confined space. A moment later, the woman fell, her momentum broken, her body toppling backwards.

'I got her!' Fasil's man said. There was pride in his voice. Then, more sheepishly, he said, 'All praise to Allah.'

Fasil looked at him scornfully. 'Get out there and make sure that she is finished,' he said. The man looked at him apprehensively. 'We don't want her shooting at the plane if she is only injured. Make sure she is dead and then get our things out on the tarmac and ready to go.' The man nodded at him and began to move. His bodyguard was a useful creature to have around, he knew, though he viewed him as devoid of any creativity or independent thought. He wondered whether that was what happened to those who had truly experienced the touch of God.

He followed his man out of the shack, and stood watching the plane. It was at the far end of the runway, and he assumed, given the wind conditions, that it would turn and come back to them so that it could take off into the wind. With the short runway, they would need every advantage if they were going to get out of the valley and off to Canada.

He still held the wooden box that contained the Cloak. He would let his man handle the guns and other baggage, but he wasn't going to let anyone else take possession of the Cloak. There was too much at stake, and even the closest loyalties were corruptible in Afghanistan.

His bodyguard walked slowly toward the shrubs to find the body of the Phelan woman, Fasil called to him, 'Jabar, hurry! We will be leaving soon!'

The man, who was almost at the edge of the tall grass where the tarmac ended, turned and waved in annoyance. 'Maybe you wish me to shoot her ghost?' he called back derisively.

As the words left his mouth, a gunshot rang out. Fasil looked over at him, assuming that he'd finished off the American woman. The bodyguard stood there, at the edge of the tarmac, his gun pointed out into the vegetation. 'What happened, Jabar?' Fasil called. 'Is the woman's ghost tougher than you believed?' The bodyguard began to turn, and Fasil expected another witless retort. It didn't come, though. He teetered, took one step, and crashed to the ground.

DAVID HOSP

At that moment, gunshots erupted at the far end of the runway, and the plane began to swerve. Fasil heard glass shattering. 'Shit!'

Fasil, still clutching the box with the Cloak in one hand and his gun in the other, dove for cover. He remained very still, waiting. He had been in enough battles to know that his survival would depend primarily on his wits and his patience.

Cianna was lying in the grass twenty feet from the spot where she'd pretended to fall victim to the distant gunshot. Originally she'd planned to take up a new position and fire off some more long-distance shots, but she quickly realized that Fasil's man was actually coming to look for her. At that point, she had a better idea. She stayed still and waited. He was standing there at the end of the tarmac, fewer than ten yards from her position. She'd been afraid to move, assuming that he would see her and get off the first shots. Her opportunity came when he turned to Fasil. He was no longer looking in her direction, and she had enough time to raise her gun and fire it.

The look on his face was one of pure shock. It hadn't occurred to him that there was a possibility that he had missed her – that she had faked being hit by his bullet. He scanned the grass with glassy eyes, but it was clear that he had no ability to see beyond a few feet. Then he collapsed, and she heard the gunplay at the end of the runway. She crawled to her knees, and looked out at the scene unfolding on the tarmac.

The plane was weaving from side to side. She could see Toney and Akhtar emerging from the brush, running at the plane, firing their weapons. It seemed as though the plane stalled for a moment, then the engines were gunned, and it lurched forward, sending Toney and Akhtar diving out of the way. The plane bucked and lurched, and turned steeply to the right, headed into the bushes. Even from her distance, Cianna could see the silhouette of the pilot slumped over the controls. The plane gathered speed as it headed off the tarmac. Once in the brush, it hit a rock and flipped forward, hanging there, balancing on its nose like a drunk circus animal, before toppling to its side.

Cianna turned her attention to Fasil. He had no one left to help him; no one to protect him. He was lying on the tarmac, taking cover behind a stack of bags outside of the small shack. Morrell and Toney's man were at the far end of the runway, moving toward the shack, guns drawn to prevent Fasil from taking cover there.

Cianna got to her feet and started moving across the runway, pointing her gun at the bags. 'It's over, Fasil!' she yelled. 'Come out from behind there!'

He screamed something in Farsi she didn't understand, put his gun over the top of the bag and fired wildly. Cianna ducked down. Morrell and Toney's man fired at the bags from the far side of the runway, and Fasil returned fire toward them.

'It's not worth it!' Cianna called. 'You're not getting out of here!'

Fasil screamed and fired two more shots in Cianna's direction, forcing her to take cover again. Even as her head was down, she saw him scurry to the other side of the runway. He had the wooden box in one hand and a gun in the other, and he moved quickly. A trail of bullets followed him, ricocheting off the cement, but it didn't appear that any of the shots found their mark.

'He's making a break for it!' Cianna shouted. She was on her feet, running so fast it felt like her lungs were on fire. She had to get to him before he made it up the slope on the other side of the second peak. If he reached the trees, he might be able to disappear. 'Come on!' she screamed to the others, who followed.

She could still see him through the shrubbery, his head bouncing into sight and then ducking down low. It was enough for her to track him, though, and she could tell that she was gaining on him. She was tempted to call out to him again, but she knew it would do no good, and her chest already felt like it was going to explode.

She paused for a moment and looked up to follow his direction. She could see that he had come to a spot where the path diverged. The main path continued to the west at a gentle slope and wound around back to the top of a steep rise. A second path went straight up the hill, meeting the longer path higher up the slope. It was a treacherous stretch of steep rock, but it was a shortcut and less than half as long as the main path.

Cianna turned and shouted to the four men following her. 'Stay with him!' she ordered them. Turning, she stuck her gun into the back of her pants, and started moving up the rocky cliff as quickly as she could. At first, the slope was manageable, and she could take the path upright. As she continued to climb, though, the rock face became steeper and steeper, and she started using her hands to pull herself along. Several times she thought that she had made a mistake in taking the shorter path, but she pushed on.

It took only a few minutes for her to reach the crest and pull herself over the edge and onto the main path. She was gulping for air, doubled over as she tried to gain her bearings. She looked up and down the path, but could see no one. She coughed as she cursed herself, wondering whether her eyesight had deceived her. Perhaps the two paths really didn't meet up, and this was a different trail. Or perhaps Fasil had found another offshoot and had headed in a different direction. In any event, there wasn't any sign of her quarry, and there was little she could do about it.

She stayed bent there for another moment, catching her breath, loosing a few more curses before straightening up to head back down the trail to see whether she could pick up the chase again. As she did, though, she heard a noise coming from down the path, around a turn blocked by a large boulder. She had no time to react before Fasil was there, standing in front of her, ten feet away, puffing his way up the mountain. He still had the box in one hand and his gun in the other, but his focus was on the ground as he picked his way carefully along the trail.

She raised her gun and took aim. 'Stop!' she shouted.

It startled him, and he tripped over a loose stone as he looked up at her. He fell to his knees and the box toppled out of his hand and landed on its side next to the path. He looked at it, and then back at her. He started to raise his gun, but she emphasized her aim, moving forward with the barrel directed at his heart. 'No, no,' she said.

He lowered the gun, but didn't drop it. 'You do not understand the wrath that you will bring down upon yourself!' he said angrily.

'Drop your gun.'

'I am saving my country!'

'I said, drop it!'

He looked at her in a rage, every muscle in his body tense. With all the fury in his soul, he screamed at her, *'Qatala armad zaniya!'*

She heard the words and found herself back in Kandahar, being pelted with rocks and spit as she stood there, a line in the sand protecting those who were willing to take the risk of standing up for their most basic rights. She saw the little girl writhing in pain, dying in her mother's arms as the skin darkened and peeled away from her face. 'You,' she said quietly.

He raised his gun, still screaming, but it never got higher than his waist. She fired into his chest, and he toppled back onto the path, dropping his gun. She walked over to him and looked down into his eyes. His hatred was still there, burning into her. She pointed her gun at his forehead. He nodded at her and closed his eyes. 'It is as it will always be,' he said.

She could feel her finger tighten on the trigger. There was no noise, no distraction, nothing to startle her. Only her anger and her hatred and her need to exact revenge for her brother, and for Nick O'Callaghan, and for Saunders, and for the little girl who had died on a Kandahar street. She took a deep breath, held it, took aim, and tightened her finger again. She wasn't sure for how long she held that breath. It could have been thirty seconds, or a minute, or two. But when she released it, it took with it some measure of her hatred, and she lowered her gun.

Fasil opened his eyes and looked at her. There was

disappointment in them – no, not just disappointment, but a sense that she had betrayed him. She looked up and saw that Toney and Morrell and Akhar were all standing there, twenty feet away, watching the scene in silence.

Cianna put her gun on the ground. 'He's yours,' she said.

'You do nice work,' Toney said. 'We have a lot to talk about.'

'I don't think so.'

Without another word, she walked past the men on the mountain and headed alone down the slope and away from the death and mayhem that had seemed to follow her most of her life.

EPILOGUE

Cianna Phelan sat in the passenger seat of the rusted Nissan Sentra in front of the tavern on L Street in South Boston, staring straight ahead. Her fingers picked nervously at a loose tab of vinyl peeling back from a crack on the armrest. It had been two weeks since the shoot-out in the mountains, and she had spent most of that time on her own. She was only just starting to feel able to talk to others. 'Thanks for bringing me here, Milo,' she said.

'No problem,' he said. 'Do you want me to come in with you?'

It was nice of him to offer. She knew that he did not really want to come into the tavern with her. Confrontations made his stomach churn, she knew, and she marveled once again at his choice of profession. 'No thanks,' she said. 'I can handle this myself.'

He turned to look at her. 'You're going to leave, aren't you?'

She didn't look back at him, and she said nothing.

He took a deep breath and blew it out through his fingers. 'Maybe it's just as well,' he said. 'This line of work is getting to be too dangerous. I need to find something else. If you leave, it gives me an excuse.'

She finally looked at him. 'Oh, please, Milo. What else would you do?'

'I don't know.' He shrugged. 'Maybe I'll open an Asian-fusion restaurant. If the yuppies keep moving in at the rate they have been, you never know; I could make a run of it.'

'The townies would burn it down if they even thought there was a chance. Hell, I'd burn it down if I thought it might succeed.'

'I could be a cop,' he offered.

'No you couldn't.'

'No, I couldn't,' he agreed. He looked away from her. 'Maybe I'll just take some time off. I don't need a job, really. I never told you this, but I'm pretty rich. Family money. I'm not proud of it, but it's true. The car, the shitty apartment, all of it . . . it's just for appearances.'

'No one with money has your haircut,' she said.

'Hey, it's a style,' he protested. He was silent for a moment. 'I really have money, though.'

'I know.'

'I'm serious.'

'I know.'

'Oh.'

She patted his knee. 'You don't have anything to prove to me,' she said. 'You don't have anything to prove to anyone else, either. Be who you are.'

'Is it that obvious?'

'No. Not to everyone else.'

'In that case, there's something I should tell you. It's something I never even told my parents. It's something I think I'm still struggling with myself.'

'Yeah?'

'I'm black.'

She laughed. It was the first genuine, full-throated laugh she'd managed in a long, long time. 'No, Milo,' she said. 'You can be just about anything you want to be in this world. Except that. You are, without question, one of the whitest people I have ever met.'

'Latino?'

'Not even on taco night.'

He sighed. 'Ah, well. I'll just have to be me.'

'It's more than enough.' She opened the door and got out.

He leaned over and called to her out of the open passenger window. 'For what it's worth, I'll miss you if you leave. We did some good things.'

'I'll miss you if I leave, too,' she said. 'And, yeah, we did.'

It was a working-class place, and it smelled of grease and stale coffee. Bill Toney looked painfully out of his element sitting at a table at the far end of the room, his shirt starched and his hair neatly combed. He saw her as soon as she walked in, and he started to stand, but thought better of it. The waitress, a woman somewhere between her fifties and her eighties, with the look of someone who would never give up the fight, no matter how bad things got, nodded to her. 'You want a table?' she asked.

'I'm with him,' Cianna said, nodding at Toney.

'Really?'

'Thanks.'

'I'll bring you some coffee. You probably need it.'

Cianna walked over and sat down across the table from Toney. 'Do you have it?' she asked.

'All business,' he commented. 'I like that. Reminds me of Jack. I always liked him; though he'd never believe it.'

The reference made her pause. It took a few seconds for her to phrase the question. 'How is he doing?'

Toney looked at her, his eyes narrowing for a moment. Then he shrugged. 'He's a lot better than he deserves to be. An inch to the left, and Sirus's round would have taken out his heart. An inch to the right, and it would have shattered the spine. I'm not saying it's a picnic at the moment, but he'll walk again. Knowing Jack, it won't slow him down at all. He's already reviewing op reports and cursing out anyone who outranks him.'

'Will he see me?'

Toney hesitated. 'In time, I'm sure. He doesn't want people to see him the way he is right now. It's not just the physical aspect of it. Ainsworth recruited and trained Jack. To Jack, Ainsworth *was* the Agency, and the Agency is Jack's life. He's got a little work to do to come to terms with what happened. He asked me to tell you to wait.'

Cianna nodded. 'You have to come to grips with the past before you can really deal with the present. No one knows that better than me.'

Toney reached into the briefcase and pulled out a file. 'Speaking of the past, here, take this. This is the last copy,' he said. 'All others have been destroyed.' He smiled at her.

'Bullshit,' she said. 'What about the one you kept for yourself?'

His smile faded. 'That's just for insurance.'

'Against what?'

He swizzled his coffee. 'Against whatever.' He pushed it over toward her. 'It won't matter to anyone else. As of this moment, you are no longer an ex-convict. How does it feel?'

She took the file and put it in her purse. 'You could have mailed this to me.'

'And trust the Post Office?' He tried a smile again, but she wasn't having any of it. 'I told you, we have opportunities to talk about. The kind of opportunities that need to be discussed in person.'

She could feel him looking at her, but she wasn't willing to go there. Not yet. 'What happened to the Cloak?' she asked.

'Akhtar took it back to the mosque in Kandahar.'

'Just like that?'

'Well, it was a little more complicated than that. He was accompanied by several of the military's best men to make sure things went smoothly, and the Cloak itself was smuggled back into the mosque in the middle of the night so no one would see it and wonder. As far as the Afghans are concerned, the Cloak never left its home. Better that way. If people over there even suspected that Americans had stolen the thing . . .' He blew out a low whistle. 'In that sense, it was an effective plan. I'll give Ainsworth that.'

'And Akhtar? He's okay?'

'As okay as anyone who has pinned his hopes for happiness on the notion that Afghanistan may somehow get its shit together and learn to live in peace can be, I suppose. His man Gamol looks like he will win the regional elections in a walk. He's probably the best option, but he's far from perfect. You've been over there, you've seen what it's like.'

She nodded. 'I have.' She looked down at her coffee. 'What happened to Fasil?'

Toney's face darkened. 'You'd need clearance for me to tell you that. You don't have clearance. Yet.'

'And the rest of it?'

'The rest of it was fairly simple. Lawrence Ainsworth died of a heart attack. He will be buried next to his son in a quiet ceremony with the official thanks of a grateful nation for all he did over the course of his lifetime. Sirus Stillwell was killed yesterday in Afghanistan while out on patrol. The key is deniability.'

'And Jack sits in a hospital recovering from . . . what? A bad climbing accident? No one outside of the intelligence community will ever know the nature of his sacrifice?'

'It's the job he chose. People don't go into this business seeking individual glory, because it's never going to come. The credit for any success you have will, by necessity, be given to others. Any failure will be yours alone. That's the deal, and everyone who joins up accepts it. That's why they are the bravest people we have working for us. And the most dangerous.'

'Sounds like a great life.'

'No,' Toney said slowly. 'It's a shitty life. But it's a great calling, and a great cause.' He took a long look at her. 'Is it something you are interested in?'

She didn't answer at first. 'Why?'

'Why what?'

'Why are you asking me?'

'Because I have seen you in the field, and I know you have the skills. You have the physical and mental strength and the ability to kill when necessary. That was what you

419

were being trained for, after all. It would be as though you were picking up right from the moment everything went to shit. You'd be making a great contribution to your country.'

She glared at him. 'With people like you and Ainsworth running things, I'm not sure whether I want to make that contribution.'

He smiled back at her. He was a good-looking man, but he had an oily unattractive smile. It was a smile she didn't trust. 'Yes you are,' he said. 'For all its faults, this is still the greatest country in the world.'

'Damning us with faint praise, aren't you?'

'The world is a fucked-up place. Like it or not, it takes dedicated people to try to keep it together. The only question is: are you one of those people?' He'd finished with a rhetorical flourish, clearly expecting that the power of his patriotism could not fail to win her over.

She finished her coffee and stood up, picked up her purse, which contained one of two final copies of her criminal record. 'Thanks for this,' she said. 'I appreciate it.'

'That's it?' he demanded, dumbfounded.

'I'll think about it.'

'What's to think about? I'm giving you the chance to change the world – potentially to alter the course of history. What could be more important than that?'

She looked at him, knowing that he would never understand. She decided to try it anyway. '*The biggest changes happen in the smallest places,*' she said.

'What the fuck does that mean?' Toney sputtered.

'It's the motto for the organization I work for. I never really understood it either. Not until now.' She walked to the door and looked back at him. 'I'll let you know. And thanks again.' She left before he could say anything.

Once out on the street, she decided to walk back to her apartment through the projects where she'd grown up. It was unusually warm for the season. The temperature had crept up into the sixties, and Southie had come alive for a brief moment. Kids played on the sidewalks in their shirtsleeves, squeezing the last hours out of what would be one of the final real nice days before winter set in. Outside bodegas and local restaurants, tables had been set up, and people loitered there, having coffee and sausages, looking at the blue sky like a lover saying goodbye.

As she rounded the corner onto Mercer, she saw a group of kids playing kick the can in the street. There was one little girl apart from the others, sitting on the steps. She was skinny and had bruises on her knees. Her face was dirty enough that the tracks where the tears had fallen recently stood out like angry warpaint.

It took a moment for Cianna to recognize her, and another for her to come up with the girl's name. Once she had it, though, she walked over to her. 'Maggie?' she said in a soft, friendly tone. The girl looked up at her with distrust and anger, as though she regarded all adults as the enemy. 'Your name's Maggie, isn't it?' Cianna ventured farther. 'I know your mom, Jenny. We . . .' She stumbled, but only for a moment, as she recalled that awful scene at the apartment, and then seeing Jenny still with Vin the drug dealer a few days later. 'We worked together once.'

Hearing her mother's name seemed to soften the girl's attitude a little. She looked away, and then put her head down.

'Do you know where your mom is, honey?' she asked.

The little girl pointed to a window on the second floor of the apartment house behind them. 'Up there,' she said. 'She told me to stay here.'

Cianna looked around her own neighborhood, and thought about her childhood. There hadn't been much of it, and what there had been was not pleasant to recall. She thought about Nick O'Callaghan and all that he had done for her. She thought about how she'd at once protected and belittled her younger brother Charlie. It hit her how, with just a little more attention, a little more effort, it could have all been so different.

She looked back down at the little girl. 'Maggie,' she said. 'Look at me.' The little girl lifted her head and Cianna could see the hopelessness that seemed to go all the way to the bottom of the girl's soul. 'I'm going to go up there and bring your mother out, okay? How would that be with you?' A spark appeared in the depths of the despair, and the girl nodded. 'Good,' Cianna said. 'I have a few things I need to talk to her about, and she may be a little tired and angry when she comes out, but together we'll try to make her better.'

She put her hand out, and slowly, hesitantly, the little girl took it. Cianna shook the hand and smiled. 'Okay,' she said. 'Just stay here and be brave.' She let go of the little girl's hand and walked up the front stoop. As she reached for the doorbell, she checked her coat pocket for the revolver she'd kept with her since Saunders had given it to her. With any luck she wouldn't need it, she thought. But in this line of work, it was nice to know it was there.

ACKNOWLEDGEMENTS

Thanks to the many people who helped me throughout the writing of this book. To all the wonderful people at Macmillan, but especially Natasha Harding, Will Atkins, Ruth Carim, Ellie Wood, Rob Cox, Maria Rejt and Camilla Elworthy, thanks so much for your hard work. A special thank you to Trisha Jackson, my spectacular editor, who helped me keep the effort on track. Undying thanks to Aaron Priest and Lisa Erbach Vance and all of the people at the Aaron Priest Literary Agency, and Arabella Stein, my agent in London: a writer could have no better support group.

Finally, thanks to my family: My wife Joanie, who does such a wonderful job keeping everything else in my life from collapsing, Reid and Samantha, Mom and Dad, my brother Ted, and my extended group of family and friends who are the best part of my life. I appreciate everything you do.

extracts reading groups
competitions books new
discounts extracts
extracts
competitions discounts
books
new events
events books reading groups
extracts
new reading groups
interviews
events extracts
discounts books
new books events
events new
discounts extracts discounts
www.panmacmillan.com
extracts events reading groups
competitions books extracts new